1001 Dark Nights Bundle Three

Four Novellas
By

Lorelei James
Lara Adrian
Christopher Rice
Julie Kenner

1001 Dark Nights

EVIL EYE
CONCEPTS

1001 Dark Nights Bundle 3
ISBN: 978-1-682305720

Roped In: A Blacktop Cowboys® Novella by Lorelei James
Copyright 2014 LJLA, LLC

Tempted by Midnight: A Midnight Breed Novella by Lara Adrian
Copyright 2014 Lara Adrian LLC

The Flame: A Desire Exchange Novella by Christopher Rice
Copyright 2014 Christopher Rice

Caress of Darkness: A Dark Pleasures Novella by Julie Kenner
Copyright 2014 Julie Kenner

Foreword: Copyright 2014 M. J. Rose

Published by Evil Eye Concepts, Incorporated

Sign up for the 1001 Dark Nights Newsletter
and be entered to win a Tiffany Key necklace.

There's a contest every month!

Go to www.1001DarkNights.com to subscribe.

As a bonus, all subscribers will receive a free
1001 Dark Nights story
The First Night
by Lexi Blake & M.J. Rose

Table of Contents

One Thousand and One Dark Nights

Once upon a time, in the future…

*I was a student fascinated with stories and learning.
I studied philosophy, poetry, history, the occult, and
the art and science of love and magic. I had a vast
library at my father's home and collected thousands
of volumes of fantastic tales.*

*I learned all about ancient races and bygone
times. About myths and legends and dreams of all
people through the millennium. And the more I read
the stronger my imagination grew until I discovered
that I was able to travel into the stories… to actually
become part of them.*

*I wish I could say that I listened to my teacher
and respected my gift, as I ought to have. If I had, I
would not be telling you this tale now.
But I was foolhardy and confused, showing off
with bravery.*

*One afternoon, curious about the myth of the
Arabian Nights, I traveled back to ancient Persia to
see for myself if it was true that every day Shahryar
(Persian: ش ا ی ر , "king") married a new virgin, and then
sent yesterday's wife to be beheaded. It was written
and I had read, that by the time he met Scheherazade,
the vizier's daughter, he'd killed one thousand
women.*

*Something went wrong with my efforts. I arrived
in the midst of the story and somehow exchanged
places with Scheherazade — a phenomena that had
never occurred before and that still to this day, I
cannot explain.*

Now I am trapped in that ancient past. I have taken on Scheherazade's life and the only way I can protect myself and stay alive is to do what she did to protect herself and stay alive.

Every night the King calls for me and listens as I spin tales. And when the evening ends and dawn breaks, I stop at a point that leaves him breathless and yearning for more. And so the King spares my life for one more day, so that he might hear the rest of my dark tale.

As soon as I finish a story... I begin a new one... like the one that you, dear reader, have before you now.

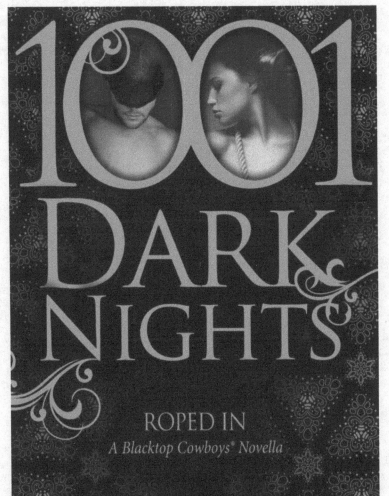

1001 DARK NIGHTS

ROPED IN
A Blacktop Cowboys Novella

LORELEI JAMES

Prologue

Steer wrestler Sutton Grant knew the instant he threw himself off his horse he was in for a world of hurt.

He'd miscalculated the distance and his rate of rotation. The last thing he remembered before he hit the steer was he could kiss this year's world championship title good-bye.

He woke up in the ambulance, his head pounding, unable to move any part of his body but his eyes.

Fuck.

Try and move.

I can't.

Was he paralyzed?

He couldn't be.

What if he was? He'd never hurt like this. Never.

But the fact he could feel pain had to be good, right?

Maybe the intense pain is your body shutting down.

If he was paralyzed, who would shoulder the burden of caring for him for the rest of his life? He didn't have a wife or a girlfriend. Would responsibility fall to his family?

Oh, hell no. He'd put them through enough with his last rodeo mishap.

Mishap? Don't you mean accident that kept you out of commission for a year? Do you remember living at home and seeing the worry on your parent's faces?

That'd been worse than the months of physical and mental recovery. Then he'd had the added burden of seeing their happiness vanish after he'd healed and had informed them he planned to return to the sport.

His mother's voice drifted into his memory. *You're still going to do this even if it hurts, maims, or kills you?* He'd responded, *Even then.*

He still saw the tear tracks on her face, the subtle shake of her head. And he'd still gone off anyway, chasing the gold buckle, putting his body through hell.

I take it back! I didn't mean it!

Right then and there, Sutton made a bargain with God:

Please Lord, if I survive this with my body intact, I swear I'll give up bulldoggin' forever. No lie. I'll be done for good.

White lights blinded him and for a brief instant, he thought he'd died. A voice he'd never heard before whispered to him, *promise accepted.*

Then darkness descended again. The last thing Sutton remembered was wiggling his fingers and toes and whispering a prayer of thanks.

Chapter One

Eight months later...

"You ain't supposed to be out there doin' that," Wynton shouted.

Sutton looked across the paddock at his older brother and scowled. He tugged on the reins but his horse Dial wouldn't budge. Damn stubborn horse; he had to be part mule.

"I've got a ridin' crop you can borrow," his younger brother Creston yelled from atop the corral fence.

"I'm surrounded by smartasses," Sutton informed Dial. "And apparently I'm a dumbass because I never learn with you, do I?"

Dial tossed his mane.

After he climbed off his horse, Sutton switched out the bit and bridle for a lead rope. Then he opened the gate between the paddock and the pasture, playfully patting Dial's flank as the gray dun tore off.

Dial actually kicked up his hooves in glee as he galloped away.

"Yeah, I'll miss our special time together too, asshole."

Asshole. Man, he was punchier than he realized if he was calling his horse an asshole.

Sutton sauntered over to where his brothers waited for him, surprised that they'd both shown up in the middle of a Friday afternoon—with a six-pack. Wyn and Cres both ranched with their dad, although as the oldest, Wyn had inherited the bulk of the ranch work decisions. It appeared he'd changed the rule about working a full day—every day, rain, shine, snow, come hell, high water, or wild fire.

"What's the occasion? You here to borrow money?" he asked.

"Good one. Glad to see they didn't remove all of your funny bone after surgery," Wyn said dryly.

"Hilarious." Sutton quirked an eyebrow at Cres. "Got something smart to say?"

"Yeah. You know you ain't supposed to be doin' anything that'll further injure you. When we hadn't heard from you all week, we figured you were up to no good. And I see we were right."

"It wasn't like I was bulldoggin'."

"This'd be a different conversation if we'd seen you doin' that." Wyn handed him a beer. "We ain't trying to bust your balls, but goddammit, Sutton. You almost fucking died."

"*Again*," Cres added.

"Well, I ain't dead. But don't feel like I'm alive, either." He sipped the cold brew. Nothing tasted better on a hot summer day.

"Should we be on suicide watch?" Wyn said hesitantly.

Sutton had a mental break the last time he'd been injured, so his family kept an eye on him, and he knew how lucky he was to have that support. "Nah. It's just this sitting around, healing up stuff is driving me bugshit crazy."

"The way to deal with your boredom ain't to get in the cage with your demon and go another round."

Sutton squinted at Cres. "You callin' my horse a demon?"

Cres rolled his eyes. "No, dipshit. Your demon is the need to prove yourself. Regardless of the cost."

His gaze met his youngest brother's. Growing up, Wyn and Cres joked about Sutton being the mailman's kid because he was the only one of the three boys with blue-green eyes. Both his brothers and his parents had brown eyes. Sometimes he wondered if that outsider status is what lured him into the world of professional rodeo and away from working on the family ranch.

He sighed. "I appreciate your concern, I really do. I'm just frustrated. Makes it worse when I hafta deal with Dial. He's a temperamental motherfucker on his best days. I don't trust anyone to work with him after that last go around with the so-called 'expert,' which means he ain't getting the proper workout for a horse of his caliber."

"A few months cooling his hooves shouldn't have changed his previous training that much. Breeders take mares out of bucking contention, as well as barrel racing, when they're bred. Sometimes that'd be up to two years."

"I know that. But Dial? He ain't like other horses. Gelding him didn't dampen that fire; if anything, it increased his orneriness."

"I'd be ornery too if some dude sliced off my balls," Wyn said with a shudder. Then he looked at Sutton. "So that other bulldogger, the guy with the weird name...what happened the weekend he borrowed him?"

"Weird name." Sutton snorted. "That's rich coming from a guy named *Wynton.*"

"Fuck off, *Sutton*," he shot back. "I think Mom was high on child birthin' painkillers when she picked our names."

"Probably. You talkin' about Breck Christianson? He tried to help me out during the Western Livestock Show in January while I was still laid up."

"Yeah. Him." Wyn looked at Cres. "Don't know if I ever heard you talk about what went down that week you were there with him and Dial."

Cres rested his forearms on the top of the fence and his hat shadowed his face. "It was a damn disaster in the arena. Dial wouldn't do nothin'. Seriously. That high-strung bastard stayed in the damn chute. The one time he left the chute, he charged the hazer's horse. Breck traveled to Denver specifically to get a feel for Dial before the competition, but he ended up sticking with his own mount."

"Huh. Surprised you stayed in Denver for the whole stock show since it meant you had to take care of demon horse while you were there."

Cres shrugged. "I never get to see the behind the chutes action for a week-long event. It was interesting and everyone was friendly."

"So Breck took good care of you?" Sutton asked.

Cres choked on his beer.

Wyn patted him on the back. "You okay?"

"Yeah." *Cough cough.* "A bug flew in my mouth." Another cough. "Breck introduced me around."

Sutton nudged his shoulder. "Breck introduce you to his buckle bunny pussy posse?"

Before Cres responded, Wyn interrupted. "Cres wouldn't know what to do with the ladies. The kid is all work and no play. He probably spent all his time hidin' in the horse trailer."

"I ain't a kid," Cress said tightly. "And don't assume you know what I got up to because you don't. Anyway, Breck knows everyone." He looked at Sutton. "He introduced me to Saxton Green, that other bulldogger you get mistaken for all the time. He's built like you, even looks like you, but he sure don't act like you. That man is fuckin' wild."

Sutton groaned. "Do you know how many times I've had to defend myself against something Saxton did? It sucks. That's about the only time I don't mind that the other competitors call me 'The Saint.'"

"Other competitors, and everyone else involved with the rodeo circuit, including the women, call you 'The Saint' because you're the one who acts like a freakin' monk," Wyn pointed out helpfully. "Damn man. How do you turn down all that free pussy?"

"It ain't free, trust me," Sutton retorted.

"Wyn, leave him alone," Cres said. "Stop acting like you've got it rough and ain't getting your fair share of tail. Women are lined up in your driveway to get a piece of you."

Wyn smirked and raised his beer. "It's good to be me."

Cres rolled his eyes. "Oh, and I also met the couple who raised and trained Dial before you bought him."

That piqued Sutton's interest. "Chuck and Berlin Gradsky? Really?"

"They were in the arena when Breck was having a hard time with Dial. Neither of them even tried to step in. They said the only people who had any effect on him was you and their daughter who'd trained him."

London Gradsky. He hadn't thought of her in a couple of years. The surly brunette who'd thrown a shit fit when her parents had sold Dial to him rather than just continuing to let him compete on the horse. She'd accused him of taking advantage of her parents, caring about his career above the welfare of the animal. Then she'd launched into a diatribe about how self-absorbed he was for pushing to have the stallion castrated without considering the long-term gains for breeding. After calling him a dickhead whose belt buckle was bigger than his brain, she'd stormed off.

Chuck and Berlin explained away her behavior, fondly referring to her as their headstrong filly. They were proud that she'd struck out on her own as a horse trainer rather than just expecting to get a primo position at Grade A Horse Farms because her parents owned the business. But still, London's accusations had stung. What he wouldn't give for her expertise now. Although it'd been three years since their altercation, he doubted the feisty firecracker would let bygones be bygones. "Well, it's obvious I need help."

"What about that Eli guy?" Wyn said. "Didn't you say he's some kind of Native American horse whisperer?"

"Eli is top notch. But Dial's temperament is particularly bad around other horses. He took a chunk outta the alpha horse the one time I left him there—this was after Eli put him in a pasture by himself and he jumped the fence. So Dial is no longer welcome."

"I have faith you'll figure something out that doesn't entail you bein' on the dirt with him."

Cres straightened up and moved to toss his bottle into the shooting barrel. "To be blunt, as much as we care for our animals, bro, they are tools. Tools are replaceable. You are not. This last time you nearly went into kidney failure, liver failure, and they talked of removing your spleen. Both me'n Wyn would've offered up a kidney or even a damn lung for you. You know that. We'd rather not have to face that choice again."

"We're askin' you not to do something that'll put you back in the hospital for another six weeks followed by months of recovery." Wyn gestured to the ranch house and the area around them. "You've got a nice place to hang your hat, money in the bank, the kinda looks that get any woman you want into your bed, and family nearby. Ain't nothin' wrong with that life."

Sutton watched his brothers drive off. He put the three bottles left from the six-pack into the fridge in the garage, knowing he'd be less tempted to drink them all if he had to leave the house to get them.

He changed clothes, flipped on the ball game for some background noise, and snagged his laptop. He typed London Gradsky in the search engine. The top result read:

London's Bridge To Training A Better Horse

Seriously? That was the worst fucking business slogan he'd ever heard. He clicked on the link.

Hers was a simple website. Contact info via e-mail or phone. Testimonials about her training successes. Links to horse brokers and breeders—no surprise Grade A Horse Farms topped the list—but nowhere did London list her lineage. Interesting.

Lastly, he saw a page with a schedule of summer events.

Sutton scrolled the page. Evidently, London put on training clinics on the weekends during the summer at local fairs and rodeos. For fifty bucks, she'd spend thirty minutes assessing the horse and rider before offering training recommendations.

The cynical side of his brain remembered her cutting words to him and weighed in with: *What are the odds she recommends herself as the horse trainer who can miraculously fix bad habits and riders?*

But his optimist side crawled out of the dark hole it'd been hiding in since the accident and countered with: *Her business wouldn't last long if she didn't get results, and the horse training world in Colorado would shun her if she was a shyster.*

It looked to him like she'd been putting on these summer clinics for at least a couple years. And every time slot was booked, as well as several people on standby for an open appointment. He scrolled down to the current week's schedule and his heart skipped a beat.

Score.

She'd be in Fairfax, Colorado, this weekend. That was only thirty miles from here. And score again. Her last slot of the day was still open.

With zero hesitation, he typed in D.L. A-ride and hoped liked hell she had a sense of humor.

And that she wouldn't chase after him with a horse whip when she realized who he was.

Chapter Two

Worst. Morning. Ever.

London Gradsky glared at the busted coffee maker. She'd spent twenty minutes fiddle-fucking around with the thing to try and get it to work. Giving it up as a lost cause, she'd chucked the whole works outside.

No coffee in her cozy camper meant she had to go to the exhibitors' and contestants' tent to get her morning jolt of caffeine. Since she'd just planned on quickly ducking in and out, she hadn't combed her hair, washed her face, brushed her teeth, or changed out of her pajamas.

And motherfucking, son of a bitch if *they* weren't there, Tweedledee and Tweedletwat. Making cowpie eyes at each other while people looked at them with indulgent smiles. She could almost hear the collective sigh of the women in the tent when Stitch gently wiped a smear of powdered sugar off Paige's cheek then kissed the spot.

Paige giggled and nuzzled him. Her tiara caught on the brim of his cowboy hat, which sent the newly anointed golden couple's admirers scurrying forward to help them out of such a huge pickle.

Of course no one pointed out how stupid it was that Paige actually *wore* a fucking tiara to breakfast. The man-stealing bitch probably wore it to bed. Then London drifted into a fantasy where Paige had donned the tiara when she gave Stitch a blowjob and it cut the hell out of his abdomen.

"Sending eye daggers at her while eye fucking him ain't smart, London," her on-the-road partner in crime Melissa "Mel" Lockhart said behind her.

"I'm not eye fucking him, I'm eye fucking him *up*."

"Doesn't matter, because that's not how anyone will see it. Come on, let's get out of here."

London allowed herself to be led away. As soon as they were out of screeching range, she exploded. "How in the fuck am I gonna survive this summer, Mel? When every time I turn around I see them sucking each other's faces off? What does he see in her?"

Mel didn't answer. She appeared to be hedging, which was not her usual style.

"Just spit it out."

"Fine. That girl is a bonafide beauty queen. Everyone says she'll be the next Miss Rodeo America and people treat him like he's a prince— the heir apparent to take that All Around title at the CRA Championships in a few years. They are a match made in PR heaven. What don't you get about that?"

"I don't get how that asswipe could dump me, via text message, after he does one fundraiser with her because it's true love? Bullshit. No one falls in love in a night." London paced along the metal fencing. "I wanna choke her with her stupid 'Miss Rodeo Colorado' sash and then tie it around his dick until it turns blue and falls off."

Mel's hands landed on London's shoulders and then she was right in her face, her brown eyes flashing concern. "This has gotta stop, London. What the hell did you see in him anyway? He's looks like Opie from *The Andy Griffith Show*. I think the only reason you ended up with him in the first place is because you were lonely and wanted a dog."

"He's a damn hound dog who needs to be put down," she muttered.

"Not true, because we both know that man did not rock your world or even the damn camper when you two got down and dirty. He doesn't know how to be a horndog."

London couldn't argue that point.

"Seriously sista, you're starting to scare me with all these violent scenarios you spout off like horror poetry. Stitch scratching an itch with Paige the underage is not the end of the world. I think the real issue here is you need to get laid by a man who knows what he's doing. And you're putting out this I-will-rip-your-dick-off vibe to any man who starts sniffing around you."

That wasn't true…was it?

"Find a hot guy and fuck him 'til he can't walk. Then you'll be back to strutting around with your head held high instead of acting like a whipped pup."

"You're right."

"Of course I am. Now take a minute and breathe."

London closed her eyes, inhaled for ten counts, exhaled for ten, and reopened her eyes to gaze at her friend.

The freckle-faced redhead wore a smug look. "Better?"

"Much. Thank you." Then her gaze narrowed. "Hey, you just did that thing my mother always does. Did she give you instructions on how to get me to cool off?"

"Yes, and I asked her—but she didn't offer up her magic mom trick freely."

"When were you hanging out with my mother?" London demanded.

"Uh, since she *owns* my cutting horse, I see her more than you do."

"She may own your horse, but I trained Plato so he'll always love me best."

"Even my color blind horse can see what you're wearing is all kinds of wrong because you look like a leprechaun hag. Where *did* you get those god-awful green pajamas?" Mel leaned closer. "Do they have frogs on them? And sweet baby Jesus on a Vespa...are those frogs baring lipstick-kissed butt cheeks?"

"Yep. Nana gave them to me after Stitch ditched me. Said toads like him could kiss my ass."

"Appropriate I guess, but still hideous. Come to my horse trailer. I've got coffee and everything to banish that outer hag." She smirked. "You're on your own getting rid of that inner hag."

"Fuck off."

"You love me."

"I really do." She looped her arm through Mel's. "Let's start making a 'get London laid' list of candidates." She paused. "You still got your little black book of rodeo circuit bad boys?"

"Yep. It's even color coded by cock size, which circuit they're on, and their ability to last longer than eight seconds."

* * * *

London was hot and tired, but exhilarated after six hours of working with horses and their riders. About three quarters of her clientele were kids under fourteen. It was gratifying, proving to novice equestrians that their animal was under their control. Contrary to belief, she picked up very few new regular clients at fairs and rodeos. The problems she helped with were rider related rather than horse related. The horse issues would take more than a thirty minute fix.

She checked her sign-up list, surprised to see her last opening had been filled. Weird name. D.L. A-ride. No gender or age listed. Was it a joke? D.L. A-ride. She watched the gate for a horse and rider to approach.

After two minutes she closed her eyes, breathing in the familiar scents of hot dirt and manure and livestock, with the occasional whiff of diesel fuel and something sugary like cotton candy or funnel cakes or Bavarian almonds.

"Excuse me," a deep voice said behind her. "I'm looking for London Gradsky?"

London pushed off the fence and turned around, but the *you found her* response dried on her tongue. Holy balls was this man hot. Like off the charts hot. Two days' worth of dark scruff couldn't hide the sharp angles of his face. Strong, almost square jaw, ridiculously full lips. The guy wore a ball cap and dark shades. A short-sleeved polo in ocean blue accentuated the breadth of his shoulders, the contours of his chest and... Holy smoking double barrels, welcome to the gun show; his biceps were huge. His forearms appeared to have been carved out of marble. She stopped herself from dropping her gaze to his crotch. Had Mel sent this man her way?

"I'm London. Do I know you?" *Please don't tell me you're a long lost cousin or something.*

"Yeah. We met a while back." He paused. "I signed up for the last class slot because I needed to talk to you."

Needed. Not wanted. Her skepticism reared its snappish head. "Who are you?"

He encroached on her space, completely throwing her body into shadow and tumult. Then she waited, breath trapped in her lungs for the moment when he tore off his sunglasses.

Eyes as blue as the Caribbean stared back at her.

Fuck me. She knew those eyes. She'd dreamt of those eyes. Although last time she'd seen them up close she'd wanted to spit in them. "Sutton Grant."

"I reckon a once-over like that is better than the fiery look of hatred I expected." He grinned.

That grin? With the damn dimples in his cheeks and in his chin? Not fair. She was *such* a sucker for a devil's smile boosted by pearly whites. But she'd considered him devil's spawn after his dealings with her family. In her mind she'd attributed cloven hooves, demon horns, and a forked tongue and tail to him.

Which pissed her off because the man was a piece of art. A real piece of work, too, if he thought she'd let bygones be bygones just so she could stare slack-jawed at his perfect face, spellbinding eyes, and banging body.

"You lied to get a meeting with me?" She snorted. "I see you're still the same manipulative bastard who follows his own agenda."

He took another step closer. "I see you're still the same brat who jumps to conclusions."

"Yeah? I'm not the one in a piss-poor disguise, douche-nozzle."

"Douche-nozzle...I don't even know what that is."

"Look in the mirror, pal." Her gaze flicked over him. "A ball cap, a polo shirt, and...no freakin' way. Are you wearing *Mom* jeans, Sutton Grant?"

He shot a quick look around and said, "Keep your voice down. No one has recognized me and I'd like to keep it that way."

"I'll bet your girlfriend picked this outfit because it is guaranteed to keep you from getting laid. Like ever."

He scowled. "I don't have a girlfriend. Now can we skip the insults and cut to the chase? Because I really need to talk to you."

"You scheduled the time and it ain't free." London held out her hand. "Fifty bucks for thirty minutes. The clock starts ticking as soon as you pay up."

Sutton dug in his front pocket and pulled out a crumpled fifty. "Here."

"Shoot."

"It's about Dial."

"What did you do to him?"

"It's more a problem of what I'm *not* doin' with him. Due to my injury, he's been benched the last eight months."

Now she remembered. Sutton had gotten badly hurt late last fall during his circuit's last qualifying event for the CRA Finals and ended up with life-threatening internal injuries. "What do you want from me?"

"I'll hire you to work with Dial, get him back up to speed, since I'm still sidelined."

"So he'll be in top condition when you're back on the circuit?"

A funny look flitted through his eyes and he looked away. "Something like that."

"Why me?"

"Because we both know the only people who've been able to work with him have been you and me."

She sucked in a few breaths and forced herself to loosen her fists. "This wouldn't be an issue if you hadn't browbeaten my folks into selling Dial to you outright. When the breeder owns the horse and a rider goes down, other people are in place to keep the horse conditioned. That responsibility isn't pushed aside."

"You think I don't know that? You think I'm feelin' good about any of this? Fuck. I hired people to work with him and the stubborn bastard chased them all off. A couple of them literally."

London smirked. "That's my boy."

"Your boy is getting fatter and meaner by the day," Sutton retorted. "I'm afraid if I let him go too much longer it'll be too late and he'll be as worthless as me."

Worthless? Dude. Look in the mirror much? How could Sutton be out of commission and still look like he'd stepped off the pages of *Buff and Beautiful Bulldogger* magazine?

"I hope the reason you're so quiet is because you're considering my offer."

London's gaze zoomed to his. "How do you know you can afford me?"

"I don't. I get that you're an expert on this particular horse and I'm willing to pay you for that expertise." Sutton sidestepped her and rested his big body next to hers—close to hers—against the fence. "I know it'll sound stupid, but every time I grab the tack and head out to catch Dial to try and work him, even when I'm not supposed to, I feel his frustration that I'm not doin' more. I ain't the kind of man that sees a horse—my horse—as just a tool. Your folks knew that about me or they wouldn't have sold him to me for any amount of money."

"Yeah. I do know that," she grudgingly admitted, "but you should also know that I wouldn't be doin' this for you or the money, I'd be doin' it for Dial."

"That works for me. There's another reason that I want you. Only you."

"Which is?"

His unwavering stare unnerved her, as if he was gauging whether he could trust her. Finally he said, "Strictly between us?"

She nodded.

"If it's decided I'll never compete again, you're in the horse world more than I am and you'll ensure Dial gets where he needs to be."

London hadn't been expecting that. Sutton had paid a shit ton for Dial, and he hadn't suggested she'd help him sell the horse to a proper owner, just that she'd help him find one. In her mind that meant he really had Dial's best interest at heart. Not that she believed for an instant Sutton Grant intended to retire from steer wrestling. First off, he was barely thirty. Second, rumor had it his drive to win was as wide and deep as the Colorado River.

As she contemplated how to respond, she saw her ex, Stitch, with Princess Paige plastered to his side, meandering their direction.

Dammit. Not now.

After the incident this morning, she'd steered clear of the exhibitor's hall where the pair had handed out autographs and barf bags. She felt the overwhelming need to escape, but if she booked it across the corral, it'd look like she was running from them.

Screw that. Screw them. She was not in the wrong.

"London? You look ready to commit murder. What'd I say?"

She gazed up at him. The man was too damn good-looking, so normally she wouldn't have a shot at a man like him. But he did say he'd do *anything*...

"Okay, here's the deal. I'll work with Dial, but you've gotta do something for me. Uh, two things actually."

"Name them."

How much to tell him? She didn't want to come off desperate. Still, she opted for the truth. "Backstory: my boyfriend dumped me via text last month because he'd hooked up with a rodeo queen. Because he and I were together when I made my summer schedule, that means I will see them every fucking weekend. All summer."

"And?"

"And I don't wanna be known as that poor pathetic London Gradsky pining over her lost love."

Sutton's eyes turned shrewd. "*Are* you pining for him?"

"Mostly I'm just pissed. It needs to look like I've moved on. So I realize your nickname is 'The Saint' and you don't—"

"Don't call me that," he said crossly. "Tell me what you need."

"The first thing I'd need is you to play the part of my new boyfriend."

That shocked him, but he rallied with, "I can do that. When does this start?"

"Right now, 'cause here they come." London plastered her front to his broad chest and wreathed her arms around his neck. "And make this look like the real deal, bulldogger."

"Any part of you that's hands off for me?"

She fought the urge to roll her eyes. Of course "The Saint" would ask first. "Nope."

Sutton bestowed that fuck-me-now grin. "I can work with that." He curled one hand around the back of her neck and the other around her hip.

When it appeared he intended to take his own sweet time kissing her, she took charge, teetering on tiptoe since the man was like seven feet tall. After the first touch of their lips, he didn't dive into her mouth in a fake show of passion. He rubbed his half-parted lips across hers, each pass silently coaxing her to open up a little more. Each tease of his breath on her damp lips made them tingle.

She muttered, "Kiss me like you mean business."

Those deceptively gentle kisses vanished and Sutton unleashed himself on her. Lust, passion, need. The kiss was way more powerful and take charge than she'd expected from a man nicknamed "The Saint."

Her mind shut down to everything but the sensuous feel of his tongue twining around hers as he explored her mouth, the soft stroking of his thumb on her cheek, and the possessive way his hand stroked her, as if it knew her intimately.

Then Sutton eased back, treating her lips to nibbles, licks, and lingering smooches. "Think they're gone?" he murmured.

"Who?"

He chuckled. "Your ex."

"Oh. Right. Them." She untwined her fingers from his soft hair and let her arms drop—slowly letting her hands flow over his neck and linebacker shoulders and that oh-so-amazing chest.

Their gazes collided the second she realized Sutton's heart beat just as crazily as hers did.

"So did that pass as the real deal kiss you wanted? Or do I need to do it again?"

Yes, please.

Don't be a pushover. Let him know who's in charge.

London smoothed her hand down her blouse. "For future reference, that type of kiss will work fine."

Sutton smirked. "It worked *fine* for me too, darlin'."

His face, his body, his voice—everything about him tripped her every trigger. The man would be hell on her libido.

Or you could be hell on his. Take Mel's advice. Getcha some mattress action. See exactly what it'd take to get "The Saint" all hot under the collar.

When she smiled at him, his body stiffened. "Why do you look so nervous?"

"Because that devious smile you're sporting is scary. So let's skip what it means for now. You said you needed two things from me before you'd agree to work with Dial. First is this boyfriend fake out stuff. What's the other?"

"I need a place to crash. Since I'll be working with your horse every day, I'll be crashing with you for the summer."

Chapter Three

Crashing with him?

What the bleeding hell?

He opened his mouth to protest and London laughed. "Dude, you oughta see the look on your face!"

"So you were just dicking with me?"

Her smile dried. "Sorta."

"Explain...sorta?"

"Okay. Fine. I've been living in my camper since Stitch ditched me."

"Stitch? Seriously? Your ex's name is Stitch? Is he really funny or something?"

London rolled her eyes. "No. His given name is Barclay or something stupidly stuffy. The year he turned five he was in the emergency room for stitches like ten times. The doctor said they oughta change his name to Stitch and it stuck. Anyway, I didn't have any place to go after his breakup text."

"Why didn't you go home? I've been to your house. It's huge." He paused. "Did you have a falling out with your parents?"

"No. But I'm twenty-seven. Returning home...I'd feel like a failure. I've been on my own for years. I only gave up my apartment because I was practically living at Stitch's anyway." She looked away. "I thought the relationship would be permanent. When it turned out not to be? I should've followed my mom's advice to always take care of myself first and to not give away things for free."

"Meaning...why buy the cow when you're giving the milk away for free?" he teased.

"No. Meaning I trained Stitch's horse. That's part of the reason he's done so good on the circuit this year."

His gut clenched. "He didn't pay you?"

She shook her head. "Worse. I didn't charge him." Absentmindedly, she traced the polo logo on his left pec and his nipple hardened. "I've been meaning to look for a place to live that's centrally located, but my summer schedule is busy and I don't seem to have enough time."

"But you'd have time to work with Dial?"

"Yes, especially if I'm onsite with him. I just need a place to park my camper. That's it. I won't bother you at all. My morning training appointments don't start until ten. I'm usually done by six in the evening." Her gaze hooked his. "Wait. You don't live at home, do you?"

"No. I have my own place. Why?"

"I just thought maybe your injuries were such that you moved home again so your family could help you out. I remember my mom mentioning—"

"The last time I injured myself in the arena was five years ago, and yes, *that* time I did return home. As soon as I dealt with some issues, I finished the house I'd started to build for my ex. After I'd changed the layout so it was what I wanted not what she'd demanded."

London's hazel eyes softened. "Glad to see I'm not the only one with baggage from an ex."

"You have no idea."

"Then tell me."

"Why?"

"If we're involved I'd know stuff like this. Plus, I'm nosy. So dish on the biggest bag."

Christ, she was pushy. "I met Charlotte when I started competing professionally in college. We were young. She knew what she wanted. I was too...green to see it."

"See what? That she just wanted you for your green?"

"Clever. She wanted a man who made a good living but was gone all the time. After my career setback and the injuries that required multiple surgeries...I was off the circuit. That meant no money coming in and I'd be underfoot expecting her to take care of me. She bailed on me the second week of my recovery."

"Harsh. That sucks."

Sutton let himself get a full look at this woman he'd spent a good five minutes kissing. High forehead and cheekbones. Dark eyebrows and eyelashes. Her eyes were more green than brown. With her auburn hair and fair complexion he expected to see freckles, but her skin was smooth. Flawless. Her lips, when they weren't flattened into an angry line, were pink and lush and way too tempting. If he had to describe her heart-shaped face with one word he'd say...sweet.

"Why the fuck are you gawking at me, bulldogger?"

And...not so sweet. Undeterred, he traced the curve of her neck, intrigued by how her pulse jumped at his touch. "Because it's one of the first times you've let me. And darlin', you *are* a pretty sight when you ain't scowling at me."

She blushed. But she didn't move away from his touch. "Can I ask you something?"

"Sure."

"Were you ever a player?"

"How would you react if I said yes?"

London considered him for a moment. "I'd be surprised."

"Why?"

"You seem more settled than the last time we crossed paths."

Wrong. He'd never been more unsettled, which was proof people saw what they wanted. "Not to disagree, but you were so busy painting me as the enemy back then that's all you saw. I'm not a bad guy; I was just trying to prove myself in the arena. Any of the player stuff I get accused of is because I get mixed up with Saxton Green."

She snorted. "I've met him. He doesn't hold a candle to you." London realized she'd paid him a compliment and backtracked. "Well, hate to burst your bubble, pal, but you'll still be proving yourself to me."

They realized, simultaneously, they were still body to body, face to face. But when London tried to bolt, Sutton wouldn't let her. "Steady. Don't want the people watching us to think we had a tiff after that kiss, would we?"

Her eyes widened. "Do you think there are people watching us?"

"I know there are, because darlin', that was some kiss."

Her lips curved into a smile. "Yes, it was."

Sutton pressed his lips to her forehead. "Let's head to your camper to finish this discussion in private before my thirty minutes are up."

London retreated, took his hand and said, "This way."

On the walk to where the competitors and exhibitors had set up camp, London said hello to several people but didn't introduce him, and luckily no one recognized him.

Her camper was the pull-behind kind—not fifth wheel sized, but the funky silver-bullet Airstream type. He noticed it was still hooked up to her truck. "When did you get here?"

"Late yesterday afternoon." She unlocked the camper door. "After you."

Sutton hadn't known what to expect when he'd stepped inside, so the vibrant color scheme filled in the blanks about what kind of person London was in the hours off the dirt.

Crafting stuff covered every inch of surface area across the small table. "I function in creative chaos and don't normally have visitors."

"What'd the smashed coffee pot on the ground outside do to get tossed out?"

"Quit working."

"Ah." He leaned against the wall while she packed things away. "You're lucky you've got this much space. Bad thing about bein' on the road is there's never enough room in the living quarters of a horse trailer."

"That's why my mom insisted I get this. She has no problem hauling horses, but she insists on sleeping in a hotel."

"Smart lady."

"So, Sutton, what do you do during the day at home since you aren't training or on the road?"

"Physical therapy some days," he lied. Those days were behind him. "Other days, I'm a great gate opener when my dad and brothers need extra help on the ranch."

London looked up sharply. "You don't ranch?"

He shook his head. "Growing up a rancher's kid, I never saw the appeal, just all the damn work."

"I hear ya there. I didn't date ranchers' kids because I never wanted to be a rancher's wife." She sorted beads and strips of twine into a plastic catch-all container with dozens of different compartments. "Does this feel awkward to you?" she asked without meeting his gaze.

"What? Me bein' in your camper?"

"That, and the fact that we'll be spending a lot of time together over the next few weeks. An hour ago, we were strangers who'd spoken just one time and now we've played a pretty intense round of tonsil hockey, and here we are alone."

He laughed. "If I think too hard on it, yeah, it'd seem weird. But I approached you, London. I figured that my offer would catch you off guard."

"As I'm sure my counter offer did you."

"Yeah. Well, I ain't exactly sure how that'll work."

London's shoulders stiffened.

"That came out wrong. What I meant is we're acting like a couple only on the weekends?"

"Saturdays are my workshops, so I'd like you to be around after my sessions end."

"Not before?"

"I don't expect world champion steer wrestler Sutton Grant to stand around holding my clipboard and collecting payments."

"You'd be surprised at what I'd do to get a sense of purpose these days," he said dryly.

She smiled and kept packing stuff away. "If the rodeo finals are held on Sunday, there's usually a dance Saturday night. I'd like to put in an appearance because that'd be normal for me. And since we're together..." She glanced up at him. "Speaking of, what will we tell those nosy people who ask how we ended up falling in *lurve* so suddenly?"

Sutton scratched his chin. He really needed to shave. And make sure he didn't dress like a bum. No daily schedule meant he'd gotten lax on dressing the cowboy way, as he'd done for years. "How about the truth? I was havin' behavioral issues with Dial. I knew you'd trained him so I asked you for help. We spent a lot of time together and that's our *lurve* story."

"Perfect." She snapped the locks on her huge plastic tote. "Done."

"What is all that anyway?"

"Like I said, creative chaos. I'm the super high-energy type, which means I always need to be doing something. Making jewelry forces me to focus and slow down. It's a hobby, but since I'm so task oriented, I'm very prolific."

He could see that. "How many pieces you finish in a night?"

London shrugged. "At least two. Some nights as many as ten."

"Sweet Christ, woman. What do you do with them?"

"They're in plastic tubs in the bedroom. Hell, I think there might even be some tubs on the bed. Not like the bed has seen any action lately."

We could remedy that. Right now.

She seemed embarrassed by her confession. Before she fled, Sutton hooked a finger in her belt loop, stopping her.

"Whoa there. No running away. Especially not in here since there's no room for me to chase you, darlin'."

Her eyes blazed. "Let go."

"Nope. You're gonna tell me what you meant when you said the bed hadn't seen any action."

"That's none of your damn business."

"Wrong. Every low-down dirty personal detail about you is now my business bein's we're a couple in *lurve*." To reinforce his point, he crowded her against the cabinet. "If I remember correctly, you said your ex broke up with you a month ago. So it's been a month since that mattress has had a real pounding?"

"That mattress has been jostled and bounced, but it's *never* been pounded."

Sutton quirked an eyebrow. "Stitch too much of a gentleman to give you a good hard fuck?"

The fire in her eyes died. "Just drop it."

"How long's it been for you, London?"

"Four months."

"Motherfuckin' hell. What was wrong with that asswipe? He had sexy you in his bed and he left you alone for three goddamned months?"

"Yes. Apparently he was getting what he needed from Paige so he didn't touch me. I made excuses for his behavior. He was stressed, I was too pushy, I was too kinky. You name it, I took the blame." She sighed and studied the logo on his shirt again.

"No sirree. You ain't takin' the blame for him bein' a total douche-nozzle."

That brought a smile.

"And I will tell you something else."

"What?"

"I will take complete blame for this." Sutton's mouth crashed down on hers. With every insistent sweep of his tongue, with every sweet and heady taste of her, his pulse hammered and his cock hardened. He imagined hoisting her onto the counter and driving into her, finding out firsthand where her kink started and how hard she'd let him push her. The second kiss was hotter than the first. Once the embers started smoldering, it wouldn't be long before they ignited.

She kissed him back with the same hot need. By the time they ended the kiss, they were both breathing hard and staring at each other with something akin to shock.

Then London nestled the side of her face against his chest. "Okay. Wow. Normally I'd say, whoa, let's take a step back, but all I can think is I'd rather take a running step forward straight to my bedroom."

"In due time, darlin'."

"You busy right now? Or are you just out of condoms?"

He stroked her hair and smiled against the top of her head. After a bit he said, "Yeah, I'm out of condoms. Haven't needed them."

She lifted her head and looked at him. "What? A hot, built guy like you ain't getting any at all?"

"Nope. You said it's been four months for you? I've got you beat. It's been over nine months for me. Since before my accident."

London's skeptical gaze roamed over his face. "Are you just saying that to make me feel less shitty?"

"Why would you think that?"

She slid her hands up his chest and curled her fingers around his jaw. "Because you look like this."

He blushed. "Now you're just bein' ridiculous."

"You can't honestly tell me you don't have women hitting on you all the freakin' time."

"Not lately, bein's I've been holed up at home recovering. Ain't a lot of women prowling around my place. My dogs tend to run them off."

"Sutton. I'm serious."

"So am I." He counted to five. "Women don't want to see a man struggling to put himself back together. It's easier to go it alone. I found that out the hard way the first time." He tugged her hands away from his face, sidestepping her and the topic. "So is there a dance tonight?"

His abrupt subject change perplexed her. "Yeah, but I'd decided to skip it."

Sutton angled his head toward her box of jewelry supplies. "Got other plans?"

"Maybe." London pointed to the back of the camper. "Got a mattress that needs pounding. And darlin'"—she gave him a hungry, full-body perusal—"you look completely recovered to me."

"Much as I'd love to take you up on that offer, ain't gonna happen today."

"Why not?"

"Because even before my injury I wasn't the kind of guy to indulge in indiscriminate sex." That made him sound like a total pussy. He made light of it. "That's why they call me 'The Saint,' remember? Plus, I'm gonna make you at least buy me dinner first."

"There's a box of Corn Pops in the cupboard. And the milk is fresh." She waggled her eyebrows. "I'd totally give it away to you for free."

He laughed. "Taunting me won't change my mind."

"So saintly you is leaving *just* when it's starting to get interesting?"

"Yep. I said my piece. Come by tomorrow when you get done here.

I'll be around." He picked up the clipboard and scrawled his address and phone number in the last box where she'd written—*D.L. A-ride.* "Didja get my joke?"

"Dial a ride? Yes. Not funny."

"I've heard that before too."

"What?"

"That I lack a sense of humor and I'm always too serious about everything. So with that..." He headed for the door.

London grabbed his hand. "Did I scare you off by being too aggressive? Is that why you're slinking outta here like a scalded cat?"

"No." He said, "No," again more forcefully when her eyes remained skeptical. "I like that you know what you want—I'll never judge you for that. This all happened fast. You kissed me once; I kissed you once. I'm guessing the heat between us surprised us both, and hot stuff, ain't no doubt there's an inferno between us just waiting to ignite. We both need to think about it and decide how far this is gonna go before it blows up in our faces. But it's not happening an hour after we reconnected. And not ten steps from a bed."

"For the record, can I say I hate that you're right?" She plucked up the clipboard and clutched it to her chest. "I didn't even like you an hour ago. Now I'm pissy that you won't test the bounce factor of my mattress, so obviously my head isn't clear."

"Lust and reason rarely go hand in hand." Sutton let his gaze move over her, making sure she knew he liked what he saw. "Let's let reason win today."

"Fine. But it doesn't feel like much of a victory."

"For me either, sweetheart."

After Sutton exited London's camper, he headed straight for his truck. Unlike past years on the rodeo circuit, no one stopped him to chat. No one recognized him. That would've bothered him when he'd been trying to make a name for himself. Now it just drove home the point he was done with the world of rodeo.

Or he would be, as soon as Dial had regained some of what he'd lost. Only then could Sutton find an owner that saw the workhorse beneath the spirited nature.

The drive to his place passed quickly. At home he fed Dial and talked to him about London, mostly out of habit. There were times on the road when Sutton had felt his horse was his only friend—totally fucked up, but true. Dial wasn't just a tool to him. Most of the time the opposite was true. Dial needed the challenge of those moments on the dirt. Sutton needed the moments on the dirt as a means to an end.

Over the years, socialization had gotten easier for him, but in the beginning on the circuit, he'd remained in the background, barely speaking because he'd always been painfully shy. Early on most folks considered him conceited, but he couldn't help people seeing what they wanted to. Rather than hit the wild parties after a competition, he hid in his horse trailer and watched DVDs.

That's not to say Sutton didn't have friends—just none of them, with the exception of Breck Christianson, were professional rodeo competitors. Plenty of buckle bunnies had sniffed around him from day one. But he'd understood early on that it wasn't him personally those women saw, but him as a meal ticket.

After Charlotte dumped him and he'd survived his recovery, he'd returned to life on the blacktop and lost some of his reserve. He hadn't gone hog wild as much as he'd learned to separate love from sex. Being in a serious relationship at such a young age hadn't given him any experience with no-strings-attached, let's-fuck-just-because-it-feels-amazing kind of sex and he quickly became a huge fan of it. But even then, his sexual exploits were nowhere near what his fellow road dogs were indulging in. And he'd yet to find a woman willing to let him explore his darker side. So, he'd let her set the initial parameters and then he'd push the sassy cowgirl's boundaries.

As he walked back up to his house from the corral, it reminded him how much he loved being at home. His house was his one indulgence. Basic on the outside. But inside? Big rooms, open space. A man his size needed room to move around. And because he'd had the house built from the ground up, he'd installed an underground shooting range. The basement, dug a level deeper than most, was literally his fortress. The concrete bunker that ran a 100 yards beneath his house was completely soundproofed and fully ventilated. He could fire ten clips from an AR-15 and anyone sitting in his living room wouldn't hear even a small pop.

His private shooting range wasn't something he broadcasted, lest he get called a gun nut or a freak preparing a bunker for the end of days—neither of which were true. But he'd always been drawn to guns. Not for hunting, not for collecting, but for the actual skill it takes in shooting all types of firearms. If he hadn't been offered a college scholarship for rodeo, he would've gone into the army. And he'd taken perverse pleasure in turning the indoor "dog run" that Charlotte insisted on for her stupid poodles into a regulation competitive shooting range with all the bells and whistles he could legally buy.

Not only had the shooting range saved his sanity during his recovery period this go around, but being home for longer than a week at a time, he'd had a chance to hang out with other guys with the same passion.

Passion. He'd had passion for his sport and passion for his hobby, but passion for a woman had been missing long before his accident.

It'd shocked him how quickly passion had sparked to life with London Gradsky today. He liked the challenge of her. His thoughts scrolled back to that day she'd given him what-for when she'd found out he'd bought Dial. The fire flashing in her eyes, the over-the-top hand gestures. He admired that she didn't hold back her true nature.

She might be used to getting her own way on the dirt, but guaranteed he didn't get roped into this situation without planning to take some risks of his own.

Chapter Four

Winning four steer wrestling world championships must've paid well because Sutton Grant had a gorgeous house. A ranch style with southwestern elements. The corral spanned the distance between the house and the big metal barn-like building on the left side. A three-car garage on the right side balanced out the sprawling structure.

It was obvious this house had no full-time female occupant. No flowers or landscaping beyond a few bushes beneath the front windows. The reverse U-shaped driveway was unique, giving her the choice to pull up to the garage, follow the wide swath of blacktop and park in front of the house or pull up to the metal outbuilding.

Before she could decide which would be the best parking option, Sutton strolled out the front door sans shirt. When she tore her gaze away from his muscled torso and saw he was wearing pants—pity that—and that he was barefoot, she hit the brakes hard. Nothing on earth was sexier than a bare-chested barefoot man in faded jeans. Nothing.

Sutton meandered over.

She unrolled her window but gazed straight ahead at the garage door instead of his mesmerizing chest.

"Hey. I wasn't expecting you so early."

"Did I interrupt something? Because I can come back."

"Why would you think you interrupted something?"

Because you're half-dressed and I'm pretty sure if I look down at your holy fuck washboard abs, I'll see the top button on your jeans is undone. Then I'll imagine you were lounging naked in bed when you heard a car pull up and you're probably commando beneath those body-hugging jeans.

Jesus. She even sounded like a breathless twit in her head.

"London. Why aren't you lookin' at me?"

"Because you've got way too few clothes on." *And I've got way too many ideas on what to do with a hot, half-naked man.*

A rough-tipped finger traced the length of her arm down from the ball of her shoulder, pausing to caress the crease in her elbow, and continuing down her forearm and wrist, stopping to sweep his thumb across her knuckles. "You could even things up, darlin'. Get rid of that pesky shirt and bra."

"I'm not wearing a bra," slipped out.

Sutton sucked in a sharp breath. "Prove it."

London's head snapped around so fast she might need to find a neck brace. Her indignation vanished when she saw his dimpled grin.

"That gotcha to look at me."

"Jerk."

Keeping his eyes on hers, he gently uncurled her fingers from her grip on the steering wheel. "Let's start over. Good afternoon, London. You're lookin' pretty today. I'm happy to see you. There's a concrete slab on the far side of the barn where you can park your camper."

"Thanks."

"You're welcome."

Sutton continued staring and touching just the back of her hand in a manner that should've been sweet but sent hot ripples of awareness vibrating through her. "Uh, I'll just go park now."

He released her hand and her eyes. "Need help?"

"Nah. I've done this a million times." She drove along the front of the house, cutting the turn wide when she started down the driveway. Then she put it in reverse and cranked it hard, perfectly lining it up alongside the building. After she climbed out of the truck, she saw Sutton had already unhooked the camper from the ball hitch. "Thanks."

"My pleasure. You wanna grab the stabilizer blocks?"

She lifted them out of the back of the truck and set them on the ground.

Sutton had them in place in seconds. Then he stood and brushed the dirt from his palms.

Her focus had stuck on how the muscles in his arms flexed. Given his bulked up state, it didn't look like the man had spent the last eight months recuperating from injuries.

"London?"

She met his amused gaze. "Did I say something?"

"Not with your mouth, darlin', but you are sayin' a whole lot with them burning hot eyes of yours."

"Sorry."

"Don't be. You need help hauling anything into the house?"

London frowned. "No. But if you'll show me where I can plug in—"

"No." Then Sutton crowded her, trapping her against the side of her camper with his arm right by her face. "I'm a single guy with a four-bedroom house. There's no reason for you to stay in your camper."

Good Lord his muscles were even more impressive this close up. What weight exercise did he do to get that deep cut in his biceps? She could probably stick her tongue halfway into that groove. Then she could follow that groove down... Way down.

Stop. Mentally. Licking. Him.

"London?"

She cleared her throat. "I can think of a reason."

"What?"

Scrambled by his nearness, she said, "I snore really loud."

"I'll wear earplugs."

"I get up at least twice every night to use the bathroom."

"You have a private bathroom in your room."

"I'm messy. Really messy."

"I have a housekeeper."

She was losing this battle. *Think, London, because if you can't come up with a plausible reason to stay out of his house, guaranteed you'll be in his bed.*

"That's what I'm hoping for."

Her gaze zoomed to his. "What are you hoping for?"

"That you'll end up in my bed. Or I'll end up in yours."

Jesus. She'd said that out loud.

Grinning, he pushed back. "Come on. I'll show you the guest room."

She followed him inside. The entrance opened up into a big foyer with tile floors. Beyond the pillars separating the entrance from the hallways going either direction, she saw a great room with a fireplace, a man-sized flat screen, and puffy couches. Windows overlooked a patio. The living area melded into an open kitchen and small dining room. No bachelor bland in Sutton's abode. The colors were masculine; rust, dark brown, and tan, yet the coffee table, dining room table and chairs, and end tables were light rough-sawn wood.

"What a gorgeous space. Did you decorate it?"

"Not on your life." He snagged a black wife beater off the back of the sofa and yanked it on over his head. "I told my mom what I wanted, well, mostly what I *didn't* want, and she supervised since I wasn't around much."

"She lives close by?"

"A few miles up the road. This house is actually on the far corner of the ranch."

"Handy."

"My brothers each have their own places too."

"There are worse things than having your family as your closest neighbors."

Sutton flipped a switch and light flooded the hallway. "We've never had a problem with it. What about you? I don't remember how many siblings you've got."

"Two. My older brother, Macon, is an attorney in Denver. My younger sister, Stirling, received her masters' degrees in biology, genetics, and animal science." London held her breath, waiting for the inevitable question. *What's your degree in?* Yeah, she bristled at being the lone Gradsky kid without a college education. Instead, she'd chosen the "school of hard knocks" route.

"So you're a middle child, too?"

She slowly exhaled. "Yep."

"My oldest brother, Wynton, ranches with our dad, as does my younger brother, Creston."

"Wynton, Sutton, Creston; masculine names for strapping western ranching sons."

He leveled her with a look. "I'd think a woman named London wouldn't poke fun."

"I'm not. What are your folk's first names?"

"Jim and Sue. Mom wanted something unique for us, but personally I'd rather be Bill or Bob or Joe." He took a few steps down the hallway. "Here's the bathroom."

"At least your mother didn't go with a theme. My dad's full name is Charleston Gradsky, and he hates it so he goes by Chuck. But that didn't deter Mom from picking a southern city as my brother's name."

"So you're London because she's Berlin? Why didn't she name your sister Paris?"

She whapped him in the arm. "Too easy. She narrowed her choices to Stirling, which is a town in Scotland, or Valencia, a town in Spain. She hated the idea that Valencia could be shortened to Val. God forbid one of her kids would have a somewhat normal name."

"Wynton never uses his full name. He's gone by Wyn since he

started school. Same with Cres. But ain't no way to shorten Sutton."

"Or London."

They smiled at each other.

Sutton opened his mouth to say something then shook his head. He turned and started down the hallway. They passed two closed doors and he opened the third. "This is the guest room." He pointed. "Bathroom is through that door."

"This is really nice." The space was simple, tan walls with oak trim and oatmeal colored Berber carpet. Centered on the longest wall was a big brass bed sporting a Denver Broncos bedspread. Next to it was a nightstand with a matching orange and blue desk lamp. Opposite sat an antique dresser with a TV on top. Shades covered the windows, leaving the room cool and dark—just like she liked it. Some summer nights her camper was like sleeping in a tin can. "You've convinced me to crash here, although I'll point out it's a good thing I'm not a Kansas City Chiefs super fan."

"Bite your tongue, darlin'. Them's fightin' words."

She peeked into the bathroom. Same Broncos theme. When she looked at him again, she casually asked, "Where's your room?"

"At the other end of the hallway. There are two bedrooms on this side and two on that side." He smirked. "So yes, your room is as far from mine as it gets."

How was she supposed to respond? Good? Or that sucks?

"Need help unloading your stuff?"

"No. My stuff is scattered throughout my camper, and I need to dig it out first."

"Okay. If you need anything, holler." Then he left the room.

London used the facilities and figured out the bare minimum of what she'd need. She practically tiptoed down the hallway, leaving the front door unlatched so she wouldn't disturb Sutton with the door slamming.

She had packed a suitcase—full of dirty clothes—and set it outside hoping laundry privileges were included in her guest status. She unearthed a duffel bag and shoved the few clean clothes inside along with her makeup bag. Her laptop bag held all of her electronics and charging cords. Then she figured she'd need her boots and hat, which were in the back of her club cab. Since she'd be dealing with Dial, a notoriously stubborn horse, a crop would come in handy. She rooted around under the seat until she found it.

Looking at the pile, she wished she'd taken Sutton up on his offer of help. She slipped the strap of the duffel over her left shoulder and the laptop strap over the right. Hat on her head, boots teetering precariously on top of the zipped duffel, she reached for the suitcase handle.

"You'd rather sprain your damn neck than accept my help?"

She whirled around. Her hat, boots, and crop went flying. "Don't sneak up on me like that!"

Sutton picked up her riding crop and muttered, "I oughta use this on you."

"Okay."

He shot her a look.

She didn't break eye contact. Neither did he.

Then he offered her a mysterious smile, grabbed the suitcase and rolled it to the front door.

Whew. Talk about a hot moment. Scooping her hat onto her head, she trudged behind him. She met Sutton in the hallway. "When you're done getting settled, I'll be in the kitchen."

I don't know if I'll ever be settled around you.

Not only was he...oh, a fucking dream man with those looks, those eyes, that body, enough amazing attributes to make any man cocky, he rarely acted that way. If she didn't know better, she'd swear the man was...shy.

Nah. He couldn't be.

Why not? Why do you think you know him? You've met the man one *time. You've heard your parents talk about him, but you've had exactly one hour-long conversation with him.*

But he hadn't shied away from kissing her or from accepting her challenge to act like her boyfriend. And he'd all but told her she was crashing in his house, not her camper.

Those were the actions of a self-confident person, not the shy, retiring type.

Since when are those traits mutually exclusive?

Maybe she should stop staring at the closed door like an idiot, clean herself up, and go talk to him.

London changed from shorts into jeans. Hopefully the flies weren't bad and she wouldn't regret wearing a T-shirt instead of switching to a long-sleeved blouse. She tried to run a comb through her hair since she'd had the windows down on the way here, but the brush got stuck so she finger-combed it into a low ponytail. Not the best look, but she was headed into the pasture for the next couple of hours and bad hair days were why God had invented hats.

As she wandered down the hallway, she expected to hear the TV or maybe music, but the house remained quiet. She turned the corner into the kitchen and saw bags of groceries strewn across the quartz countertops. Whoa. That was a lot of food.

Sutton slammed the cupboard door and spun around. He seemed startled to see her. "Oh. There you are. That was fast."

She shrugged. "I travel light. And I'm not much of a primper anyway." Which is probably part of the reason her ex upgraded to a more feminine model. "What's all this food for? You having a party? Feeding an army?"

He ran his hand over the top of his head in a nervous gesture. "The food is for you, actually."

"All of it? Do I look like I eat like a fucking Broncos linebacker or something?" she asked sharply.

"No. Jesus." Bracing his hands on the counter, he hung his head. "Look. I suck at this kinda stuff, okay? I never have anyone stay with me, say nothin' of a woman. I figured I oughta stock up on girl food— yogurt, salad, fruit, diet soda, double-stuff Oreos—but I reached the checkout and realized I'd bought nothin' for me. Then I worried maybe you didn't like the stuff I'd picked so I ended up buying more. Now I'm staring at it, embarrassed as hell, knowing you'll see all this food and think I'm some kind of freak for assuming we'll eat together at all."

Oh yeah. The man really was shy and unsure. And very, very sweet, worrying how *she'd* take *his* thoughtfulness in providing food for her. Impulsively, she ducked under his arm and set her hands on his chest. "Sutton Grant. You are a saint and a total sweetheart, and forgive me for acting like a thankless dick."

"You're not upset?"

"Only that you'd assume I eat girl food. Dude, I'm meat and potatoes all the way." His heart thumped beneath her palm but he didn't touch her. "Then again, I eat salad and other healthy stuff so I can eat Oreos."

"I also bought cookies and cream ice cream."

She licked her lips. "Another fave of mine. I always say I'll have a little taste, but it never works out that way. I end up wanting more."

"I know how that goes," he murmured.

His gaze seemed stuck on her mouth.

As much as she wanted him to kiss her, she knew he wouldn't. Not without a clear sign from her. "How about I help you put these groceries away?"

He retreated. "I'd appreciate it."

"Then I'll head out and catch Dial and see where we're at."

Chapter Five

Dial proved to be his usual dickish self to London.

Which was a relief. Sutton half expected the gelding would make him look like a fool by being compliant.

London suggested Sutton stay on the outside of the corral that way Dial knew she was in charge.

It took her thirty minutes to catch him and put a halter on him. Dial didn't fight the saddle, but he needed the riding crop to get him moving.

For the next hour, he watched, mesmerized as London worked Dial over with a combination of firmness and a loving touch. He'd expected her to reward the horse with oats after she unsaddled him, removed the training bit and bridle, and thoroughly brushed him down. But she merely looked into his eyes and stroked his head as she spoke to him.

For once, Dial stood still.

Yeah, Sutton wouldn't move either if London had her hands all over him as she murmured in his ear.

Since the moment she'd driven up, her interest in him still apparent after he'd given her some time to think it over, he realized that pretending they were crazy about each other wouldn't be a problem.

London bounded across the corral, her dark ponytail swinging behind her. She was long and lean—it looked like a strong wind could knock her over, so it was hard to imagine her forcing her will on animals five times her size. He'd watched as she'd approached Dial, and her presence exceeded the size of her body.

She exited through the gate and he walked over to meet her halfway. "You all right?"

"Sore."

"Where?" he asked, alarmed.

"Don't worry. Just my arms and neck, nothing serious. Dial gets it in his head to resist and he pulls like a damn draft horse."

"You're welcome to use my hot tub if you think it'll help loosen your muscles."

London tipped her head back and squinted at him, raising her hand to block the sun. "You being a nice guy ain't an act, is it?"

"You run into guys like that? Where it's an act?"

"Guys who are assholes beneath the slicked up public persona? Yep. That's how most of them are."

Sutton started walking toward the house. "I didn't see the point in maintaining a public and a private face. If it wasn't for sponsor's requirements, I wouldn't have any public presence in the world of rodeo."

"So the perfect day at the rodeo for you?"

"Do my runs. Take my turn as a hazer. Collect my check and visit with the rodeo officials and coordinators. Hop in my truck and haul my horse home. Then have a beer on my back patio and reflect on my performance—whether I win or lose." He shot London a sideways glance. "Pretty boring, huh?"

"Not at all." When she looped her arm through his, he managed to keep his feet moving instead of stumbling over them. "Attitudes of entitlement among the rodeo participants is why I rarely take jobs with them. They want me to fix a horse in a day, when the problem's usually been years in the making. They've watched 'The Horse Whisperer' way too many times and they believe that shit is real."

"You mean that one session with Dial didn't cure him?"

"Not. Even. Close."

"Dammit. Way to dash my hopes. You're fired."

London hip-checked him.

They fell silent on the rest of the short walk, but London didn't pull away until they reached the patio. "This is such a great space. No neighbors, no traffic noises, no cattle. I could sit out here for hours and just enjoy the solitude."

"Hang tight. I'll grab us a couple of beers."

"Sounds good."

When Sutton returned, he saw that London had ditched her hat and her boots. With her face aimed toward the sky, her dark hair swaying in the breeze, a slight smile on those full lips and the sexy way she spread her toes out in the patch of sunshine, he was absolutely poleaxed. Not only by lust, but by the premonition this would be the first of many times they'd be together like this.

You wish.

When she opened her eyes and smiled at him, lust muscled aside any feelings of destiny. He ached to see her mouth wrapped around his cock. He wanted to see the diamond pattern from the metal table imbedded in her skin after he pinned her to it and fucked her hard.

"Sutton? You okay?"

"Yep." He handed her a Bud Light.

"This is perfect. Thank you."

He sipped and asked the question that'd been weighing on him. "So what's the deal with Dial?"

She expelled a long sigh. "He's got deep-seated anxiety about his ability to perform, not only to the level he's reached, but on any level at all. He feels he's being punished for a mistake that clearly wasn't his fault. And in horse years, that punishment seems like years instead of months. So he's resentful of you and the only way he can show that resentment is by not doing what you ask or demand of him."

Sutton's jaw dropped. "Are you freakin' kidding me?"

London laughed. "Of course I'm bullshitting you, bulldogger. Sheesh. That kinda psychobabble about a horse's psyche is a bunch of horseshit—pardon the pun. Dial hasn't been worked with for months. He's rusty. He's ornery. Does he miss being a workhorse and doin' what he was trained to do? No idea. Alls I can do is hope the training we both did over the years kicks in at some point." She swigged her beer. "It ain't a one day fix. But hell, maybe he'll snap back to it and he'll be ready to hit the dirt in a week."

There was his nightmare scenario.

She leaned forward and pulled a folded piece of paper out of her back pocket and dropped it in front of him. "Take a look at those numbers."

"What's this?"

"My rates."

He unfolded the paper. Stopped himself from whistling when he saw the amount. London Gradsky commanded a pretty penny for working with pretty ponies.

"Of course, I wrote that out yesterday before you offered me room and board."

"So do you need a pen so you can refigure the amount?" he teased.

"Nice try, but no. The dollar amount stays the same, but I'll double the amount of time I work with Dial until there are results."

"Sounds fair." He offered his hand and she shook it.

A meadowlark trilled and she smiled. "Your house is centrally located to how far I have to drive to my clients. I will be so glad not to have to leave my camper at a campsite."

"I'll be a snoopy bastard and ask why you've distanced yourself from Grade A Farms. Your folks know about you living in your camper, parking at different campsites every night?"

"No. And please don't tell them." She paused. "My parents are great people. No complaints on the familial relationship. But their business goals are different than mine. They breed horses and sell them. They're shrewd in that they demand stud and genetic shares from those sales, but refuse to get into the sperm collecting and artificial insemination portion of the business. For a while they were trying to fit each high-end horse to the specific rodeo discipline. I was all for that."

"They don't do that anymore?"

"Nope."

"What happened?"

"My big shot lawyer brother stuck his nose in. He created a spreadsheet that showed how much money they lost in a five-year period by doing it that way and cross referenced it with the number of national champions who were using Grade A livestock to compete. They were losing capital for a few lousy bragging rights. They revamped their policies, which is why they had no issue selling Dial to you."

"So you weren't really pissed off at me for suggesting they castrate Dial?"

"Oh, I was plenty pissed off at you about that. I'd had my sights set on breeding him with a gorgeous paint. She was sturdy, sweet-tempered, and would've done fine with the beast mounting her. Anyway, that was when I knew I had to fully strike out on my own. While some aspects of what I do are still the same, I'm not in the same place, day in, day out. My clients are varied, not just monied rodeo stars. Plus, I've tried other training disciplines, not just the ones my dad used." London nudged his knee with her foot. "You played a part in me making that decision."

"Then I think I deserve a deeper discount on your services."

She laughed. "Don't push your luck."

Sutton stood and held out his hand. "Time to earn your keep, whip cracker."

London took his hand without hesitation. "Which is what?"

"Helping me get supper on the table."

＊ ＊ ＊ ＊

Later that night they sat side by side on the swing on the patio, watching the flames crackle in the fire pit.

They'd shared a meal together, cleaned up together, and talked about everything under the sun, except rodeo and horses. Sutton expected she'd bring up the other part of their deal, acting like a couple. One thing he hadn't been clear on was whether they were telling their families they were involved or if the only place they were "out" was on the weekends at the fairgrounds. The other thing he needed to know? If London was trying to get Stitch back. He was onboard to help London save face, but he wouldn't be happy if she planned on returning to her ex. He'd played the chump before.

But as the evening wore on, he hadn't asked because it'd been easy—ridiculously so—how well they got along.

Maybe because they were both on their best behavior. Maybe it was something else that Sutton was too superstitious to name. Tempting to let this easy camaraderie lie, but he needed to know exactly where he stood with her. "Did you see Stitch and Paige last night or today?"

"No. I pretty much avoided everyone. Stayed in my camper and worked on some jewelry."

"Why?"

"I figured a few people saw that kiss at the rodeo grounds and I didn't want to explain it. Or you. I wanted to make sure we were on the same page—hah! Poor word choice, being on *that* Paige since that's now Stitch's job—before we put ourselves out there in public."

He nodded.

"So I'm really grateful you opened up your home and we can get to know each other as friends."

Fuck. There was the word he'd feared. "Friends?" he repeated. She sure as fuck hadn't wanted to be friends when she'd practically tackled him to her bed.

"Yeah. I mean you were right to put the brakes on us yesterday. I'm more impulsive in my personal life than I should be. Just like you said, you're the calm, quiet voice of reason. So if we spend this week getting to know each other, on, ah—another level, our relationship will seem less suspicious this weekend when we're together."

"Less like we're literally doin' a horse trade to get something that each of us wants?"

She laughed. "Exactly. Being friends puts us more at ease."

"Because it's all about appearances." That came out with a bitter edge.

"It has to be. I don't want to get caught in a lie. Wouldn't that be the most mortifying thing you can think of?"

No, the most mortifying thing I can think of is getting friend-zoned by you in the first four hours of play.

Damn. No wonder he didn't put himself out there. Good thing he'd asked about their parameters before he'd made a move.

But Sutton had to respect her for taking the time to consider her boundaries when she clearly had none yesterday. Yet, the bottom line for him hadn't changed. He needed London to work his horse—no matter how much he wanted to work her over in his bed nine ways to Sunday.

Friends. He could do that. Hell, he oughta be used to it by now.

But fuck if he wasn't tired of denying himself, even when it was his own damn fault. Demanding she stay with him in his house. Cooking for her. What people said about him was true. He was too damn nice and accommodating, but he did have an ulterior motive—hot kinky sex. But he didn't want London to feel obliged to fuck him, which sounded ridiculous in his head and would sound even more idiotic if he said it out loud. He needed to retreat, regroup, before he stuck his boot in his mouth.

Sutton forced a yawn and then stood. "Sorry. It's getting late."

London's eyebrows shot up. "Late? It's only eight-thirty."

Shit. "Huh. Well, it seems later than that which is a sign I should call it a night."

"Oh. Well. Sure. Do you mind if I stay up and wash some dirty clothes?"

"Help yourself to whatever you need."

"Thank you. I was afraid I'd be walking around naked tomorrow morning since everything I own is dirty."

Do not think about naked and dirty and London in the same sentence.

Friends, remember?

Repeat it. F-r-i-e-n-d-s.

Still, this was gonna be a long damn week.

Chapter Six

Now London understood why people called Sutton Grant "The Saint."

She'd been trying to get under his skin—okay mostly she'd been trying to get into his Wranglers—for the past four days and the man hadn't been tempted even once, as far as she could tell.

They spent their free time together. She stuck close while he cooked supper, tasting and touching and forcing him to feed her little tidbits. She wore pajama short shorts and a camisole that showed a lot of her skin when they watched TV. When he'd mentioned suffering from a sore neck, she'd offered to give him a massage, but he'd spoken of the personal massager his therapist had lent him. When she'd noticed his razor-stubbled face and volunteered to shave off the scruff, he'd just smiled and said he'd pick up razors next time he went to town.

A saint.

But...London knew he watched her. He watched her work with Dial—from a distance. He watched for her truck to pull into the drive at the end of her workday—from a distance. He watched her doing beadwork—from a distance. But he watched her watching TV up close and personal. He watched her all the damn time.

But that's all the man did. Watched.

What the hell was he waiting for?

Maybe he's been watching you for some sort of sign.

She'd had a huge fucking neon sign over her head from the moment they'd met that flashed "Available Now!" What more did he need?

Maybe he's not attracted to you.

Wrong. She'd felt his attraction when he'd kissed her. It'd been hard to miss or ignore as it'd dug into her belly.

Maybe he wants to stick to your business deal.

So he was saving his performance for the weekend when he'd have to be all over her?

Performance. Why did that word turn her stomach? Because she wanted it to be more? To be real?

It'd felt real on Saturday as those amazing eyes of his had eaten her up the way she knew his mouth wanted to. It'd felt real on Sunday, seeing his shy, flirting side behind the serious persona. But Monday morning he'd acted buddy-buddy—she'd half expected him to give her a noogie—and it'd been that way between them ever since, no matter how much she tried to turn the sweet saint into a red-hot sinner.

After London parked at Sutton's place, she opted to keep her sour mood to herself and headed straight for the corral rather than stopping inside the house first.

The day had turned out to be a scorcher. She stripped out of her long-sleeved shirt to just her camisole. Grabbing her tack out of the barn, she draped it over the metal railing. She looped the rope around her neck and whistled twice, surprised when Dial came trotting over. They played catch and mouse for a bit, not in an ornery way, but playful and she was happy to see the reappearance of that side of the horse.

This first week she'd planned on earning Dial's trust. He'd balked but each day made a baby step. Pushing too hard too fast caused backsliding into familiar behavior.

Maybe that's what's going on with Sutton. You're pushing a man to get what you want. What if that's not what he wants?

She'd get to the bottom of it tonight.

Since Dial had shown improvement, London decided to treat him with some oats. She'd sprinkled too many in the bucket and reached in to scoop some back out when Dial tried to crowd her to get his face in the bucket.

"Hey, rude boy, back off." She turned to move the bucket aside and she felt a sharp, hard nip on her upper arm. "Motherfucking son of a whore!" She swung the bucket up and dropped it on the other side of the fence. Something hot and wet flowed down her arm. She expected to see horse slobber but it was blood.

So much for the old wives' tale about horses bolting at the scent of blood. Dial just stared at her, unmoving, his tail flicking back and forth, trying to intimidate her.

Fuck that.

London rose up, making herself as big as possible, staring him right in the eyes. "Back off," she said sharply. "Now."

Dial backed up.

She walked over to where she'd left her shirt. Her arm stung. Small, hard horse bites hurt worse than anything, tender flesh caught between that powerful jaw. It'd been a while since a bite had broken the skin.

"London?"

Shit, shit, shit. She'd hoped she could get inside and cleaned up before seeing Sutton. No such luck.

"What's wrong?" He tried to grab her injured arm to spin her around and she hissed at him, cradling her elbow with her hand. "What the hell happened?"

"Dial bit me."

"Lemme see."

"Not a big deal. It'll be fine once it's cleaned out."

"Let me fucking see it, London. Now."

She glanced up at him.

Fury blazed in his eyes when he saw the blood. "Let's go inside and I'll take a closer look." He gently lifted her arm until it was parallel with her shoulder. Then he grabbed her shirt from her free hand and held it beneath the bite to catch the blood. "Hold it like this. Did he get you anywhere else?"

"He's not like a wolf or a dog with sewing machine teeth that just keep attacking. One chomp and that's it."

Muttering something, he looked over at the corral then back at her. "Come on."

Sutton kept his hand on top of hers beneath the wound as he led her into the house through the patio door. She expected he'd stop in the kitchen but he directed her down the hallway opposite of her wing, into his bedroom. She got an image of heavy wood furniture before she found herself in a large bathroom.

He seated her on the toilet—the lid had already been down, an extra point for that—and propped her forearm on a towel on the countertop. "How bad does it hurt?"

"You don't need to make a big deal about this. And don't worry. I won't cry."

Then Sutton was right in her face. "You don't have to be the tough chick with me. Now tell me how bad it hurts."

"It stings. Worse than my foot getting tromped on but not as bad as getting bucked off and landing on my ass."

"That's a starting point." He pushed a loose hank of hair behind her ear. "Sit tight while I dig out my first aid kit."

While Sutton rummaged in a tall cabinet, she checked out the space. No bland white fixtures, tiles, or vanity in here. Gray cabinets with black accents. The countertop was black, the sinks were gray. The walls of the glass-fronted walk-in shower were frosted, but behind that she could see the walls were speckled with the same color scheme. The space was wholly masculine yet classy.

"You ready for me to clean this out and gauge the damage?" he asked softly.

"Shouldn't I ask for your medical qualifications first?"

"Helicopter medic in 'Nam. Did two tours in the medical corps during the Gulf War, then a stint in Iraq and Afghanistan."

London smiled. "And some people say you don't have a sense of humor. Wait, is it considered bathroom humor if you actually crack jokes in the bathroom?"

"Now who's the funny one? So it's okay if I poke around?"

"Take off your belt so I have something to bite down on."

She watched as he uncapped a bottle of antiseptic. Every muscle in her body tightened.

"You weren't kiddin' about needing the strap, were you, darlin'?"

Whoa. She could take that the wrong way—but so could he. She said nothing and shook her head.

"Maybe you'd better look away and focus on something else."

London locked onto the visage that'd distract her—Sutton's handsome face. She knew he'd shaved this morning but dark stubble already coated his cheeks, jaw, and throat. She'd fallen into a fantasy where he left beard burns on her throat as he ravished her when he said, "Doin' okay?"

"I guess." She hissed at the stinging spray.

"This stuff will kick in soon and it has a numbing agent."

"How bad does it look? Is the skin flapping so I'll need stitches?"

"No. The bleeding's mostly stopped now." He pressed a gauze pad over the mark.

"Fuck that stings."

"Almost done."

The way he said it... "No, you're not. And if that's the case? I'd rather sit on the counter than the toilet. Then you won't have to bend down and get a crick in your neck." She stood before he could argue. But he curled his hands around her hips and hoisted her up. She automatically widened her knees so he could step between them.

When he reached for her arm, the backs of his knuckles brushed the outside of her breast and her nipple immediately puckered. Because Sutton had his head angled down, she couldn't tell if he'd noticed or not.

But she noticed everything about him. The scent of clean cotton mixed with the darker scent of oil emanating from beneath his starched collar. His full lips were parted as he concentrated on his task, but his breathing stayed steady. She wanted to run her fingers through his dark hair, trap his beautiful face in her hands and suck on those lips until his mouth opened for her kiss. Whisper secrets in his ear while his hair teased her cheek.

Mostly she wanted to ask the question that'd been burning on her tongue for days.

Do it.

"Are you ever going to make a move on me?"

That caught his attention. "What?"

"That wasn't a question to be answered by another question. Just tell me the truth."

Sutton lifted his head. "Where's this coming from, *friend?*"

Hey, was that sarcastic? She squinted at him. "It's coming from the fact we're supposed to be acting like boyfriend and girlfriend and you haven't kissed me or touched me beyond a friendly pat since we were in the camper, and I'm pretty sure kissing and petting is something we need to practice. A lot. So to recap, you haven't touched me since Saturday. It is now Wednesday."

"I know what day it is, London," he said testily.

"Oh yeah? Do you know what I call it? Hump day."

Silence as Sutton taped a chunk of gauze over the bite.

"I thought you'd at least crack a smile at that."

"It's really fucking hard to smile when you're bleeding in my bathroom because my douche-nozzle horse took a bite of you. Sometimes I think that nasty motherfucker deserves to spend his life isolated, and I don't know why I give a shit that he's properly trained since I'd like to ship him off to the damn glue factory."

"He didn't do it on purpose," she said softly.

His angry eyes finally met hers. "The fuck he didn't."

Seeing that fierceness? For *her?* Immediate lady boner.

"Can I tell you a secret, Sutton?"

"What?"

And then she couldn't do it. Couldn't tell him that Dial had shown remarkable progress in just four days. Because if she told him that...then what was his incentive to keep her here?

None.

She couldn't take that chance.

Even if she just had one quick run-in with Stitch this weekend, he'd see firsthand that she wasn't crying in her camper over him. That she'd hooked up with a hot man who sometimes stared at her—when he thought she wasn't looking—like he'd already stripped her naked and was fucking her over the back of his couch.

If it made her a douche-nozzle to fantasize about the shock on her ex's face when he realized his loss was a better man's gain, then so be it; she'd take it.

"London?"

"I like the way you say my name. Classy and dignified, with a hint of sexiness. Makes me wonder how it'd feel to have your mouth on me when you moan it."

"Jesus, London, knock it off."

She frowned. "Okay, that wasn't sexy at all."

"I'm not trying to be sexy with you right now," he snarled—in a decidedly sexy way, not that she'd point that out.

"You should be!" She poked him in the chest. "We're in *lurve*, remember? We are in the throes of a new relationship and that means we oughta be talking about fucking all the time."

"Do you always say the first damn thing that pops into your head?" he demanded.

"Pretty much. No reason to beat around the bush when you could be touching my bush, if you get my drift. See, alls I'd have to do is scoot my butt to the edge of this counter and you could slide inside me. After we're done eating supper, you could spread me out on the dining room table and have me for dessert." She allowed a small smile. "Or I could have you."

"Is there a point to your teasing?"

"That's the thing," she mock-whispered. "I'm not teasing."

While he stood staring at her—*through* her really—she saw his eyes darken as he imagined the exact scenarios she'd just detailed. Then his eyes turned conflicted and a little frosty. "Bullshit."

"What?"

"You're bein' a cock tease. You said you wanted to be *friends*, remember? Wasn't what I wanted, wasn't what I thought you wanted, but I've stuck to those parameters. So we're friends. But every damn time you touch me or get close to me and say such blatantly sexual things, the last goddamn thing I'm thinking about is bein' your friend.

I'm a man, not a fucking saint, as I've heard you mutter loud enough for me to hear. You bein' all cute, flirty, funny, and sweet ain't helping me keep the parameters *you* set Sunday night."

Her jaw dropped. "*That's* what you got from our conversation Sunday night? That I just wanted to be friends with you?"

"How else was I supposed to take it?"

"Like it was the talk you demanded we have *before* we got involved on any level! That we'd discuss it. I said *friends* because I didn't think you'd appreciate me saying I'd rather ride *you* all damn night than your horse. And you jumped to the conclusion that *all* I wanted to be with you was friends? Bullshit. You ran away and pouted, bulldogger, when you jumped up and went to bed."

"What should I have done instead?"

"This." London curled her hand around the back of his neck and pulled his mouth to hers. No sweet kiss, no teasing. She fucked his mouth with her tongue like she wanted him to fuck her body. A hot, wet, drawn-out raw mating.

Sutton clamped his hand on her ass and jerked her to the edge of the counter, pressing his groin to hers. Kissing her without pause, holding her in place so he could ravage her mouth and her throat.

After his lips blazed a trail to her nipple, and he sucked on it through the fabric of her cami, she pulled back. "Tell me, bulldogger. Does that feel like I just wanna be friends with you?"

"No. Now give it back. I'm not done with it."

She started to laugh, but it turned into a moan when he pinched the wet tip with his fingers as his mouth reclaimed hers.

Holy hell could the man kiss. And touch. And rub and grind and get her so hot and bothered with her clothes on that she might've had a teeny orgasm right there.

Four loud raps sounded on his outer bedroom door, followed by, "Sutton? Come on. Dad's waiting in the truck."

Sutton froze. Then he broke the kiss and gazed into her face. Any chance she'd had of making light of the situation evaporated when she saw the sexual heat smoldering in those turquoise eyes.

When he brought his thumb up and traced the lower swell of her lip, the intensity pouring from this man might've set off another mini O.

"Sutton? Who's at the door?"

"Cres. We're taking Dad out to the Moose Club for poker night."

"Shouldn't you get going?"

"Yeah. In a minute." He pressed a kiss to her lips, then her chin, then her cheeks. "I'll be back late."

That's when she knew they were done for tonight—all night. She hopped down from the counter. "Thanks for the first aid. I'll go lie down now, but have fun with your family and I'll see you in the morning."

London pushed him out of his bathroom and locked the door.

Let him meet his brother with a hard-on. It'd serve him right for being an idiot.

Friends. What the hell had he been thinking?

* * * *

Sutton's cell phone rang on his nightstand early the next morning, yanking him from a hot dream where he'd taken London up on her offer of an after-dinner treat—except in his version they were on the rug in front of his fireplace, him having his dessert while she also had hers. Sixty-nine usually didn't appeal to him, but in his dream, he didn't have to concentrate on both giving and receiving pleasure—just being naked with her was the pleasure. Warm skin beneath his hands, her skilled mouth, the long trail of her hair teasing up the inside of his thighs...

His phone kept buzzing.

He answered, "Yeah?"

"Grant? It's Ramsey."

Ramsey? Why the hell was his shooting buddy calling him so early? "Do you know what the fuck time it is?"

"Seven. I thought you ranching/cowboy types were up when the cock crows."

"I'm not a rancher, as you well know, so fuck off."

Ramsey laughed.

"What's up? Is your shooting range under fire?"

"Ha. Ha. You're fucking hilarious first thing in the morning."

"Why else would you be calling me? Wait. Are you offering your favorite customers free day passes?"

"You wish. And you're more than just a customer." Ramsey paused. "Look, this might seem like it's coming outta the blue but the truth is we both know that we've skirted this subject for months, so I'll just say it straight out. You're dealing with some heavy shit as far as getting back on track with your career. I recognize restless, man. So I'm not convinced that you want to return to that life on the road."

Sutton had no idea where this conversation was coming from. Wasn't like he'd gotten shitfaced with Ramsey and spilled his guts.

Maybe your lack of enthusiasm about returning to rodeo isn't as disguised as you believe. Your brothers mentioned the same thing in passing. More than once. "Now you've got my attention."

"I appreciate every time you've pitched in and helped out at the gun range. I've hinted around that I could use you on a part-time basis. You've been polite but vague on whether you'd seriously consider it. So maybe you won't give a damn, but I've run into a tricky situation, hence the early morning call."

"What situation?"

"My full-time range master, Berube, got orders and he's being deployed in a month. His deployment will last a year. That leaves me short a range master."

"Which makes me feel your pain as a customer and your friend, but why are you telling me?"

"Because you're an expert shot. You're very knowledgeable about guns without being a know-it-all asshole or a reckless dick."

"But I'm not a range master."

"You'd be a shoo-in to pass the range master's exam—the firearms range testing portion anyway. There's also a written test, but since you've earned a college degree, I'm sure that won't be a problem either."

Ramsey didn't hand out praise lightly, and Sutton found himself feeling proud of something for the first time in months.

"It's short notice, I know, but I'd planned a boys' night out for my instructors at my cabin to discuss the future growth of the gun range. Every guy who works for me will be there, so if you're even remotely interested in the position, this'd be the ideal time to get answers directly from the ones who work with me."

"Just one night? Or an all weekend thing?" He couldn't flake out on London. She expected him to play his part as her boyfriend.

"Just one night. Weekends are our busiest time so we'll be back at work tomorrow."

Two knocks sounded on the door. Then it opened and London walked in.

More like she sashayed in, wearing a see-through flimsy black thing that left nothing to the imagination. He could make out every muscled inch of her toned legs, the slight flare of her hips. Her flat belly and defined abs. Strategically placed bows hid her nipples but not the sweet curve of her tits.

"Sutton? I hope I'm not interrupting. I heard you talking in here so I assumed you were up. Look, I can't figure out the coffee pot. It keeps beeping at me every time I hit start."

Mostly Sutton heard, *blah blah blah* which translated to, "Look at my perky tits," followed by *blah blah blah*, "look at these naughty red panties that barely cover my pussy," and then *blah blah blah*, "look at my sexy bedhead and imagine holding this tangled hair in your fists while I suck your cock."

Fuck me. *Fuck me twice.*

"What the hell? Did you just tell me to fuck off?"

His rational train of thought had hit a fucking brick wall named London Gradsky.

"Sorry, no, I didn't say that. Gimme five minutes and I'll call you right back." Sutton tossed the phone on his bed without checking to see if he'd actually ended the call. "What. In. The. Name. Of. All. That's. Holy. Are. You. Doing. Half. Fucking. Naked. In. My. Bedroom?"

"I told you! Were you even listening to me?"

Not the words falling from your mouth when your body is speaking its own language loud and clear. He cleared his throat. "I was on the phone, so I missed most of what you'd said. What's the problem?"

"Your coffee pot hates me. I can't figure it out."

"I'll be right there after I slip some pants on." And after he whacked off so she didn't see how hopeful his dick was at seeing a hot, half-naked woman in his room first thing in the morning.

"Fine."

She turned to flounce out and he noticed she wore a thong. So she treated him to a full look at that perfect ass of hers before the crabby, horny man inside him yelled out, "And you'd better put some damn pants on too!"

Even with morning wood it only took him a minute to rub one out in the shower. He brushed his teeth and packed his overnight bag before he exited his room.

In the kitchen, he was both relieved and annoyed to see London had donned a robe.

"Took you long enough," she groused. "You've had coffee ready for me every day this week, so I don't think you understand the importance of coffee in my life. I'm a bitch on wheels without my morning caffeine fix."

"I saw the poor, unfortunate coffee maker that failed to do your bidding, so I'm aware of your demands. Watch and learn." He dumped the beans in and set the lid on the filter basket. "Line up these arrows. This is a grind and brew model. If the arrows aren't lined up, then it won't work at all."

"Oh. Thanks. Now it makes sense."

He smothered a yawn. "You're welcome."

"What time did you get home last night?"

"Late. Dad likes to cut loose on poker night. Especially if he wins. If I'd gotten home earlier, I planned on..." His gaze swept over her, from bedhead to pink-tipped toes. "Never mind what I'd planned 'cause it's a moot point now. That phone call earlier was a reminder that I have a prior commitment. So I'll be gone all day and tonight."

"But you *will* be back by tomorrow? You're coming to the Henry County Fair and Rodeo with me this weekend?"

"Yes. But I'll have to meet you there."

"Promise?"

He scowled. "I'm a man of my word, London."

She scowled back at him. "You'd better be. And where are you going on such short notice anyway?"

Away from temptation. At least for one night. While I figure out why in the hell I like you so much and I've only known you five days. And why that make-out session last night in my damn bathroom was more erotic than any sex I've had in years. "I'm headed out for a retreat."

"A spiritual retreat? Is that why they call you 'The Saint?'"

Sutton rolled his eyes. "I'm called 'The Saint' because I carried a Saint Christopher medallion my grandmother gave me when I first joined the pro tour. The guys saw it and ragged on me endlessly."

"Good to know. I'm assuming the name fit your lifestyle back then?"

"At first they tried calling me 'The Monk' but it didn't stick."

"Why not?"

He pinned her with a look. "Because there's a big difference between bein' a saint and a monk. And newsflash, darlin'... I'm neither."

Flustered, London poured a cup of coffee while the pot still brewed.

"How's your arm today?"

She faced him and shrugged. "Doesn't feel too bad."

"So you're working with Dial this morning?"

"That's what I get paid to do."

His cell phone rang again. He checked the caller ID. Ramsey. Impatient bastard. He tucked his phone in his pocket. "I've got to go. Do you need anything before I do?"

"No."

"You're sure? No issues locking up?"

"I've been in a house in the country by myself before, Sutton."

If she'd shown any fear, he'd open up the locked door and assure her that she was far better protected than she could fathom.

"Wait. There is one thing I want."

When Sutton's eyes met the heat in hers, he knew exactly what she wanted. To avoid temptation, he curled his hands around the straps of his duffel bag and took two steps backward. "I can't. Not now."

"Why not?"

"Because the second I put my hands and mouth on you, we ain't goin' anywhere for the rest of the day. And night. We may even miss the entire Henry County Fair."

A sexy smirk curled her lips. "Then you'd better get going."

Chapter Seven

After London had loaded up her camper and hit the road toward Henry County Fairgrounds, she'd had way too much time to think. And all her thoughts were focused on one super-hottie, Sutton Grant.

Like...what did he do during the day? He wasn't involved in his family's ranching operation. Did he obsessively work out, trying to speed up his rehab and return to competition form? Because heaven knew, the bulldogger had the most banging body she'd ever seen up close and personal. Well, sort of up close and personal. Not that she'd gotten to do more than drool over his sculpted chest, arms and abs, even when the tempting man walked around his house half-naked.

She pondered other things Sutton could be doing with his time. Doing pay-per-view porn in his bedroom? Yeah, she'd pay to see that. Or maybe he was just watching XXX Websites all day. Maybe he played video games. She'd met her fair share of guys who were addicted to their X-box or PlayStation.

Why don't you just ask him?

Yeah, that'd go over well since he'd been so forthcoming about where he was going.

London froze. Wait a damn minute. Had Sutton been purposely vague because he'd set up a bootie call and didn't want her to know? Every time his cell phone rang this week, he'd excused himself to take the call in private.

But hadn't he told her that he hadn't been with a woman since his accident?

And you believed him? A harsh, sarcastic bark of laughter echoed in her head. *Because no man has ever lied about sex.*

Dammit. Had he played her?

Since Stitch had dumped her, she'd second-guessed everything about her attractiveness to the opposite sex, her personality, her sexual skills, and how she conducted herself on a professional level. In her twenty-seven years she'd never been the type of woman who needed validation from a man or a relationship to feel worthy of either.

Sutton Grant had better fall in line. Because he needed her more than she needed him.

* * * *

London had arrived early enough to score a primo parking place in the area specifically marked for rodeo contestants, stock contractors, exhibitors, and vendors. Being part of "tent city" was one of her favorite things about summer rodeo season. Nothing like sitting in front of a bonfire, drinking beer, laughing and talking about horses, rodeo, and the western way of life with other likeminded souls.

She tidied up the camper, deciding if Sutton showed, she'd let him sleep in the bed tonight since his big body wouldn't fit on the convertible sleeping area up front. But she'd be lying if she wasn't hoping they'd share that lumpy mattress sometime this weekend.

Then she changed into an outfit that made her feel sexy and desirable—a sleeveless lavender shirt embellished with purple rhinestones, her beloved b.b. simon crystal encrusted belt, her Miss Me jeans with black studded leather angel wings on the back pockets, and a pair of floral stitched Old Gringo cowgirl boots. She fluffed her hair, letting it fall in loose waves around her shoulders. After applying heavier makeup and a spritz of tangerine and sage perfume, she exited the camper.

The heat of the day hung in the air but the lack of humidity made it bearable. Still, an icy cold beer would make it better. London bought a bottle of Coors and wandered through tent city to see who was around.

The second person she ran into was Mel. "Hey, girl. If I'd known you were already here I'da brought you a frosty beverage."

Mel smiled and kept brushing down her palomino. "It's okay. I've gotta run Plato a bit so I'll take a rain check."

"Deal." London sipped her beer and looked around.

"Please don't tell me you're here so you can spy on Stitch and Paige."

London snorted. "As if. I don't give a hoot about them."

"Since when?"

"Since you told me I needed to get laid. A new guy barged into my life and swept me off my feet last weekend."

Mel stopped brushing Plato's back. "Are you kidding me?"

"Nope. He's hot, he's sweet, and he's crazy about me." London said a little prayer: *don't you let me down Sutton Grant, or so help me God I will superglue your dick and balls together in your sleep.*

"Uh-huh," Mel said skeptically. "But this guy that's so hot for you isn't from around here, is he? So I can't meet him."

"Wrong. He'll be here." She hoped.

Before Mel could demand more details, Stitch's best friend Lee—nicknamed Lelo on the circuit because of his association with Stitch—meandered over. He still wore his back number from the slack competition. "Hey Mel."

"Lelo. How's it hanging?"

"They ain't dangling low at all when I see you. They're high and tight and raring to go."

Mel muttered something.

When it became obvious to Lelo that Mel didn't intend to banter with him, he looked at London. "Hey. What's up?"

"Not much. What's up with you?"

"Askin' around, seein' where the parties are tonight."

A challenge danced in Mel's eyes. "Really, Lelo? Because I heard that Stitch and Paige were having a *huge* party at their campsite before the fireworks kicked off."

Lelo's mouth opened. Then snapped shut.

"I thought maybe you'd come by to invite me personally," Mel continued.

He looked between Mel and London. "Well, I, ah—"

"And since London is here, it'd be rude of you not to include her in that invite, doncha think?"

Jesus, Mel was a shit-stirrer sometimes. And precisely the reason they got along like gangbusters.

"I don't know if that's such a good idea, Mel, bein's they...dammit, you know why I can't invite her," Lelo blurted.

"Because London and Stitch used to date?" Mel flashed her teeth at London. "Water under the bridge, Lelo, since my girl here has herself a new boyfriend."

Shut your face, Mel, shut it right fucking now.

Lelo's eyes went comically wide—as if he hadn't considered that a possibility.

Which pissed London off. Big time.

"You don't say?" he said to London. "I thought you were still—"

"Hung up on Stitch?" Mel supplied. "Huh-uh. That's some bullshit Stitch and Paige have been spreading around so people don't hate him because he fucked London over."

"Mel," London warned.

"What? I'm sick of Opie and Dopie hinting around that you're some broken-hearted chump. Girlfriend, you are hot as lava and you were always way, way above Stitch's pay grade."

Lelo's focus bounced between them like he was watching a volleyball match. Then he said, "So who is this fella you're seein'? Anyone we know?"

Just then someone shouted her name. Someone with a deep, sexy voice.

London sidestepped Lelo and looked down the walkway between the horse trailers. There he was. The quintessential cowboy. And he stood less than fifty yards away. "Sutton?"

"Whatcha waiting for, darlin'? C'mere and gimme some sugar." He held his arms open.

Grinning, she ran toward him. He caught her and spun her in a circle before settling his mouth over hers. She twined her arms around his neck and gave herself over to his kiss.

And what an intoxicating kiss it was. His mouth teased, seduced, inflamed. By the time he eased back to brush tender kisses over her lips and jaw, her entire body shook.

Sutton whispered, "Sorry I'm late."

She nuzzled his neck, wishing she could pop open the buttons on his shirt and get to more skin. "You're here now."

"Did you think I wouldn't show?"

"The thought had crossed my mind."

He forced her to look at him. And her knees went decidedly weak staring into those crystalline eyes of his. "I said I'd be here. I'm a man of my word, London."

Sliding her arms down, she flattened her palms on his chest. "But when you left yesterday morning, you acted pissed off. So what was I supposed to think?"

"That I'm a man of my word," he repeated. He curled his hand around her jaw, denying her the chance to look away. "Ask me why I left my own damn house."

"Why'd you leave?"

"Because my willpower to finish the 'friends' conversation

vanished the instant you showed up in my room wearing them baby doll pajamas that oughta be illegal, looking so fucking cute and sexy I had to sneak into my bathroom and whack off before I taught you how to use the coffee maker."

Her mouth dropped open.

"Surprised?"

"Very. You've seemed so...unaffected."

A growling noise rumbled from him before his mouth descended and he kissed the life out of her. She was so damn dizzy when he finally relinquished her lips, she had to fist her hands in his shirt just to keep from toppling over.

Then his breath was hot in her ear, sending shivers down the left side of her body. "Does that seem unaffected to you, sweetheart?"

"Ah. No."

"Good. Maybe you oughta offer me a little reassurance this ain't one sided."

London wreathed her arms around his neck and played with the hair that fell to his nape. "I've left my door cracked open every night, hoping you'd see an open door as an open invitation. I imagined the look on this gorgeous face if you caught me diddling myself."

His eyes darkened. "What did you imagine me doin' if I caught you?"

"Barging in, tying my hands to the brass headboard and driving me crazy with my vibrator before you pounded me into the mattress like you'd promised."

Another low-pitched growl reverberated against her skin. "You and me are gonna get a few things straight tonight. But probably not until after I fuck you hard at least once and swat your ass for you ever doubting me."

Sutton swallowed her gasp with another bone-melting kiss.

When he finally released her lips, she murmured, "You know, I'm not busy right now."

He laughed and pulled back slightly. "How about you introduce me to your friends first? Then I'll feed you."

"You don't have to do that."

"What? Meet your friends?"

"I want you to meet my friends, but you don't have to feed me since you cooked for me all week."

Sutton traced the bottom edge of her lower lip with his thumb. "I've liked having you around this week, London. More than I thought I would." After another kiss, he stepped back only far enough to drape his left arm over her shoulder.

They started toward Mel and Lelo. Mel wore a look of shock only less obvious than Lelo's.

"Did you tell your friends about me?" he asked softly.

"Just that I'd met a hot man. I didn't give them your name in case you didn't show up and I'd have to find me a new guy on the fly."

His arm fell away briefly so he could slap her ass. He grinned when she yelped. Then he whispered, "Oh ye of little faith. 'Fraid I'll have to punish you for that lapse."

"A hot lashing with your tongue or a spanking? Luckily, I'm good with either."

He nipped her earlobe. "Good to know. But it's not like I'm gonna let you choose which one *I* prefer."

"Funny."

"I wasn't joking. Now that you've shared your rope fantasy, I'll add it to mine that involves…you'll just have to wait and see, won't you?"

Holy. Hell. Heat licked the inside of her thighs.

Mel and Lelo stood side by side in front of Plato. Before London could offer introductions, Lelo blurted out, "Man-oh-man, you're Sutton Grant."

Sutton extended his hand. "Yes, I am. Who're you?"

"Lee Lorvin, but everyone calls me Lelo. It's so great to meet you. I'm a huge fan."

"Thanks."

Lelo stared and just kept pumping Sutton's hand until Mel shouldered him aside.

"Hiya handsome," she cooed. "I'm Mel Lockhart, London's fellow road dog. I too am a huge fan. I watched you win the CRA championship in Vegas the year Tanna Barker also won for barrel racing."

"Nice to meet you, Mel. Glad you were entertained that year."

"Uh, *yeah*, hard not to be jumping up and down outta my seat when you set the record for the fastest time."

London glanced at him, and the man seemed embarrassed by the focus on him. And she wanted to rub Mel's face in the dirt to see if that'd erase her expression of lust.

"So you're a barrel racer?" he asked Mel.

"No. I'm in the cutting horse division. Not as glamorous as the rodeo events people pay to see, but I do well."

"Bein' able to cut cattle out of a large herd is far more challenging and entertaining than any scheduled rodeo event," Sutton said. "It's a real skill that's needed in ranching."

London inwardly sighed at Sutton's sweetness in making sure Mel knew her competitive event was appreciated. What kind of man did that?

"Are you about healed up and ready to get back to competing?" Lelo blurted out, interrupting the conversation.

She felt Sutton stiffen beside her, but outwardly he stayed cool. "I'm in the 'wait and see' stage right now." He turned and kissed London's temple. "Luckily, I sweet talked London into working with my horse again while I'm at loose ends."

"That's right," Mel said. "I remember Berlin told me that London initially trained your horse at Grade A Farms."

"I knew she was the only woman for the job. I just had to convince her to take me on."

"You do have some interesting methods of persuasion, bulldogger."

He laughed. "You're gonna give your friends the wrong impression of me, darlin'."

"Not me," Mel quipped, "because I'm sure hoping you've got a dirty-minded, sweet-talking single brother."

"I've got two."

Mel's lashes fluttered. "They as big and good-looking and charming as you?"

"Mel!" London said with fake admonishment.

"What? It can't hurt to ask." She scooted closer to London to whisper, "You decide to get laid and the next thing I know you've hooked up with the smokin' hottie known as 'The Saint?' Girlfriend, I'm so proud of you I might just bust a button."

Lelo made a noise and they realized he was still staring slack-jawed at Sutton.

"Lelo, you're gonna catch flies if you don't shut your big trap," Mel drawled.

"Sorry. It's just...Sutton Grant. Your runs are damn near perfect. That's why folks call you 'The Saint' because you never screw up."

"Oh, I wouldn't say never. And that's not the only reason I've been called that." He sent London a conspiratorial wink. "But it doesn't apply this week, does it darlin'?"

"Stitch is gonna flip his shit when he meets you."

Ooh, mean-girl London clawed her way to the surface. "Pity then that I'm not invited to Stitch and Paige's party, isn't it?"

Lelo's mouth opened. Closed. Opened again. Then he cleared his throat. "Uh, well, maybe I spoke outta turn. I'm sure Stitch don't have no hard feelin's if you don't, London."

Sutton sent her an amused look. "Up to you darlin', what we do tonight. You know if I had my way we'd head to the camper right now and wouldn't leave until..." His heated head to toe perusal was as powerful as an actual caress. "Until tomorrow. Late tomorrow."

"Looks like you're shit outta luck, Lelo," London said breezily, laughing as Sutton started pulling her away.

Behind Lelo's back, Mel mouthed, "Call me you lucky bitch."

"You know where we'll all be if you change your mind," Lelo shouted after them.

* * * *

"That was fun."

Sutton draped his arm over her shoulder. "How far's your camper?"

She hip-checked him. "Friends first, then food, remember?"

"Right. And I'll bet we aren't skipping Stitch's party?"

"You bet your sexy ass we're not. It's not like we have to stay long, but you do need to put in an appearance for your adoring fans."

"And rub it in Stitch's face that you're no longer pining after him and you've moved on with me?"

London stopped, forcing Sutton to stop.

He faced her. "What?"

"I don't want you to get the wrong impression, Sutton."

"I'm not."

"Are you sure?"

"I don't know darlin', maybe you'd better spell it out for me."

London inhaled a fortifying breath and let it out. "About this deal. After seeing Lelo's reaction to you—to us—I'm glad that other people who've been looking at me with pity will be looking at me in a completely different light when they see us together."

"But?"

She inched closer and twisted her hand in the front of his shirt. "But my reason for wanting you to fuck me until I can't walk isn't for anyone's benefit but mine."

"And mine," he said softly. His eyes searched hers. "So I didn't misread the situation?"

"That what's been happening between us in private the past six days is only to make us look like a real couple in public?"

"Yeah."

"Until I saw you today, I wasn't sure. No, that's not true. I wasn't sure until after you kissed me and told me you'd had to go away because you couldn't *stay* away from me. That's when I knew there's nothing fake about the heat between us."

Sutton curled his hand around the side of her face and gave her a considering look.

"What?"

"You have good insurance on that camper? Because we're gonna set the inside on fire tonight."

The inferno in his eyes nearly torched her clothes. Right there in front of the white tent proclaiming "Jesus Saves." Tempting to shout, "Can I get an amen?!" and then crack jokes about her burning bush.

Instead she slipped her arm around Sutton's waist and pecked those delectable dimples. "Feed me first, bulldogger, then we'll get naked and test the combustible point of the mattress."

Chapter Eight

Sutton couldn't take his eyes off London. He'd catch himself staring at her mouth or those long, reddish-brown curls, or the flex of the muscles in her arm even when she just lifted her fork to eat.

She'd catch him gawking and as a reward, or hell, maybe it was punishment, she'd eye fuck him and run her tongue around her straw until his cock swelled against his zipper.

He leaned forward and grabbed her hand, bringing her knuckles to his mouth for a soft kiss. "You really think we'll make it through the party and the dance?"

"Who said I wanted to go to the dance?"

"You did. Last weekend. You said you always go."

"To the Saturday night dances. It's Friday night."

He raised his hand to the waitress. "Check, please."

London laughed. "Down boy."

"Been a while for me, darlin', and I'll need a round or five to build up my stamina."

"Don't scare me. I do have to climb on a horse the next two afternoons."

"Too bad for you. I plan on making you plenty saddle sore." He smirked. "I'm looking forward to kissing it and making it all better."

She turned her hand, threading their fingers together. "We need to get our minds off sex at least for a little while. Tell me something about you that's surprising."

Besides that I've been cleared to ride and I've been lying to everyone the past four months?

"No pressure. I'll rephrase. I'll go first. I've never been pierced. Your turn."

"Okay. I don't have any ink tattoos."

"But you've had a few rodeo tattoos."

"Yep. Your turn."

"I don't like anything butterscotch flavored."

"I do. Bring on the flavored body paint, baby. I'll lick you clean."

She groaned. "You are killing me. This was supposed to take our minds off sex."

"Darlin', I can't look at you and not think about all the ways I want to make you come. And if you'd prefer that I smear the body paint on your nipples or between your thighs?"

"Both." Her eyes heated. "I'm guessing the application would be as pulse-poundingly erotic as the removal."

"No reason to rush a good thing." He nibbled on the inside of her wrist. "It's your turn."

"My brain is stuck on whether I'd finally start liking the taste of butterscotch if I sucked it off your tongue after you licked it off me."

"Let's test that theory."

"Now?"

"I saw a bottle of butterscotch syrup at the ice cream place. I'll distract them. You swipe it and shove it in your purse."

"'The Saint' contemplating a heist for a dirty sexual scenario? I'm shocked. And more than a little turned on."

"Excuse me. Are you Sutton Grant?"

His gaze reluctantly moved from London's molten bedroom eyes to the guy standing at the end of the table. "That's me."

"I thought so, but I knew you were on the injured list for this season, so I was surprised to see you. Especially here at such a small-potatoes rodeo." He paused. "Are you competing?"

"Nope. I'm here with my girlfriend." He angled his head at London. "She runs a horse clinic."

The guy glanced over at London, and she gave him a finger wave.

"Oh. Wow. Sorry. Didn't mean to interrupt," he said with zero sincerity. "But as long as I'm here, can I get you to sign this?" He shoved a piece of paper at Sutton.

"Sure. What's your name?" Sutton made small talk as he scrawled his name and the date across the program. As soon as he finished, he saw there were several more people who'd lined up. He smiled and kept signing. This was part of the gig for a man in his position, with four championship buckles—the very buckle most of these guys would give their left nut to have a shot at.

After they were alone, he stood and threw some bills on the table. Then he offered London his hand. "Come on."

It'd gotten completely dark. The musical and mechanical sounds from the midway echoed with distortion and the bright lights sent the entire area aglow. "You wanna hit some of the rides before we crash the party?" He swung their joined hands. "Might be romantic to grope each other at the top of the Ferris wheel."

"Not romantic at all because I am a puker. No spinning rides for me."

"Poor deprived girl," he whispered. Then he tugged her into a darkened corner between two storage sheds, pushing her up against a modular home. "How about if I try and get that pretty head of yours spinning another way." Sutton kissed her, starting the kiss out at full throttle. Not easing up until she bumped her hips into his, seeking more contact.

God, she made him hard. He'd never wanted a woman this much, this soon. What sparked between them might be fueled by lust but it also went beyond it—which is what'd sent him running.

For now, he'd focus on that lust.

His hands squeezed her hips and then moved north to her breasts. He broke his lips free from hers and dragged an openmouthed kiss down her throat. When the collar of her shirt kept him from sampling more of her skin, he tugged until the metal snaps popped.

No bra. Nothing to get in the way of taking every bit of that sweet flesh into his mouth to be sucked and licked and tasted.

Her breath stuttered when his teeth enclosed her nipple. She knocked his hat to the ground as she clutched the back of his neck, pressing his mouth deeper against her.

Sutton shoved his thigh between hers. Immediately she rocked her hips against that hard muscle.

"Yes. Right there."

He lost track of all sanity as he nuzzled and suckled her sweet tits, stopping himself from jamming his hand down her pants and feeling her hot and creamy core as he got her off with his fingers. Choosing instead to get her off this way, because fuck, there was something primal about making her come nearly fully clothed.

"Harder."

London's head fell back against the building and she softly gasped his name as he gave her what she needed.

She'd clamped her thighs around his leg so tightly he felt the contractions in her cunt pulsing against his quad. He felt the matching pulse beneath his lips as he drew on that taut nipple. Felt her short nails digging into the back of his neck.

Fucking hell this woman tripped all his wires.

When she loosened her grip on him, he planted kisses up her chest, letting his breath drift along her collarbone, smiling when gooseflesh broke out beneath his questing lips.

"You are no saint, Sutton Grant."

"Nope." He nuzzled the curve of her throat.

"Mmm. Keep kissing me like that while I fix my shirt."

"I'm happy you didn't wear a bra."

"No need for me to wear one, well, probably ever."

"Lucky me."

She rubbed her lips across his ear, raising chills across his skin. "Brace your hands on the building by my head."

"Why?"

She nipped his earlobe. "Because I wanna kiss you."

As soon as he complied, he angled his head so she could better reach his lips.

But London dropped to her knees and started working on his belt.

"Sweet Christ, woman. What are you doin'?"

"Giving you a kiss."

"My mouth is up here."

"That's not where I wanna kiss you."

Any blood left in his head surged to his groin. The one teeny part of his brain that wasn't giving him mental high-fives managed to eke out, "What if someone comes up behind us?"

"You really care about that?" *Pop* went the button on his Wranglers. *Zip* went his zipper. She pulled back the jeans and shifted his boxer-briefs so his dick slid through the opening.

"Fuck, not really. Just giving you an out—holy fucking hell," he said when her hot mouth closed around his cock.

When she eased back and off him, he actually whimpered.

"Oh, bulldogger, you're just big all over, aren't you?"

Before he formed a coherent sentence, she sucked him to the root.

Again.

And again.

And again.

His body throbbed with the need for release. God. It'd been so long.

"London," he managed, "I'm about to..." That warning tingle in his balls lasted barely a blip before his cock spasmed and unloaded. Each hot spurt jerked his shaft into her teeth.

Her mouth worked him until he was utterly spent. He started to feel lightheaded, realizing he'd held his breath. After gulping in oxygen, the fuzzy sensation faded, but he still felt rocked to his core.

Then London was in his face. "Sutton, you'd better do up your jeans."

"Sure." Still in a daze, he pushed off the building. He kept his gaze on hers as he tucked in, zipped up, and buckled. Then he leaned in and kissed her. "Thanks."

"My pleasure."

"Fair is fair though, darlin'."

Her eyes widened. "What do you mean?"

"I wanna taste you. Undo your jeans."

"Sutton—"

"Now."

London's obedience surprised him as well as pleased him. Excitement tinged with fear danced in her eyes as she loosened her belt and unzipped, peeling the denim back. "I don't think—"

He slammed his mouth down on hers. Kissing her with a teasing glide of his tongue and soft licks, he pressed his palm over her belly, slowly sliding his hand over the rise of her mound and into her panties. When his middle finger breached the slick heat of her sex, he smiled, breaking their kiss. "You're wet," he said, his breath on her lips.

"Yes."

"It's so fucking hot that you're wet after blowing me." He followed the slit down to her center where all the sweetness pooled. After swirling his fingertips through her cream, he worked his hand out. Then he pushed back so only a few inches separated their faces and brought his hand up, letting her see the wetness glistening there, hyperaware they were close enough she could smell her own arousal.

Sutton slipped his fingers into his mouth and sucked the sweet juices, briefly closing his eyes to savor this first taste of her.

Before he completely pulled his fingers free, London was right there. Licking his fingers, tasting herself on him, sucking on his tongue. The kiss could've soared past the combustible stage, then neither of them would've been able to stop. But something made him hold back, turn the kiss into a promise of more to come as he dialed down the urgency. Easing back, he let his hands wander, wanting all of her but willing to wait until he could have her the way he needed.

London sensed the shift too. She fastened her jeans and fixed her belt. Her gaze finally hooked his, but he couldn't read her.

He traced the edge of her jaw. "What?"

"You pack a powerful punch, Sutton Grant."

"Same could be said about you, Miz Gradsky." Knowing they needed a break from the intensity, he reached down and grabbed his hat and settled it on his head. "You still wanna hit the party?"

"Of course. Now we've got a really good excuse for being fashionably late."

"So if someone asks where we've been?"

"I'll say we were messing around and lost track of time." She smoothed her hands over her hair and straightened her clothes. "It's the truth."

They returned to tent city hand in hand. The party wasn't hard to find.

Several guys stopped London to chat, and he had a surge of jealousy even when she introduced him right away. But they both discovered it wasn't necessary since he knew a lot of the people hanging around. Except the kids in line for the keg all looked younger than eighteen. Seemed like so long ago that he'd been the new kid on the circuit. Back then, seeing guys who were the age he was now had seemed so ancient.

Finally, they reached the spot by the fire where the couple hosting the party held court.

Sutton had only seen the pair last week from a distance. Stitch was a substantial guy—although Sutton had him by a couple inches—and he appeared to be four or five years younger than London, which is why Sutton didn't do a double take at seeing his baby-faced girlfriend. She was cute, miniature in stature. But her blonde hair, as big as the state of Texas—a phrase his friend Tanna used to say—added some height. He wondered if someone had warned the young thang about the perils of standing too close to the fire doused with that much hairspray. Or about the fuse-like dangers of the synthetic beauty queen sash she wore loosely draped across her chest.

Besides, Sutton was way more interested in this Stitch guy, the douche-nozzle dumb enough to dump long, lean London for pint-sized Paige.

Like most bulldoggers, Stitch was solid, but he'd gone a step further, bulking up to the point he'd lost his neck. Nothing else about him seemed remarkable, save for the fact the guy was bow-legged. Probably made Sutton an ass to wish the dude was cross-eyed, with buck teeth and nearly bald beneath his cowboy hat too, but there it was.

Sometimes he wasn't a nice guy.

London's hand tightened in his. "Sutton."

"What?"

"Stop growling."

"Sorry." *Not at fucking all.* "Just feeling a little territorial, darlin'."

"I can see that. So can everyone else."

"Good."

Lelo elbowed Stitch and his entire body stiffened.

Then Stitch dropped his arm from Paige's shoulder and skirted the fire pit, heading toward them. He offered his hand first and Sutton automatically followed suit. "I can't believe *the* Sutton Grant is here at my campsite. I can't believe I'm meeting you. Man, I'm such a huge fan! Your run in Vegas was legendary. It was a dream to get to watch history being made."

"I appreciate you saying so."

"When Lelo said you were here, I thought he was pulling my leg. He's such a prankster."

"Maybe *his* name oughta be Stitch," Sutton deadpanned.

Stitch's eyes clouded for a second. He didn't get the joke.

Sutton kept his expression cool. As much as he appreciated Stitch's enthusiasm, it bothered the crap out of him that neither the man nor his girlfriend had acknowledged London.

Paige pushed her way between them and offered her hand, while keeping a proprietary hand on Stitch. "Hi. I'm Paige. We're happy you could stop by our party."

"We appreciate the invite."

Paige glanced at London, then refocused on Sutton. "I'm sure London has told you all about us, but we had no idea she'd met someone new."

Sutton smiled at London. "Don't know where you got the impression that London and I just met. I've known her for three years. We reconnected when I asked her to work with my horse, since she'd trained him at Grade A Farms." He brought their joined hands up and kissed the back of her hand. "And what a reconnection it's been."

London let her secret smile speak for her.

"Good to see you, London," Stitch said politely. "You're looking well."

"Thanks, Stitch."

Then Stitch launched into a barrage of questions that normally would've amused Sutton, but he was just so damn distracted by the woman by his side. The scent of her. The tiny taste of her still lingering on his tongue. The bonfire had nothing on the heat that rolled off her body. Then she started feathering her thumb across the inside of his wrist. Back and forth. Pressing into the vein to feel his pulse, teasing the sensitive spots as if it was his cock.

Enough. He wanted the real thing.

When Stitch took a breath, Sutton bent his head to whisper. "Let's go."

"We haven't been here ten minutes."

"I can be inside you in under ten minutes," he countered with a silken growl.

"We just wanted to drop in and say thanks for the party invite," London announced to Stitch and Paige, "but we've gotta get."

Sutton didn't bother masking his grin.

"But you just got here!" Stitch protested. "You haven't even had a beer yet."

"Thanks for your hospitality, but maybe next time. Nice meeting you."

"Maybe we'll see you at the fireworks?" Stitch said hopefully.

Sutton glanced into London's heavy-lidded eyes. "We'll be far too busy making our own fireworks to care about someone else's, won't we darlin'?"

"Yeah, baby, we will." She reached up and touched his cheek. "I missed you last night."

Looking into her eyes, Sutton knew none of this was for show—this moment, although played out in front of dozens—belonged only to them. "Same here. Let's go."

Chapter Nine

London felt Sutton's hot breath on the back of her neck as she fumbled with the key to unlock the camper. She closed her eyes, trying to calm down because this was it, this was where all the sexual teasing and banter had led to...being naked with Sutton Grant.

Holy fucking shit was she ready for this?

"London?"

"I'm sorry. I'm shaking so hard I can't get the key in the lock."

"Let me." He didn't grab the key, he just curled his body around hers, steadying her, making his hand an extension of hers. Metal clicked and the door popped open. He pressed a kiss below her ear and murmured, "After you."

She shuddered at the deep timbre of his rough and sexy voice.

"Should I be concerned about your hesitation?"

"No. Just stop whispering in my ear. It's distracting me."

"Mmm. Sweet thang, I'm gonna have so much fun telling you every dirty little thing I plan to do to you." He made a half growl against the side of her throat. "Then doing it." He sank his teeth into her skin and growled again. "At least twice."

That prompted her to take that first step inside. The door slammed behind them.

Sutton kept his hands on her shoulders as she led him to the bedroom. She'd cleaned off her bed but it hadn't improved the area much. Suddenly, she worried this might not be the best idea.

Then that liquid sex voice melted into her ear again. "Stop."

"What?"

"Whatever negative thoughts that're keeping us from climbing in that bed and crawling all over each other." He pressed his hips into her backside. He tilted her head to the right and moved his hands over her collarbones to the front of her blouse and popped the buttons. One. At. A. Time.

As soon as he'd undone the last button, he slowly turned her to face him.

Keeping her eyes focused on her task, she undressed him in the same leisurely manner, enjoying the feel of his hot skin and contours of his muscles beneath her hands. All she could think about was feeling the press of his weight against her, feeling the musculature in his back with her fingers as he moved above her.

"You're killing me with that look in your eyes, London."

"The look that makes it very clear I want to lick you up one side and down the other?" She angled her head, breathing on the tight tip of his nipple before her lips circled it.

"Ah, Christ."

"You like that."

"Mmm. I'd really like it if we could speed things up." His hands followed the contours of her sides to the curve of her hips.

"What's the rush?"

"You," he whispered across her bared shoulder. "I wanna feel you—all of you—around me. Been wanting that for days."

That's when Sutton took matters into his own hands. He stepped back far enough that she could see him yank off his boots and socks. Then he unbuckled his belt and unzipped his jeans. He lifted one, sexy dark eyebrow, silently asking why she wasn't stripping.

London had an overwhelming rush of shyness. It was one thing to want him so desperately, to want to rip off his clothes and feast on him, to get lost in passion, to reach for each other in a haze of lust...so how had they gone from that to...this? Lowering her chin, she allowed her hair to fall over her face.

Rough-skinned hands cupped her shoulders. Then his fingers were beneath her chin and his avid mouth landed on hers, reigniting that passion. He kissed her with authority and greed while he stripped her out of her remaining clothes. His hands were everywhere, pinching her nipples, squeezing her hips, clamping onto her ass. They fell back onto the bed with Sutton on the bottom, breaking their fall.

His cock had gotten trapped between their bodies. Raising herself up on all fours, she automatically started rocking against it, kissing him frantically as the tips of her breasts rubbed against the hair on his chest.

Two sharp slaps on her ass burned like hell—but it caught her attention. She gasped, "What—"

"Scoot up."

Confused by another abrupt halt to their intimacy, her eyes met his. "Why?"

"I want your pussy on my face."

She blushed.

"London," he said with a sharper tone than she'd ever heard from him, "get on up here girl, before I smack that fine ass of yours again."

"B-but I've never—"

"Don't care. That little taste of you wasn't near enough." He held onto her inner thighs, pulling her up his body while he pushed himself down the bed. He slid his hands around to her butt cheeks and pressed her mound against his mouth.

Any thoughts London had about awkwardness vanished the instant that tongue came out.

A relentless tongue that licked her up one side and down the other. Probing her folds. Swirling inside the opening to her sex and then plunging deep. Teasing her clit with alternating soft flicks and licks.

His hands were hard, his fingers digging into her skin. The wet lapping noises of his mouth on her sex mixed with her soft moans and echoed in the tiny space.

Sutton pulled back to kiss the inside of her thigh. Then he nipped it hard and she cried out. It startled her more than hurt her, but even the tiny sting sent a shot of heat through her.

He made that sexy growling noise against the stinging spot. "Shoulda known a tough woman like you would like a little rougher play." Then he nipped the other thigh a bit harder.

London's gasp turned into a groan when he settled his hot, sucking mouth over her clit.

It'd been so long and he was so freakin' good with that naughty mouth of his. The tingling sensation immediately radiated down her spine, sending every hair from the back of her neck to her tailbone on full alert.

She threw her head back and said, "Oh-god-oh-god-oh-god don't stop! Please. That's so..." The orgasm hit—then it expanded and exploded. Each hard contraction had her knees quaking and her arms shaking.

When she opened her eyes, she realized she'd lowered herself completely onto Sutton's face and was probably smothering him. She tried to scramble back. "I'm sorry—"

Another hard whap landed on her butt and he scooted out from beneath her to stand at the end of the bed. "Never apologize for coming like that. Sweet heaven that was so damn sexy."

Next thing she knew he'd caged that big, strong body around hers. She arched into him. She might've purred.

Sutton's lips skimmed her earlobe. "I want you." His hot breath burrowed inside her ear. "Want you like fuckin' crazy." Then the tip of his tongue traced the shell of her ear. "Want you hard and fast this time." He kissed the hollow below her ear and her pulse skyrocketed. "Next go will be slow, sweet, and sweaty, okay?"

"Okay, yes, please."

He pushed back and she heard the crinkle of a condom wrapper. Then his knees moved between hers and work-roughened hands traveled the back of her thighs, stopping to tilt her ass to a better— God, hopefully deeper—angle. The tip traced her slit once before he wedged his cock inside her fully in a steady glide.

She'd held her breath, waiting for a hard thrust. So when Sutton layered his body over hers, all heat and muscle and strength, the air left her lungs in a long groan. He nudged aside her hair and planted openmouthed kisses from the nape of her neck to the ball of her shoulder and back.

Gooseflesh rippled across her body.

"You're so sexy, London. You drive me out of my ever-lovin' mind." Sutton curled his hands around her hipbones and pulled himself upright. His slow withdrawal lasted two strokes before he was ramming into her.

As much as she'd envisioned their first time together being face to face with their mouths fused and their hearts racing in unison as he rolled his body over hers, this was better. More intense. She rocked back into him. The slap of skin on skin and the rhythmic squeak of the bed created a sexual cadence that had her clenching around his pistoning shaft. Each time she bore down he'd make a deep, sexy noise of masculine satisfaction.

After about the fifth time, he said, "London. I can't hold off."

"Just a couple more. Please, I'm so close again."

Sutton quit moving, but he stayed buried balls deep inside her. He leaned over and murmured, "I'll getcha there. Squeeze me hard, baby. Really hard."

As soon as she released her tightened pussy muscles, his hand cracked on her butt and her cunt spasmed on its own.

She cried out, not in pain, but because that extra stimulation shoved her closer to the edge.

"Beautiful. Again."

London did that four more times, bore down, then felt the heat of Sutton's hand as she let go of her clenched inner muscles. Her body took over and she started to come wildly. The orgasm radiated out from her core, electrifying every inch of flesh. Every nerve ending flared to life.

That's when Sutton moved, plunging into her in the same tempo as the blood throbbing in her sex. Once her peak waned, he ramped up his pace, holding her steady as he shouted his release. Such a rush, feeling his big body shuddering behind her and the hard jerk of his shaft against her swollen pussy walls.

Then he went completely still.

Once he'd caught his breath, he caged her body beneath his again, pressing his chest against her from shoulders to hips. He nuzzled the back of her head and expelled a sigh. "You okay?"

"Way, way, way better than okay, Sutton."

"Me too. Lemme ditch the condom. Be right back." He kissed her again and withdrew.

She withheld a hiss, but her arms gave out and she collapsed on the bed.

Gentle hands turned her over and two hundred plus pounds of hot, hunky cowboy loomed over her. His kiss was so sweet and packed with such gratitude that she couldn't help but reach for him, twining her fingers in his thick hair. Running her palm down his spine and getting a handful of his muscled ass.

This man was full of surprises. Over the past week she'd learned to appreciate his quiet sense of humor, as well as his stillness. He was thoughtful and deliberate—such a welcome change from the rash and selfish assholes she'd dated in the past. He listened instead of jabbering on, but he could knock her down a peg if she needed it. He had a protective streak and yet he could soothe her with a simple touch. He loved animals. He was close to his family.

All those things would be more than enough to capture her interest. But add in his stunning good looks—although he tried to downplay them—his holy fuck body, and now learning he had a raunchy, bossy side behind the bedroom door, and she'd lost any hope of not falling madly in love with Sutton Grant.

Love. Jesus. What was wrong with her? No one falls in real true love in six days.

So this overwhelming sensation of satisfaction and excitement had to be a lust high, the happy discovery of sexual compatibility...not the kind of life-affirming love she wanted.

True to his intuitive nature, Sutton immediately sensed the change in her mood. He didn't do anything by half-measures. She should've recognized that right away. While that trait usually had her running the opposite direction, now she clung to it and to him.

"London. Sweetheart. What's wrong?"

Tell him.

Don't be an idiot.

She squeezed him more tightly. "I like being with you like this. And I'm kicking myself we haven't been doing this at every possible opportunity all week."

Soft lips brushed her forehead. "I was thinking the exact same thing."

"Oh yeah? What else were you thinking?"

He rolled them until she was on top, straddling his groin. His hand grabbed a fistful of hair and he tugged her head back, baring her throat. "I'm thinking I watched you riding my horse this week—and I've never been so jealous of a horse in my life. So after I get a chance to taste these sweet tits, I'll wanna see how well you ride me."

"That right?"

"Mmm-hmm. And baby, if you're really good, next time you can be guaranteed I'll wanna try out that riding crop on you."

Chapter Ten

Sutton towel dried his hair and watched London sleeping. Not a graceful sleeper. She was a sprawler. And she hadn't lied about being a snorer. She'd twisted the sheets into a knot, exposing her bare leg, allowing him to see the love bruises he'd sucked on the inside of her thighs. Damn if those red and purple marks didn't look sexy against her pale skin. Before they'd called it a night, he'd checked her ass to see if he'd left marks there from the whacks he'd given her. But he'd just found a few reddened hot spots and thumb and finger shaped bruises on her hips, cheeks, and the backs of her thighs.

A wave of want rolled over him, staring at the beautiful siren he'd worn out last night and who'd wrung him out. He'd never been fully able to explore his kink with any woman, besides a few slaps on the ass here and there—rarely during sex—and some limited rope play, one hand tied to the bed sort of thing. But London wanted more.

And heaven help him he wanted more too, and couldn't wait to see where the need for more would lead them.

Her arms moved overhead in a long morning stretch. She sighed softly and opened her eyes, zeroing in on him first thing. She smiled. "Hey, handsome."

"Hey yourself, gorgeous."

"How long have you been standing there watching me sleep? Because if I'm drooling, I swear it's a new thing since I finally had a drool-worthy man in my bed last night."

Sutton returned her smile. "I've been up fifteen minutes. Took a quick shower. I've been watching you because it's so fucking hot how you just give yourself over in bed whether you're asleep or awake."

London glanced away.

"Did I say something wrong?"

"No. You said something exactly right." Her hazel eyes were alight with happiness when she looked at him. "Last night was amazing. Beyond anything I ever imagined. But what I always wanted. I wasn't sure how you'd react this morning. Make sense?"

"Perfect sense. It's that way for me too. That's why I've been standing here watching you."

"Seriously?"

"Yeah."

She brushed her hair from her face but didn't attempt to cover up her breasts as she waited for further explanation.

But Sutton was done talking. For now. "I imagine you want coffee?"

"Mmm. A man who will spank me during sex, make me coffee the next morning, and looks that damn good in a floral towel?" She sighed gustily. "Score one for team Gradsky."

He laughed. "Coffee will be done by the time you get cleaned up."

While London took a quick shower, Sutton called Ramsey at the gun range and asked the sample tests be e-mailed to him right away so he could study for the range master test. If he failed, he was out nothing. After he hung up, he really wanted to share the possible change in his life with someone, but his excitement dimmed when he realized he couldn't tell anyone. Especially not London. Things were on an uphill swing with them—not just because they were burning up the sheets. And besides, she'd been working with Dial less than a week. Doubtful the horse had made great strides in such a short amount of time.

As soon as London stepped out of the back room, fully dressed, Sutton wrapped his arms around her. She melted into him, sharing the sweet type of morning kisses he craved. "You smell great and I know firsthand that you taste even better."

"Stop blocking my access to coffee."

They sat at the small table in the front, which he noticed for the first time had been completely cleared. "Where's all your jewelry stuff?"

London blinked at him as she gulped coffee.

"London?"

"It's around."

"Not around here. Where is it?"

"Don't get mad."

He fucking *hated* when women said that because it was guaranteed to blow his top. "Where is it?"

"You had way more room at your place and I knew you'd be staying here this weekend, and we needed the space, so I hoped it wouldn't be that big of a deal if I moved it into your house. Temporarily."

"Why would I be mad about that? You've already brought some of it in."

"I don't know. Most guys get weird about their latest squeeze infringing on their space."

"I'm not most guys, sweetheart." His gaze hooked hers, silently asking, *calling yourself my latest squeeze is insulting to both of us, doncha think?*

She turned away to pour herself another cup of coffee.

He let it go. "What's on the agenda today?"

London snagged a clipboard before she sat. "I'm booked solid but I did leave myself two hours for lunch."

"What did you and Stitch used to do during breaks?"

That surprised her—almost as if she'd forgotten about him. "We didn't get breaks at the same time very often. But he always wanted to wander through the crowds. See and be seen." She shrugged. "As long as I get fed, I don't care what we do."

"Need me to hang around the corral and help you out today?"

Another look of surprise. "Why would you wanna do that?"

"It's gotta beat sitting alone in the camper."

"Don't you want to go...?"

"To watch the rodeo contestants and stock contractors? Nope. To the midway? Nope. Go chat up all my great buddies still running the blacktop? Oh, right. Hanging with them guys never was my scene." Sutton leaned over and tugged on her ponytail. "Looks like you're stuck with me."

She smiled and stole a kiss. "Looks like. Let's hit it."

* * * *

It should've been boring, watching London working horses, conferring with young riders and their parents. But there was such enthusiasm surrounding her, as well as strength and confidence that he couldn't focus on anything else except her. Wanting her, needing her, taking her.

The instant her break started, he herded her toward the camper. She fumbled with the keys again, but in her defense he did have her body pressed up against the door leaving her little space to maneuver.

"Sutton. What are you doing?"

"I'm about to fuck you right here against your camper door in broad daylight if you don't get us inside."

"This door is flimsy. If you wanna fuck me hard, I'd suggest we hit the floor."

The door flew open. Somehow they managed to get it shut and locked before they were on each other.

And the floor held up just fine.

* * * *

Afterward, they strolled hand in hand through the exhibitors' hall. If Sutton would've had his way they would've spent the last hour of her break alone inside the camper. It bothered him that even after their intimate connection, which London admitted she'd never had with another lover, that she was still on the *look-at-my-new-man* kick with Stitch.

That's what you signed on for. Showing her you are the better man is the best way to combat any feelings she might still have for him.

London stopped at a jewelry stand. She chatted with the owner, asking about square footage rental charges, revenue, venue commission percentage kickbacks. All the while Sutton stayed so close behind her he could feel the rumble of her laughter vibrating against his chest.

Finally she said, "Thank you so much for your time."

As soon as they were out of earshot, Sutton said, "Do you know her?"

"No. But I'm interested in whether running a seasonal jewelry storefront is profitable."

"You thinking about starting one for the jewelry you've been making?"

London stopped and faced him. "Do you think it's a frivolous venture? A waste of my time and energy?"

He framed her face in his hands. "No. If you love making the jewelry you'll keep doin' it regardless if it's profitable. You're savvy enough to talk to the people in the trenches before you make any decisions. Sweetheart, that is just smart business. Anyone who tells you otherwise needs their head examined before getting their ass kicked."

"You are so..."

"What? Don't leave me hanging here."

"Surprising. You're smart, with the perfect mix of raunchy and sweet."

Sutton leaned forward to graze her lips, tasting her and breathing her in. "Will it scare you off if I admit I'm really crazy about you?"

"No. Will it scare you off if I say I really need you to kiss me right now like you are that crazy about me?"

"C'mere and gimme that mouth." He deepened the kiss, keeping the passion simmering below the surface.

She kissed him back with the single-minded absorption in the moment he'd come to expect from her. Everything but her faded away.

He had no idea how long they'd been lost in the kiss until he heard a throat clearing behind them.

Reluctantly releasing her lips, he let his hands fall way.

London opened her eyes and stared at him, equally dazed.

"No offense, but you two are kinda blocking the aisle."

Sutton looked over his shoulder and saw Stitch standing there, his hands in the front pockets of his jeans, his gaze on London.

His suspicions kicked in. Had London asked him to kiss her like that only because she'd seen Stitch?

Dammit. None of what'd been happening between them was playacting on his side. Was it on hers?

London wrapped her arm around Sutton's waist and they faced Stitch. "Oh, hey, sorry. We'll get out of the way."

"No, no that's okay. I had a few questions for Sutton anyway, if he's got time."

"Gosh, that'd be swell, but we were headed to the midway so I can win my lady a prize." Sutton leaned forward and confided, "London has this theory that faithful men are as mythical creatures as unicorns, so I'm gonna prove her wrong. And win her the biggest stuffed unicorn I can find as a daily reminder that I am the man she can count on."

Poor kid looked confused as hell.

Over the course of the weekend, Stitch wore that expression a lot.

Chapter Eleven

The second week that London shared Sutton's living space was markedly different than the first week.

They spent a large portion of their time naked—in every room in the house. London never knew what to expect from Sutton either in bed or out of it. The first afternoon back from the Henry County Fair, he'd borrowed one of his brother's horses so they could ride together. Which had been fun, even when she kept an eye on Sutton to make sure he didn't show off, act all macho and hurt himself—not that the man seemed injured at all. He was in better physical condition than any man she knew. It also meant that she'd met his brothers, who'd been equally shocked to meet her.

Then the following night he'd grilled steaks and they'd sat outside beneath the starry sky and had fallen asleep entwined together on his puffy outdoor chaise lounge.

The one night he'd left her alone because he had mysterious "other commitments" she found herself watching the clock as she crafted eight necklaces, anxious for him to come home. The man had been so impatient to have her he'd practically swept all her beads off the kitchen counter like in one of those romantic movies. But the way he'd fucked her on the counter had been hot and nasty—X-rated—not a romantic thing about it, thank god.

They'd watched TV together. Cooked together. Danced around the house and the patio in the moonlight together. They'd made love in every position imaginable. Sometimes their interludes included kink—London still remembered the high from when he used ice on her after he'd bound her hands and how he'd heated up all the cold spots with his hot mouth. Sometimes their interludes were just hot and fast—new lovers who couldn't keep their hands off each other. Sometimes Sutton woke her up in the middle of the night, loving on her with such tenderness she wondered if she'd dreamt it. Which was a real possibility because not one night in the last week had he spent the entire night in her bed.

London continued to work with Dial, but she'd cut the horse's training sessions short because there wasn't much more she could do with him. Not that she could tell Sutton that yet. Partly because just after two short weeks she wasn't ready to close the deal she'd made with him. For one thing, whenever she asked the bulldogger if he'd been cleared to compete, he changed the subject, so she knew he was hiding something. But what? Did it have anything to do with her?

The one wrinkle in their intimacy was Sutton hadn't invited London to move into his bedroom. If they made love in a bed, it was hers in the guestroom. Even if Sutton fell asleep with her afterward, when she woke in the middle of the night or at dawn, the man was gone. That didn't mean he'd just crashed in his bed. No. That meant gone—she couldn't find the man in his house.

She hadn't tried to track him down, figuring if he needed time alone outside or wherever, then it wasn't her place to disturb him.

In the last day he'd become restless, but in a brooding manner. London suspected mindless chattering would get on his nerves so she...did exactly that. Jabbered on and on until he'd threatened to gag her. She'd retorted if he gagged her, he'd better plan on spanking her too.

That's how she ended up gagged with her own thong, her hands roped up with pigging string, bent over the back of the couch as Sutton whacked her bare ass until she came. Twice. Then he replaced the gag with his cock and she'd sucked him off, loving the sharp sting as he pulled her hair, which countered the gentle caress of his thumb on her jaw as he released in her mouth.

Afterward, he'd carried her to her bed and spooned her. She'd soothed him, but he still wasn't quite himself.

Right before she dozed off, she murmured, "Sutton, baby, you know you can talk to me about anything."

"I know. I just...can't. Not yet."

When she'd awoken in the morning, Sutton was gone.

As the weekend loomed, she didn't give a damn if they ran into Stitch and Paige or not. After being with Sutton, she knew even if Stitch came crawling back on his hands and knees she wouldn't take him back. She didn't want him. Hell, she'd never wanted him like she wanted Sutton. So any time Sutton asked about a specific plan to make Stitch jealous, she changed the subject.

Tit for tat, my man. You tell me what you're hiding and I'll admit you ruined me for all other men and I'm milking the training in the hopes you'll fall for me as hard as I've fallen for you.

* * * *

These late nights were killing him.

Sutton had agreed to help out his family by haying the field closest to his house. Cutting and baling was tedious work and left him more tired than if he'd run a marathon.

But he couldn't say no to his brothers—they'd pulled his ass out of the fire plenty of times. He couldn't say no to London—being with her was always the high point of his day. So the only time he had to practice the shooting requirements was after normal people went to bed. Add in the practice written tests, which weren't as easy as Ramsey claimed, and he'd been skating by on two hours of sleep a night.

Since last weekend's county fair was only forty-five minutes from his place, London decided to make the drive to her clinics every day rather than stay overnight.

Sutton had breathed a huge sigh of relief because it gave him the extra time he needed to study and prepare for the range master test. It also indicated that London had moved on for real in the make-Stitch-jealous game.

They'd entered the third week of their deal, trade—whatever it was. If he could make it through the next ten days, he'd be golden. Hopefully he'd pass the test, then he could come clean to London and his family about his future career plans and settle into a real relationship with his hot-blooded horse trainer. She'd seemed a little distant the past couple of days.

He'd managed to get two hours of dead-to-the-world sleep. Upon waking, he crept into the guest bedroom, intent on putting his wide-awake state to good use—waking London up with his face between her thighs. Nothing revved his engines like sucking down her sweet juice first thing in the morning.

The first time she came, she'd arched so hard against his mouth that his teeth had pressed into her delicate tissues. The tiny bite of pain had her fingers gripping his hair as the orgasm pulsed through her.

Then he'd instructed her to grab onto the headboard and hold on.

The wait for orgasm number two, when she couldn't direct him at all, was much longer. Sutton took his time exploring her reactions. Suckling just her pussy lips. Jamming his tongue into her hole. Lightly flicking the skin surrounding her swollen clit but avoiding direct contact with the pulsing bundle. Slipping two fingers into her wet cunt, he spread her open and feasted until she begged him to let her come. When he relented and focused entirely on her clit, London's body quivered and she'd screamed her release.

Her pussy walls were still pulsating when he rammed his cock in deep. He paused for a moment, watching the sunbeams fall across her face. Probably, he should've made love to her with a gentle wake up.

But Sutton was too far gone. "The Saint" that London teasingly called him was still sawing logs; his beast was ravenous for a hard morning fuck. The headboard banged into the wall as he relentlessly hammered into her, sweat dripping into his eyes, his jaw tightened in anticipation with every stroke into that tight, wet heat. His fingers curled over hers on the brass bars, the backs of her thighs pressed against his chest. Her calves on his shoulders provided extra resistance as he drove his cock into her over and over.

After he'd spent himself—physically and emotionally—he unhooked their hands from the headboard and placed a soft kiss on each of her anklebones, then slowly lowered her legs to the mattress. He planted more kisses up the center of her body. Looming over her, he pecked her once on the lips. "Good morning, beautiful."

"Helluva way to start the day, bulldogger," she said with a satisfied feminine sigh. Her fingertips scraped the stubble on his cheeks. "I like the way this feels on the inside of my thighs."

When she kept petting him but didn't speak, he said, "Something wrong?"

"No. I was just happily surprised to have you in my bed this morning."

Sutton suspected this question would come up. He wasn't sure how to answer it. "We shared a bed in the camper for two nights on two different weekends." And it'd killed his back.

"But we didn't get much sleep. Oh. Now I get it. That's why we're in separate bedrooms? So you're not tempted to fuck me all the time and we can rest between rounds to keep it hot and exciting?"

"Smartass."

Her eyes clouded. "Why don't you want to sleep in the same bed with me? Do I snore? Did I fart?"

"Why're you taking the blame?" He kissed the frown line between her eyes. "I don't wanna fight with you. It's not a big deal that our sleep patterns don't mesh."

London slid out from beneath him and perched on the edge of the bed. "You're right. It's not a big deal. And it won't matter tonight because I won't be here."

"What? Why not?"

She stood and slipped on her nightgown. "Commuting from here will work most days, just not today."

Sutton studied her. Something else was going on with her. "And tomorrow? Are you coming back here before we head to the Jackson County Fair?"

London fiddled with the bow on her nightgown strap. "We'll see."

The idea of her not being here, not talking to her, not touching her, kicked him into sort of a red rage. She was not inserting herself into his life so completely, making him fall for her, and then just walking away, leaving him so crazy about her that he'd do anything to keep her.

Anything except telling her the truth.

He yanked his sweatpants on and pulled his T-shirt over his head. "We're not doin' this."

"Not doing what? Being honest with each other? You're the one who's keeping to himself. If I didn't know better, I'd think you were sneaking off and trying to rope and ride in the middle of the damn night. But since I haven't seen you out in the barn at all in the last weeks since I started working with Dial, I know that's not where you've been keeping yourself.

Sutton hesitated all of ten seconds. "You really wanna see what I've been up to and where I've been?"

"Yes!"

"It'll change things between us."

London cocked a hand on her hip. "Some things need to change between us, Sutton."

"Fine." He snagged her hand. "Don't say I didn't warn you."

They stopped in front of the door at the far end of the hall. He opened the little box next to the doorframe that looked like a thermostat and punched in a code. The locks disengaged and he turned the door handle.

"After you."

London said nothing as she ducked inside.

After the door shut and latched behind them, he flipped on the main lights and led her down the stairs, keeping his back to her.

The space had been completely finished. Textured walls, acoustic ceiling, tile flooring, a built-in gun vault, locking cabinets for ammo. Tall benches lined the walls with a pegboard between the bench and the cabinets. The corner held a reloading station.

Sutton loved the absolute silence in his hidey hole. Once that upper door closed, he was vacuum-sealed in. The apocalypse could happen above him and he'd be oblivious. For that reason, so he didn't venture into "survivalist" territory, he didn't keep so much as a can of soda down here, say nothing of cases of weanies and beans and plastic jugs of water.

The actual range had been built from huge circular sections of concrete culverts. The targeting system was on an electronic pulley that ran along the top and bottom, allowing him to change the size, angle, and the distance of the practice targets with the push of a button.

It'd been an unconventional choice, foregoing a traditional basement family room, but he never regretted creating this for himself.

"Omigod! What is this place?"

Sutton hated—*hated*—London's wide-eyed look of horror as her gaze encompassed the space, as if she expected to see electrical tape, mini-saws, an array of pliers, dental instruments, and other devices of torture. "It's a gun range."

"*Inside* your house?"

Technically it was under his house, but he said, "Yeah."

"You have a fucking *gun range* inside your house?" she repeated.

It wasn't like she hadn't been raised around guns—her dad was a huge gun collector. He'd even invited Chuck to come over and shoot. He forced himself to keep his tone cool. "So? Some people have photography studios or theater rooms or a woodworking shop." He shrugged. "Shooting is my hobby. So I had a regulation range put in."

"But...isn't that illegal?"

"Jesus, London. You think I'm the law-breaking type? You think I would've showed it to you if I was trying to keep it on the down low?"

"Don't get snappy with me. I didn't realize people could have a gun range inside their house!" she snapped back.

"It's not that uncommon," he assured her. "I had dozens of designs to choose from. I first got the idea when a guy on my college rodeo team showed me his dad's inside shooting range."

"I assume the guy lived in a rural area like this?"

Sutton shook his head. "In town. Don't know what the building code restrictions are there, I know I had to jump through some hoops here to get approval and to pass inspection afterward."

London marched up to him and jabbed her finger into his chest. "Why didn't you tell me about this?"

"Because—"

"This is where you've been disappearing to at night?"

"Mostly. Some nights I work out. And I didn't think it'd be in my best interest to tell my houseguest that I was down here target shooting while she slept."

Her eyes narrowed. "What if I would've stumbled down here in the middle of the night? Would you've shot me as an intruder?"

"For Christsake, London! I'm not a fucking trigger-happy rube! And you can't just *stumble* down here because the area is secured with a coded locking system and a self-closing door. That means even if you get pissed off, know the code and come down here looking for my Smith and Wesson .460 to do some real damage to me, unless you chop off my thumb to get biometric access to my gun vault, you ain't getting nothing but even more pissed off."

"Don't even joke about that."

"I'm not. And see that?" He pointed to the red ambulance light on the ceiling. "If someone opens the door while I'm down here, it triggers an alarm. I cannot be caught unaware." Then he pointed to the range itself. "That enclosed space is bulletproof. I can't shoot out, no one can shoot in. I also have a secret panic alarm that goes straight to the sheriff's department."

"God. It's like I'm in Dr. Evil's underground lair."

He clenched his jaw and bit out, "Dr. Evil? Seriously?"

"No. But goddammit, Sutton, you had to expect I'd be freaked out by this."

She had him there.

"This"—she gestured around the space without breaking eye contact with him—" is an important part of who you are, isn't it?"

"Yeah."

"Why didn't you tell me? Not just about the James Bond underground thingy, but that you—"

"Had something in my life besides bulldoggin'?"

"Yes."

Not accusatory or hurt, but more curious. So he really felt like a total fucking heel for keeping this from her, too. "Because shooting has always been just mine in a way that bulldoggin' never will be. I do it for enjoyment. It's the one thing that's kept me sane during this last recovery."

They were nose to nose, breathing hard, staring at one another.

"Are you a good shot?" she asked softly.

"Darlin', I put a gun range in my basement. What do you think?"

Then she took a step back and her gaze roamed over him, head to toe, the return journey much slower as she seemed to catalog every inch of him, as if she was seeing him for the first time. When their gazes met, something had changed in London's eyes.

"Jesus. What now?"

"Do you ever wear those special military clothes when you're down here shooting?"

He frowned. "You mean like camo?"

"No." Her eyes were firmly on his chest. "The kind of clothes that black ops guys wear. A tight black T-shirt and black cargo pants tucked into biker boots, and a belt with a place for your gun, ammo, and maybe a pair of handcuffs? Ooh, and those mysterious wraparound sunglasses."

Sutton watched as she bit her lip. Then it dawned on him. She was turned on by the idea of him packing heat.

His cock went as hard as steel.

This was a far better reaction than fear. And if she wanted to play gun range taskmaster and novice shooter? He'd give it a whirl.

"When's the last time you fired a gun?" he asked gruffly.

"It's been a long time. And I never was very good at it."

He crowded her. "We'll change that right now."

"What? I'm in my damn pajamas!"

"So? Gimme your hand."

"Sutton—"

"In here I'm the teacher, and darlin', you *don't* get to argue with me." He snatched her hand. "A Glock will be too big for you. Let's start out with a thirty-eight."

"Thirty-eight what? Shots?"

"Thirty-eight caliber." His eyes searched hers. "You really don't know anything about guns?"

"Besides they're loud and dangerous? No."

A slow grin spread across his face. "That's what makes them so fun."

Her palms slid up his chest. "So the question is you gonna show me how to handle your big gun?"

In that instant, Sutton knew total acceptance. He knew those voices in his head telling him what he felt for her had gone beyond just lust and amusement and straight to love hadn't been taunting him. Still, he kept his tone light. "The one I want you handling has some heft to it. It heats up real fast."

"Show me."

He bent down and brushed his lips across the top of her ear. "You will listen to me and do exactly as I say."

She swallowed hard. "Yes, sir."

"Feel free to look around while I get out the guns and ammo." Sutton opened the safe and removed one gun—a thirty-eight Ruger revolver. When he turned around, London was staring at him. "What?"

"You are the most fascinating man I've ever met. And I've just touched the tip of the iceberg with you. I wonder what other secrets are beneath the surface."

"It's always the quiet ones you have to worry about," he joked.

"Sutton. I'm serious."

"Me, too. Come on. Let's load and shoot." He unlocked the gun cabinet and took down the box of bullets. He flipped the cylinder out and shoved in six bullets. "This first round I'll have you watch. Then I'll get you situated to shoot." Sutton snagged his ear protection and the plastic eye protection from the pegboard. There were half a dozen other sets of ear and eye protection hanging there, and he handed her the smallest set. "You can stand behind me and watch. And pay attention, sweetheart, 'cause there's gonna be a test."

Sutton ducked into the shooting area and started the ventilation system. He chose a target, picked the range, and hit the button that sent it back to his coordinates. He moved his neck side to side, shrugged his shoulders, and dropped them down as he widened his stance. Once he'd picked up the gun, he inhaled a slow breath and released it before he fired. Six times. He punched the button and the target returned. He'd clustered his shots, pretty damn perfectly if he did say so himself. Practice was paying off for him. He faced her.

Crazy woman smiled and gave him a double thumbs-up.

After he left the shooting area, London said, "I know you want me to have a turn, but I'd really like to see you do that again."

"Fine. Let's reload. You're doing it this time. And be careful because the barrel is hot."

"Why don't you just take the box of ammo in with you?"

"It's a safety protocol. Don't reload where you shoot. Full clip going in, empty clip going out. I follow that even when I'm down here by myself."

"Such a rule follower you are, Mr. Grant."

"On most things? Yes." He let his hot gaze sweep over her sexy, pajama-clad form. "But I wanna break all the rules when it comes to you, darlin'.'"

Sutton shot another round. Then he brought London into the shooting area and did the clichéd instructor move where he stood behind her, his arms alongside hers as she pointed the gun. He adjusted her stance. He whispered instructions in her ear. She wasn't easily distracted, which was a good sign. But she was aware of his hard cock nestled against her ass as he maneuvered her into position.

Gun loaded, he stood behind her as she sited the target. She fired off all six shots in rapid succession. The target showed five hits, so one shot had gone wild.

"Let's go again. That's not bad."

By the sixth round, London had become more comfortable.

But Sutton's pleasure receptors had overloaded. He was in his gun range with a sexy woman who wore very few clothes and delighted in making "big gun" and "quick on the trigger" and "hot barrel" jokes while sending him—and his cock—smoldering looks. Add in the scent of gun smoke that hung in the air around them and the buzz in his ears from the gunfire, and he was in bad shape. He needed her right fucking now.

"Sutton? Are you okay?"

When his gaze collided with hers, she gasped. "Baby, let's do something about that. But you've gotta put away your toys first."

As soon as he'd locked away the revolver and box of bullets, he was on her. Kissing her desperately, fumbling with her clothes, needing her skin beneath his hands while his body covered hers. Owned hers.

Sutton took her down to the floor on her hands and knees on the rug in front of the lone easy chair, his cock, head, and heart pounding. The violent need for her had him hiking her hips in the air, pinning her shoulders down with one hand while the other guided his cock between her legs.

But something stopped him.

He glanced down at London, the sexpot who was always up for anything, and he knew she deserved better than this. She liked it as rough and raunchy as he did, but right now he wanted to give her more of himself. "London. Sweetheart. Turn over."

A haze of lust had already clouded her eyes. "What's wrong?"

"Nothing. I just wanna look into your eyes when I'm loving on you." He levered himself over her. Those muscular thighs of hers automatically circled his waist. He tilted her pelvis and pushed inside her slowly, feeling her snug pussy walls relax to let him in. His hand shook when he brushed her hair off her face. "You are so beautiful." He kissed her with awe. The gentle mating of their mouths sent warmth flowing through him. "Beautiful and sexy. Sweet and nasty. Is there a more perfect woman on the planet for me?"

"Sutton."

"I think not. I can say it, but I don't think you believe it. Let me show you."

He kissed and touched and tasted her, dragging out the pleasure until their bodies were both slick with sweat.

Her fingers dug into his ass and her back bowed off the floor when he kicked up the pace. "Please, I can't take any more, this is..."

"For me too. Move with me."

She did. They were in perfect synchronicity.

When he hit that tipping point and the first wave of pulsing heat erupted, he'd been tempted to close his eyes.

But London's whispered, "Look at me and let me see you let go," had him locking eyes with her.

It was one of the most startlingly intimate moments he'd ever experienced.

His entire being shook in the aftermath. He nuzzled and kissed her, needing that grounding contact with her warm skin. "Thank you," he murmured against her lips.

"Can we just stay like this for a little while?" London nibbled on his jawline. "I'm not ready to return to the real world yet."

"Of course." He rolled so she was on top, wishing he had a blanket to cover her.

After a bit, she said, "You know, these benches would be a great place for me to work on my jewelry."

"Yeah?"

"Yeah. Then sometimes I could be down here and keep you company while you're shooting."

"I'd like that." More than she knew.

Chapter Twelve

London glanced at her watch. Where was Sutton? He should've been here fifteen minutes ago.

The funnel cakes were tempting. Rather than give in to her desire for fried dough covered in powdered sugar, she wandered to the next vendor site. The tent blocked the heat of the day and a fan from the back blew the first cool air she'd felt since she'd sat in her truck this morning.

She stayed there, pretending to look at the racks of handmade jewelry.

A familiar voice said, "London?"

Don't turn around. Maybe he'll go away.

"Never thought you were into jewelry. I'da bought you stuff like this if I thought you'd wear it."

I didn't need you to buy me stuff like this. I made stuff like this, dipshit, or don't you remember?

"You got your earplugs in or something?" Stitch clapped her on the shoulder, forcing her to face him.

"Oh hey, Stitch. What are you doin' here?"

"Killin' time until tonight."

"Without Paige?" came out a little snotty.

"Yeah. I wanted to surprise her with a little something." He paused. "Probably be wrong of me to ask for your help, huh?"

Do you think, fuckwad?

London shocked even herself when she said, "She'd probably like anything with sparkles or rhinestones."

"Paige does like her pink stuff."

They stood side by side, looking at jewelry—for her ex-boyfriend's new girlfriend. Talk about bizarre. London spied a lapel pin with a rhinestone crown on it. Tacky, but perfect for a princess. "I think she'll dig this."

Stitch nodded. He fingered the points on the crown. "So you and Sutton Grant, huh?"

"Yep."

"He's a good guy."

"That he is."

"I've always admired him. A lot. I watch his performance tapes all the time. His runs are picture perfect." He chuckled. "Except for that one last year. I was happy to see he didn't have permanent injuries. Man, he wrecked bad. You normally only see that in rough stock events."

"Sutton is fortunate."

Silence stretched between them. Then Stitch blurted, "Dammit, London, I'm so sorry that things ended up the way they did between us."

She looked at him, half expecting to see him wringing his hat in his hands. His blue eyes were filled with wariness; his cheeks were red with embarrassment. That's when she remembered why she'd fallen for the cute cowboy in the first place. Stitch was a sweet guy. Their four-year age difference hadn't mattered to her, but now she realized they'd always been in different places in their lives. While she patted herself on the back for lighting a fire in his Wranglers, in truth she'd been more his teacher for sex and dealing with his horse than his girlfriend. As much as it pained her to admit it now, she understood why he'd wanted something different.

They'd had some good times together. But if she really thought hard about it, she'd always known in her heart that they weren't right for each other for the long haul.

So was she repeating the pattern with Sutton? Training his horse and having hot, kinky, wild sex with him?

No. There was an emotional connection she'd never had with a man before. And she suspected Sutton felt it too. But since she'd blurted out her love for Stitch within the first month, this time, when it mattered, she'd be more cautious.

"London?"

She realized she'd gotten lost in her thoughts. "Sorry. I just wish you'd talked to me instead of sending me a lousy text message. Was that your idea or Paige's?"

He blushed. "Mine. Paige knew I was with someone when she and I first started hanging out. When we realized we wanted to be more than friends...I just ended it right then so we could be."

"You didn't think I'd be upset? Or that I deserved an explanation?"

"What was I supposed to say? Especially since we'd spent more time apart than together those last couple months."

"Is that when you and Paige started seeing each other?"

"Yeah, but as friends. And just so you know, because we never talked about it, Paige and I didn't... I mean we weren't...We hadn't..." He blushed harder.

Good lord. How had she ever ended up naked with this guy? "You and Paige weren't bumping uglies while you were still with me?"

"No! I'd never do that." His fist closed around the piece of jewelry. "I liked you, London. A whole lot. But meeting Paige... I never felt anything like it. She's just the one. And she feels the same way about me." Stitch's blue eyes met hers. "This ain't a fling with her."

"Like it was with me."

He nodded.

Just then, something inside her shifted. If she had to lose out—although now she suspected it was just getting dumped that'd had her seeing red—she'd rather lose out to true love.

"So are you gonna be mad at me forever? Cause we'll be seeing each other for years yet if we're both working the circuit."

She grudgingly said, "No. But I'd be happy if you talked to Paige about keeping her animosity leashed. She doesn't have anything to worry about when it comes to me."

"I'll talk to her about backing off."

"That'd be good. I'm..." *Just say it.* "Happy for you finding the real deal."

"You are?" His eyes nearly bugged out of his head.

"Hard to believe, but yes. Because now, after being with Sutton for such a short time, I know it can happen."

Stitch grinned. "Cool." Then he pulled her into his arms for a hug. He whispered, "Thank you for the forgiveness, London. I never meant to hurt you."

"I get that now." Before she could step back, they were ripped apart.

An infuriated Sutton demanded, "What the fuck is this?"

"I, ah, well, London and I—"

"Tryin' to get back into her bed and into her life, weasel? Guess what? It ain't ever happening because I'm there now and I take up a lot of goddamned room, and I'm not goin' anywhere. *Ever*."

"Sutton!"

He got right in Stitch's face. "Are you one of them guys who only wants what he can't have?"

Stitch stumbled back.

London could tell that Stitch's vocal cords had frozen in mortification from being dressed down and physically intimidated by his idol. So naturally she jumped in to protect him. "Leave him alone."

Sutton's gaze snapped to her. "Why are you defending him?"

"Because you are bein' an ass. And in public."

"Tell me I didn't just see this man with his arms around you."

"Oh, for Christsake."

"I saw it. I watched you and him all cozied up, chatting like it was old home week." He glared at Stitch. "Where's your girlfriend?"

"Uh, she and I—"

"Broke up?" Sutton supplied. "So that leaves you free to—"

London covered Sutton's mouth with her hand. "Shut your face before you say anything more ridiculous than you already have." When he tried to jerk away, she twisted the fingers of her other hand into his shirt and hissed, "Asshat." Then she looked over her shoulder at Stitch. "Sorry. I'm pretty sure he's been at the bar all afternoon."

"Oh. Well, then, I'm gonna git." He sent Sutton an odd look then threw his shoulders back. "Treat her right. She deserves it."

Sutton growled something.

London didn't move her hand until after Stitch had paid for his trinket and left.

They glared at each other.

He opened his mouth and she held up her hand. "Me first. You really thought I'd start up with him again?"

He loomed over her. "You were fucking *hugging* him, London. And it wasn't a bro hug, it was a lingering hug."

"Lingering hug," she repeated. "Wow. I didn't know there was a scale that denoted what kind of hug it was by its length. And double wow that you have somehow memorized that scale."

"I know what I saw," he said stubbornly.

"Then you need fucking glasses."

"Hey, you two get outta here," the woman behind the tables yelled. "You're scaring off my customers."

"Fine." London spun on her boot heel and stormed out of the tent. Of course Sutton followed. His hand circled her biceps and he turned her back around. "I deserve a goddamn explanation."

"And I deserve a goddamn apology for your lack of faith in me."

He laughed. "Lack of faith? Sweetheart, the only reason we ended up together was to make that man jealous. You succeeded. Every time I've asked you if you'd go back to him if he showed interest again, you've hedged."

"Because it's a stupid question."

"No, it's a legitimate question."

"No, this is a legitimate question. You really think the only reason I'm still with you, four weeks after we made the deal, is because I'm trying to lure Stitch back? Everything we've done and said when no one's been around us was us playing a part? None of it was real?"

"You tell me," he said coolly.

Just like that, London stepped back. "How about when you figure it out you come find me." She stormed away from him.

"How about I'd better find you in my damn corral, working with my horse," he shouted at her.

For the love of God. Seriously? They were shouting at each other like angry teens now?

And she'd never understood the phrase *the devil made me do it*, but at that moment she was so mad that she lost control of rationality. "Don't hold your breath because I'm done with your horse."

"Explain what the hell that means."

"Dial is as trained as he's gonna get."

"And you just decided that right now when you're pissed?"

London shook her head.

"How long have you been keeping that from me?"

"Since the end of the second week."

Shocked, he said, "Why?"

"Because I didn't want to leave you, jackass," she snapped. "I've been in this situation before. After you got what you wanted from me I figured you'd boot my ass out."

"You really think the only reason I wanted you around, four weeks after we made the deal, is because I want you to train my fucking horse?" he shot back.

How dare he throw her words back in her face? "You tell me. If you'd bothered to come out and watch me work Dial, you would've known two weeks ago that I was done. But you stayed away because you never intended to get back on that horse and compete again, did you?"

He bit off, "No," with zero hesitation.

"When were you gonna tell me?"

"When I had some other things squared away in my life."

"Was I one of those things?"

A muscle ticced in his jaw. "Are you gonna let me explain or just jump to conclusions?"

"Like you did with Stitch?"

"This is getting us nowhere. Can we—"

"No. I need to cool down before I say something out of anger that I don't mean."

"London. If we don't do this now—"

"Then we'll do it later." She jabbed her finger at him. "Don't you give me an ultimatum, Sutton Grant."

"I'm not. But please wait."

She didn't. She kept walking until she reached her camper.

Once inside, it was tempting to break into her emergency bottle of tequila.

Instead she breathed slow and deep to stave off her tears. Part of her expected that Sutton would come barreling into her camper, snarl about putting her over his knee to get her attention, but he didn't show.

She held out on checking her phone until after opening ceremonies—but no missed calls or text messages.

In fact, she didn't see him or hear from him that night.

Or the next day and night.

Or the next day.

Since London had a key to his house, she headed there first after the rodeo ended Sunday afternoon. No sign of him. But she could tell he'd been there. She could tell it'd been at least a day since he'd tended to Dial because the headstrong gelding came right up to her. He didn't make her chase him down.

Once she returned inside, she punched in the code and entered his private domain, ready to read him the riot act if he was hiding from her. If Sutton had been in his underground shooting range, she couldn't tell because the place was always spotless. Granted, she hadn't expected Mr. Responsible to suddenly leave firearms lying about, but there wasn't even an empty ammo box in the garbage.

After locking the door, she wandered into the kitchen. But she was too melancholy to fix herself food. Wasn't long before anger replaced her melancholy. The man's avoidance was ridiculous. Did he really think she'd just pack up and leave because she didn't have a conversation on *his* time frame? Did he really believe she'd let this issue stand between them when she was in love with him?

Wrong.

She might be hardheaded but she wasn't a fool.

The man had one more day to come to his senses or she was calling in the big guns.

Chapter Thirteen

Sutton was running late—a rarity for him, so he hoped she didn't give him grief for it. He scanned the tables in the restaurant. When he saw her, he smiled. There'd been a time when his pulse would've quickened, but now that his heart belonged to another, he just had a genuine sense of happiness at seeing her.

He wandered to the back booth where she'd set up camp with a stroller, a car seat, and a diaper bag.

As soon as he loomed over her, she drawled, "Forgive me if I don't get up, but as you can see my hands are full."

"I see that. Will your bruiser of a husband punch me in the face if I kiss your cheek?"

"He's not here right now. He'll be back in a bit, so kiss away, hot stuff."

Sutton kissed Tanna's temple. "I've got you all to myself, Tex-Mex? Well, besides this little guy." He peered at the face peeking out of the blanket. "Handsome papoose you birthed."

Tanna whapped him on the arm. "Papoose. With Fletch's Native American background and my Mexican, August Bruce Fletcher has gorgeous coloring." She sighed and stroked her baby's chubby cheek. "He has gorgeous everything, doncha darlin' boy."

He slid in the booth across from her. "So his full name is August Bruce Fletcher?"

"After his daddy and his grandpa. But we're calling him Gus."

"How old is Gus now?"

"Three months."

"How are you doin' with the new mom thing?"

Tanna's entire face lit up. "Fantastic. I had a rough pregnancy and ended up having a C-section because the kid weighed in at a little over ten pounds, but he's such a good baby. Such a joy in our lives." She looked away from Gus long enough to say, "If you think I'm smitten with our boy, you oughta see his father with him."

Sutton grinned. "I'd give anything to see the big, bad animal Doc baby-talkin'."

She snorted. "Not happening."

The waitress stopped by to refill Tanna's coffee and take Sutton's order. "Just a Coke," he said, "but keep them comin'."

"Wild night?" Tanna asked.

"Nope. Just a long one. Lots of tossing and turning."

"Well, you look good, if that's any consolation. But you always look like you stepped out of a magazine ad trying to sell rugged men's aftershave to men who have no hopes of ever lookin' like you."

"Stop flirting with me Mrs. Fletcher."

Tanna laughed. "Sorry. Habit. So what's up? Not that I wasn't happy to hear from you, but I was surprised."

"I figured you would be. Is it weird I considered it a sign that you'd be in Denver visiting your brother right when I needed to talk to you?"

"Not weird at all." She reached over and squeezed his hand. "I was lost and in an unhappy place three years ago. Thanks to you—and Fletch—I'm now happier than I've ever been. So anything you need from me, name it."

He squeezed her hand back. "I just need the same thing you did—to talk to someone who's been there."

"What's goin' on? Start at the least confusing place for me."

"My accident late last fall? When I came to in the ambulance and I couldn't move, I was scared out of my mind that I was paralyzed. I made a deal with God that if I didn't end up a permanent cripple that I'd never compete in steer wrestling again."

Tanna whistled.

"Obviously I recovered. I've been recovered for a helluva lot longer than anyone knows. My docs gave me the all clear four months ago. My family thinks I'm still on physical restrictions—because that's what I've led them to believe. I've pulled through two bad wrecks and some heavy emotional shit, so yeah, I'm keepin' my heavenly promise. But that's left me in limbo, not knowing what to do with myself if I'm not bulldoggin' for a living."

"I hear ya there." The bundle on her lap squirmed and squeaked and she rocked in the booth. "What else?"

"Dial has been shunted aside since the accident. I figured he'd be okay taking it easy for a couple of months. When the docs gave me medical release, I immediately took him out and tried to put him through his paces."

"How'd that go?"

"Not well. Mostly because my brothers happened to come by and check on me, saw me racing hell bent for leather on my horse, and lost their minds. At that point I coulda told them I'd been medically released and I was fine to resume training. But in the back of my mind? That little voice reminded me training was pointless because I'd promised to give it up and I had no freakin' idea what to do with my life."

"And this tug of war has been goin' on since that day?"

"Yep."

"It's gone beyond you faking a limp and constantly complaining about your sciatica to your family?"

"I see you ain't lost that smartass humor."

"Gotta take my shots when I can." She smirked. "But I'll behave. Go on."

"I hate that Dial became a problem horse because of my lie. I even went so far as to hire London Gradsky to help me get Dial back on track." He didn't want to tell her this next part, but in for a penny, in for a pound. "And I've fallen head over heels in love with the woman."

Tanna stopped moving and didn't start again even when Gus fussed. "Are you shittin' me, Sutton Grant? You and the horse trainer? I thought she hated you for convincing Chuck and Berlin to sell Dial to you."

"She did. But she's a horse woman to the core, Tanna. She trained Dial in the first place. At first she had uh...other reasons for agreeing to help me."

"Should I ask about them other reasons?"

"That's more her deal than mine. But it was a deal I agreed to. Spending all our time together...she's practically livin' with me. She's sexy, sweet, funny, and that girl has a mouth on her that don't quit— evidently that's a trait in a woman that attracts me"—he laughed when Tanna flipped him off—"and damn if I don't like playin' house with her. A lot."

"Does she know you're in love with her?"

Sutton smiled. "Talk about déjà vu."

"What?"

"I asked the same thing of Fletch that day he came to watch you race around barrels at full speed."

"What'd he say?"

"That you couldn't be around him and not know how he felt about you."

Her brown eyes softened. "I was crazy in love with that man then too, but I wouldn't admit it to him either. So the question is, has the tough babe wielding the horsewhip softened up some and is she in love with you?"

"I have no idea. This all happened so damn fast. Who the hell falls in love in a couple of weeks?" Agitated because he didn't do this spilling his guts thing, Sutton let out a slow breath. "Go ahead and laugh."

"Not on your life. But I am gonna play devil's advocate for 'The Saint.'"

He blinked at her. "Okay."

"I have to err on the side that says the horse whisperer—or should I say horse whipper?—is madly in love with you too. How could she not be? You are the real deal, a genuine gentleman and one of the greatest guys I've ever known." She winked. "Even if you are a little shy and reserved for my taste."

"I'da given my left nut to hear you say that to me years ago." He'd been so crazy about Tanna, even when she'd been crazy about Fletch, but he hadn't harbored illusions that they'd ever be together. That just reminded him he had a long history of betting on the wrong horse— when it came to women. Reading more into situations and relationships that weren't there. So he erred on the side of caution. "I just...worry that if London had feelings for me, they'll change like Charlotte's did when she realized I'm no longer interested in living life on the road pursuing another championship."

Tanna angled forward. "You listen to me, Sutton. Charlotte was a star-fucker; she doesn't deserve a thought beyond that. I take it London found out you're putting 'former bulldogger' on upcoming resumes?"

"We had a big damn fight and I didn't even tell her that I knew in the hospital I'd never intended to compete on the circuit professionally again. She asked why I hired her. I saw it in her eyes, she thought everything was lies and manipulation—and she stormed off refusing to discuss it."

"Ever?"

"No. She said she needed to cool down. Then I had to go out of town and everything is just fucked. Been a long couple of days."

Fuck. He needed to get the hell out of here. What made him think this was a good idea? He drained his soda and stood. "Sorry. Wasn't fair to dump all this on you when you've got so much on your plate already."

"Sit your ass down, Sutton. Now."

He sat.

"You came here because you want my advice, not to hear me condone or condemn what you've been doin', right?"

"Right."

She smiled at her baby when he grunted and squeaked. "My precious boy here has changed my life and the way I look at every little thang. So *he* was my promise to God, so to speak. Fletch and I tried for a year to get pregnant. I swore that if we were blessed with a child, I'd slow down. Take a year off from the circuit."

"Are you rethinking that?"

"Right now, I couldn't give a damn if I *ever* compete in barrel racing again. On any level." Tanna looked up at him. "I have four world championships. The number of women who can lay claim to that can be etched on the head of a pin." She bit her lip. "Okay, that ain't true. I still tell tall Texas tales if I can get away with it. The point is, the deals we make with ourselves, the promises we break, all lead to one question: how many championship gold buckles are enough?"

"My brother asked me that same question."

"Did you answer?"

"Nope. Mostly because I was trying to downplay the truth."

"Which is?"

"Even without the injury and the promise I made, I was ready to move on from the road to rodeo glory bein' the only life I had."

Tanna said, "Aha!" loud enough to startle Gus. The baby screwed up his face and wailed. "Sorry my sweet." She brushed her lips across his forehead. After the baby had settled, her gaze met Sutton's. "Once you stop faking your injury, what are your options as far as a career? Ranching with your brothers?"

"They'd let me be part of the operation if I asked."

"But you ain't gonna ask."

"No. I like living close to family and having some acres to spread out on and helping them out in the busy season, but the day to day grind of ranching ain't for me."

She raised a brow. "Still didn't answer the question, bulldogger. What's your college degree in?"

"Business. Not ag business, just an associate's degree in business administration." He sighed. "My dad wanted me to have something to fall back on after I stopped chasin' points and purse."

"And do you?"

He shrugged. "Maybe."

"Don't make me come over there and box your ears to get an answer. Beneath the baby spit up, I'm still a born and bred Texas cowgirl, ready to kick some ass."

"I never doubted that for an instant, Tex-Mex." He took a moment to gather his thoughts. "A buddy of mine is waiting on whether I'll pass the tests that'll clear the way for me to come to work for him at his gun range."

"That's great! See? You've got options."

"First I have to pass my range master certification."

"So? Eli told me you're a deadeye with any kind of weapon."

"It helps when you have a shootin' range in your basement," he said dryly. "Not much else for me to do while I was laying around, lying about going to rehab and stuck in my house. I told myself I was killing time, but—"

"You were preparing for the future," she finished. "So get your shit together, Sutton. Talk to London. Talk to your family. Talk to your friend. Don't put any of it off any longer."

"She givin' you some of that tough love that you gave her a few years back?" Fletch said.

Sutton jumped. How had he missed the big man approaching them?

Fletch reached down and plucked the baby from Tanna's arms—after he gave his wife a steamy kiss. A long, steamy kiss.

Sutton laughed. "Still marking your territory?"

"Always." He cradled the bundle to his chest. "Hey, little man. You been good for your mama?"

"An angel, like always," Tanna said, smiling at her husband and son.

"I can walk around with him if you guys wanna finish your talk," Fletch offered.

"Nah, man, that's okay," Sutton said, standing up. "Your wife set me straight, which is what I needed."

"You did me a good turn. I'm happy to pay it forward," Tanna said softly.

"Agreed. Anything I can do, just ask," Fletch said. "I owe you, too."

"There is one thing..." He laughed when Fletch groaned. "Since my bulldoggin' days are over, I'll need to find a good fit for Dial. So if you know anyone who's lookin', send 'em my way."

Fletch pinned him with a look. "Chuck and Berlin Gradsky wouldn't buy him back?"

"Doubtful. He'd been a thorn in their side for a few years—before you castrated him—and since he and I were well matched they were happy to get rid of him."

A pause hung in the air. Then, "Sweet Jesus, that's something else that London doesn't know," Tanna said. "That you didn't pressure her folks into selling Dial to you. They wanted to get rid of him."

"Yeah, well, she wouldn't have taken that well since she trained him. It'd be a double blow for her."

"Sutton. You have to tell her that too, when you're telling her everything else."

"It's not my place."

"It is. Does she know you're planning on selling Dial?"

"She does now that she told me Dial has been done training for weeks and the only reason she stayed around was because of me."

"Sounds like she loves you, which means this is fixable," Tanna said, standing to hug him and then give him a quick shove. "So go fix it, dumbass."

Chapter Fourteen

Barn therapy.

That's what she needed.

London pointed her truck toward her parent's place and drove. Half an hour later she was in the shed, slipping on waders, an apron, and gloves. She loaded her tools in the wheelbarrow and started in the stall at the farthest end of the barn.

Two cleaned stalls later, she realized she wasn't alone. She turned toward the gate and rested her arm on the handle of the pitchfork.

Her mom hung over the gate. She smiled. "Barn therapy?"

"Yep. Learned it from the best."

"When you're done slogging through the shit—real and imagined—come on up to the house."

"Will do." London returned to her task. After she finished another stall, she called it quits. She cleaned up in the barn bathroom. Since the barn at Grade A Horse Farms cost on the high side of five million dollars to build, it boasted cool amenities, including a full-size shower in both the women's and men's restrooms.

After London drove the mile between the training facility and the private Gradsky family home, she wasn't surprised to see her mom waiting on the porch.

"Would you like tea?"

"That'd be great, Mom." She flopped on the canopy swing and sighed.

"I'd say I was pleasantly surprised to see you, but I haven't heard from you in a while so I figured you'd visit soon." She handed London her tea in her favorite rainbow swirl and polka dot glass.

"Thanks."

"You're welcome. Thank you for tackling those stalls. They always seem to need more maintenance than the others."

"Some kids do too," London muttered.

"Yes, your brother is always harassing me for legal advice for his toughest cases."

She smiled.

"Talk to me, sweetheart. What's the problem?"

"Sutton Grant is the hottest, sexiest, sweetest, most wonderful guy on the planet."

Her mother sipped her tea. "Doesn't seem like much of a problem to me. So I'll ask how does this affect you?"

"Because he's also the most exasperating. And I'm kinda, sorta thinkin' that I'm half in love with him, maybe a little bit."

"Kinda, sorta, maybe?" she repeated.

London blew out a breath. "Okay. Completely, totally, hat over boot heels in love with that man."

When London kept brooding, her mom said, "London Lenora Gradsky. If you don't start talking right now and give me every detail a mother needs, I will bend you over my knee."

She froze. Hard to believe how much she liked it when Sutton had spanked her. He'd been so...intense. So in tune with what she needed and wanted she hadn't even had to ask. And then afterward, so sweet and loving.

"I'm waiting," her mom singsonged.

Where to start? "After Stitch dumped me for that tiara-wearing terror, everyone thought I was suicidal. I wasn't. Yes, I was pissed, but what kind of freakin' jerk breaks up with the woman he's practically living with via text? Jerks like him. I got tired of the pitying looks and wondered how I'd survive the summer since I'd see them every weekend, and then Sutton showed up at one of my seminars. He hadn't been working Dial at all since he'd gotten out of the hospital after his accident."

"Dear Lord. I bet Sutton was fit to be tied because he's all about that horse."

"He was and I initially told him no way because I hated how he pestered you and Dad to sell him Dial. Part of me was thinking 'what goes around comes around, pal' but another part of me was feeling cocky because he had come to *me* for help." She gulped her tea. "This is where it gets tricky." After she gave the rundown about their "deal," she looked over at her mom.

Berlin Gradsky wore a smile that scared London.

"What?"

"That's my girl."

"You're not...upset?"

"That you used your brains to get revenge and make money and getcha some of that hot man honey?"

"MOTHER!"

"What? Sutton Grant is built, good-looking, thoughtful, and genuine. How could I be upset with you getting with a man like him? In fact, I'm thinking tears of pride and joy are gonna start flooding the table at any moment."

London rolled her eyes.

"Keep going because I suspect we hit the problem part of this talk."

"Yeah. So he insists I move into his guest bedroom. He's all cool and laid back, which bugged me to be honest. I wanted him to want me for real. So I put it aside and worked with Dial. And our first official appearance as a couple was so convincing that behind closed doors..." She sighed. "Sutton hasn't forgotten how to ride entirely."

Her mom lifted her glass for a silent toast.

"The more time I spend with Sutton, the more Stitch and that whole thing just fades away. It seems Sutton and I are headed into real relationship territory, but I feel he's holding something back from me."

"I imagine he's tired of that same old question of when he'll start competing again."

London nodded. "He didn't ask me how the training is going with Dial. Which I took as I wasn't doin' a fast enough job and he feels he can't push me because we're sleeping together. But now...the man admitted he won't be competing again and he's been having me work with his horse so he can get rid of it."

"Oh dear."

She drained her tea and chomped on a piece of ice. "He can't sell Dial. I didn't train his horse for someone else, I trained it for *him*."

Her mother shook her head. "I know you've got an independent streak, sweetheart, but there's where you've stepped over the line. You trained Sutton's horse. Period. Whether he sells it or rides it himself is immaterial. He's paying you for a service." Her eyes narrowed. "He *is* paying you?"

"Of course." Not that she'd cashed the checks.

"There's your answer for that part of the problem."

London locked her gaze to her mother's. "You have no ill feelings toward Sutton at all for him demanding you sell Dial to him three years ago?"

"You somehow got your wires crossed because your father and I don't give in to demands—be they horses', kids', or customers'. We sold Dial to Sutton because they complemented each other. Dial was a nightmare horse, sweetheart. I don't know why you don't remember that. We were over the moon that Sutton wanted to take him off our hands. Sometimes I think your father would've paid Sutton to take him."

London's mouth fell open. "What? But *I* trained him."

"We're aware of that."

"So you're saying the reason Dial is such a nightmare is because of me? Of how I trained him?"

"No." Her mom set the glass on the tray and took London's hands in her own. "You and Sutton were the only two people we'd ever run across who could control that horse. The only two. We even had Dial castrated in an attempt to change his behavior and that changed nothing. We were at a loss. You know how we handle a horse like that."

"You get rid of it."

"Exactly. Sutton offered to buy him and we accepted. We knew you'd take it personally, honey. But we all know that a well-trained horse isn't always a well-behaved horse. That's Dial. When he's on the dirt he's focused, a champion, ready to do what he's been trained to. But the instant his hooves are out of the arena? He's difficult. You would've kept trying to change that behavior to the exclusion of training other horses. We had to get rid of him." She squeezed London's fingers. "I know that situation was the catalyst for you to strike out on your own entirely. Your father and I couldn't be more proud of you."

"While I appreciate that...it is sort of embarrassing that I've been wrong all along."

"About us resenting Sutton Grant? Absolutely. *You* resented him. And I worry you've gotten sucked back into that cycle of trying to fix a horse that has limitations."

She'd never considered any of this and it sent her reeling.

But didn't Sutton ask you that very first day if he couldn't utilize Dial after he'd been retrained, if you'd be willing to help find him a new home?

Yes. But she hadn't believed him. In fact, she'd done exactly what her mother claimed she'd done: she'd set out to prove Sutton wrong.

"Damn. I am a fucking idiot."

"No. You just added the complication of love to an already

complicated situation."

"What do I do now?"

"Talk to Sutton. Tell him you know that we happily handed over Dial to his care. Tell him you'll help him find another bulldogger to sell to who can handle a horse who performs well but won't ever acclimate to a normal environment outside the arena." She cocked her head. "What about Stitch?"

"Oh sure, Mom, suggest that Sutton sell a horse with behavioral problems to my *ex-boyfriend*. There's no chance that Sutton would oh, hope the horse would hurt Stitch because he hurt me?"

"Sounds like Sutton is pretty protective of you?"

"Yes. Which is sweet and sorta hot, in a Neanderthal way. Sutton and I had words about a freakin' hug Stitch gave me. That's when it came out he wouldn't be competing anymore. I was mad; he was annoying as fuck. I asked for some time and I'll be damned if he didn't give it to me. It's been four damn days! He's not answering my texts or my calls. I don't know how to fix it."

"He hasn't been to his house?"

"Not when I've been there."

"Does he still have that underground shooting range?"

Again, London was shocked. "You *knew* about that?"

"Of course. It's his pride and joy. He invited your dad over to shoot." A sneaky and slightly evil looking smile spread across her mom's face. "I know one way to get a man back home, and you won't even have to get on your knees."

"MOTHER!"

"What? I mean getting on your knees to beg him. Good lord. You have as dirty a mind as your father. Anyway, call Sutton and leave him a voicemail."

"I've tried that."

"Ah ah ah. But you haven't told him that you feel so bad about what happened between you two, and you know he's upset, so you've decided to do something nice for him to open those lines of communication."

"Like what?"

She paused for effect. "Polish all his guns."

"Oh shit."

"Then tell him you've used a Brillo Pad to shine up the metal parts, but you aren't sure if you should use furniture polish or car wax on the wood parts. I guarantee you'll get his attention."

"Mom. That is brilliant. Twisted, but brilliant." Totally impossible to do with the biometric locks on the vaults, but it'd get her point across. London leapt up and hugged her. "Thanks for listening. But I'll admit you scare me sometimes."

Berlin Gradsky delicately sipped her tea. "I have no idea what you're talking about."

Shining his gunstocks with furniture polish? ... when

Chapter Fifteen

Shining his gunstocks with furniture polish?

That woman had a warped sense of humor. Seriously fucking warped.

Which was probably why he was seriously fucking in love with her.

Sutton didn't bother pulling into the garage. He parked on the concrete slab and barreled into the house. Shouting wasn't his style, but he found himself doing it anyway. "London Gradsky, you better not have put a single spritz of Lemon Pledge on my shotguns or so help me God I'll—"

"You'll what?" she said from the living room where she was sprawled out on the chaise, drinking a beer.

His eyes narrowed. Hey, wait a second. London was knocking back the special brew he'd brought back from Germany two years ago.

"Still waiting," she said and then took a big swig.

"Where are my guns?"

"Safely locked away in their velvet lined, dehumidified gun cases I presume."

He crossed his arms over his chest. "Then why'd you send me that threatening text?"

"Threatening text? When I said I was gonna help you out by cleaning up your guns? That was me being nice, asshole."

"If that's you bein' nice, darlin', I'd hate to see you when you're bein' nasty."

London leapt to her feet. "You're about to find out."

"Bring it, cowgirl. And bring me that damn beer you stole. I haven't had a taste of it."

She smirked. Then she tipped the bottle up and drained it. She wiped her lips with the back of her hand and belched.

"You are the most annoying fucking woman on the planet."

"So does that mean you missed me?" she asked softly.

Here was the moment of truth. "Yeah. I missed you like a limb."

"Sutton."

"London. I know we need to talk, but c'mere and gimme a kiss 'cause the last few days have sucked without you."

He didn't wait for her to come to him. They met halfway, and he wrapped her in his arms for several long moments, reminding himself of how well they fit together, in so many ways.

"I missed you too, bulldogger."

Sutton twisted his hand in her hair and tipped her head back to get at that sweet, hot mouth of hers. The kiss heated up, and he paused to say, "I like how that beer tastes on you."

"Stop talking and kiss me some more."

He did just that. But as much as he wanted to let the passion between them expand, letting it show her how he felt about her, he needed to say the words. "London," he murmured against her lips.

She flattened her hands on his pecs and pushed, putting distance between them. "Uh-oh. That's your serious voice."

"I have different voices?"

"Yep. There's your *Jesus, woman* tone, which means you're exasperated with me. There's your *Hey, sweet darlin'* rasp that means you're about to strip me naked. Then there's your *C'mon, sweetheart* taunt that means you're teasing me. And there's the softly spoken *London*, which means...I'm never exactly sure what I'm in for with that one." She raised her gaze to his. "So if you do plan to tell me something good that'll make me smile, weep with joy, and throw myself into your big, strong arms, let's get through the bad stuff first." She touched her lips to his. "There's things we both need to get off our chests."

He pressed a kiss onto her forehead. "Sounds fair. Kitchen or living room?"

"Living room. That way if you really piss me off I'm farther away from the knives and you have time to run."

Yep. He so loved this woman.

London held his hand and led him to the sectional couch. After he'd settled himself in the corner, she immediately stretched out on top of him, nestling the side of her face against the center of his chest, pressing her hip between his legs. Being body to body, where he could touch her at will but wasn't staring directly into her eyes as he made his confessions, would make those confessions come easier.

Sutton ran his hand down her arm. "Is this okay for you?"

"It's perfect for me." She kissed his pectoral. "Start when you're ready."

He reflexively tightened his hold on her hip. "You won't take off?"

"Nope. Unless you tell me you're part of some religious sect where they allow you to have as many wives as you want, because I don't share well at all."

"Me neither." He marshaled his thoughts and decided to get the worst over first. "The reason I have no intention of ever competing as a professional steer wrestler again is because I made a deal with God that if I survived the wreck, I'd walk away from the sport for good. I'm keeping my word because in that moment I finally realized how lucky I am." When she didn't laugh or call him an idiot, he told her the story. "So no one knows what really went down. Not my family, not my sponsors, not the CRA."

"How long have you been medically cleared?"

"Four months. My brothers busted me trying to work with Dial right after I'd been released. I chose to perpetuate the lie. No idea why I did. Seemed smart at the time. Then it just steamrolled. But you know better than anyone what happens to a highly trained horse when it's allowed to run amok. Needing your help with Dial was completely sincere."

She traced the edge of his shirt pocket. "I know. I knew when you didn't balk at pretending to be my boyfriend as a stipulation of me helping you that you were desperate."

"Not the word I'd use..."

"After the first time we kissed, I knew I was in big trouble with you."

"Why?"

"Because I didn't give a damn about Stitch anymore."

"But I thought you did and I kept pushing us into bein' more visible as a couple—"

"When all I wanted was alone time with you, my hot man. So you believe me when I say Stitch means nothing to me? That conversation you interrupted—"

"That overly friendly hug," he corrected with a growl.

"Was just a hug between friends. I didn't only ask you to pretend to be my boyfriend to make Stitch jealous. I needed my ego bolstered after being dumped. I never wanted Stitch back. I guess I didn't make that clear."

He sighed. "How did this get so fucked up?"

"Because we both kept following our own agenda. How long did you plan to keep me training Dial?"

"Until you said he was back to normal or that you couldn't get him there." His hand traveled back up her arm and he brushed her hair from her shoulder. "Then I remembered why your folks agreed to sell me Dial in the first place—because you'd keep working with him to the exclusion of every other animal in their stable. So I was selfish, hoping it'd take you a long damn time to retrain him."

"Because...?"

"Because I fell in love with you. I hoped if you had more time with me, you'd fall for me too—when I wasn't second guessing myself that no one really fell in love in a week." He felt her smile against his chest.

London lifted her head and looked at him reverently—and they weren't even naked. That had to mean something, right?

"Talk to me."

She ran her fingertips over the stubble on his cheeks. "I expected you to say you didn't think this was real because you were my rebound man."

"Shit. I should've been worrying about *that* too?"

She laughed. "No." Then she sobered. "Here's the truth. Dial is as good as he's ever gonna get. At least under my training. I've been pretending that he hasn't made much progress because I didn't want to leave you."

He grinned so widely it hurt, then he wondered if he might've pulled a muscle.

"I've been milking this job. But not for money. Every check you wrote me is uncashed. I also suspected you weren't being truthful because you let me be. You weren't gauging Dial's progress. A guy antsy to get back on the dirt would've been out there every day harassing me for faster results."

"You didn't take my hands-off approach as that I trusted you to do the job I'd hired you for?"

"Nope."

"Damn."

"But I'd hoped that you were keeping me around because you were starting to feel things for me since I'd fallen in love with you."

Sutton kissed her then, knowing he'd remember this moment for the rest of their lives.

"So what now?"

"You move in with me."

"Like we're roommates?"

"Fuck no, we won't be roommates. And we ain't playing house either. This is for real."

"I can move my stuff into your room?"

"Woman, half your shit is already in my room—don't think I didn't notice." He held her chin and feathered his thumb over her lips. "Dream come true having a woman like you in my bed every night."

"A woman like me?"

"A hot, feisty, sexy cowgirl who loves me for me. Not because of the championship buckles, the fame, or the money. "

"The money is a nice bonus. But will you be in our bed with me every night? Because that's been another thing we haven't discussed. Your need for space."

"Baby, it's not about me needing space; it's about me needing more time. For the past month I've been haying with my brothers, and keeping you thoroughly fucked to entice you into staying with me forever, and that wears a man out. So the only time I could study for the test I'm taking to become a range master was in the middle of the night. The only other thing that's been constant in my life besides bulldoggin' is my love of guns. My buddy Ramsey owns an indoor/outdoor gun range. The first week you were here he told me one of his range masters is getting deployed for a year. He asked if I'd be interested in taking the test and filling in. Then when the guy returns from deployment, he'll find me a permanent position if I like working there. So that's where I've been the past two days, taking the written test, which wasn't fun at all, and sharpening my skills here and at the range for the firearms qualification portion, which will be the fun part."

"It's a really exciting change and opportunity for you, Sutton! How awesome you get to do another thing that you love to make a living."

That shit-eating grin spread across his face again. She got it. She got him in ways he didn't have to explain. "Thanks. I planned on telling my family after I told you."

"Will you make an official announcement about retirement from the CRA?"

"Most likely. I've been avoiding my PR person, so I'll talk to her about it."

"That leaves just one thing left to deal with." She paused. "Dial."

He brushed her soft cheek with his knuckles. "I asked my buddy who's a veterinarian in Wyoming to keep his ear to the ground for anyone interested in a championship bulldogging horse. Dial needs to work, so I prefer he went to a qualified candidate. Payment, lease, whatever is all secondary to me at this point." He paused. "Why? Do you already have someone in mind?"

"No, but I agree it's better to wait than just shipping Dial off and cutting your losses. As long as folks in the rodeo world know you're serious about finding the right competitor for him, you *will* have interest. Whether it's the right interest? Dial is the best judge."

"I'll defer to my expert horsewoman. But I'll point out you didn't think Dial had the best judgment when he chose me."

"You'll still be harping on that years from now, won't you?"

Sutton liked that London was already imagining a future for them. "Maybe. Unless you agree to keep working Dial until he's found a new home."

"Hell no. He's *your* horse. You can put him through his paces every day. Besides, I'm officially not your horse trainer any longer."

"Mmm. But you will keep that ridin' crop? Cause I have a feeling you're the type of woman who'll need a whack every once in a while to keep things interesting."

Epilogue

Three months later...

"I can't thank you enough." Stitch kept pumping Sutton's hand as he spoke. "He'll be in good hands. You'll never have to worry he ain't bein' well taken care of."

"That's why we're letting you take him," London said sweetly. Then she laughed. "Well, not *take*, exactly."

Stitch nodded, his gaze zipping to his horse trailer as if he couldn't believe what it held. Then he met Sutton's eyes again. "You're really okay with payments starting in January?"

"This year is a loss for me, at least professionally"—he sent London a wicked smile—"on the personal front, it's been a bang-up year." London melted when he wrapped his arm around her shoulder. "I've no problem waiting until you're starting a new season."

"That's just...awesome, man. Thanks." Stitch smiled at London, his gaze zeroing in on the big sapphire ring on her left hand. "I heard you two got engaged. Congratulations."

"Thank you," London said, sneaking a peek at the ring Sutton had given her just one short week ago. In typical Sutton fashion, his proposal had been a little offbeat; he'd tied the ring at the end of a fancy ribbon and looped it around the barrel of her new shotgun, begging her to make an honest man of him.

"Have you set the date?"

London said, "No" the same time Sutton said, "Soon."

"Good luck." Then Stitch climbed in his rig and drove off.

Sutton kissed her temple. "Whoda thunk, huh? That Dial would take to Stitch and vice versa?"

"Stitch is a good guy."

"Just not the guy for you," Sutton said with a growl.

God, she loved that possessive tone. She loved that the shy man wasn't shy at all about showing her every day, in so many different ways, how much he loved her and how happy she made him.

And she was more than happy to return the favor. To be the woman he could count on to love him through the good times and bad.

He draped his arm over her shoulder. "What's on the agenda tonight?"

"We could pick up and clean the shell casings for the new line of bullet jewelry I've started."

"Pass. I get enough shell casing clean-up duties at my day job. What's my other option?"

"Hanging out in front of the fireplace. Playing cards."

His eyes lit up. "Strip poker?"

"No, you cheat."

"Me?" he said innocently. "I'm 'The Saint,' remember? I don't cheat."

"Ain't no one calling you that anymore, bulldogger."

"Thank God." He pulled her closer and his lips grazed the top of her ear. "To be honest, I don't care what we do just as long as I'm with you."

She sighed. "I'm so crazy in love with you."

"Same goes, sweetheart."

Acknowledgments from the Author

A big yee-haw! and tip of my hat to the wonderful, marvelous Liz Berry and MJ Rose for asking me to be part of the 1001 Dark Nights project!

When I saw the list of authors who'd signed on, I was…humbled and excited and now I'm thrilled because I can call so many of them my friends. That October weekend was a blast and I can't wait to do it again – although this time I will pull my arm back when Cherise Sinclair assures me the rubber flogger "doesn't hurt that much" and I will be 100% prepared for dinosaur porn readings, jello shots, amazing southern cooking (bacon every day!) field trips, beach walks, wine tours and late nights gab sessions with my roomie Julie Kenner.

Extra thanks to Liz Berry who never balked at my crazy texts and just went with it when I made changes to the story/plot/characters…again. This one is for you darlin'…

About Lorelei James

Lorelei James is the *New York Times* and *USA Today* bestselling author of contemporary erotic romances in the Rough Riders, Blacktop Cowboys, and Mastered series. She also writes dark, gritty mysteries under the name Lori Armstrong and her books have won the Shamus Award and the Willa Cather Literary Award. She lives in western South Dakota.

Connect with Lorelei online:

Website: http://www.loreleijames.com/

Stripped Down
A Blacktop Cowboys® Novella
By Lorelei James

Coming September 1, 2015

From *New York Times* and *USA Today* bestselling author Lorelei James, a new steamy story of the Blacktop Cowboys...

The heat is on when feisty cowgirl Melissa Lockhart challenges playboy rancher Wynton Grant to a game of sexual truth or dare...who will come out on top?

Also from Lorelei James

Rough Riders Series

LONG HARD RIDE
RODE HARD PUT UP WET
COWGIRL UP AND RIDE
TIED UP, TIED DOWN
ROUGH, RAW AND READY
BRANDED AS TROUBLE
STRONG SILENT TYPE (novella)
SHOULDA BEEN A COWBOY
ALL JACKED UP
RAISING KANE
SLOW RIDE (free short story)
COWGIRLS DON'T CRY
CHASIN' EIGHT
COWBOY CASANOVA
KISSIN' TELL
GONE COUNTRY
SHORT RIDES (anthology)
REDNECK ROMEO
COWBOY TAKE ME AWAY

Blacktop Cowboys Series

CORRALLED
SADDLED AND SPURRED
WRANGLED AND TANGLED
ONE NIGHT RODEO
TURN AND BURN
HILLBILLY ROCKSTAR
ROPED IN (novella)

The Mastered Series

BOUND
UNWOUND

SCHOOLED (novella Dec 2014)
UNRAVELED (March 2015)

Individual Titles

RUNNING WITH THE DEVIL
DIRTY DEEDS
WICKED GARDEN (Three's Company novella)
BALLROOM BLITZ (Two to Tango novella)
MISTRESS CHRISTMAS (Wild West Boys novella)
MISS FIRECRACKER (Wild West Boys novella)
LOST IN YOU (sexy contemporary novella)

1001
DARK
NIGHTS

TEMPTED BY MIDNIGHT
A Midnight Breed Novella

NEW YORK TIMES BESTSELLING AUTHOR
LARA ADRIAN

CHAPTER 1

He had lived for more than a thousand years, long enough that few things still held the power to amaze him. The sea at night was one of those rare pleasures for Lazaro Archer.

Standing on the third-level bow deck of a gleaming, 279-foot private megayacht off the western coast of Italy, Lazaro braced his hands on the polished mahogany rail and indulged his senses in a brief appreciation of his moonlit surroundings.

Crisp, salty Mediterranean air filled his nostrils and tousled his jet-black hair. The late summer breeze was cool tonight, gusting rhythmically toward the Italian mainland. Dark, rippling water spread out in all directions under the milky glow of the cloud-strewn moon and blanket of stars. Far below, waves lapped fluidly, sensually, against the sides of the yacht where it floated, engines silenced as it waited at its destined location on the Tyrrhenian Sea.

Lazaro supposed the luxurious vessel he stood aboard would take the breath away from just about anyone—human or Breed. Being born the latter, and first generation Breed besides, one of the vampire nation's eldest, most pure-blooded individuals, Lazaro had known his fair share of wealth and luxury.

He'd once had all of those things himself. Still did, if he could be bothered to care.

He left everything he once had back in Boston twenty years ago, after the most precious things in his long life had been taken from him. His blood-bonded Breedmate, his sons and their mates, a houseful of innocent children...all gone. His only surviving kin was his grandson,

Kellan, who'd been with Lazaro the night the Archers' Darkhaven home was razed to the ground in a heinous, unprovoked attack by a madman named Dragos.

Lazaro exhaled deeply, no longer feeling the raw scrape of grief whenever he thought of his slain family. The anguish had dulled over time, yet his guilt was always with him, scarred over like a physical wound. A hideous, permanent reminder of his loss.

Of his life's greatest failure.

If his existence had any meaning now, it belonged to his work with Lucan Thorne and his fellow Breed warriors of the Order. As the commander of the Order's operation in Rome these past two decades, Lazaro had little time for self-pity or personal indulgences. He had even less opportunity for pleasure, rare or otherwise.

Which was the way he preferred it.

He dealt in justice now.

At times, he dealt in death.

Tonight, he was representing the Order on a less official basis, on the hopes that he could facilitate a secret meeting between two of his trusted friends. One of them was Breed, a high-ranking American member of the Global Nations Council. The other, the megayacht's owner, was human, an influential Italian businessman who also happened to be the brother of that country's newly elected president, a politician who had won his office with tough talk against the Breed. If the meeting with Paolo Turati took place as planned tonight and was deemed a success, it would be the first step toward forging an alliance with one of the vampire nation's most vocal detractors.

As for Byron Walsh, the Breed male had been one of Lazaro's colleagues in the States, even before the GNC had tapped Walsh for his current diplomatic post. As leader of his own Darkhaven in Maryland, Walsh's social circle had occasionally intersected with Lazaro's in Boston. There had even been a time, one bitter winter, that Walsh's family came to visit Lazaro's at their Back Bay mansion.

A long time ago, back when Lazaro had a Darkhaven. Back when he still had a family kept safe under his protection.

It had been even longer since Lazaro Archer had played emissary for any cause. He hoped like hell this clandestine introduction wasn't a mistake.

Seventy-odd miles behind him was the seaside town of Anzio, where Lazaro had joined Turati on his yacht a couple of hours ago. Up ahead of them, an even farther distance, the island of Sardinia glittered with light against the darkness.

A smattering of other large yachts and watercraft bobbed in the vast space between Turati's vessel and the island, but it was the low drone of a motorboat that captured Lazaro's full attention. The size of a small cabin cruiser, the yacht tender had departed from an idling vessel in the distance and was heading Lazaro's way. He watched the chase boat approach from out of the inky darkness, its navigation lights dimmed as instructed, flashing three times as it crossed the water toward them.

His Breed colleague from the States did not disappoint. Byron Walsh was arriving as promised, and right on time.

Lazaro nodded, grim with relief.

He turned away from the rail and headed down to the yacht's main deck salon where Turati waited. On Lazaro's directions and assurances, the gray-haired billionaire had brought just two men from his usual security entourage. The yacht's crew of fifty had been reduced to a bare dozen, just enough personnel to operate the vessel.

At Lazaro's entrance to the lavish salon, Turati glanced up, wiry brows lifting in question. "He comes?" the old man asked in his native tongue.

Lazaro answered in Italian as well. "The boat is on the way now." As tonight's host did not speak English, Lazaro would personally translate for the duration of the meeting, if only to ensure that the conversation didn't inadvertently stray into unfriendly waters.

Paolo Turati was one of a small number of humans Lazaro considered a friend. He was also one of the few humans who didn't look upon the Breed as a race of monsters in need of collaring at best, or, at worst, wholesale extermination.

Granted, the fear wasn't without cause. For millennia, the Breed existed in the shadows alongside their *Homo sapiens* neighbors. In the twenty years since Lazaro's kind was outed to man, trust between the two races on the planet had been anything but easy.

That trust became even more complicated a couple of weeks ago, when a violent cabal calling themselves Opus Nostrum smuggled a bomb into a very important summit gathering of Breed and human dignitaries.

If tonight's introductions went well, the Breed would gain a supportive voice and a much-needed ally in their efforts to keep the peace between man and vampire all around the world. If it went poorly, the Order's efforts to broker peace could ignite the smoldering war that Opus Nostrum seemed to want so badly.

"I hope your friend from Maryland comes to this meeting with the same intentions as I do," Turati said, apprehension in the flat line of his mouth, even though the old human's eyes held Lazaro in a trusting look. "If I like what I hear tonight, I will do what I can to persuade my brother to at least entertain the idea of talks with the GNC and Lucan Thorne. After all, everyone's goal is peace, not only for ourselves, but for our generations to follow."

"Indeed," Lazaro replied. His acute Breed hearing picked up the faint, approaching growl of the boat carrying Byron Walsh. "He's arriving now. Wait here, Paolo. I'll go down to meet him and bring him up."

Turati frowned then shook his head. "I will join you, Lazaro. It seems only proper that I greet Councilman Walsh personally and welcome him aboard along with you. I would do no less for any invited guest."

Lazaro inclined his head in agreement. "A fine idea."

He waited patiently as the old man stood and smoothed his custom-tailored navy suit and creamy silk shirt. By contrast, Lazaro was dressed in what he'd come to regard as *Order casual*—black slacks, light-duty combat boots, and a fitted black patrol shirt.

And although he was first generation Breed and more than deadly with his bare hands alone, he carried a blade concealed in each boot and had a semiautomatic 9mm pistol strapped to his right ankle. He didn't expect trouble from either of the two men or their few staff present at tonight's meeting, but he'd be damned if he didn't come prepared for it.

Together, he and Turati left the grand salon on the yacht's second level, making their way down a polished brass stairwell that spiraled elegantly onto the lower deck. The boat carrying Walsh was coming around the stern as Lazaro and Turati arrived on the aft deck to meet it.

A suited bodyguard stood at attention on the motorboat, just outside the cabin's hatch. He was Breed, as big and menacing as any one of Lazaro's kind. Turati's steps hesitated at the sight of the unsmiling guard. The two men comprising the Italian's own security detail now stood behind their employer, pulses spiking with a tension Lazaro felt as a palpable vibration in the air.

He gave a solemn nod of greeting to Walsh's guard, the signal as good as his word that Walsh would be safe among friends tonight. The guard turned, opened the hatch to murmur an "all clear" to the boat's occupants.

Byron Walsh appeared in that next instant. Dressed less formally than Turati, the Breed diplomat emerged from the cabin in a crisp white shirt with rolled-back sleeves and fawn-colored slacks. Although Walsh was formidable-looking, over six feet tall and heavily muscled, like all of their kind, his relaxed attire softened his edges.

As did the smile he gave as he disembarked from his tender and stepped onto the deck of Turati's yacht. Walsh's friendliness seemed genuine, even if his smile didn't quite reach his eyes. There was an undercurrent of anxiety about him, as if he hadn't yet decided if he was stepping onto safe ground or a nest of vipers.

"Lazaro, my old friend, it's been too long. Good to see you," he greeted briefly, then extended his hand to the evening's host. "*Signor Turati, buona sera.*"

"Paolo," Turati offered as the two men shook hands.

"Thank you for agreeing to this meeting," Walsh continued in English. "And please forgive the cloak-and-dagger aspect of our introduction tonight. Unfortunately, there are those who might prefer to keep our people at odds, rather than embrace the peace that you and I both hope to achieve."

Lazaro murmured a quick translation, to which Turati smiled and replied in kind. "Paolo says he is honored to have the opportunity to talk and share ideas with you, Byron. He would like you and your men to be comfortable as his guests inside now."

Walsh held up his hand, gesturing to wait. "A moment, if you will. We're not all present just yet." He pivoted to look at his pair of Breed bodyguards behind him. "Where's Mel?"

"Right behind me a second ago," one of his men answered.

Lazaro scowled, confused, and not a little concerned that Walsh had apparently brought a third member of his entourage when the agreement had explicitly called for balance on both sides of this informal summit. He shot a questioning glower at his friend—just as a head emerged from the cabin below.

A head covered in long, luscious waves of fiery red hair.

"I'm sorry," the woman offered hastily as she made her way out. "I had to sit down for a second. I'm afraid I'm still trying to find my sea legs."

She came out of the cabin completely then, and every pair of eyes on deck rooted onto her like the tide pulled toward the moon. Not even Lazaro was immune.

Christ, not even close.

"Ah. There you are, darling." Walsh pivoted to assist her off the smaller vessel.

Darling? Lazaro vaguely recalled hearing that Byron Walsh had lost his mate in a car accident three or four years ago. Had he taken another lover so soon? Whether she was a Breedmate or human female, Lazaro couldn't be sure.

More to the point, what the hell was Walsh thinking, showing up with her unexpectedly to a meeting of this importance? Lazaro had worked on Paolo Turati for months before the man finally agreed to open the door to talks with a member of the GNC. Walsh himself had been reluctant to trust the kin of a government leader who made no secret of his suspicion and distaste for the entire population of the Breed. Lazaro could not imagine what had possessed Walsh to treat this unofficial summit as a goddamned pleasure cruise.

If grabbing the Breed male by the throat and demanding an answer to that very question wouldn't turn an already awkward situation into a potential disaster, Lazaro might have uncurled his fists at his sides and done just that. Instead, he stared, silent and fuming. He'd deal with his friend's apparent lapse in judgment later.

"Careful now," Walsh cautioned his uninvited companion. "Watch your step, sweetheart."

Hell, every male present was watching her step. She was tall, elegant, with bountiful curves that filled out every body-skimming line of a conservative—yet damned sexy—charcoal gray skirt that skimmed her knees and showcased her long, shapely legs. She wore a garnet-colored silk blouse unbuttoned midway down her sternum, just low enough to tease at the generous swell of her bosom.

At the base of her throat was a small scarlet birthmark in the shape of a teardrop falling into the cradle of a crescent moon. So, the voluptuous beauty was a Breedmate, Lazaro noted with displeasure. Had she been simply human arm candy for the councilman, Lazaro would have no qualms at all about turning her sinfully formed behind right back around and sending the motorboat away with her inside.

But a female born with the Breedmate mark commanded deeper respect than that from one of Lazaro's kind. And although he was more warrior now than gentleman, there was still a part of him that held rare females like this one in high regard. And if she was in fact mated to Byron Walsh, then Lazaro had no bloody right to stare at her with a smoldering crackle of interest heating his veins.

As her slender-heeled pumps settled gracefully on the deck, she lifted her head and glanced up to look at him and the other men. Her mane of lustrous, flame-bright hair framed a delicate oval face dominated by large green eyes and soft, sensual lips.

She was, in a word, stunning.

The face of an angel and the kind of body to tempt a saint.

And based on the sudden hush of focused male interest on the deck of Turati's yacht, there was hardly a saint among them.

Lazaro shut down his own awareness of her with abrupt, violent force.

Walsh took the woman's hand and led her forward. "Lazaro, you'll remember my daughter, Mel."

In a flash of memory, Lazaro envisioned a gangly tomboy about seven years old who'd come with her adopted parents to the Archer Darkhaven one winter. Freckle-faced, scrawny, and possessed of more courage than good sense, the way he recalled it now.

Nothing like the curvaceous, poised woman he saw before him here.

"Melena," she corrected her father gently, her lush mouth bowing in a polite smile as she offered her hand in greeting first to Turati, then to Lazaro. "I'm my father's personal assistant. Tonight I'll also be translating for him." She turned the full strength of her smile on Turati, speaking now in flawless Italian. "I hope you don't mind. Between you and me, Daddy's Italian is only slightly better than his French, which isn't saying much."

Turati chuckled, his aged eyes twinkling as he drank in the sight of Melena Walsh. The pair immediately began a light, effusive chat about Italy and its numerous areas of superiority over all things French. Lazaro didn't want to be impressed with the young woman, but he couldn't deny her language skills—or her charm. Paolo Turati was no pushover and it had taken her less than a minute to have the old goat eating out of the palm of her soft white hand.

Still, this wasn't a social call.

There was real business to be done tonight.

Lazaro cleared his throat in effort to break up the uninvited distraction. "Your offer to translate is appreciated, Miss Walsh—"

"Melena, please," she interjected.

"But it won't be necessary," Lazaro finished. "As this meeting is confidential and a matter of global security as well, all interpretation will be handled personally by me. I trust you understand."

She glanced at her father, an anxious flick of her eyes.

"I'll be more comfortable knowing Mel is nearby," Walsh replied. "As you say, Lazaro, there is much at stake in the world, and I would hate for my clumsy words to convey anything less than what I truly mean. Likewise, before I leave tonight, I would like to be sure that I've understood everything Paolo intends me to know."

"You don't trust that I am capable of assuring you of both those things?"

"Melena's come all this way to assist me, Lazaro."

"And she's welcome to wait on board in one of the other salons until the meeting is finished." Lazaro met his old friend's gaze, tried to decipher some of the apprehension he saw in the Breed male's eyes. "If you don't like my decision, take it up with Lucan Thorne when you return to the States."

Turati was frowning now, lost by the rapid back-and-forth in English. "Something is wrong?" he asked, directing his question to Lazaro in Italian, even though he could hardly tear his gaze away from Melena. "Tell me what is going on."

"Miss Walsh will join us after the meeting concludes," Lazaro informed him. "She was unaware of the sensitive nature of this arrangement and has agreed that I should provide the necessary translation assistance as planned."

Melena glanced down, and Turati's face pinched into a deeper frown. He stepped toward her, his mouth pursing under his silent contemplation. When she looked up at him, the old man grinned, hooking a thumb in Lazaro's direction. "Shall we ask him to join us after the meeting instead?" he whispered in Italian. "I would much rather listen to your voice for the next few hours than his, my dear."

She smiled but started to shake her head. "Thank you, Mr. Turati, but I cannot—"

"You can, and I insist that you do. You and your father are both my guests here tonight. I'll banish neither of you from our meeting." Turati slanted a sly glance at Lazaro. "I won't banish you either. Come, let's go inside now."

Lazaro sent the motor boat away with a dismissing wave as he waited for the Walshes, Turati, and the two pairs of bodyguards to head back up to the yacht's main salon. Then, with a low curse and a vague, but troubled, niggling in his veins, he fell in behind them.

CHAPTER 2

The meeting was going far better than they could have hoped. Especially considering Melena had nearly been banned from the room before it even started.

Her father and Paolo Turati had talked without interruption for a couple of hours—serious conversations ranging from cultural misconceptions among the Breed and mankind, to the volatile political climate that existed between the two races. They'd discussed their hopes for a better future and confessed their shared worries about what that future might look like if the mistrust that festered on either side of Breed/human relations were allowed to continue.

Or worse, if it were encouraged to spread—something the failed terror act at the GNC peace summit in Washington, D.C., two weeks ago had seemed orchestrated to do.

The two men hadn't solved the world's many problems in the space of two hours, but they did seem to be forming a genuine respect and fondness for each other. With the heavier subjects behind them, Melena happily translated as they moved on to trading anecdotes from recent travels they'd both enjoyed and talk of their children. Mundane, comfortable conversations peppered with easy smiles, even bouts of laughter.

If her father had reservations about his trip overseas for this covert audience, those concerns seemed all but evaporated now. And he had been more than apprehensive, Melena had to admit. He'd been on the verge of paranoia in the days leading up to this meeting.

He worried that betrayal awaited him around every corner—not so much groundless panic, but a hunch he couldn't shake. Born with limited precognitive ability, her father's hunches, good or bad, all too often proved to be fact.

Every Breed vampire was gifted with a preternatural talent unique to himself. The same held true for Breedmates like Melena, women who bore the teardrop-and-crescent-moon mark and had the rare genetic makeup that allowed them to blood-bond with one of the Breed in an eternal union and bear his young.

It was Melena's specific extrasensory ability that brought her along with her father tonight, more so than her translation skills. She'd needed to see Paolo Turati in person in order to assure her father of the human's intentions. And she'd been satisfied in that regard. *Signor* Turati was a good man, one who could be trusted at his word.

Melena was glad she could be there to allay her father's worry, even if her presence had met with the glowering disapproval of the Breed male who'd arranged the important introduction.

For the duration of the meeting so far, Lazaro Archer had loomed in brooding silence at the peripheral of the megayacht's opulent main deck salon, as distracting as a dark storm cloud. While he'd allowed her to translate as Turati insisted, it was obvious the raven-haired Gen One Breed male wasn't happy about it.

No, he was furious. He wanted her gone. And she didn't need to rely on ESP to tell her so.

From the sharp stab of his piercing indigo gaze, which had been fixed on her each time she dared a look in his direction, Melena guessed it wasn't often he found himself not in absolute control of any given situation.

She could personally attest to Lazaro Archer's commanding, take-charge demeanor. She had witnessed him in action firsthand once. She'd been just a child, but to say he left an impression was an understatement.

Memory yanked her back to a cold winter night and a foolish dare gone terribly wrong. She could still feel the frozen water engulf her. Could still see the blackness that filled her vision as her head struck something hard and sharp with her fall.

Idly, Melena ran her fingertips across the scar that cut a fine line through her left eyebrow. She didn't realize she was being spoken to until she saw both her father and Paolo Turati looking at her in expectation.

"Oh, I...I'm sorry," she stammered, embarrassed to have been caught drifting. Especially with Lazaro Archer there to notice it too.

"Would you repeat that last part for me, please? I want to be certain I get it correct."

Her father chuckled. "Sweetheart, I just asked if you might like to take a short break. We've been going on for hours without a rest. I'm sure we all could use a few minutes to relax a bit."

"Of course," she replied, then pivoted to translate for their smiling host.

As she rose from the antique sofa, both men politely stood with her. Lazaro Archer took the opportunity to stalk out of the salon. She watched him disappear into the darkness outside.

"Would you like some wine?" Turati asked her, his Italian words infused with pride as he gestured to a collection of bottles encased in a lighted cabinet the length of one entire wall of the salon. "My family owns three vineyards, one dating back nearly a thousand years. I would be pleased if you would join me for a glass of my favorite vintage."

Melena smiled back at him. "I would enjoy that very much, thank you. But first, may I ask where I might find a restroom, please?"

"Certainly, certainly." Turati snapped his fingers at the pair of bodyguards who'd been hanging back obediently for the duration of the night. Continuing with Melena in Italian, he said, "There is one just through that door and down the passageway, my dear. Gianni will show you—"

"No, that's okay." She shook her head at the approaching guard, unaccustomed to so much fawning and more than capable of finding her own way. "Thank you, but I'm sure I can find it on my own. Will you all excuse me?"

With a reassuring glance at her father and a nod to Turati, Melena headed out of the salon and into the passageway. The private restroom at the other end was every bit as sumptuous as the salon, with gilded trim and elegant millwork, gleaming mirrors, and a wealth of original art on the walls.

As she came out of the single stall a few moments later and washed her hands, she couldn't help but pause to check her reflection in the polished glass. Her light copper hair was wind-tossed and thickened from the humidity of the sea. Her skin was milky beneath the freckles that spread out over the apples of her cheeks and marched across the bridge of her nose. And the aura that radiated off her was imbued with shades of green and gold.

Hope.

Determination.

She tried not to notice the faint pink glow that simmered beneath the stronger colors of her psyche. Her curiosity about Lazaro Archer had no place here. Her awareness of him as a dark, dangerously attractive male, even less. She'd come to assist her father; that was all.

And besides, the grim representative from the Order had given her no reason to think he'd even noticed her tonight, other than as a nuisance he was eager to relieve himself of at the earliest opportunity.

Every time she looked at him, he'd been cloaked in a haze of unreadable, gunmetal gray. Coupled with his intimidating gaze, the effect should have been enough to make her keep a healthy distance.

Instead, as she left the restroom, rather than returning straight to the salon again, Melena pivoted in the opposite direction. Toward the aft deck, where she'd seen him go.

He stood alone at the rail in the dark, a stoic figure, unmoving, forbidding. His large hands were braced wide before him. His immense, black-clad body leaned slightly forward as he gazed off the stern of the yacht over the endless blanket of rippling water beyond.

Melena took a silent step toward him, then hesitated.

This was probably a bad idea. She should go back inside and focus on what she was supposed to be doing. She had no business with Lazaro Archer, even if there was something she'd been wanting to say to him all night. For much longer than that, in fact.

But from the rigidity of his stance, she could see that he was in no mood for conversation. Probably least of all with the interloper who'd shown up uninvited and inadvertently defied his authority over the meeting.

Her feet paused beneath her, Melena started to pivot around to leave him to his solitude.

"You're doing well in there." His deep voice arrested her where she stood. He didn't bother to look at her, and although the compliment was completely unexpected, it came out more like a growled accusation.

"Thanks." Tentatively, since there was no point in trying to avoid him now, she crossed the deck to join him at the railing. "I like *Signor* Turati. And I have a good feeling about this meeting. I think my father has made a true friend here tonight."

Lazaro grunted. "I'll be sure to inform Lucan Thorne that you give your blessing."

Melena exhaled a short sigh. "I'm not trying to minimize the importance of this meeting. I understand what's at stake—"

"No. You couldn't possibly," he replied, finally swiveling his head to look askance at her.

And oh, Lord. If she thought Lazaro Archer was intimidating from across the room, up close he was terrifying. His midnight-blue eyes glittered as dark as obsidian in the moonlight, ruthless under the ebony slashes of his brows. His strong nose and sharp cheekbones gave him a ferocity no human face could carry off, and his squared, rigid jawline seemed hewn of granite.

Only his mouth had an element of softness to it, though right now, as he looked at her, his broad, sensual lips were flattened in an irritated scowl.

"How old are you?" he demanded.

"Twenty-nine."

He scoffed, his dark gaze giving her a brief once-over. Based on the fierce ticking of a tendon in his already ironclad jaw, she guessed he didn't particularly like what he saw. "You've barely been out of diapers long enough to understand how important it is to have peace between the Breed and humankind. You were only a child when the veil between our world and theirs was torn away. You didn't wade through the blood in the streets. You didn't see the death, the brutality inflicted on so many innocents by both sides of this war." He blew out a curse and shook his head slowly back and forth. "You can't possibly comprehend how thin the thread is that holds back an even uglier war now. Nor can you know the lengths to which some people will go to rip that thread to tatters."

"You're talking about Opus Nostrum," Melena said quietly. A flicker of surprise in those narrowing indigo eyes now. "As my father's personal assistant, he trusts me completely with all of his GNC business. I collect data for him. I summarize reports. I attend most of his meetings, as well as compose the majority of his speeches. I'm also his daughter, so of course, I'm well aware of the attempted bombing at the summit he attended a couple of weeks ago. I know Opus wanted to take a lot of lives at that event—Breed and human. I also know the Order's primary objective now is to unmask the members of Opus's secret cabal and take the terror group down."

Lazaro grunted but seemed less than impressed. "If you came out here to recite your credentials, Miss Walsh, let me spare you the effort."

"You all but challenged me to tell you," she pointed out.

"And all you've done is confirm what I already knew about you. I have a job to do here too, and you've been standing in my way all night." He glanced back out at the water. "I'm sure your ample charms will find a far more receptive audience back in the salon."

Ample charms? Was that a cut on the fact that she actually had curves and a figure, or could he possibly mean he found her even a little bit interesting?

"I didn't come out here to...Jesus, never mind," she stammered. "Forgive me for disturbing you." Frustrated, Melena pushed back from the railing. She started to pivot away, then paused. Glanced over at him one last time, her own anger spiking. "We've met, you know. You don't remember me."

Why she felt stung by that she really didn't want to consider. When he didn't respond after a long moment, she decided it was probably for the best. God knew, she would be better off forgetting the night she nearly died too.

She turned and headed back across the deck.

"I remember a reckless child doing something stupid," he muttered from behind her. "A silly little girl, being somewhere she damned well didn't belong."

Rather like the way he seemed to regard her now, she thought, bristling at the comment.

"I was seven," Melena replied, swinging a look over her shoulder at him. Lazaro hadn't moved from his position, was still staring out at the black water. "I was seven years old, and you saved my life. I'd be dead if not for you."

"Saved you? Christ." He exhaled sharply, as if the idea annoyed him. "I'm not in the habit of saving anyone."

Something about the way he said that, the quieting of his tone, and the almost raw edge to his words made her drift back toward him. She rubbed a chill from her arms as the recollection of her accident washed over her with fresh terror.

"Well, you did save me. You pulled me out of that frozen pond and you saved my life." He didn't look her way at all, hardly acknowledged she had returned. "My family was in Boston, visiting at your Darkhaven. A bunch of us kids were playing outside that night, mostly boys—your grandsons and young nephews and my older brother, Derek. Unlike me, they were all Breed, and as the only girl with them besides, it took all I had to keep up."

Sometimes she felt as though she were still competing, still struggling to prove her worth in everything she did. She realized she held others up to her same impossible standards too. Her parents had pointed it out to her on numerous occasions. So had more than a few of her exes.

Now here she was, making a point to remind this arrogant man of the stupidest thing she'd ever done in her life.

Melena let out a soft sigh as she stood next to Lazaro once more. "The boys didn't want me there with them at the pond, but I followed them anyway. They started daring each other to walk farther and farther out onto the ice."

"Idiots, all of them," Lazaro grumbled. "Winter came late that year. The pond hadn't yet frozen toward the center."

"Yes," she agreed. "And it was very dark that night. I didn't realize the ice wouldn't hold me until I was already too far out. I stepped onto a thin section, and it broke away underneath me."

The curse Lazaro uttered was ripe, violent. But the look he finally swung on her was oddly tender, haunted. To her complete shock, he reached out and grazed the pad of his thumb over her scarred eyebrow. "You'd hit your head on something."

"The edge of the ice was jagged," she murmured, her throat going a bit dry for the mere second his touch had lingered on her face. When his hand was gone, she shivered, though not from anything close to a chill. "I went down very quickly. God, the water was so cold. I could hardly move my limbs. I panicked. I couldn't see anything. When I tried to swim back up, I realized I was trapped under the ice."

Lazaro was listening intently now, his expression impossible to read. His aura forbid her too, the dull gray haze blurring the edges of his broad shoulders and strong arms, haloing his dangerously handsome face like a brooding cloud against the darkness of the night that surrounded him.

"I remember everything started to go black," Melena said. "And then...there you were. In the water with me, pulling me to the surface. You dived into that frigid pond and searched until you found me. Then you brought me back to your Darkhaven."

"You were bleeding," he said, his gaze returning to the scar above her left eye.

Melena nodded. "Your Breedmate, Ellie, helped my mother patch me up."

Both women were gone now. Melena's adoptive mother, Byron Walsh's mate, Frances, had been killed in a senseless car accident a few years ago. Lazaro's kind-hearted, beautiful Breedmate, Eleanor, had suffered a far more brutal end. Killed just a couple of years after Melena had met her, along with the rest of Lazaro's family who'd been home at his Boston Darkhaven the night of an horrific attack.

His gaze hardened, going distant at the mention of his lost mate. It took nearly all of Melena's self-control to keep from reaching out to offer comfort to him now.

If she didn't think he'd snap her fingers off at the roots, she might have braved it in spite of his forbidding glower.

And yet, there was something more in his eyes as he looked at her. As much as she was drawn to him tonight, she couldn't help feeling that he was aware of her too. Not as the hapless girl he'd fished out of a frozen pond, not even as the grown-up daughter of a colleague and friend.

He was annoyed with her tonight, no question. Given a choice, he'd probably still prefer her gone. But Lazaro Archer was also looking at her the way a man looked at a woman. And she couldn't deny that his interest made her pulse trip into a faster tempo.

"What are you doing here, Melena?" His gruff question caught her off guard.

Did she even know the answer to that? She shrugged lamely. "I guess I just...I don't think I ever got the chance to thank you—"

"No." He cocked his head slightly, those unsettling eyes narrowing shrewdly now. "I mean, what are you doing here at this meeting? As skilled of an interpreter as you are, I think we both know there's something you're not saying."

She stared at him, wondering how he'd gone from looking at her like he wanted to touch her—maybe even kiss her—to pinning her in a suspicious glare. Maybe he hadn't been ignoring her all evening, but silently assessing her, even now.

Part of her wanted to tell him the truth. That she'd been a psychic insurance policy, to make certain her father wasn't walking into a trap with Turati or his men, regardless of the Order's assurances. Lazaro would be furious to hear it, no doubt. That she and her father had defied diplomatic protocol to insert her into a top secret meeting without the knowledge or permission of the Order or the GNC? She didn't even want to consider the ramifications of that, for her or her father.

And anyway, it wasn't her place to publicly voice her father's fears or suspicions, not even to Lazaro Archer. If any of Byron Walsh's colleagues knew how paralyzing his paranoia had become lately, he would surely lose his position on the Council. Her father lived for his work, and Melena would not be the one to jeopardize that for him.

"I don't know what you mean," she murmured, hating that she had to deceive Lazaro. "And I really ought to get back inside now."

"You're protecting him. From what?" Lazaro took hold of her by the arms, preventing her from escaping his knowing stare or his questions. His large hands gripped her firmly, strong fingers searing her with the heat of his touch. "What is your father trying to hide?"

"Nothing, I swear—"

He wasn't buying it. Anger flashed in his eyes. Behind his full upper lip, she glimpsed the sharp points of his emerging fangs. "Tell me what he's afraid of, Melena. Tell me now, before I go in there and haul his ass out here to tell me himself."

"It's nothing," she insisted, finding it impossible to break Lazaro's hold or his stare. "It doesn't matter anyway. He had no reason to be afraid tonight. Turati's intentions are good, he means no harm to—"

She wasn't able to finish what she was saying because in that same instant, Lazaro tensed. His head snapped up, eyes searching the dark sky. Some of the blood seemed to drain out of his grim face in that fraction of a second.

"Fuck," he snarled, his grip tightening on Melena's arms. *"Goddamnit, no."*

He lunged into motion, yanking her against him protectively. His arms wrapped around her. He then tumbled her over the railing of the second-level deck along with him...

Just as a screaming object arrowed down from the sky.

It hit the yacht, a direct, dead center strike.

The vessel exploded. On the deafening boom of impact, Melena crashed into the hard waves with Lazaro. Engulfed by the cold, horrified by what she was seeing, all the air left her lungs on an anguished cry. She tried to break away, but Lazaro held her close, refusing to let her swim back up to find her father.

Together she and Lazaro sank deep into the water, falling down, and down, and down...

Far above them, a hellish ball of flame had erupted on the surface. Fiery chunks of debris dropped into the sea everywhere she looked.

There was only ruin left up there.

The yacht and all of its occupants obliterated in an instant.

CHAPTER 3

By Lazaro's guess, they had been in the water roughly two hours before Anzio's cliff-edged shore was finally within sight. Bleeding from shrapnel wounds and battered by the long journey, he was close to exhaustion—even with the preternatural strength and speed of Breed genetics at his command.

Melena was faring far worse. She was limp against him, having fallen unconscious somewhere around the halfway point of their swim. Although she wasn't entirely mortal either, her human metabolism could not cope with the prolonged exposure in the cold seawater.

In that regard, Lazaro was doubly fortunate. Being Breed had given him another advantage. The same one that had allowed him to pull Melena out of the frozen pond twenty-two years ago. His ability to withstand extreme temperatures had given him the strength to search for her under the ice and pull her to safety before she drowned.

He hoped he hadn't lost her tonight.

Lazaro held her close at his side as he paddled the last few hundred yards with his free arm. As soon as his bare feet were able to touch ground, he repositioned Melena in both arms and ran her toward the empty, moonlit beach.

The bulky cliffs that lined the shore loomed just ahead. Several large caves were burrowed into the rock—black, yawning mouths that had once been part of an ancient Roman emperor's crumbled stone villa that was a thousand years in ruin. Lazaro carried Melena inside one of the caves, past a littering of rough rocks and pools of tidal water, to a spot where the sand was soft and dry underfoot.

As he set her down, he couldn't help revisiting the night he'd carried a lifeless little girl into his Darkhaven in Boston. He'd remembered every minute of it, despite the indifference he'd feigned with Melena earlier on the yacht. She had been a seven-year-old child that first, and last, time he saw her before tonight. Back then, she had been as helpless and fragile as a baby bird to his mind. He'd rescued her the same way he would have done for any innocent child.

But now...

Now, Melena Walsh was a grown woman. She was as enticing a woman as he'd ever seen—even more so, with her lovely face and thick red hair, and all of her soft, feminine curves that drew his eye even as he carefully arranged her unresponsive, alarmingly chilled body on the sand.

And as fiercely as he'd wanted to save her life in Boston, he wanted to save her now.

Not the least of his reasons being his need to know what secret she was keeping from him. She'd been on the verge of telling him in the seconds before the yacht was blown to pieces. If that secret had anything to do with the attack tonight, he was going to see that Melena answered for it.

Lazaro felt in his bones that Opus Nostrum was behind the brazen act. Whoever did it knew just who and where to strike. But how did they know? Both parties were meticulously screened by the Order. Lazaro had personally vetted everyone in attendance, right down to the last man on the vessel's crew tonight. He'd approved them all.

Except Melena Walsh.

He gazed at her in the cave's darkness, his Breed eyes seeing her as clearly as if it were midday. She was beautiful, stunningly so. She was poised, intelligent, erudite. And he'd seen her wield her charm without effort over Turati and the rest of the men at the meeting.

Lazaro couldn't deny he'd been equally affected. More than affected, despite his unwillingness to give it reins. A woman like Melena would make a deadly asset, if allied with the wrong people.

He didn't want to think she might be his enemy, intentional or otherwise.

The fact that she'd nearly gotten killed tonight along with everyone else made it impossible to imagine her presence on the yacht could have had anything to do with the catastrophe that followed.

She would give him the truth, but first he had to make sure she stayed alive to do so.

Lazaro scowled at her sodden, bruised condition. Her skirt was shredded, her shoes lost like his somewhere between the yacht and the shore. Her blouse was in tatters, the burgundy colored silk dark with seawater...and blood. Fortunately, most of it was his.

Her hair drooped lifelessly into her face. Lazaro smoothed away some of the drenched red tangles, letting out a low curse when he saw how white her skin was. Her lips were slack, turned an alarming shade of blue. She had contusions on her forehead and chin. Blood from a scalp wound trailed in a bright red rivulet down her temple.

Fuck.

His vision honed in on that thin scarlet ribbon, everything Breed in him responding with keen, inhuman interest. The fact that she was a Breedmate made her blood an exponentially greater temptation to one of his kind.

Melena's blood carried the subtle fragrance of caramel and something sweeter still...dark cherries, Lazaro decided, his lungs soaking in a deeper breath even though it was torment to his senses.

His fangs punched out of his gums, throbbing against the firmly closed line of his lips. His vision sharpened some more, his irises throwing off a rising amber glow that bathed her paleness in warmer light. His own skin prickled with the sudden surge of heat in his veins.

If Melena opened her eyes now, she'd see him fully transformed to the bloodthirsty, otherworldly being he truly was.

If she opened her pretty, bright green eyes, she would know that his desire for her didn't stop at just her blood. He didn't want to think what kind of base creature he was that he could feel lust and hunger for a bruised, bloodied woman who'd just lost her father and nearly her own life too.

The truth was, he'd felt these same urges back on the yacht too. He hadn't wanted to admit it then either.

For all he knew, she could belong to another Breed male. Hell, she could already be blood-bonded to someone, a thought that should've relieved him rather than put a rankle in his brow. It would be pointless to let himself wonder, then or now. He wasn't about to act on either of his unwanted needs. Least of all with a woman bearing the Breedmate mark.

Since Ellie's death, he'd found other women to service him when required. Humans who understood the limits of his interest. More importantly, humans he could feed from without the shackle of a blood bond.

Instead here he was, shackled to the rescue and safekeeping of a woman he didn't fully trust and had no right to desire.

On a rough curse, ignoring the pounding demands of his veins, he stripped off his ragged black combat shirt and hunkered down in the sand alongside Melena. She moaned softly as he wrapped his arms around her. Her raspy sigh as she instinctively settled into his heat was an added torment he sure as hell didn't need.

Jaw clamped tight, pulse hammering with thinly bridled hunger, Lazaro gathered Melena to his naked chest to give her body the warmth it needed.

CHAPTER 4

She woke from an endless, cold nightmare, a scream lodged in her throat. She couldn't force out any sound, and when she dragged in a sudden gasp of air, her lungs felt shredded in her breast.

No, not her lungs.

Her heart.

All at once, the details flew back at her. The explosion. The fire and debris. The cold, black water.

Her father...

No, he couldn't be gone. Her kind and decent father—that strong Breed male—could not have been wiped from existence tonight.

Betrayed, murdered. Just as he'd feared.

Her father was dead.

Some rational part of her knew there was no other possibility, but accepting it hurt too much.

She tried to move and found herself trapped in a cocoon of warmth. Thick arms encircled her. Arms covered in Breed *dermaglpyhs*. The elaborate pattern of skin markings could only belong to one man.

"You're all right, Melena." Lazaro's deep voice rumbled against her ear. "Lie still. You need rest."

She felt him breathing, felt his large body's heat all around her. And God, she needed that heat and reassurance. Every particle of her being wanted to burrow deeper and just close her eyes and sleep. Try to forget...

But her father was out there in the dark. Left behind in the frigid water, while she was safe and protected in the shelter of Lazaro's arms.

She opened her eyes and took in her surroundings as best she could in the lightless space around them. She smelled the sea and wet rock. Felt soft sand beneath her.

"Where are we?" Her words came out like a croak. She swallowed past the salt and soot, attempted to extricate herself from the comfort she couldn't enjoy. She ached all over. Could barely summon strength to move her limbs.

"I brought you to Anzio. We're in a cave at Nero's villa ruins."

She had no idea where that was, only that it had to be a good long distance away from the yacht. "How long have we been here?"

"A few hours."

An irrational panic crushed down on her. "Why did you let me sleep for so long? We should be out there, searching for them!"

His answering curse vibrated against her spine. "Melena—"

"I have to get up. We have to go back for him, Lazaro. For all of them."

On a burst of adrenaline, she managed to slip out of his loose embrace. She sat up, registering dimly that her clothing was damp and ruined, torn open in more places than it was held together.

And Lazaro was only half-dressed. Just his black pants, clinging to him in tatters as well. No shirt on his bare, *glyph*-covered chest and muscled arms. There were numerous bruises on his torso and shoulders. When he sat up too, she noted that a healing gash in his thigh had bled through the material of his pants.

"There's no reason to go back, Melena. There's no chance of survivors."

She didn't want to hear him confirm the terror churning inside her. "No. You're wrong!" She made a clumsy falter to her feet. Lazaro stood with her, catching her by the arms before her sluggish legs could buckle beneath her. She didn't have the strength to break out of his hold again. "You *have* to be wrong. I have to go back and find him. My father—"

Lazaro shook his head. His handsome face was grim with sympathy and something darker. "I'm sorry, Melena. The missile strike was a direct hit. There was nothing left."

Some of her hysteria leaked out of her under his grave stare. She couldn't hold back the grief, the tears. It all flooded out of her on an ugly, shuddering sob. And then her knees did give out, and she sank back down to the sandy floor of the cave.

Lazaro's warm hands were still clasped on her arms as he crouched down in front of her. She couldn't stop the wracking anguish, no more than she could keep herself from pitching forward into his arms, clinging to him as she wept.

He held her there, for how long, she didn't know.

She only knew that after she didn't think she could cry anymore, or hurt any worse, he was still holding her. Still keeping her upright when the rest of her world was crumbling all around her.

"Why?" she murmured into his bulky shoulder. "My God, he knew this. He was so afraid he was going to die soon. Who would do this to him? Why?"

Lazaro gently pulled her away from him, his ebony brows knit in a tight scowl. "Your father feared for his life?" Confusion flashed across his features, then settled into suspicion. "Damn it. Why didn't he tell me this? We spoke several times before the meeting. He had plenty of opportunity to say something if he felt he was in danger in any way."

Melena shook her head, heartsick. "He didn't know who he could trust. He'd been having premonitions, sensing some kind of betrayal. He knew he was going to die soon. He didn't know when, or where the betrayal would come from. He wasn't sure of anyone anymore."

"Not even me," Lazaro replied. "Jesus Christ, why didn't he cancel the damned meeting? He could have made any excuse."

"I told him the same thing. But it was too important to him. And he didn't know what would happen tonight. Neither one of us knew." She thought back on the time she and her father spent with Paolo Turati. She had detected no hidden agendas. No duplicity or harmful intent in any one of them.

Lazaro was studying her in unreadable silence. "You need to tell me the truth, Melena. Beginning with why your father brought you with him tonight."

She gave him a weak nod. There was no more reason for her to keep it from him. Her father was gone. He had nothing left to lose if word of his paranoia became public. Melena no longer needed to protect him. "I've been traveling with him everywhere for months now. He can't bear to go—he *couldn't* bear," she corrected herself quietly, "to go anywhere unless I was there to assure him no one meant him any harm."

"How so?"

"You were right that it wasn't only my translation skills that brought me here tonight. It was my ability to see people's auras. I can tell at a glance if someone's intentions are good or not."

"Your Breedmate talent," Lazaro murmured. There seemed to be a trace of relief in his tone. "So, when you looked at Turati and the others on the yacht tonight?"

She shook her head. "There was nothing to fear from any of them."

"Did your father voice his concerns to any of his colleagues in the GNC?"

"No."

"Anyone outside the Council?"

"No one," she replied, certain of it.

Lazaro grunted, and she could see his gaze go distant as his mind began to churn on the information. She knew he and the Order would not let this attack go unmet, and there was a vengeful part of her that longed to see the guilty tortured to within an inch of their sadistic, cowardly lives.

"Make them pay, Lazaro."

"They will," he answered solemnly. "Whoever had a hand in this, they will be found. There will be justice."

Her tears started up again, but they were quieter now, filled with more rage and resolve than bereavement. She hadn't been prepared for Lazaro's tender touch. She held her breath as he caught her chin on the edge of his fingertips and lifted her gaze to his. He stroked her cheek, his thumb sweeping away the wet trail of her tears.

She could sense his tenderness went deeper than mere concern.

She could see the evidence of that truth in the crackling sparks of amber that were lighting in the deep sapphire of his irises. She could see it in his *dermaglyphs*, which surged with dark colors across every muscled inch of his torso and arms, the intriguing swirls and arcs of the *glyphs'* pattern changing hues before her eyes.

And if all of that weren't enough, she could see his intent in his aura, which formed a smoldering glow around him now, confirming the astonishing fact.

Lazaro Archer wanted her.

No sooner had the thought entered her mind than he leaned down and brushed his lips over hers. Her breath was already shaky and thin, but as his mouth pressed against hers, her lungs dried up on a slow moan. The kiss was tender, careful, no doubt meant to console or soothe her.

It did both, but it also inflamed her.

Heat raced through her at the feel of his mouth on hers. She didn't want to feel it—not now, not when her heart was breaking over the loss of her father and fear still held her in a firm grasp.

But Lazaro's arms were stronger than any of that. His gentling, but arousing, kiss made her melt against him with a desire she could hardly reconcile.

And he broke away much too soon for her liking.

His Breed pupils had narrowed to the thinnest vertical slits. And when he ground out a vivid curse, the tips of his fangs gleamed white and razor-sharp.

"Fuck." He let go of her. "That shouldn't have happened. I apologize."

"Don't," she murmured, her voice a raspy whisper. Desire was singing through her veins—uninvited, maybe, but too powerful to be denied. "I didn't mind, Lazaro. I...liked it."

"Christ, don't say that." He blew out a harsh breath, then drew back from her as though she had scorched him too, and not in the good way he'd ignited her. "You do not want to say that to me, Melena. For the good of both of us."

He got to his feet in abrupt, stony silence. As he stood, she noticed that the gash in his thigh was still bleeding. While he'd been looking after her these past few hours, he'd neglected his own injuries. He seemed oblivious to it, walking over to examine a comm unit that lay on a nearby rock. He shook the device, swearing as water dripped out of it.

"That wound on your leg needs attention, Lazaro." He was Breed, Gen One besides. She knew his body would heal itself, but even a vampire needed help sometimes. "You need to feed soon."

"Is that an invitation, Miss Walsh?" The comm unit clutched in his fist, he snarled down at her, baring his teeth and fangs. God, they were huge. Terrifying, and he damned well knew it. His aura seethed as menacingly as the rest of him. When she shrank back a little where she sat, he gave a dark chuckle. "No, I didn't think so. Smart girl. Do us both a favor and don't concern yourself with what I need."

His anger confused her, almost as much as his unexpected tenderness of a moment ago. And the fact that he wanted to push her away when he was the only reason she was alive right now kind of pissed her off too. She stood up, refusing to be cowed by his bluster.

"Why shouldn't I be concerned? You just saved my life—for the second time, in fact. So, forgive me if that makes me care about you just a little bit."

When he scoffed and took a long stride away from her, she followed after him. When she put her hand on his shoulder, he rounded on her with a hiss. "Just because you're alive, doesn't mean you're safe with me. Don't make the mistake of thinking I'm some kind of hero."

He didn't give her the opportunity to reply. On a furious glower, he pivoted to stalk toward the mouth of the cave. "Stay put. I'm going to see about sending a signal and getting us out of here."

Melena watched him prowl out into the darkness, his kiss still warming her lips and his harsh words ringing in her ears.

Don't make the mistake of thinking I'm some kind of hero.

Didn't he know? She'd been thinking of him that way for most of her life.

CHAPTER 5

One of Lazaro's comrades showed up less than an hour later to retrieve them in a big black SUV. Melena had hardly been introduced to the Breed warrior who drove them—a towering male with a mass of loose golden curls and a dimpled, quicksilver smile that instantly softened his strong, square-cut jaw. She thought he'd said his name was Savage, but in her opinion, he looked more like a fallen angel. If fallen angels wore combat patrol gear and bristled with blades and heavy firearms.

The warrior seemed already aware of who she was and how she'd come to be in his Order commander's company, although he didn't so much as try to ask. It was obvious from Lazaro's menacing silence during the ride to wherever they were heading that conversation with her was neither welcomed nor encouraged.

Where they'd been heading was Rome.

More specifically, the Order's command center in that city.

Melena tried not to gape when she realized that's where Lazaro had brought her. Neither the late-night sight of the illuminated Colosseum nor Pantheon had inspired more than a lingering look as they passed the monuments, but when the SUV approached a gated, secured mansion compound nestled in the heart of the sprawling city, Melena couldn't help but sit up a little straighter in her seat and draw in her breath.

The stately white brick mansion with its elegant, carved marble detailing and old bronze fixtures looked as timeless as the city around it. But it didn't take long to understand that the structure's antiquity ended at the street. This was a modern fortress, beautiful and sturdy and impenetrable. Inside the massive gates, motion sensors followed the SUV's progress toward an underground parking garage around back.

Once they got out of the vehicle, Lazaro sternly instructed her to follow him. The warrior who drove them lingered behind, leaving her alone to his commander's dubious care.

Lazaro took her not into the living quarters of the compound, but to another wing of the estate that seemed to be where the warriors conducted Order business. She heard two male voices in one of the rooms they passed along the corridor, but her escort didn't slow his pace at all.

Actually, it didn't seem that he could get rid of her fast enough for his liking.

A few minutes later, Melena found herself abandoned to a vaguely medical-seeming room. The small space contained the hard bed she sat upon, and next to it a single chair. Glass-fronted cupboards mounted to the wall opposite her appeared to house bandages and other field dressing supplies.

She wasn't sure how long she sat there, feeling awkward and unwanted in Lazaro's domain. At some point, she dozed, still exhausted from her ordeal and the raw grief that clung to her. A couple of times, she'd glanced toward the window in the infirmary room door and saw one of the warriors stride past. The gorgeous blond who brought her there had smiled through the glass as he walked by. Another Breed male, a mean-looking warrior with a shaved head and a jagged facial scar that made him more suited to the name "Savage" than his friendly comrade, spared her only the briefest, disinterested glance.

But it was a different warrior altogether who finally came into the room. Hulking and immense, he had a mane of shoulder-length brown waves and skin the color of sun-kissed golden sand. Arresting sky-blue eyes scrutinized her from within his ruggedly handsome, exotic face. "Melena. How are you feeling?" As big and imposing as the Breed male was, he somehow moved with the easy, feline grace of a jungle cat as he approached. His voice was rich and deep and cultured. "I am Jehan."

"Nice to meet you," she replied, her manners on automatic pilot.

"Commander Archer sent me to see if your injuries need tending. I must apologize that we're not equipped for treating wounds outside of the Breed, but I can get you medicine for your pain. There are ointments I can prepare to make the contusions heal faster."

Melena shook her head. "Thank you, but no." Compared to the pain of her grief and fear following the attack, and the lingering exhaustion from what she suspected had been hypothermia back in the cave, her assortment of cuts and bruises were a minor issue. "I'm okay."

He eyed her skeptically, folding his *glyph*-covered muscled arms over his chest. "You've endured quite an ordeal. You're certain there is nothing you need?"

Melena gave a vague shrug. She wasn't certain of anything at the moment. Part of her wanted to bolt for the door and find the fastest way out of this nightmare, back home to Maryland. Another part of her just wanted to crawl under the covers of the bed and scream.

"I know this can't be easy," Jehan said, genuine concern in his low voice. "And I am sorry for your loss."

"Thank you." Although she was well-versed in multiple languages, she couldn't quite place his unusual accent. His name was old French, if she wasn't mistaken, but the formal way he carried himself and the way he spoke had her curious. "Where are you from, Jehan?"

"All around," he answered cryptically. "But it's Morocco you hear in my voice. My father's homeland."

That explained it. He had the kind of voice that made her imagine moonlit desert plains and the spicy fragrance of incense and woodsmoke. "Your mother wasn't Moroccan, though?"

"Born and raised in Paris," he confirmed, his sensual mouth curving at the corners. "She and my father met in France. After they were mated, he brought her back with him to our tribe's Darkhaven in his country."

"Your tribe?"

Jehan's dark brows quirked. "A relic of a term." He shrugged it off, but something mysterious flickered in his mesmerizing gaze. "My father's Breed line is very old. Its roots go deep into Moroccan soil. Burrowed in almost as stubbornly as the old man's heels."

"What about you?" Melena asked, genuinely curious.

Jehan inclined his head, almost courtly in its tilt. "To my father's eternal regret, his eldest son's feet refused to stay put. Despite the shackle of obligation he's tried to affix to them."

As they spoke, the door opened again and the blond warrior came in. He grinned, his hazel eyes bouncing off Jehan for a second before fixing on Melena. "I see Prince Jehan is already trying to dazzle you with his long, boring pedigree."

Melena swung a questioning look on the enigmatic warrior. "Prince?"

Jehan grunted under his breath, but didn't deny it. "What are you doing here, Sav? You know damned well Lazaro's orders were that no one enter this room or speak to Melena without his permission."

Melena wanted to be offended by the news of that domineering command, but her two visitors were a welcome distraction from everything else going on. Not the least of which being Lazaro Archer's stinging rejection of her in the cave. A sting that hurt all the worse for his tenderness when he touched her...kissed her.

"We weren't properly introduced," Sav said. "Ettore Roberto Selvaggio."

His dimples deepened along with his heart-stopping smile. His Italian accent seemed to deepen as well, the kind of accent that probably ensured he never wanted for female company.

"Melena Walsh," she replied. "I thought I heard Lazaro call you Savage."

"Lazaro?" he echoed.

She felt color rise to her cheeks. "Your commander. Mr. Archer. Whatever I should call him," she muttered. The man who saved her life, awoke an irresistible desire in her, but made her feel as if he might have rather left her behind in Anzio a few hours ago. "I think he despises me."

The two Breed males now exchanged a look. Jehan was the first to talk. "Don't let him scare you. It's just his way."

"Come on, man," his comrade said. "It goes a bit deeper than that."

Melena glanced at them both. "What do you mean?"

"The way I heard it, Archer's never been the same since he lost his family back in Boston twenty years ago," Sav said. "He blames himself, I imagine."

"Why would he do that?" She couldn't begin to guess how Lazaro could hold himself even the least responsible for what happened to his kin. "The Darkhaven was attacked while he wasn't home. It was razed to the ground."

"Yes," Jehan agreed soberly. "And now imagine you have the incredible gift of walking into even the most extreme temperature and emerging wholly unscathed. But you're not there when the attack on your own loved ones takes place."

"You have the ability to save some of them—maybe all of them," Sav added. "Instead, you lose them all in one fell swoop."

Melena couldn't speak. She wasn't even sure she was breathing as the weight of what she'd just heard settled on her.

She hadn't known about Lazaro's Breed gift. Now it made sense, of course. His ability to search for her for so long in the frozen pond all those years ago. The fact that he'd swum across nearly half of the

Tyrrhenian Sea to save her tonight, impervious to the cold, unlike her.

He'd saved her twice, but had been unable to save the ones he loved. Including his blood-bonded Breedmate.

"He will not be pleased if he knew we told you," Jehan warned grimly.

Sav gave a nod. "Probably want to stake both of us out in the sun. Or worse." He glanced at Melena. "So, not a word, yeah?"

"Okay," she murmured woodenly. But oh, God, her heart ached for Lazaro now.

"Enough about him," Sav said, grinning as if he wanted to lighten the grave mood. "You asked about me, if I recall. So, to answer your question, yes. Most people who know me call me Savage."

She took his bait, needing to put her sympathy for Lazaro on a higher shelf. He wouldn't want it anyway. "Why do they call you that? You seem nice enough to me. Are you usually mean or something?"

"Or something," he said, the glint in his eye and the playful, seductive hue of his aura providing all the correction she needed.

Jehan snorted. "He's a legend in his own mind. Pay no attention to him."

Sav barked a laugh. "Envy isn't a good look for you, Highness."

"And you may kiss my royal ass, peasant."

Melena found herself smiling with them. She took in their banter and warm, welcoming faces, not realizing until then how much she needed to feel she was among friends.

She needed her family, which was now reduced to just one other person. Her Breed brother, Derek, had been living in Paris for the past year, bouncing between England and France on one business venture or another.

Melena hadn't seen him since he left, hadn't even spoken to him for several long weeks. She couldn't imagine the anguish it would cause him to learn their father had been killed. Before he heard it anywhere else, she wanted to be the one to break the news to him. She wanted to spare him the unnecessary grief of thinking she had died along with everyone else tonight.

"Do you think it would be possible for me to try to reach my brother somehow?" she asked the two warriors. "He's traveling and I need to let him know—"

"Is there a reason half my team is not where I expect them to be?" Lazaro's deep, furious growl interrupted the conversation without warning. He stood in the open doorway, looking every bit as ferocious as a Gen One Breed male could. His sapphire eyes were thunderously dark, except for the flashes of amber outrage sparking in their depths. "Out. Both of you. Now."

Sav and Jehan departed on command.

Leaving Melena to face Lazaro's rage by herself.

She waited for him to lay into her too, but he didn't. He merely stared at her, a tendon ticking hard in his jaw. His aura was as stormy as his glower, back to the gunmetal haze that she found so difficult to read.

His animosity seemed clear enough. He didn't want her in his command center any more than he'd wanted her in his presence on the yacht or at the cave.

And she wanted to be somewhere safe now, even if that meant returning to her father's empty Darkhaven in the States. "I don't want to be here," she murmured. "I need to get in touch with my brother Derek, and I need to go home."

"Out of the question." His answer was firm, flat. Unyielding. "I've spoken to Lucan Thorne. Before you go anywhere else, he wants me to bring you to the Order's headquarters in Washington, D.C. He'll talk with you there, debrief you."

"I already told you everything I know. What more can I tell him?"

Lazaro didn't answer. "We leave tomorrow evening, Melena." He started to go, then pivoted back to her. "In the meantime, I won't have my team distracted by the fact we have a Breedmate underfoot. I'll make a place for you in the villa. You'll stay there until we depart for D.C."

CHAPTER 6

Melena had been moved out of the command center's infirmary to the living quarters of the mansion hours ago. Lazaro's team had gone back to their business as instructed. The morning passed with discussions of Order objectives and priorities. Chief among those priorities being to ensure that reports of the tragic, "accidental" explosion on board Paolo Turati's yacht didn't brush up against the truth that it was, in fact, a stealth missile attack.

And while no one yet had stepped forward to publicly claim responsibility, there wasn't a shred of doubt among the Order's entire organization that the killings were surely instigated by Opus Nostrum.

Halfway through the afternoon in Rome, the warriors were now dispersed to prepare for their patrols that coming evening, everyone focused on task and ready to carry out their missions.

And yet the female under their roof remained a distraction.

For Lazaro, that is.

He made his way through the corridors in a foul mood. He didn't want to think about her. He didn't want to think about his irritation over finding Sav and Jehan chatting her up earlier, making her smile in spite of everything she'd been through. He didn't want to think about the anger that had shot through him in that moment—the blast of pure male possessiveness that he had no right to feel.

And he sure as hell did not want to give another moment's thought to the kiss he stole from Melena back in the Anzio cave. He'd had no right to take that liberty either. But was the kiss truly stolen if she didn't seem to mind that he did it?

She'd told him she enjoyed it, for fuck's sake.

His blood rushed a bit faster, disturbingly hotter, at just the thought. And a lot of that blood was making a swift run south. It pounded through his veins like liquid fire, settling in his groin when he recalled how soft and inviting her mouth had been under his.

Melena had more than liked his kiss. She'd welcomed it. Wanted more.

Wanted him.

Christ, he couldn't get away from her fast enough after that kiss. He still couldn't put enough distance between them for his peace of mind. How he was going to manage the long hours between now and their departure for D.C. tomorrow evening, he had no damned idea.

More than likely, he'd be spending that stretch of time with a constant hard-on and a fevered hunger that bordered on madness. He needed to exorcise that hunger, and soon. He was on his way to the weapons room to sweat out some of his aggression with his blades and pistols when one of his men met him in the corridor.

Trygg had been the only one of the unit with sense enough to avoid their pretty, uninvited guest. The bald, menacing looking Breed male carried a long, cream-colored box in his arms. "Package you ordered this morning just arrived."

Lazaro grunted as he took the box from the most intimidating member of his team.

"You want me to deliver it to her?" Trygg suggested.

"No." The reply came out too quickly, too forcefully, but there it was. Melena had been through enough of a scare already; she didn't need a brutal killer like Trygg showing up at her door, even if he did it with an unlikely gift in his hands.

Besides, Lazaro had placed the order for her as something more than just a courtesy. He supposed he'd been hoping it would also serve as some kind of apology. He'd been a warrior for twenty years, but he liked to think there was still some sense of decency in him. Given the way he'd treated Melena so far, she might be hard-pressed to agree.

"I'll bring it myself," he told Trygg. The vampire merely stared, his shrewd eyes unblinking, far too knowing. Lazaro tucked the long box under his arm. "There is something you can do. Locate Derek Walsh. Melena said her brother's been spending his time between Paris and the United Kingdom. When you've got a bead on him, let me know."

Trygg gave a slight nod. "Done."

Lazaro stalked through the command center to the attached, four-story residential quarters. The Roman villa had ten bedrooms, but

Melena had been placed in the largest suite in the estate. It was also the one place where he knew neither of her newest admirers would be tempted to seek her out.

Paused outside the closed door of his private quarters on the top floor, Lazaro noted she'd left the tray of food he'd delivered hours earlier untouched. It didn't appear she'd even come out to look at it.

He listened for movement on the other side. Hearing nothing, he rapped his knuckles on the carved wooden door. He waited, feeling both awkward and annoyed.

When he knocked again and got no response, he started to get concerned.

He opened the door and peered inside. "Melena?"

His suite spanned the entirety of the villa's fourth floor. He didn't see her anywhere, not even in the spacious bedroom. He dropped the box on the end of the king-sized bed, then noticed the door to the en suite bath was cracked open.

Through the thin wedge, he saw her slip into a terry robe, apparently having just stepped out of the tub. He caught an unexpected glimpse of her bare skin—delectable curves, lovely breasts peaked with dusky peach nipples...the hint of dark curls at the V of her creamy thighs.

Ah, damn, she was gorgeous.

Everything male in him responded as swiftly—and as obviously—as everything Breed in him. His pulse jackhammered, the drum filling his ears with a rush of hot need. The tips of his fangs dug into his tongue, and as he stared at her, his gaze grew heated as his pupils thinned with his hunger and his cock thickened with desire.

Until he spotted the bruises that still lingered on her. His own wounds had healed, thanks to his Gen One metabolism, but Melena still carried numerous contusions on her ribs and delicate belly.

"Fuck." Lazaro's growled reaction made her look up sharply. Too late to pivot around and leave. Too late to pretend he hadn't just crept into the room and stood there ogling her in open lust. Or to hope she wouldn't notice how powerfully she affected him.

Her expression was guarded, wary. She opened the door wider, but he noticed how tightly she now gripped the edges of the robe at her chest. When Lazaro took a step toward her, she slipped out of the bathroom and into the larger space of the bedroom.

With some effort, he curbed the presence of his fangs. His vision was still awash in amber, but he could feel his pupils resuming a less feral state. And as for the state of his arousal, that was a more difficult thing to hide, let alone suppress. But while his body was still thrumming with awareness—and want—of her, his primary interest in that moment was Melena's well being.

"Jehan was supposed to look after your injuries when you arrived," he muttered angrily. "He's skilled with ointments and herbs. He should've given you something to help you heal."

"I told Jehan I was fine. And I am...or at least, I can try to be, once you and the Order allow me to go home."

Lazaro ignored the pointed complaint, even if it had merit. "I see you didn't eat anything either."

"What do you care?" she tossed back, her fine auburn brows pinched together.

"I care, Melena. For now, you're under my watch. It's my responsibility to ensure that you're comfortable and healthy. That you're fed and clothed." He gestured toward the boutique box on the bed. "I arranged for some things to be sent here for you from one of the local shops."

She cast a sidelong glance toward his gift, then back toward the bathroom where her ruined skirt and blouse lay in rags on the tile floor. Warily, she drifted over to the bed and lifted the lid off the box. She glanced inside, then one by one, pulled out the skirt and pants, then the blouse and sweater he selected for her.

"I didn't know what you'd prefer," he murmured.

She lifted the charcoal gray, fine-gauge sweater first, then the pair of black slacks. The understated classics of the collection, which didn't surprise him. She glanced at the two pairs of shoes he'd purchased as well, taking out the elegant Italian flats. "These are all in my sizes. Perfectly in my sizes." She slanted him a guarded look. "I wouldn't think you'd paid attention long enough to notice."

"I noticed." Lazaro slowly approached her near the bed. "I should be focused on a thousand other things right now. Instead, here I am. Noticing everything about you, Melena."

If she had flinched at all when he came to stand beside her, Lazaro would have somehow found the strength of will to leave her in peace.

If she had resisted even a little when he lifted her chin on his fingertips and drew her gaze up to his—if she had looked into his transformed Breed eyes with anything close to fear or uncertainty—he would have forced himself to let go of her and refrain from ever touching her again.

But Melena did none of those things.

And when he slowly lowered his mouth to hers, this time, not even he or his iron will could pretend the desire that arced between them was anything either of them would be able to deny.

He kissed her, hard and hungry. Any illusions he might have had for taking things slowly with her, or giving her a chance to get away before he pounced, were all but obliterated once their lips and tongues had come together.

A fresh surge of molten need scorched through his veins, and all at once it didn't matter to him that getting involved with Melena Walsh was the last thing he needed to be doing.

He wanted her.

She wanted him—he knew that even in the cave.

And the fact was, he'd already let himself get involved, whether or not they allowed this undeniable, if untimely, desire for each other to flare any further out of control.

Melena awakened a need in him that he hadn't felt in a long time. A new kind of need, something white-hot and irresistible. She had done in less than a day what no other woman before her had managed to do in two decades.

She made him feel alive again.

Lazaro growled and took her mouth in a deeper kiss. She moaned, reaching up to burrow her fingers into the short hair at his nape. Her soft curves felt like heaven against him, even through the barrier of their clothing. Her mouth tasted warm and sweet. Her body arched into his, pliant, consenting.

Welcoming.

Hot with need.

He smoothed his hand down her throat, breaking their kiss as his thumb grazed over the Breedmate mark nestled in the hollow between her collarbones. He lifted his head to look at it—to remind himself of what she was and why he could not allow himself anything more than this desire they shared.

"I should ask you if there is someone else," he uttered thickly. He dragged his smoldering gaze back up to hers. "I should ask, but right now I don't think I'll give a damn if you say there is."

"No." She gave a faint shake of her head, her breast rising and falling with each rapid pant of her breath. "There's no one. Not for more than a year. And even then, I never wanted anyone like this..."

He registered that sweet confession with a growl that vibrated deep in his chest.

He kissed her again, gathering her face in his hands while his mouth moved intensely, hungrily, over hers. Being Gen One, his appetites were stronger than most. With Melena all but undressed and willing in his arms, those appetites were on the verge of owning him. It was only the dim knowledge of her lingering injuries that kept him in check.

And she wasn't helping in that regard.

Meeting each thrust of his tongue, parting her lips to take him deeper, she stoked his arousal even further. Her body pressed against his, heat igniting everywhere they touched. He couldn't resist the loosened opening of her robe. His hand slipped inside to feel the softness of her skin. Her pulse banged against his fingertips, strong and certain. Erotic and primal.

Melena groaned in pleasure. Her voice rasped sensually against his mouth. "I like the way you kiss me, Lazaro. I like the way you touch me."

Holy hell. Her words made fire erupt in his already molten blood.

With fangs filling his mouth and his cock gone hard as granite behind the zipper of his pants, Lazaro moved his hand to cup the buoyant underside of her breast. A hot, pent-up sigh gusted out of her as he caressed her bare skin beneath the slackened robe. Her nipple was pebbled and erect, a temptation he lightly tweaked, then rolled between his fingers. Melena's grasp at the back of his neck tightened, her fingers curling into his hair as a moan leaked through her parted lips.

Every taut fiber of his being ached with the need to put his mouth on her silken skin, to feel all of her. Taste all of her.

His hands obeyed that need, reaching up to gently ease the robe off Melena's shoulders. It slipped down her arms, baring her to the waist. She was so lovely. Porcelain skin dusted with a smattering of sweet, peachy freckles and lush, feminine curves that begged to be savored.

The purple contusions and mending cuts on her torso and abdomen drew his eye just as intensely. Rage for whoever did it swirled through him like a fierce tempest. When he thought of how close she'd come to being lost in the explosion along with everyone else, that rage turned murderous and black.

But tenderly, he let his fingers light on a couple of her worst bruises. She flinched a little and some of his fury snarled out of him. "It hurts?"

"Only a bit." When he drew his hand away, she caught it, placed his palm atop her bare breast. "I don't want you to stop touching me."

His cock jerked in response, more than eager for him to oblige her. He filled his hand with her breast, then took her mouth in another deep kiss.

But feeling her, kissing her, only made him ache to explore some more.

His entire Gen One being throbbed with the need to claim, to possess.

He drew the robe off her completely. Let it fall in a pool at her feet. For one indulgent moment, he soaked in the sight of her through his amber-drenched, fevered eyes.

Then he lifted her off her feet and spread her out beneath him on his bed.

CHAPTER 7

Melena sank down onto the soft mattress and watched, wide-eyed and trembling, as Lazaro prowled up the length of her naked body.

It wasn't fear that gripped her. Nothing even close to fear.

Her every nerve ending had come alive—gone dizzyingly electric—under his careful, caressing touch and the sensual promise of his lips and tongue as he'd tenderly explored her skin.

Now, lying exposed to him completely on the bed while he remained clothed, she wasn't uncomfortable in the least. And whether that made her a wanton harlot or a daring fool, she didn't know. Nor did she care in that moment.

She wasn't nervous or uncertain about anything she was doing with this man.

She wanted more.

He sent the boutique box to the floor with a sweep of his strong arm, making more room for them. She jumped, breath catching at the animalistic power that poured off Lazaro in palpable waves. She'd never felt so much energy and heat focused on her.

In her handful of failed relationships, no other man—Breed or human—had stirred her passion so easily, so masterfully. *Difficult to please*, more than one lover had called her. And they'd been right. None of them had taken her breath away. None of them had been able to hold her interest, in or out of bed, for more than a few months.

Then again, they weren't Lazaro Archer.

She'd never been in the presence of a Gen One male with carnal hunger in his eyes.

And Lazaro's hunger was intense.

His eyes were twin coals, locked on her as he positioned himself above her, braced on his strong fists on either side of her head. His fangs gleamed razor-sharp, enormous and fully extended.

And while his *dermaglyphs* were obscured by his black shirt and combat pants, she knew they had to be vivid with deep colors—not unlike the pulsating, blood-red aura that radiated from him as his consuming gaze drank in her nakedness from forehead to ankle.

He spread her legs with his thigh, nudging her open to him. As he covered her, the rigid length of his arousal ground against her hip. Her pulse sped up, tripping as he gave her a meaningful thrust of his pelvis, those smoldering amber irises burning her up.

He took her mouth in a slow but demanding kiss. He took her lip between his teeth, sucked her tongue deep into his mouth. Kissed her until she was panting and writhing beneath him, grasping at him with needy hands. "Now, I'm going to taste you, Melena," he murmured against her slack mouth. "Every last creamy, delectable inch of you."

And then, heaven help her, he proceeded to do just that.

He started with a maddening sweep of his tongue just below her ear. She shivered, even though her blood was on fire for the heat of his lips and the gentle, but unmistakable, rasp of his fangs as he dragged his mouth down to the curve where her neck and shoulder met. He suckled and nipped, working his way to her breasts. Kneading them in strong hands, tonguing the tight buds at their peaks, he didn't move on until she was moaning with pleasure and aching for more.

Her back arched into him as he began a slow and steady exploration of her rib cage and abdomen. He took care around her bruises, astonishing tenderness from a Breed male who had lived ten lifetimes and counting, whose own otherworldly body was virtually indestructible. Yet he navigated her minor wounds as though he were handling glass.

That moved her deeply, even more than his passion had overwhelmed her.

Melena reached down, cradling his dark head in her hands while his kiss traveled lower.

Across her stomach, onto each hip bone, over the quivering tops of her thighs. She trembled as his mouth blazed a slow path down the entire length of her right leg and ankle, then returned up her left calf, to her knee and the tingling flesh of her inner thigh.

If he wanted to make her wet and vibrating with the need to have him inside her, Lazaro could have stopped right after their lips had met for the first time here in his bedroom.

But it was patently clear from the wicked look he shot up the length of her nude body that he was only getting started.

His head lowered between her spread legs. When the heat of his breath rushed out against her sex, she shuddered. When his lips touched down and his hot, silky tongue cleaved into her slit, she let out a strangled cry.

Fingers gripping the coverlet on each side of her, she held on for dear life as Lazaro licked and kissed and fucked her senseless with his ruthlessly skilled mouth.

She came in mere moments, pleasure shooting through her in wave after glorious wave. She didn't know if she sighed or screamed or both. She only knew that while her body was still floating in a million tiny shards of bliss, Lazaro started climbing back up to her on the bed.

He stroked her face, watching her—smirking in obvious satisfaction, for God's sake.

Then his grin was gone as quickly as it had arrived, and he covered her mouth with his, kissing her hard and deep and wild.

He drew back on a curse, his breath sawing in and out of his lungs. He stripped off his clothing and boots in mere seconds. Then he pivoted back to her, gloriously naked. He found his place between her thighs again and held himself there, unmoving, watching her. Considering her in some way.

His big body threw off waves of heat and power. The *glyphs* that traced his bulky shoulders and muscular arms continued onto the contours of his chest and rippled abdomen. They pulsed vividly on his skin, alive and flooded with color.

Those Gen One skin markings trekked farther south as well. The thick, long shaft of his cock was circled with *glyphs*, their hues flushing even deeper as Melena admired him with unabashed approval.

God, he was immense. Magnificently so.

And sexy as hell.

She rose up to touch his face, cupping his stern jaw in her palm when a scowl thundered across his expression. "It's been a while for me too," he said, then gave a small shake of his head. "I'm not sure I can be as gentle as I'd like for you. The last thing I want to do is hurt you."

Melena saw the torment in his aura, even if his body was being driven by a stronger need now. He didn't want to let her in, but he couldn't shut her out either.

He cared, even though he wanted to deny it.

She thought back to what he said to her in the cave. That just because he'd helped her stay alive, didn't mean she was safe with him.

Melena had never felt more protected or secure with anyone in her life.

And she'd never known anything so raw and consuming—so impossible to deny—as how it felt being with Lazaro.

She wrapped her hand around his nape and pulled him down in a deep, scorching kiss. With her other hand, she sought out his cock and grasped it firmly, pumping his length in sure, steady strokes. She didn't let go of his mouth or his penis for a good long moment. When she did, she gave him a smile against his parted lips and the fangs that now filled his mouth even more than before. "See?" she told him. "I'm not going to break."

He uttered a low, vicious curse that sounded to be half relief and half anguish.

Then he positioned himself at her body's entrance and drove home, deep and slow and long, all the way to the hilt.

He filled her so completely she could hardly summon her breath. Then he started to pivot in and out, rolling his hips in controlled, tantalizing swivels that dragged a curse out of her too. Sweet pressure spiraled within her core as he pushed her toward another climax. He didn't go gently, instead driving into her so far and fully, it was all she could do to hold on to him and let her body shatter in his arms.

Lazaro watched her as she came, his eyes locked on hers. She couldn't look away. The power of the connection was too intense. He felt it too—he had to have felt it.

As his own release built, then broke on a coarse shout, he kept his gaze fastened on hers too. It was so intense, so startlingly real, this thing coming to life between them.

If anything had the power to terrify her, it was this.

The feeling that she had already given herself to this man. A man who had pretended he barely remembered her when he first saw her on Turati's yacht.

A man who warned her not to get close to him, all but threatened that he would only hurt her.

And here she was, giving him her body.

Staring into his eyes as she surrendered the most intimate part of herself to him, and imagining that she could so easily let herself fall. That maybe she already had. Maybe the men in her past had been right. They would never have been good enough for her.

Because all along, what she wanted them to be was someone like Lazaro Archer. Brave. Loyal. And yes, heroic, even if he refused to accept that truth.

She didn't need him to be perfect, because even through the haze of affection and searing desire, she knew he would never be perfect. He didn't need to be. Not for her to want him like she did. Not for her to feel so right, so safe and contented in his arms.

Oh, God...could she be falling so fast?

Did she dare?

Melena finally broke his gaze then, turning her head away from him to the side, bewildered by her epiphany.

Her heart was pounding hard, making her carotid tick palpably in the side of her neck.

She didn't have to look back to him to know that Lazaro's amber eyes had drifted to that fluttering vein. She felt the heat of his stare. Then she heard a dangerously low growl curl up from the back of his throat.

She went very still, terrified he might bite her.

Terrified he wouldn't.

"Lazaro?" she whispered, uncertain what she was about to ask him to do.

She slowly pivoted her head back to look at him and saw torment in his handsome, otherworldly face. And fury. He drew back from her on a hiss.

His expression was wild looking, intense...and his smoldering aura told her he was balanced on the razor's edge of a rigidly held, but tenuous, control.

* * * *

What the fuck was he doing?

Lazaro came to his senses as if physically struck. He was still buried inside Melena's hot, wet heat, his pulse still charged and racing. His cock was still hard, still greedy, even after the climax that had ripped through him with brutal ferocity.

And he'd been reckless enough to let his fevered gaze drift to the vein that throbbed so enticingly in the side of her vulnerable throat.

Christ.

He'd nearly lost control—something he never allowed to happen. Not once in twenty years had he even been tempted. His guard was always up, his will impenetrable.

Even then, he'd made a habit of avoiding women like Melena, females with the Breedmate mark. To drink from one of her kind would tie him to her singularly, irrevocably. He would always crave her. He would always feel her in his blood, in the root of his soul...unless death severed the bond, as it did when he lost Ellie.

Why the thought didn't freeze his thirst or shrivel his desire for Melena, he didn't want to know. And he sure as hell wasn't going to sit there pondering that fact as she gaped at him in mute terror.

"Damn it." He pulled out of her on a roar. As difficult as it was to deny himself the feel of her silken grip on his shaft—as much as he wanted to have her now, still, again and again—he needed the separation more.

What he needed was to put as much distance as possible between her soft, inviting body and the blood hunger that was suddenly twisting him in vicious knots.

He got off the bed to collect his clothes.

"What are you doing?" Melena asked from behind him. When he began to dress, he heard her slide across the sheets. "Talk to me, please."

He couldn't form words, let alone push them out of his mouth. He still wanted her too much, and he feared that if he let himself cave to that need now, he might not be able to reign it back in. He zipped up his pants, ignoring the persistent bulge of his uncooperative arousal. His hands moved hastily, aggressively, as he donned his shirt, then bent to retrieve his boots.

He had plenty of human females he could call upon to slake his needs. A pity he didn't think to do that before he made the mistake of putting himself alone in the company of a Breedmate as tempting as Melena.

And what a feeble fucking rationalization that was.

Nothing would satisfy him more than to dismiss his near-mistake as something that might have occurred with any female sporting the teardrop-and-crescent-moon birthmark. Far more troubling to realize that it was *this* woman who tempted him like no other.

Melena Walsh would continue to tempt him for as long as she remained in his care, under his dubious protection.

He didn't know how a woman who'd come into his life so unexpectedly—not to mention temporarily—was making him hungry for things that would come with a very permanent price.

"You're just going to walk away then?" She stood beside the bed, watching him prepare to make his escape. For a long moment, she said nothing more, her silence ripe with hurt and confusion, almost too much for him to bear. "You're not even going to acknowledge what almost happened just now?"

That he was only an instant away from taking her vein between his teeth? Or that every particle of his being was so ravenous for a taste of her Breedmate blood, there was a chance he might still act on the powerful impulse?

The memory of her blood scent hadn't left him since he'd first caught a trace of it back in the cave. He knew what she would taste like: caramel and dark, ripe cherries. On top of the other decadent sweetness that still lingered on his tongue from his carnal exploration of her body.

Lazaro cursed roundly, a nasty profanity spoken in a language only the eldest of the Breed like him would comprehend.

"No, Melena, I'm not going to acknowledge it." He caught her gaze, knowing how cold his own must look through her eyes. Yet even as he glowered, furious with his own lack of control, his traitorous body had lost none of its interest in her. "And yes, I am going to walk away, and what happened here will not happen again."

She stared at him. "I think we both know better than that. You still want me, Lazaro. I don't need to read your aura to see that."

"This was a mistake," he snarled through teeth and fangs. "I damned well won't complicate it any more by letting it become something both of us will regret forever."

He turned and walked out the door.

Before his shaky resolve could break completely.

CHAPTER 8

True to his word, he didn't return.

She had showered and dressed, even eaten a fresh meal that Jehan had brought up to her sometime after Lazaro had gone. That was hours ago, according to the old grandfather clock in the hallway. It was well into the evening before she'd finally given up waiting, wondering...God, pitifully hoping, that he would come back and at least talk to her after the incredible passion they'd shared.

Her psychic gift prevented her from sulking over doubts about Lazaro's intentions. It wasn't that he didn't want her tonight. He'd left because he wanted her too much.

But that didn't change the fact that he was quite obviously avoiding her.

She'd since begun pacing the residential suites in the clothing he bought for her, feeling like a prisoner in a beautiful, unlocked cage. Although she had the entire fourth floor to explore, decency kept her from snooping too avidly through Lazaro's home. Not that she'd find anything very personal in his quarters, she'd realized fairly quickly.

Each room was consummately appointed with elegant furnishings and a variety of fine things. Sophisticated pieces, tasteful antiques, a wealth of heirloom Oriental rugs—the kind of things she might expect someone who'd lived as long as him would appreciate.

But there was nothing personal in Lazaro's home. Nothing modern.

There were no photographs on the bureaus or sofa tables or walls. No mementoes scattered about in any of the meticulously kept rooms.

There was nothing to remind him of the past century, let alone the past twenty years.

He lived here in a carefully curated, elegant isolation.

Her conversation with Jehan and Savage came back to her now. The fact that Lazaro had never fully gotten over the deaths of his mate and family. That he blamed himself for not being able to save them. And so he'd joined the Order and exiled himself to this place.

If he hadn't found room in his heart for anything or anyone in the past two decades, how could she hope he might let her in after just a couple of days?

She had half a mind to confront him about the way he was living his life. Maybe it wasn't her place to call him on it. Maybe she'd be better off leaving well enough alone and simply wait to return home to the States, where she had her own life to manage.

A life that no longer included her father, she thought, swamped with a fresh wave of grief to think that Lazaro's entry into her life came at the loss of someone else she loved. But even before losing her father last night, even before the loss of her dear mother years before, Melena realized that her life was missing something vital.

She had a life that, if she were truly being honest with herself, wasn't so much different from the cage Lazaro had built around himself here in Rome.

She had a nice apartment of her own at her father's Darkhaven in Baltimore. She had friends. She had lovers when she wanted them. She had colleagues at her father's office and in the GNC. She had her Breed brother, Derek. She had a full life and plenty of companionship whenever she needed it.

And yet, deep down, she was so lonely.

She saw that same emptiness in Lazaro. Maybe he saw it in her too. Maybe that's why when their gazes had locked in the midst of their release tonight, the connection had felt so real. So nakedly, startlingly real.

How could he expect her to ignore that as if it hadn't happened?

She couldn't.

And she wouldn't, not without a fight.

Whatever was building so swiftly—powerfully—between them had a chance of growing into something extraordinary. She felt that with a certainty in her bones, in her blood. And she knew she wasn't alone in that feeling.

So, like it or not, Lazaro Archer was simply going to have to talk to her. He might be accustomed to blustering and bossing his way around everyone else in his life, but she wouldn't stand for it.

Steeling herself for a battle she wasn't sure she could win, Melena left the suite on the fourth floor and headed downstairs to the mansion's main level. It was quiet down there, so she continued on, toward the connected command center of the estate.

She didn't get far.

From out of nowhere, a massive wall of muscle materialized to block her path.

It wasn't Lazaro. Not Savage or Jehan either.

She looked up and found herself gaping into the cold, hard face of the one warrior she hadn't yet met. His shaved head and jagged scar made him look even more lethal than the dark stare he held her in now.

He didn't speak. Didn't seem inclined to make even the remotest effort to put her at ease.

Melena lifted her chin in defiance. "I'm looking for Lazaro."

"He's not here." God, that voice was coarse gravel. "And you shouldn't be down here either, female."

As he spoke, Savage and Jehan came out of a nearby chamber in the corridor. Sav hissed. "Trygg, for fuck's sake. Go easy on her. Save the venom for tonight's patrol."

When the scarred vampire didn't so much as twitch in acknowledgment, Jehan stepped forward, placing himself between Melena and the warrior who bristled with a feral darkness.

Jehan squared off against his comrade, gently guiding Melena behind him. "I'm only going to say it once. Back. The. Fuck. Down."

The one called Trygg had an aura that verged on feral. The menacing haze sent a shiver up Melena's spine. She saw pain there too, buried deep, but it was a dangerous pain, as sharp as razorblades.

For a long moment, Trygg didn't move. Neither did Jehan. It wasn't clear which warrior would be the first to spill the other's blood, but there was no mistaking that cool, calm, and cultured Jehan was every bit as lethal as his barely leashed brother-in-arms.

Perhaps more so. Jehan's aura burned with a steady, unyielding resolve. He would be unstoppable in all things he set out to do. Honorable to his last breath.

Trygg seemed to know this about his teammate. He seemed to respect it. With a slow exhale, the terrifying Breed male let his shoulders relax a degree. His jaw pulsed, but he did as his comrades demanded, easing back on his heels with a quiet rumble in his throat.

Then he turned and walked away, stalking down the far length of the corridor.

"You okay?" Sav asked.

Melena nodded. "Is his problem just me, or does he despise all women?"

Sav gave her a sardonic look. "It's not just you. And it's a long, ugly story. If you have a week or five to spare, maybe I'd tell you."

No, she didn't have that kind of time. And the fact that tomorrow Lazaro would be taking her back to the States put a pang of regret in her breast. She wanted to stay a bit longer with Savage and Jehan.

She wanted to get to know them: Savage and his easy charm and gorgeous smile. Jehan, with his intriguing past and enigmatic personality. She wanted to know what obligation awaited him in Morocco, and why was he trying to outrun it. Against her own sense of logic or self-preservation, Melena also wanted to stay long enough to understand what had inspired Trygg's terrifying animosity toward women.

And Lazaro...

Would there ever be enough time in this life to unravel all of his torment and secrets and dark, hidden thoughts? Would he even allow her that, if by some miracle they did have more time? All those rooms of his upstairs, missing memories...she wanted to help him fill them back up again.

She wanted to be the one to save him this time.

"Come on," Sav said. "You really shouldn't be down here in the operations compound. Lazaro will have our balls if—"

The warrior's words cut short as a gust of cold, dark air seemed to blow in from the far end of the corridor. He was there. Melena waited to hear Lazaro growl his fury at the men, or demand to know what she was doing back in the Order's domain after he prohibited her from distracting his team.

But he didn't growl or demand anything. He just stared at her in silence, his sapphire gaze trained on her alone.

Intense. Penetrating. Focused on her with searingly sensual regard.

She trembled a little under that potent gaze, not from anything resembling fear. Seeing him there, looking at her as though no one and nothing else existed but the two of them, it was all she could do to keep from launching herself at him from down the corridor and flying into his arms.

But Melena held back. And now she noticed that there was something different about him tonight. Something different in the relaxed state of his *glyphs*, in his schooled expression.

"You were gone for a long time," she murmured. And then she did start to approach him, though not with the jubilation she felt just a moment ago. This was something heavier. Something that stung as the realization began to dawn on her. "You've fed. You went out to find a blood Host. A woman?"

He didn't deny it.

Damn him, he just stood there, watching impassively as she slowed to a stop in front of him. The array of skin markings on his arms under his rolled-back sleeves were calm, satiated. "Did you fuck her too, Lazaro?"

Behind her, Melena heard Jehan quietly clear his throat. There was brief movement in the corridor at her back, followed by the polite closing of a door as the two warriors made a hasty exit.

"Did you?" she repeated, now that it was just she and Lazaro in the passageway.

He swore, roundly, fiercely under his breath. "Don't be ridiculous."

She scoffed. "You know what's ridiculous? Sitting around waiting for you to return. Hoping that I didn't somehow push you away tonight. But how can I push you away when I never had you in the first place?"

She swept past him on a wounded, furious cry. She didn't know if he followed. In that moment, she didn't care.

But he had followed her. She had only made it to the main floor of the mansion's residential wing when Lazaro halted her by grasping her hand. "Melena—"

"You know what else is ridiculous?" she fumed at him. "Hoping you'd come back and tell me that you realize there's something serious going on between us too." She glanced away, giving a shake of her head. "It's ridiculous to expect that a man who's been living his life like a ghost for twenty years could ever admit that he actually feels something again."

Wrenching out of his light hold, she ran for the stairs. She heard him stalking up behind her, but he didn't stop her now. Her breath was heaving by the time she found herself in the center of Lazaro's palatial living room suite.

"I don't want another blood bond, Melena. I won't risk it." His deep voice sounded brittle at her back. "So, whatever you think is happening here between us, it has no future."

"Whatever I think?" She turned to face him. It stung that he wanted to diminish what they'd shared, but she didn't believe him. She could see that he cared. But he was also determined to push her away. He truly intended to spend the rest of his life alone, punishing himself for something he couldn't control. "I know about your family, Lazaro. I know you blame yourself for not being there to save Ellie and the rest of your Darkhaven."

He glared at her furiously, as if she had violated some boundary simply in speaking of the incident. "They trusted me to keep them safe. I failed them."

"You weren't there. That's all. And that's a completely different thing."

"No, not to me. And if you know so much about it, then you should also understand why I left to find a blood Host tonight. After making love with you, if I'd stayed..." He exhaled sharply. "The ifs don't matter. I don't want another Breedmate shackled to me and reliant on me for protection, for her sustenance. For her life. I won't do that to someone again. I prefer to keep my appetites restricted to human females."

Melena scoffed. "Safe women you can fuck and feed from without the risk of feeling anything."

He stared, unflinching at her jab. "It is simpler that way, yes."

"Women who leave you free to walk away and wallow in your guilt and self-flagellation."

His full lips had compressed in a flat line as she spoke, his expression hardening now. "That's right, Melena. That's exactly the kind of woman I prefer. Simple. Safe. Forgettable. What I don't want is what nearly happened between us today. I'm not going to sacrifice two decades of resolve on a couple of days of passion."

And she didn't want to hear him say that. No more than she wanted to acknowledge the regret she saw in his dark gaze, or the grim determination that emanated from the stormy color of his aura. "How fortunate for you and your martyred honor that I'll be out of your life tomorrow."

She pivoted away from him on a burst of hot anger and bitter pride.

She didn't even make it two steps.

Lazaro was suddenly in front of her. And he was fuming. He seized her shoulders, blocking her path with the muscled wall of his body and the power of his sudden fury.

Amber sparks crackled in the midnight-blue pools of his eyes as his gaze clashed and locked with hers. "The fact that you'll soon be out of my life is fortunate for you too, Melena." He drew in a breath and more fire leapt into his irises, reducing his pupils to thinning, inhuman slits. "You should be thanking me for my restraint thus far, not stomping off to pout like a petulant child."

"Let go of me." He didn't. If anything, his grip only went firmer. His face was so close to hers now, the bones of his high, angled cheeks sharpening with the emergence of his fangs. She refused to shrink under the full blast of his Gen One fury. "You call it restraint, the fact that you deny yourself the things you really want? Do you honestly think your guilt is ever going to release you if you only keep feeding it with your self-imposed isolation and pointless, hollow honor?"

A snarl curled up from his throat. It escaped through bared teeth and fangs. "You're far too young to lecture me on life and death or guilt and honor. You don't have any idea what you're talking about."

"Don't I?" she challenged hotly. And maybe a bit recklessly too, but she was so pissed off at him now, she couldn't stop. "Twenty years of licking your wounds, hiding from life? Pretending you don't need anything or anybody? One of us is acting like a sulking child, but it sure as hell isn't me."

A low, thunderous growl. That was all the warning she had. Then Lazaro's mouth came down hard on hers. His kiss was ruthless, punishing. Spiked with raw fury and violent need.

Melena felt his fangs press against her lips, against her tongue when she opened her mouth to his invading kiss. He was holding nothing back now. She felt that hard intent roll through him with the fierce drumming of his heart against her breasts. She felt it in the steely demand of his cock when he brought his arm around her back and hauled her into a brutal embrace, crushing her abdomen into the immense ridge of his arousal.

She felt the wall come up against her spine and realized dazedly that he had moved her there using the power of his Breed genetics to propel them both across the floor in an instant. Lazaro fucked her mouth with his tongue, grazed her lips with the deadly points of his fangs. His big body caged her, allowing her no room to escape, even if she tried.

"Now tell me what you know about my restraint, Melena." His voice had dropped to a timbre so low, so dangerously dark, everything reasonable and sane in her trembled with a dreadful anticipation. His merciless gaze bore into her, daring her to flinch as he bent his head toward her vulnerable throat. "Tell me about my hollow honor."

She couldn't speak. All of her senses were drawn taut, coiled to the point of breaking. His breath rushed hot and fevered across her neck, into the sensitive shell of her ear. Her pulse was racing, electricity coursing through her veins everywhere Lazaro touched her. He reached up, ran his fingertips over the scarlet teardrop-and-crescent-moon mark at the base of her throat.

"Tell me you're not afraid that I'll take your sweet, frantic carotid in my teeth right now and do exactly what I've been dying to do since I first saw you on that boat last night."

She was afraid. And for all her desire for him—despite her sense that she had been waiting all her life for him and had never realized it until now—Lazaro's fangs nestled so dangerously near her throat put an arrow of true panic in her blood.

If he pierced her vein, just one sip of her Breedmate blood would create an exclusive, unbreakable bond. He would be tied to her for the rest of his days—or until her death, should that come sooner.

One sip and he would crave no one else.

He would always feel Melena in his blood, even if they were apart. Even if miles or entire countries separated them.

One sip and there would be no other Breedmate for him, even if he drank from another woman with the mark after his connection was formed with Melena.

And if she drank from him in exchange, their bond would be a complete circle. Sustaining. Eternal. Unbreakable, except by death.

Melena held her breath, suddenly understanding the full impact of what she was inviting. Lazaro Archer, one of the eldest, most formidable Gen One Breed males in existence, his body pressed against her from breast to ankle, his enormous fangs bared and poised over her carotid.

And he wanted *her*.

Every muscled inch of him was coiled with power, all of it at the razor's edge of breaking. Desire burned in his eyes—desire for her body and for the vein that throbbed so madly near his mouth. Heat and rigid strength pulsed where his pelvis ground so demandingly into her abdomen.

He was feral and wild and nearly unhinged...and she had never known anything hotter in her life.

"Damn you for making me want you," he muttered thickly. His searing breath skated across her electrified skin like a lick of flame. "Damn you for making me want this..."

She heard his brief inhalation. Felt his head descend, his lips and tongue sealing over her skin. Then she felt Lazaro's bite.

Sharp.

Deep.

Irrevocable.

CHAPTER 9

The first hot rush of Melena's blood over his tongue slammed into him like a freight train. Warm, rich, potent. And laced with the sweetest trace of caramel and dark, ripe cherries—her Breedmate blood scent, a fragrance that had tempted him from the moment he'd first encountered it. Now that scent would call him as surely as a divining rod seeking a spring of cool, pure water.

He would feel her in his blood, everything she experienced most intensely would now echo in his veins. Her joy, her sorrow, her fears. Her hungers. Melena owned him now.

The bond he'd just activated inside him was unbreakable. She had been a distraction to his mind, will, and body before; now she would be his lifelong addiction.

And although better than a thousand years' of logic strove to persuade him that Melena's blood was a shackle he shouldn't want and damned well didn't need, the part of him that was purely male, elementally Breed, roared with the one word Lazaro never thought he would utter again: *Mine.*

He had known this feeling before. But what he had with Melena now was all the more intense for how desperately he'd tried to resist it. He groaned with possessive pleasure, knocked off his axis with a force that staggered him.

Amazed him.

Holy hell, it humbled him.

He drank more, starving for her. Twenty years of feeding from human blood Hosts went up in flames as he drew greedily from

Melena's tender vein. Her blood surged into his body, nourishing his cells as it wrapped silken bonds around his soul.

She was his. Even if his mind and will were reluctant to accept that fact, his body knew it with a ferocity he could hardly contain now. And where his desire for her had been consuming nearly from the moment he first laid eyes on her two nights ago, now it was a raging inferno that demanded its own satisfaction.

He wanted her savagely.

Needed her with a fury that left him shaking.

He realized in that moment that it wasn't only the blood bond that lashed her to him. Melena would have owned him even if he hadn't given in to his thirst for her tonight.

As unwelcome as that thought was—as unnerving as he found it, to think that she had obliterated his long-standing, iron resolve—it was a truth Lazaro could not deny.

And right now, he could not get enough of her.

* * * *

Oh, God, she was lost to this man.

She'd never known what it would be like to have a Breed male drink from her. Like so much where he was concerned, Melena hadn't been prepared.

With her head dropped back and Lazaro suckling with long, hard tugs at her carotid, she dissolved into a state of pure, boneless bliss. She held him as he drank from her, cushioning his big body as he thrust against her where they stood.

Her veins were on fire. The core of her had gone molten as well. Each demanding pull at her throat sent arrows of pleasure and need shooting through every cell of her being.

When Lazaro suddenly stopped suckling her and swept his tongue over the wounds he'd made, Melena groaned in protest. "I need you naked now," he muttered thickly against her throat. "I can't wait much longer."

Neither could she. "Yes," she gasped, her hands still clutching at him as he began to sink down before her into a crouch. He made quick work of her slacks and panties, baring her to him with the clothing pooled at her feet. On a low growl, he moved in and kissed each hipbone, then descended farther, burying his face between her thighs. "Oh, God..."

His tongue cleaved her folds, hot and wet and hungry. In long, knee-weakening strokes, he lapped and suckled, then kissed and nipped, wringing a moan from her as he drew her clit into his mouth and teased it toward a frenzy. She felt his teeth graze her sensitive flesh, felt the sharp tips of his fangs getting larger as he feasted on her with ruthless abandon.

She was quivering with hard need, on the verge of orgasm already, as he slowly kissed his way back up her body. With a deep, rolling growl, he stripped off her sweater and bra, then tossed them aside to gaze on her nakedness with burning amber eyes. Her blood stained his sensual lips a duskier hue, making his diamond-white fangs stand out in stark contrast.

He had never looked more dangerous or inhuman...nor more preternaturally beautiful.

"Lazaro," she sighed, her voice feathery, as unsteady as her legs. That sigh became a moan as he lavished her breasts and nipples with his hands and mouth, tongue and teeth.

He muttered her name in a fevered, animal-like rasp that sent her blood surging with even greater pleasure and arousal. He needed her now, as much as she needed him. On a curse he released her nipple and drew back to shuck his pants and shirt. He stood before her like an otherworldly god.

Magnificent. Terrifying. And hers.

Melena reached down between their bodies to grasp the jutting length of his cock. His shaft more than filled her hand, thick and warm and pulsing with strength. He purred deep in the back of his throat as she stroked him, then seized her mouth in a wild kiss. She could taste herself on his tongue, her blood and juices an erotic sweetness that only made her burn even more for him. She stroked him harder, craved him with a desperate ache that demanded to be filled.

"I can feel your need in your blood, Melena," he rasped against her lips. "It's alive in me now. So fucking intense. Everything you feel this strongly, I will feel too." He flexed his hips, his shaft surging even more powerfully within the tight circle of her fingers. "I need to be inside you. Put me there."

She obeyed, guiding him into the slick cleft of her body. He drove home on a savage groan, the fierce thrust making her cry out in pleasure. He gave her more, slamming in hard and urgently, his lack of restraint sending her own control spiraling away. She clawed at him as he fucked her against the wall, orgasm roaring up on her in a shocking wave of sensation.

She came fast and hard, convulsing in tremors that racked her from head to toe. As she shattered around him, Lazaro's tempo became a storm. He crashed into her with abandon, his immense body taut and shaking, so deliciously wild. He cursed against the side of her neck as his own release roared up on him. She felt him go rigid, driving deeper with every stroke, until a wordless shout tore out of him and he released.

Melena registered the hot blast of his orgasm, a heat she felt in her core and in every tingling particle of her being. She was drained and completed all at once, awash in a pleasure that rocked her to her soul.

But Lazaro wasn't finished with her yet, apparently.

Instead of pulling out, he guided her legs up around him, lifting her against him, their bodies still joined and vibrating with the aftershocks of release. He brought her into the bedroom, placed her beneath him on the big bed.

Then he began to drive her mad with desire and pleasure all over again.

* * * *

The temptation to stay with her in his bed had been all but irresistible, but after hours of making love to Melena, Lazaro finally let her sleep. No easy thing, for how much he still craved her. His desire for her soft curves and addicting heat was rivaled only by his newer thirst for her.

He didn't want to think about how strong those urges were, now that he'd indulged so recklessly—selfishly—in both.

He didn't want to think about how right it felt to lie next to her, inside of her, to hear her soft cries of pleasure or the quiet puffs of her breath as she slept so sweetly—trustingly—in his arms.

He didn't want to think about any of that when reality waited for them in D.C. in just a few short hours.

Lazaro slipped away from Melena's side to shower and get dressed, the predawn morning a prickle in his ancient Breed veins as he headed down to the command center to meet with his team. The warriors were just coming in from the night's patrol.

Trygg said nothing as he approached with the others from the far end of the corridor. The brutal warrior merely strode into the team's meeting room for the mission review. Jehan and Sav both slowed as their path met Lazaro's in the passageway. They greeted him with measured nods and sober, suspicious gazes.

"How did it go out there?" Lazaro asked them. "Any rumblings on the street about the explosion on Turati's yacht?"

Jehan answered first. "Nothing that we found. It was just a typical night in the Eternal City. A couple of club brawls to break up before they got too bloody and created a bigger problem. Handful of Breed youths feeding past curfew near the train station."

"No unusual activity at all?"

Sav glanced down, trying to suppress a grin. "Seemed like the only unusual activity going on last night was in here."

Lazaro glared, but he couldn't take offense at the truth.

"Is everything all right, Commander?" Jehan asked, ever the diplomatic professional, despite being one of the most dangerous warriors Lazaro had ever seen. "The situation with Melena seemed...difficult."

Now, it was only more difficult. Not to mention complicated. If she had cause to despise him last night after he'd seduced her then fled to find a blood Host, she had every reason in the world to loathe him for what he did a few hours ago.

And for what he had yet to do, after he saw her safely home to the States.

"Melena Walsh's welfare is no one's concern here but mine," he said, eager to shut down the topic of discussion, even though it weighed heavily on him. "The Order has difficulties of its own to worry about. For instance, does it bother anyone else that no one is stepping forward to claim responsibility for the assassinations of Turati and Byron Walsh the other night? The attack smacks of Opus Nostrum, yet the group hasn't formally declared it was their doing."

"Maybe they're waiting for the right time to own up to it," Savage suggested.

Jehan grunted, not quite convinced, if the shrewd look in his sky-blue eyes was any indication. "If it is Opus, maybe it wasn't a sanctioned attack. Maybe it was an over-zealous member looking to make a name for himself among his comrades. Or maybe it was done for more personal reasons than that. Turati was a high-profile businessman with political connections as well. He could've had any number of enemies. The same could be said of Walsh."

Lazaro gave a grim nod. The warrior could be right about any of those scenarios. And the only thing more troubling than Opus making such a bold move was the thought of a renegade agent operating from his own agenda.

Walking into the meeting room with Sav and Jehan, Lazaro couldn't help but relive the shock and horror of the rocket's destruction. And the fact that Melena might have been part of the carnage? That she had been mere seconds away from complete obliteration along with the others on that yacht?

Christ. What had shaken him that night—what had outraged him as a man and as the one entrusted with the security of those dead men—now put a cold knot of dread in his chest.

It put real, marrow-chilling fear in his bones.

Now more than ever, he needed to ensure she would be kept far out of harm's reach. And as bitter as the taste was on his tongue, he knew that anyone in the Order's orbit, or in that of the ever-expanding number of enemies seeking to incite true war between man and Breed, would always be at risk.

Like Ellie had been.

Like their sons and the dozen other family members living in Lazaro's Darkhaven who were killed on his watch.

He couldn't bear to have anything happen to Melena. She'd been through enough pain and loss already.

And so had he.

As Lazaro took his seat at the head of the conference table in the room with his men, Trygg palmed a slip of paper and slid it toward him. "What's this?"

Trygg nodded his shaved head at the note he'd scrawled. "Located her brother, like you asked." Lazaro glanced at the Baltimore, Maryland, address. "Derek Walsh is on a plane out of London as we speak. Booked the flight yesterday, after his father's death aboard Turati's yacht made international headlines."

Lazaro nodded gravely. He would've rather Melena's brother—Byron Walsh's only blood kin—had heard the news another way, but there was no fixing that now. At least her brother would be there for her. She would be home again, with family and familiar things. God knew, she had needed someplace soft to fall these past days, Lazaro thought grimly. And she hadn't exactly found that with him.

No, she'd found tears and anger and hurt.

She'd found a man ill-prepared to give her what she needed, what an extraordinary, tender-hearted woman like Melena deserved in life...and in love.

Instead of offering her comfort during her most vulnerable state, he'd growled and snapped at her. When he wasn't busy seducing her, that is.

When he wasn't selfishly slaking all of his needs on her as if he would ever be worthy of her heart or her blood.

He had no business giving in to those urges when war was still brewing all around him. So long as there were enemies killing innocents, his duty was, and always would be, to the Order. How could he have let himself slip so egregiously when it came to Melena? How could he be letting himself fall in love when he knew all too well how easily it could be ripped from his arms at any moment?

Love...

Fuck. Of all the rash impulses he had been unable to resist when it came to Melena, that would be the most foolish of them all.

Loving her would be even more selfish than the blood bond he had no right to claim and no intention of completing.

CHAPTER 10

Lazaro was gone when she woke up that morning.

He had stayed away most of the day, vanished to his command center until the time came for Melena and him to leave for the flight to D.C. that afternoon. Even on board the Order's private jet, Lazaro had remained distant, his comm unit to his ear most of the time, or his attention rooted to his work and his computer. She would have called him preoccupied, but his smoky aura had conveyed a deliberate resistance.

Hours later and thousands of miles away from everything they'd shared in Rome, Melena had sat beside him in the debriefing with Lucan Thorne and a few other members of the Order at the Washington, D.C., headquarters, feeling almost as though she were seated next to a polite, detached stranger. He'd introduced her graciously, almost formally, giving no one cause to suspect she was anything more to him than a civilian temporarily placed in his safekeeping following the attack on Turati's yacht.

He was careful not to touch her, even though heat crackled between them at the slightest brush of contact. He was careful not to let his gaze linger too long, even though his indigo eyes smoldered with awareness every time he glanced her way. He was coolly, determinedly remote.

It had made her want to scream.

She still felt that swamping urge, having since been removed from the meeting to accompany some of the Order's women in the living room of the headquarters' elegant mansion while the warriors continued their discussion in private.

"Are you sure you wouldn't like something to drink or eat, Melena?" Lucan Thorne's auburn-haired Breedmate, Gabrielle, offered a warm smile as she indicated a side table laid out with plates of finger sandwiches and tea cakes. Aromatic Darjeeling and chamomile steeped in their pots next to an elegant white china service.

Although her appetite wasn't there, everything looked and smelled delicious, and Melena was reluctant to reject the woman's kindness. "Thank you, I think I will have a little something."

She walked over from the sofa, joined by Gabrielle and two other women of the Order.

All of the Breedmates present tonight at the headquarters had been nothing but kind and welcoming. They were a family. That much was clear. And in the short time she'd been sitting with them, they'd each done their best to make Melena feel at home among friends as well.

Melena had been exhausted from her session with Lucan and the other warriors, to say nothing of the dread she felt every time she looked at Lazaro. Being around other women had helped dissolve some of that anxiety, even if it might only be for a little while.

She couldn't help watching the hallway outside, waiting for some indication that the meeting had broken so she and Lazaro could finally go somewhere to speak privately. So she could get rid of the awful feeling she had that he was somehow already gone.

Gabrielle handed her a small plate, collecting Melena from her dark thoughts. "If you'd like something more substantial, Savannah made a big pot of jambalaya earlier today. You really can't go wrong with any of her amazing cooking."

"I do have my numerous and varied talents," Savannah said, her doe-brown eyes dancing at the compliment. The beautiful, mocha-skinned Breedmate was bonded to Gideon, another of the warriors present tonight. Where her big blond-haired mate had an intense, slightly mad genius quality about him, Savannah exuded tranquility and smooth confidence.

As Melena put a few cucumber sandwiches and peach tarts on her plate, she found it next to impossible to keep from staring at the third woman in the room with them—the one mated to the warrior named Brock. Jenna looked like neither of her Breedmate companions. In fact, Melena didn't think she was a Breedmate at all, though she definitely wasn't fully human either.

Tall and athletic, Jenna wore her brown hair cropped close to her scalp. She was pretty, yet formidable in some indefinable way, and when she leaned across the sideboard to pour a cup of tea, Melena noticed an intricate pattern of skin markings at her nape. Skin markings that looked remarkably, impossibly, similar to...

"Are those tribal tattoos, or—"

"Not tattoos." Jenna's hazel eyes were smiling, but there was a note of seriousness in her voice. She turned to provide a better look. The array fanned out to cover the back of Jenna's neck, disappearing beneath the collar of her shirt. The arcs and swirls tracked upward too, well into her hairline and up the back of her skull. From the looks of it, they continued down Jenna's spine and onto her shoulders as well.

"They're *dermaglyphs*." Melena frowned, astonished and confused. Females born Breed had been unheard of for millennia. They might never have come into existence if not for the genetic experimentations conducted in Dragos's labs in the decades before he was killed by the Order. Even then, there were only a handful of women known to bear the *glyphs* and blood appetites of the Breed.

Melena found herself staring harder now, watching Jenna pile her plate with a healthy assortment of sweets and sandwiches. "You can eat all of that?"

Jenna grinned. "I'll probably come back for seconds."

"I'm sorry," Melena blurted, immediately feeling stupid and rude for letting her curiosity overrule her manners. "I just thought..."

"You thought I was Breed?" Jenna popped a tiny pastry in her mouth and gave a shake of her head. "Not quite. But I haven't been fully human for a long time either. I guess as long as Brock loves me, it doesn't matter where I end up. Together we can handle anything—and we have."

Her two friends nodded in agreement, and Melena smiled even though the sentiment was bittersweet for her. She'd believed she and Lazaro were heading toward something special like that too. Her father's death was still a raw ache in her heart, and would be for a very long time. The attack she'd narrowly survived still held her in a cold grasp. But Lazaro had helped her through.

He'd been her rock, her comfort, whether he wanted to accept that role or not. And ever since they'd left Rome, she felt that support slipping away. No, she felt pretty damned certain that he wasn't slipping—he was running away. Cutting her off with his forbidding silence and maddening stoicism.

When she finally heard his deep voice approaching with Lucan and the others, Melena's heart started pounding in a heavy, expectant tempo. She didn't know whether to be relieved or terrified when he strode to the threshold of the drawing room and those penetrating dark blue eyes found her, locking on with the intensity that would probably always kindle an instant heat in her blood.

"Melena. May I have a word with you." Not a question, not an invitation. A sober demand.

She rose and walked to meet him as the rest of the group fell into easy conversation behind them. Lazaro led her down the hall to another formal parlor. He carefully closed the door, keeping his back to her for longer than she would have liked.

Melena didn't have to see his impassive face to know he was about to crush her heart when he finally turned around to look at her. His aura was a dark cloud, the shuttered gunmetal gray from before.

Before the first time he'd touched her, kissed her.

Before he'd shown her such incredible passion and tenderness when he made love to her. And when he bit her vein and took her blood into his body, into his soul.

All of those moments seemed to evaporate as she looked at him now. They became nothing under the regretful look in his ageless eyes.

But the moments they had weren't nothing. He'd felt everything she had. He wanted her. He cared for her. He cared maybe even as much as she did for him. She could see that diamond-bright truth breaking through the muddy resistance of his aura.

Everything they'd shared in Rome had meant something powerful and extraordinary to him too. But it wasn't enough.

"Why?" she murmured, her throat dry as ash.

He didn't pretend not to understand. "I told you from the beginning, Melena. I wasn't looking for this. I don't have a place for this in my life."

"For *this*," she said. "You mean, for me. For us."

He gave a somber nod. "For everything you deserve. For everything I can't give you."

"I don't recall asking you for anything, Lazaro. I didn't even ask for your heart."

"No, but you have it," he admitted quietly. "I think you owned a piece of my heart from the night I first dragged you out of that frozen pond in Boston."

"Then why?" Damn him, but those gentle words hurt all the more when she knew she was about to lose him. "Why are you pulling away from me now? Why are you acting as if I don't mean anything to you?"

He held her gaze, his own haunted and filled with remorse. "Because it isn't fair to you, letting you think I could ever be any kind of mate worthy of you."

She couldn't help herself. She scoffed brittly. "A shame you didn't arrive at that realization before you drank my blood."

"I told you I wasn't looking for a bond, Melena." His tone was tender but firm. As resolute as his aura. "I knew I couldn't give you that promise."

"No. Because you prefer simple arrangements. No entanglements or complications. No one to tempt you into throwing away twenty years of resolve on a couple of days of passion. Isn't that what you said?"

He said nothing for a long moment, staring at her grimly. "I'd resisted the temptation for a very long time, Melena. And it was easy. Until I found you."

Maybe she should have been moved by the confession. Maybe, if he hadn't been standing there giving her all of his reasons for why he was intent on breaking her heart. Instead, she thought back on everything they'd said to each other in heated anger and passion last night.

It was true, he had tried to resist her. He'd tried to push her away before he lost his damnable restraint. She hadn't helped, but she wasn't the one pretending she could walk away from what they had—from what they might be able to build together as a couple.

Lazaro had tried to warn her that he wasn't a hero come to save the day.

He tried to warn her that she might not be safe in his arms.

And she'd ignored him every time.

Yet for all his rigid honor and long-lived control, he hadn't been able to stop himself from claiming her.

He'd pierced her vein, swallowed her blood...created a bond that no other woman would ever be able to break for as long as Melena drew breath.

And wasn't that a convenient benefit of his colossal slip of self-discipline?

"Did you use me, Lazaro?"

His ebony brows crashed together. "Use you? Christ, no. Melena, you can't possibly think that—"

"Two decades of denial gone after just two days," she reminded him. "And now, with my blood living inside you, you'll never be tempted by another Breedmate. You have no ability to bond with anyone else as long as I live, so when you walk away from me now, you're free. Free as you've never been all this time. Congratulations. I'm so pleased I could permanently scratch that annoying itch for you."

He moved so fast she couldn't track him. One moment he was several feet away at the closed door of the room, the next he was crowding her with his big body, his hands clamped around her biceps. His eyes flashed with furious amber.

"You are not an itch I needed to scratch." His voice rumbled, low and deep and hard with outrage. "Damn it, Melena. Don't say that. Don't ever believe that."

"Then what are we doing? You've been shutting me out since we left Rome. If you care for me—and I know you do, I can see it, I can feel it—then why are you pulling away?"

"Because I can't do this again. You know loss, Melena, but you don't know what it is to lose a mate. I don't ever want to know that pain again. And with you—" He blew out a harsh curse. "I've seen you nearly die twice. I don't want to know what that would feel like now that your blood lives inside me. And I don't want to be the reason you're not safe. My life is committed to the Order now. It's a dangerous life. I won't put you in the crossfire."

"Don't you think that's something I should decide for myself?"

He stared at her for a long time, silent but unswaying. "I'll see you home safely to Baltimore tonight. Your brother should already be there as well."

"You've talked to Derek? When?" Despite the fact that her heart was breaking, it perked at the mention of her brother. "Where is he? How is he? Does he know I'm okay?"

Lazaro shook his head soberly. "There was no time to contact him before we arrived. Trygg found him on a flight coming in from London tonight."

"I need to see him," she murmured. "Derek needs to know that I'm alive."

"Yes," Lazaro agreed. "We can leave as soon as you're ready."

"Then what?" she asked cautiously. "What about you?"

"Then I'll be returning to Rome."

"When?" she asked, although her dread already knew that answer.

"I leave tonight. Arrangements have already been made. The Order's jet is refueling and waiting for me to return a few hours from now."

"So soon." She exhaled sharply. "I imagine you must be eager to unload your burden and get on with your life."

"Don't think this is easy for me," he said, frowning as he brought his hand up to stroke her cheek. "It would be easier to stay, or to bring you back with me to the command center in Rome. It would be the easiest thing in the world to fall in love with you, Melena."

She swallowed hard, trapped in his bleak, tormented eyes. Afraid to believe he might love her already. Afraid he never would.

He let his hand fall away. "It's become far too easy to imagine you at my side, as my mate. But those are things I can't give you. I can't ask you to risk your life by coming into my world. People die around me. I can't allow myself to be responsible for anyone else's life—your life. Don't you understand?"

"Yes, I think I finally do." The realization settled on her with clarity now, and not a little rage. "You're not doing this out of concern for me at all. You're doing it because you're afraid. I thought you were being noble by denying yourself another blood bond all this time. I thought it was honor that made you refuse to let another woman into your heart— and I think I loved you even more because of that. But I was wrong, wasn't I? You're pushing me away now because you're scared. You're running away from something that could probably be pretty fucking amazing because you're terrified of feeling any kind of pain again. The only person you're concerned about taking care of is yourself."

He didn't deny it. He didn't try to defend or justify anything she said. He let out a slow exhalation. His jaw was set and rigid, his aura uncompromising. "Whenever you're ready, I'll take you home to your family's Darkhaven."

"No, don't bother. You're not responsible for me, remember? I'll find my own way home." She tried to walk past him and he grabbed her arm, misery smoldering beneath the resolve in his dark blue eyes. "Let me go. That's what you want, so I'm giving it to you."

"Melena..."

She wrenched out of his loose grasp. "Good-bye, Lazaro."

This time, he didn't stop her. He stood unmoving, unspeaking, as she stepped around him and walked out the door.

CHAPTER 11

An hour later, Melena sat woodenly in the passenger seat of the Order's SUV as it rolled up to her family's Darkhaven in Baltimore. The big brownstone should have been a welcome sight in so many ways, yet all she felt was sorrow when she looked at it through the tinted glass of the vehicle's window.

Sorrow that she'd never hear her father's voice inside the house again. Sorrow for the pain her brother must be feeling as he walked into the empty home, believing he'd lost not only his father but Melena as well. She didn't want to imagine Derek's anguish, being the sole blood kin of Byron and Frances Walsh, both gone now.

And yes, Melena felt sorrow for herself too. Because instead of facing all of these heartaches with Lazaro's strong arms around her and his love to hold her up if she crumbled, she would be doing it alone.

"I'm ready," she murmured, more to herself than the Breed male behind the wheel.

Lucan and Gabrielle's son, Darion, put the vehicle in park and turned a sympathetic look on her. "I'll walk you inside, Miss Walsh."

"No." She shook her head, warmed by the kind offer. Darion was as gentlemanly as he was attractive. "Thank you, but that's not necessary. My brother won't be expecting me, and I don't imagine it will be easy for him when I walk in the door and he sees that I'm alive. I'd rather do this on my own."

"Okay." Darion frowned, but gave her a nod. The dark-haired Breed male's aura was golden and kind, steadfast with the strength of a born leader. "But I'm gonna wait here until you've gone inside."

She reached over to touch his large hand. "Thank you."

Melena climbed out of the vehicle and headed up the walkway toward the front door. It was unlocked, the soft light in the vestibule a warm, welcoming beacon. She stepped inside and pivoted to wave good-bye to Darion. As the black SUV rolled away, she took a steeling breath and closed the door behind her.

She was home.

She was back on safe, familiar ground. And yet, as she walked quietly through the house, she felt like a stranger to the place. Like a ghost drifting through a life that no longer quite fit anymore.

She drifted past the front rooms and grand central staircase, unsure if she should call to Derek or wait and let him adjust to seeing her once she found him.

She didn't have long to wonder. She heard her brother talking farther down the hallway. In her father's study. Derek was on a call with someone, the low rumble of his voice drawing Melena with a relief and a comfort she definitely needed right now.

"Yes, sir, the shipment is en route and everything is in order. That's right, I saw to it personally."

Melena paused at the open doorway. Derek stood with his back to her, dressed in loose sweatpants, his brown hair still wet from a recent shower. He wasn't wearing a shirt, and although the sight of her Breed brother's *glyphs* were no surprise to her, something did make her breath catch abruptly in her throat.

Derek now sported a number of tattoos on his broad back and shoulders. Unusual-looking stars, crossed swords, some kind of black beetle—a scarab, she realized, confused by the body art that hadn't been there the last time she saw her brother. He must have gotten the tattoos after he'd moved overseas a year ago.

"It should be in your hands tomorrow, Mr. Rior—" Derek's voice dried up.

He realized he wasn't alone now. Disconnecting the call without a word of excuse, he smoothly slipped the phone into his pants pocket.

When he pivoted around, his face was slack with shock...with stark disbelief.

"Melena. My God." He frowned, gave a vague shake of his head. But he didn't rush over to embrace her. He didn't react the way she would have expected at all from a sibling who loved her, worried for her. "I don't understand. The news reports said there were no survivors. I thought you were..."

"Dead," she replied, only understanding in that instant why her brother seemed less than relieved to see her.

He hadn't expected to see her again at all.

His sickening aura told the truth. It hovered around him, oily with corruption. Foul with deceit.

"It was you, Derek." She could hardly form the words, could hardly reconcile what her senses were telling her. "You were the faceless, hidden betrayer he feared. Oh, my God...it was you who arranged for our father's death."

* * * *

Lazaro boarded the Order's private jet in a hellish mood.

He hadn't expected the conversation to go well with Melena, but damn if he anticipated the kind of pain that had lodged itself in his chest from the moment she stormed away from him. That ache was still there, cold and gnawing, creating a vacuum behind his sternum that he didn't imagine would ever be filled.

She was gone.

He'd made certain of that—for her, he wanted to reassure himself. But Melena's words still echoed in his mind. Her condemning, all-too-accurate accusation.

He was a coward.

As the jet began to taxi toward the runway, Lazaro couldn't dismiss the feeling that he was walking away from the best thing that had happened to him in a very long time.

And why?

Because of exactly what Melena said. He was afraid. Afraid to his marrow that he might let himself fall in love with her and risk cutting his heart open again should anything happen to her.

The truth was, he was already falling. Letting her go cut him open, and as he rubbed at the empty ache in his chest, he realized only then what a fucking idiot he was.

Pushing Melena away had been the most cowardly act of his long life.

He'd lived more than a thousand years. He had loved a woman deeply, fearlessly, for several centuries before he lost her. He knew what real love felt like. He knew himself well enough to understand that time, for him, was immaterial. Time could last forever, or it could be gone in the blink of an eye.

He loved Melena. And whether it had happened in a matter of days, or over the span of a hundred years, it was all the same to him. He wanted her beside him. Starting right now, if she would have it in her heart to forgive him.

On a snarl, he punched the call button next to his seat.

"Yes, sir?"

"Turn it around."

The pilot went silent for a moment. "Sir, we're next on the runway to taxi and—"

"Turn this goddamned plane around. Now." On second thought, he couldn't wait that long. He unbuckled his seat belt and stood up. "Never mind. I'm getting off right here."

"But, sir—"

He unlocked the hatch and leapt down from the fuselage onto the dark tarmac. Then he was running. Heading for the Order fleet vehicle he'd parked in the private hangar when he'd arrived.

It was just as he neared the black sedan that his senses suddenly seized up, gripped by something powerful and horrifying. His veins lit up with a piercing dread.

Not his emotions.

Melena's.

He could feel her terror rising in his blood through his bond to her.

Holy hell.

She was in danger.

She was in fear for her very life.

CHAPTER 12

Melena tried to run.

She wasn't even halfway into the hall before Derek yanked her off her feet. His hand wound tight in her hair. Pain raked her scalp as he hauled her face backward to meet his furious sneer.

"You're supposed to be dead, sister dear," he hissed against her cheek. "You and Father both in one fell swoop. I've been planning it since he confided in me about his meeting with Turati."

"You killed him, you bastard!" Melena could hardly contain her contempt or her fear. "You killed more than a dozen innocent people that night, Derek. My God, did you hate us that much or are you simply out of your mind?"

"Arranging for that rocket strike was the sanest thing I've ever done. Killing Father and Turati? Doing it while they were secreted away for a covert meeting to broker their precious fucking peace? Let's just say it won me all the respect I deserve with the people who really matter."

Melena's heart sank even further. "Opus Nostrum."

He chuckled. "I was a mere lieutenant for this past year. They barely knew my name. Now I've got a direct line to the inner circle. I'll be a part of that circle soon. This was my proof of allegiance, my demonstration of worth." Derek's eyes flashed with vicious intent as she fought against his ruthless, unyielding hold. "As for you, Melena, I couldn't very well let you see me after I joined the organization. Your irritating gift would've sniffed me out right away."

"You plotted to kill me all this time?" she asked, hating that his duplicity hurt her so deeply.

Derek shrugged, his crackling amber eyes roaming over her terrified, miserable face with a cold disregard. "At first, I thought I could just avoid you. But then Father confided in me that he'd been having premonitions of a betrayal, and I knew it was only a matter of time before one or both of you discovered my alliance with Opus Nostrum. When he later told me about the meeting and the fact that you'd be accompanying him, I knew it was my chance to act."

Bile rose in her throat as he spoke. "You're a cold-blooded murderer, Derek. You're a sick, backstabbing fuck!"

"Careful, little sister. I'm the only thing standing between you and your grave." He snagged a cord from the table lamp on the desk, sending the thing crashing to the floor. Then he quickly bound her wrists behind her back. "Don't rush me to put you in it."

With that, he wrenched her into a more punishing hold and shoved her forward. He guided her out of their father's study and down the opposite end of the hallway. Melena had no choice but to shuffle ahead of him, panicking when she realized he was taking her outside.

He walked her toward their father's GNC-issued silver SUV parked in the drive.

"What are you doing, Derek?"

He opened the back door. Shoved her into the farthest seat.

"Where are you taking me?" she demanded, hysteria bubbling up as he calmly climbed behind the wheel. "If you're going to kill me, then just do it, damn you!"

"I'm not going to kill you, Melena." His cold eyes met her gaze in the rearview mirror. "I'm going to take you to my comrades in the organization. They're not nice people, I'm afraid. You're going to wish you died in that fucking explosion."

He started the engine. Then he backed away from the Darkhaven and started speeding for the highway.

****

Lazaro gunned the black sedan through the late-night traffic on the highway, speeding like a bat out of hell for Baltimore. He didn't know what had Melena so terrified, but her fear was visceral. And it was eating him alive from the inside.

"Hang on, baby," he muttered as he dodged one lagging car and nearly sideswiped another. "Ah, God, Melena...know that I'm coming for you."

He was just about to veer toward the exit he needed when all of his instincts lit up like fireworks.

She was somewhere close—right now.

Possibly on the same stretch of highway, by the way his veins were clanging with alarm bells.

He scanned both sides of the divided lanes, a chaos of headlights and commuting vehicles. She might as well be a needle in a goddamned haystack.

And then—holy shit.

His Breed senses pulled his attention toward a light-colored SUV that had just merged on to the opposite side of the highway. The vehicle was speeding almost as fast as he'd been. In a big fucking hurry to get somewhere.

Melena.

She was inside the silver SUV. He knew it with total, marrow-chilling certainty.

And whoever had her was going to have bleeding hell to pay if she'd been harmed in any way.

Lazaro yanked the steering wheel and sent the sedan roaring into the median. Grass and mud flew in all directions as he tore across the divider and launched his car into the traffic on the other side. He floored the pedal, tearing up the pavement as he tried to catch the bumper of the vehicle that held his woman.

Flashing his lights, laying on the horn, he tried to get the attention of the vehicle bearing GNC diplomatic plates. It belonged to Byron Walsh, but Lazaro wasn't certain who the Breed male was behind the wheel. But then, as he ran up alongside it briefly, he caught a glimpse of the driver. A cold, sickening recognition set in.

Son of a bitch.

Derek Walsh.

And judging from the vampire's murderous glower, he had no intention of giving up Melena without a fight. The SUV lurched into a more reckless speed. It careened behind a semitrailer, dodging between a car of teens and a commuter bus. Lazaro could only follow, negotiating the traffic and keeping his focus trained on his quarry.

Walsh drove erratically for several miles with Lazaro chewing up his bumper. More than once, there was the opportunity to ram the bastard and send the SUV rolling, or to draw one of his semiautomatics and blast a hole in the Breed male's skull...but not with Melena inside. Not when Lazaro's heart was tied to her and every breath in his body was devoted to keeping her safe.

He hissed when Walsh narrowly avoided a collision with a car drifting into his lane. And when another near-miss snapped off the SUV's passenger side mirror, Lazaro shouted a furious curse. He saw a break up ahead—a chance to get in front of Walsh and force him into the median. Lazaro buried the gas pedal and flew past.

But Walsh saw the maneuver coming.

Instead of letting himself catch up to Lazaro, he hung a hard right and gunned it for an upcoming exit.

An exit that was under construction, littered with barrels and an obstacle course of concrete barriers.

Walsh was going too fast, too frantically.

Lazaro stomped on his brake and was whipping around to give chase again when the SUV clipped one of the barriers and went airborne, rolling into a hard crash.

All the breath seemed to suck out of Lazaro's lungs in that instant. The entire world seemed to stop breathing. Dust went up in the darkness, the haze illuminated by the beams of passing vehicles on the road.

Then, a spark of flame.

"No," Lazaro moaned, his blood screaming for Melena. "Goddamn it, no!"

He threw his vehicle in park on the shoulder and hit the ground running.

Even with his preternatural speed, he'd barely gotten within arm's reach of the wreck before the ruptured gas tank ignited. A blinding wall of flames shot skyward, heat blasting his face.

"Melena, no!"

* * * *

She couldn't breathe.

Heat all around her. Splitting pain in her skull, ringing in her ears. She opened her eyes and saw a churning, thickening cloud of gray smoke. And flames.

Oh, God. Fire everywhere.

Melena tried to move, but her arms wouldn't work. Her wrists were tied. She remembered now, awareness coming back to her. Derek had bound her. He'd driven away with her.

He and his Opus Nostrum comrades were going to kill her.

"No," she gasped, choking on smoke and heat. "Oh, my God...no!"

She started kicking, screaming, trying frantically to get free of the restraints. She couldn't loosen them. And something was crushing her in the back of the SUV. She looked up and saw the floor. Beneath her, the roof of her father's GNC vehicle.

The smoke was rolling in front of her eyes, burning them. She couldn't keep her lids open. Hurt to see, to breathe...

"Melena." The deep voice penetrated the fire and sooty air that surrounded her. She wanted to reach for it—for him—but she was trapped, unable to move. "Melena, I'm going to get you out of here, sweetheart. You stay with me, damn it!"

There was a great, groaning howl as the vehicle rocked where it had fallen. A gust of cool air, followed by a rush of hot, intensifying flame.

"I'm coming in to get you," Lazaro said.

She couldn't see him, but she felt him climbing inside the inferno. Crawling all the way to the back, where she lay broken and half-conscious.

And then she felt his strong hands make contact with her.

"Ah, Christ," he hissed, and she knew what he saw couldn't be good.

Another metallic roar filled the air, then the crushing weight that had pinned her down was lifted. Tenderly, Lazaro took hold of her. Started pulling her free of the wreckage.

"I've got you now, Melena. I've got you."

She didn't let the first sob go until she felt the warmth of his chest against her cheek. She buried her face in that comforting strength, breathed in the scent of him even as her throat screamed with pain from the smoke that choked her lungs.

And then he scooped her up in his arms and he was running. Away from the smoke. Away from the heat and the fire and the horror.

Cool night air enveloped her, filled her nose as she braved a cleansing breath. And circled around her were Lazaro's strong arms, holding her close, keeping her safe—carrying her away from certain death.

He set her down in the crisp, moist grass, while behind them came a jarring roll of thunder as a plume of fire and smoke shot up into the moonlit sky. Horns blared out on the highway. Tires screeched as traffic came to a halt at the scene of the accident.

But all Melena knew was the haggard, terrified face of the man she loved, staring down at her as he held her in a careful embrace. He tore off the lamp cord that bound her wrists and tossed it aside on a vicious snarl. When he reached down to smooth a hank of limp hair from her face, his fingers trembled.

Melena tried to speak but couldn't push sound through her lips. Her body ached everywhere, some of the pains searing, others a dull, relentless throb.

Lazaro's dark eyes were sober in his handsome face. His beautiful, sensual mouth was a flattened, grim line. "You're going to be all right, you hear me? I'm not letting you go."

She wanted to argue that he already had. That her heart was still breaking from the thought of him pushing her out of his life. Out of his heart.

He stared down at her, misery swimming in his gaze. "I'm not going to lose you, Melena."

On a curse, he brought his wrist up to his mouth and bit into his own flesh. No hesitation. No asking for permission before he put the punctures to her parted lips. "Drink."

She tried to shake her head. This wasn't the way she wanted him, coming back to save her when he had been determined to leave her. Whether he did this out of some noble sense of obligation or guilt, or simply under the power of his bond to her, she didn't want it. Not like this.

She wanted to reject the gift of his blood, of his bond, but the instant the wet, spicy warmth came in contact with her parched tongue, she greedily drank him in.

And oh, it was incredible.

Lazaro's Gen One blood flowed down her throat like pure light. She felt it strengthening her body, feeding her cells. Mending her injuries.

He tipped his head back on a strangled moan as she swallowed more of his eternal gift, his fangs gleaming, his broad shoulders and immense body silhouetted by the flames he'd walked through to save her.

It was the last thing Melena saw before a bone-deep exhaustion rose up to claim her.

CHAPTER 13

He had lived for more than a thousand years, long enough that few things still held the power to amaze him. The sight of Melena finally opening her eyes to look at him, after lying in bed unconscious for two days, was one of those rare pleasures for Lazaro Archer.

The worst of her injuries had healed. Her burns were gone. She was alive, and he'd never seen anything more welcome in all his life.

He smiled at her and gently stroked his thumb over the back of her hand as he held it. "Hello, beautiful."

"Where are we?" she asked, her voice thready.

"Still in D.C. I brought you here after the accident. I've been waiting for you to wake up so I could ask you something."

"My brother," she murmured.

Lazaro shook his head. "I'm sorry, Melena."

"He was part of Opus Nostrum," she said quietly. "He arranged for the attack on Turati and my father to prove something to his superiors. He was trying to win their recognition. And he was afraid if I ever saw him again, I'd know all of his secrets."

Lazaro and the Order had already surmised that Derek Walsh likely had ties to Opus, but hearing Melena confirm it made his blood seethe with renewed rage. "If he'd survived the accident the other night, I swear, I would've killed the bastard myself."

"He seemed so different. He'd only been away for a year, but he wasn't my brother anymore. And he had strange tattoos I've never seen before. Symbols of some kind, and a black scarab on his back."

"A scarab?" Lazaro thought back to conversations he'd had with

Lucan and the other warriors. Reports out of London about human bodies in the morgue bearing the same kind of unusual tattoo.

"Does it mean something?" she asked, worry creasing her brow.

"It might," Lazaro said, seeing no reason to shield her from his world. But he would bring her into that part of his life slowly, after they returned to Rome. If she would be willing, that is. "We need to talk about what's happening with us, Melena. About our bond."

She turned her head on the pillow, looking away from him. "You shouldn't have done it. You didn't need to come back to save me."

"Yes, Melena, I did." He reached out, catching her chin on the tips of his fingers. He brought her gaze back to him. "Do you think I could've left, knowing that you were in danger? I feel you in my blood now."

"I'm not your obligation, Lazaro. I won't be your burden or a regret you'll carry around forever."

"No, you won't," he agreed solemnly. "But will you be my mate?"

She stared at him for a long moment. Then slowly, she shook her head. "No. No, I can't do that. You're only saying it because your honor compels you to."

He swore a harsh curse. "Melena, listen to me. See me. I know you can read my intent, so open your eyes and hear me out. I love you. I want you in my life, by my side. Forever, if you'll have me."

"What about everything you said before? You didn't want another mate under your protection. You didn't want that responsibility ever again."

He blew out a bitter laugh. "And as you so accurately pointed out for me, I was being a coward and an idiot."

"I don't think I said you were an idiot," she murmured, looking up at him from under her long lashes.

"Well, I was. And as soon as I realized that, I came after you."

"Because you were worried about me. You knew I was in danger and your blood wouldn't let you stay away without trying to help me."

"No, Melena. Because I love you." He stroked her cheek. "And because I realized the only thing worse than loving you and dreading that I might know the pain of losing you in the future, was the idea of losing you now. Before we've even begun to know what we can have together."

He leaned over her on the bed and kissed her tenderly, deeply, with all the love in his ageless heart. "I love you, Melena."

"And I love you," she whispered. She held his gaze, her own so open-hearted and trusting, it took all of his control to keep from crushing her in a fierce embrace. "You've saved my life three times now. If I'm going to be your mate, that means you're going to have to let me save you sometimes too."

"Oh, love," he murmured. "Don't you know? You already have."

Acknowledgments from the Author

Several years ago, my editor at Random House forwarded me an email from a reader who'd just discovered my books and then tore through the entire Midnight Breed series in a matter of a week. Those are my favorite kinds of emails, and what made this one even more special was it came from the wife of a bestselling thriller writer whose books I also happened to love!

What a thrill and an honor it is to now call the lovely Liz Berry a dear friend, and a wonderful colleague. I'm delighted to be part of the 1001 Dark Nights collection with this novella in my Midnight Breed vampire romance series. My thanks to Liz, MJ Rose, Jillian Stein, my fellow authors and friends in this collection, and everyone else working behind the scenes to make the project possible. Can't wait to do it again next year!

Heartfelt thanks, as always, to my family, friends, and colleagues, and to my readers. None of my books would be possible without all of you!

With love,

Lara Adrian

About Lara Adrian

LARA ADRIAN is the *New York Times* and #1 internationally best-selling author of the Midnight Breed vampire romance series, with nearly 4 million books in print and digital worldwide and translations licensed to more than 20 countries. Her books regularly appear in the top spots of all the major bestseller lists including the *New York Times*, *USA Today*, *Publishers Weekly*, Indiebound, Amazon.com, Barnes & Noble, etc.

Lara Adrian's debut title, Kiss of Midnight, was named Borders Books bestselling debut romance of 2007. Later that year, her third title, Midnight Awakening, was named one of Amazon.com's Top Ten Romances of the Year. Reviewers have called Lara's books "addictively readable" (Chicago Tribune), "extraordinary" (Fresh Fiction), and "one of the best vampire series on the market" (Romantic Times).

With an ancestry stretching back to the Mayflower and the court of King Henry VIII, Lara Adrian lives with her husband in New England, surrounded by centuries-old graveyards, hip urban comforts, and the endless inspiration of the broody Atlantic Ocean.

Connect with Lara online:

Website: http://www.laraadrian.com/

STROKE OF MIDNIGHT
A Midnight Breed Novella
By Lara Adrian

Coming October 13, 2015

Born to a noble Breed lineage steeped in exotic ritual and familial duty, vampire warrior Jehan walked away from the luxurious trappings of his upbringing in Morocco to join the Order's command center in Rome.

But when a generations-old obligation calls Jehan home, the reluctant desert prince finds himself thrust into an unwanted handfasting with Seraphina, an unwilling beauty who's as determined as he is to resist the antiquated pact between their families.

Yet as intent as they are to prove their incompatibility, neither can deny the attraction that ignites between them. And as Jehan and Seraphina fight to resist the calling of their blood, a deadly enemy seeks to end their uneasy truce before it even begins….

Also from Lara Adrian

Midnight Breed Series

Masters of Seduction Series

Phoenix Code Series

LARA ADRIAN writing as TINA ST. JOHN

1001
DARK
NIGHTS

THE FLAME

NEW YORK TIMES BESTSELLING AUTHOR
CHRISTOPHER
RICE

1

CASSIDY

The first sheets of rain pound the parked cars and filigree ironwork all around her with enough power to give off spray, forcing Cassidy Burke to hurry for the cover of the nearest balcony.

When she starts to run, the giant rolls of tapestry in her arms slide back and forth, giving her no choice but to launch into what her best friend Shane would probably call "a *Cirque du Soleil* move," a desperate sideways and backward dance intended to keep the whole precarious assemblage of outstretched arms, toile-patterned fabrics, and slippery plastic coverings from slamming to the wet sidewalk.

It works, thank God; her balance is back, and just in time. No such luck with her bangs. When she puckers her bottom lip and tries to blow them out of her eyes, they remain sealed to her forehead, her hair soaked to its roots.

For several days now the French Quarter has been in a drowsy, post-Mardi Gras slump, but the heavy downpour sends it into a coma. She's the only pedestrian in sight, which makes her feel like the only human east of Canal Street. And now she's trapped, all because some silly vendor scheduled his delivery for the week before when she'd told him specifically the shop would be closed. But it's not Leonard DeVille's fault she walked to the UPS store without an umbrella or a raincoat. Still, parking is a nightmare on these narrow streets, laid as they were in the age of horse-drawn carriages, and she knew she'd need both arms free to carry the shipment back to the little gift shop she's owned for two years.

Two-and-a-half-years, she reminds herself, keenly aware, once again, that ever since she became a business owner she's tended to round down her every accomplishment, as if no achievement of hers will be good enough until Cassidy's Corner is out of the red and fulfilling Internet orders from all over the world. *Then* everything will be better; *then* she will earn the respect of her husband's fellow architects at Chaisson & Landry, men and women who currently see her as nothing more than a housewife with a love of long novels and a codependent friendship with her gay best friend. And *then* she will never have another insecurity in the world. Ever.

If she's not careful, this cruel, self-defeating line of thought will wash away her ambitions with the speed and ease of the rain sluicing through the gutters overhead.

She's not a teenager anymore. She has no business blaming others for the terrible pressure she places on herself at the start of every workday. And if she doesn't watch herself, she'll make it Andrew's fault, too. If he weren't so driven and successful, she wouldn't feel the need to compete. And if he weren't so goddamn handsome, then she wouldn't constantly feel like she didn't deserve him, that other women were whispering things behind her back, things like, "What'd she do to land that one? Does it involve splits?"

It is fear that tricks her into seeing the blessings in her life as obstacles. It is fear, plain and simple, that twines its black fingers through the love and respect she has for her husband, pulling it apart until its strands look like chains. And nothing good in her life has ever come from treating fear like a teacher.

Worse, these thoughts are just painful distractions from uncomfortable, everyday realities. Owning a business is a lot harder than she thought it would be. That's the long and short of it. And it's just easier to indulge paranoid fantasies than it is to balance the books, conduct bi-weekly inventories, and stay abreast of trade conventions where she might find that rare, expensive specialty item that will snag the attention of a tourist from Atlanta or a Garden District housewife wandering the Quarter after brunch at Galatoire's.

And then there's what happened during Mardi Gras.

Cassidy screws her eyes shut to keep the memory at bay. For a split second, she worries the effort might launch her from her body, causing her to drop the rolls of tapestry after all. To anyone peering at her through a nearby window she probably looks like she's suffering from a crippling phobia of rain, what with her furrowed brow and her rapid, shallow breaths lifting her soaked blouse. How could they possibly know she's trying not to feel the dizzying, seductive caress of her husband's breath against one side of her neck and her best friend's lips against the other?

Stop it. Everything's fine. Stranger things have happened during Mardi Gras. You're lucky it wasn't— She's at a loss for how to finish this thought. Worse? Better? Are they one and the same when you find yourself on the verge of surrendering to a threesome with your husband and your best friend?

When the smell hits her, she assumes she's having a stroke. Isn't that how it works? Burnt toast. That's what people report smelling in the moment before an artery gives way or one side of their body goes limp.

But while there is a light, toasty quality to the aroma filling her nostrils, it's more like a top note, and the smells beneath it are multiplying. In her mind's eye, she sees the petals of a blossom falling away and wonders if that's exactly what's happening; if the rain has pummeled a potted flower somewhere nearby with enough strength to peel it apart until its central bud is unleashing raw, earthy scents that are blending with the oil in the gutters. But there are no planters nearby, not on the window ledges or front steps in either direction. Maybe on the balcony overhead...? No, that's probably not right either. These smells are not of the earth. These smells are...*men*.

She cackles at the thought. Ridiculous! But it's there. And not just any men either—*her* men.

Her men? Insane to think of them in that way! Her husband, maybe. But not Shane. Not proud, gay Shane, with his endless series of casual boyfriends. It doesn't matter. Whatever title she bestows upon them, their combined essences have somehow joined her on this tiny island of dry sidewalk amidst the storm.

Here is her husband's familiar musk, tempered by a sweeter scent that reminds her of baking bread. It makes her see the dark rings around his nipples and the smooth sweep of his tan, muscular inner thigh where she loves to rest her hand after sex. Then another, less familiar set of aromas intrudes, a lighter bouquet she was accustomed to smelling from a safe distance until a few nights before. Shane is sweet olive with a hint of earthy vetiver, both of which make her see his blue eyes and the gentle angel's press in his upper lip, the startled expression he gave her after their thrilling and forbidden kiss. A kiss he gave her, in part, because her husband put his hand on the back of his neck and made him do it.

How could her efforts have backfired so badly? She tried to dispel the shocking memory of their—she wants to call it a *mistake* again, but the overpowering smells haven't waned and for some reason they make it impossible for her to hold fast to the judgment-filled word.

In her effort to forget that night—not a night really, just a few minutes before they were interrupted—she has summoned the smells of it. The smell of them. *Together.* What other explanation could there be?

The wood plank sign hanging above the entrance to the courtyard across the street is brand-new, Cassidy is sure of it. It looks weathered and old but so do the signs for most of the shops in the Quarter, and often because they've been treated to look that way. She has to squint to make out the logo, a vague outline of something that's been carved into the wood and painted gold. A flame, a tiny candle's flame, and beneath it the words, *Feu de Coeur.* She has only a few years of high school French behind her, but she thinks it means *fire of the heart*.

For a few seconds, she's convinced the sign is another piece of some elaborate hallucination. But the tiny gold flame and the store's prim French name can only mean one thing—a candle shop. And thank God, because it's an explanation. She's not having a stroke or some out-of-body experience. And she's not suffering from madness induced by almost taking an insane sexual risk with the two men she loves the most.

It's a candle shop. That's what she smells.

The rain has lessened, but not enough to justify walking across the street toward the courtyard's entrance without fear of damaging the tapestries in her arms. Still, she won't be convinced she's not crazy or delirious until she sets foot inside the shop itself.

The courtyard is home to a tiny coffee shop, a gurgling fountain, and riots of banana trees erupting from dirt squares that reveal what fragile cover the brick floor underfoot gives to the wet soil. At first, Cassidy thinks the tinny sounds of 1920's jazz are coming from the coffee shop where a gaggle of excited, rain-soaked tourists, speaking rapidly in some foreign tongue—German, she thinks, or Swedish—have gathered around an assemblage of cast-iron tables and chairs.

She's wrong. The music, a spirited counterpoint to the rain's steady patter, is coming from the candle shop she's never noticed before now.

A sign just like the one over the courtyard's entrance hangs above the tiny shop's front door. From a few feet away, she can see the rows of identical candles lining each shelf in the front window. The glass containers are so large she could pick one up in both hands and her fingers would just barely touch around its circumference.

The smells get stronger as she approaches the shop's front door, and now that she's laid eyes on what is most likely their source, it's almost impossible to believe they contain essences of her husband and best friend. Whatever oils are mixed into these dark treasures, they've simply stirred memories deep within her. That's all—fresh, not-yet-buried-enough memories.

It would be intolerably rude of her to carry the dripping rolls of tapestry inside, and she fears leaning them against the front door would be just as inconsiderate. So she tries propping them against a column a few feet from the entrance, and is still jostling them into balance when a male voice behind her says, "You can bring them in if you want."

The man is handsome in a delicate, fine-boned way. He polishes the fog from his glasses with the edge of his vest while studying her casually at the same time; his lack of nervousness at her sudden presence suggests the confidence of a storeowner. Even in a neighborhood where people have a tendency to dress as if they've walked out of another era, there is a particular otherworldly elegance to his silk vest and tailored linen slacks.

"Oh, I wouldn't! They're soaked," she says.

"They're beautiful," he responds with a smile.

"Are they? I guess. Sure. I—I'm Cassidy Burke." She grimaces and jerks a shoulder in his direction to indicate she'd like nothing more than to shake his hand if her arms were free.

With another comforting smile, the man closes the distance between them and takes the wet rolls of tapestry from her arms before she can protest. She hates the thought of him dampening his immaculate outfit. But before she can stop him, he's upended all three rolls and placed them just inside the front door of his shop.

Inside, a thick Oriental carpet covers the hardwood floor, and the shelves along every wall are gleaming, varnished mahogany that matches the burnt-umber glass containers holding each candle. But the closer Cassidy looks at the candles, the more she can make out shades of purple amidst the brown. Is the wax one color and the glass containers another? Are the two shades working together to create an effect of syrupy, luxuriant darkness?

There's no counter or register, just a little desk pushed into one of the back corners where she spots a pile of receipts and a calculator. Several wheels of brightly colored ribbon are pinned to the wall above. The store's centerpiece is a round table with a black marble top and serpentine supports lined with flecks of ivory that curl upward like jeweled snakes united in the effort of holding the table's central column upright. There's a huge vase of yellow flowers, and beneath it a silver tray with a candle just like the one on the shelves. Only this one is lit, and the smells wafting from it have caused her face to flush. They're causing something else to happen as well, and she hopes, she *prays*, the store's owner hasn't noticed. But the rain has soaked her from her head to toe, turning her blouse into a wet napkin over her fiercely hard nipples.

"Cassidy?" Shane asks. His tone is full of yearning, but she can't answer him back. Her head is spinning. Her heart is racing and there's a voice in her head that keeps crying, It's happening! This is happening! *And she can't tell if this voice sounds joyful or if it's screaming words of warning. The way Shane strokes her breast feels hesitant and awkward at first. But then she realizes the little slips of his fingertips across the fabric of her blouse and bra have a purpose; he's searching for her nipple, searching for one of the seats of her deepest pleasure.*

They're best friends, have been since they were kids. She's never kept a secret from him, and he's never asked her a question she couldn't answer. But now...but now... Somehow just saying his name in response or saying "Yes, I'm here," *will feel as good as saying,* "Keep going. I want this. I've always wanted this so much."

Her husband's tongue traces a path up the opposite side of her neck, swirls beneath her earlobe. Then his hand slides up her thigh, squeezing—encouraging— and he takes her earlobe gently in his teeth. She shudders. Her sex ignites as if she's been penetrated and—

"Cassidy's Corner," the man says. "That's your shop, isn't it?"

Amazing how such a gentle voice could snap her back into the present so quickly. "It is," she says quietly. Her cheeks must be crimson.

"Lovely place. I've been in a few times. Of course, I'm not sure if you remember. Nor would I expect you to, what with the foot traffic around these parts. And it's possible the other lady was behind the register at the time."

There's no trace of New Orleans, or anywhere southern, for that matter, in his impeccable pronunciation. His manner of speaking is refined and utterly devoid of any regional accent, like a British actor who has trained himself for American television.

"Clara?"

"Yes. That was her name. Clara. Two C's—Cassidy and Clara. What a charming name that would make!"

"Maybe. But I can't afford to give Clara a cut of the profits, so I'll stick with Cassidy's Corner."

"Indeed," the man says, laughing gently. "I'm Bastian Drake. And now that your hands are free…" He extends his, and even though it feels rude, she studies it briefly before taking it. There doesn't appear to be a single line in the man's palm. Does he spend his evenings soaking his hands in some kind of essential oil? Or maybe he uses those silly gloves Shane tried to get her to sleep with every night until she woke up one too many times with one of them on her forehead and the other halfway down the covers, a slimy trail of moisturizer in its wake.

When she shakes Bastian's hand, she's afraid he'll be able to detect the arousal in her. Something about this fear makes her feel as if she's doing something morally questionable. She wonders if lingering in some tiny, otherworldly little shop with a beautiful man who appears to have stepped out of time constitutes some kind of infidelity. She feels a warm familiarity for Bastian Drake, but no desire—no *lust*. It's thoughts of her own husband the candle before her has stirred. That's all.

Oh, if only that were all, she chides herself. *If only it was only your husband you were thinking of right now.*

"Cassidy?" *Shane asks again. She's loves the halting sound of his voice, the gentle plea. He's always been a man of impulse and action. He is rough with other men, rough with everything—keys that jam, doors that get stuck. But with her, he has always taken his time and asked for permission. But never has he asked to do something like this.*

"Cassidy?"

Her best friend's breath against her neck, his hand on her breast, her husband gently kneading her thigh and nibbling her earlobe—when she tries to speak under the delicious assault of these pleasures, all that comes from her lips is a long, ragged sigh. And that's when Andrew grabs the back of Shane's neck. Before Cassidy can say her best friend's name, his lips have met hers, his tongue has slipped inside her mouth, and even though his throaty grunt sounds startled, he's rising up off the bench to meet the full force of her kiss, his hand leaving her breast and cupping the side of her face for the first time…

"Mr. Drake?"

"Yes, dear."

"What is *in* this candle?"

He smiles. "I believe the question is, what *isn't* in that candle?"

"A riddle. I see."

"Perhaps, but not quite," he says, laughing again. "It's probably not the best business practice to put it quite this bluntly, but I'm not your average candlemaker."

"I didn't know there was such a thing as an *average* candlemaker."

"Good point. What I mean to say is that in other stores you'll find various groupings of scents. Florals on one shelf, spices on another. Not here. Here, every candle is unique."

"Interesting marketing," Cassidy says.

"Perhaps, in that it involves faith."

"Faith?"

"Not in the religious sense, necessarily. But from my perspective, I must have faith that a particular scent will find the customer it needs to find."

"How often does it work?"

"It appears to be working right now," he says.

"May I?" she asks, fingering the edge of a label that folds over like a gift card.

Bastian Drake nods. She lifts one edge and reads the message written in calligraphic script inside:

Light this flame at the scene of your greatest passion and your heart's desire will be yours.

A shudder goes through her. She's not sure if it's fear or desire or both, but the innocent sounding invitation combines with the transportive effects of the scent. Suddenly she finds herself setting the candle back on the tray slowly and with a trembling hand.

"Take it."

Bastian Drake is next to her suddenly. His smooth, pale hand has closed over hers. The candle's glass base is frozen inches above the silver tray. She braces for a waft of his breath, but none comes. Indeed, the man gives off no smell at all. Where he held the dripping wet rolls of tapestry against his chest just minutes before, his Oxford and silk vest are smooth and dry.

"I can't…"

"Why not?" he asks.

"It's…." *Too much*, she wants to say. All of it is just too much. Its heady smells, the depth of feeling it stirs within her. It's the aromatic equivalent of a bittersweet song played on a lone violin, and each note animates a desire she would like to stay dormant, the desire to once again be at the center of the raw, animal passion of the two men who own her heart.

Bastian Drake's hand still rests atop her own. The candle's base still hovers inches above the silver tray. The flame is small, but it flickers steadily. It's hard to accept that such vivid memories of such raw desire can emanate from such a tiny, insignificant spark in the universe; a spark that doesn't waver in the drafts blowing through the shop's front door.

"My darling," he says quietly. "Take it from a man who passed up

far too many gifts in his life. There is no virtue in ignoring your heart's desire. To deny it, perhaps, is a noble thing, if it will hurt others or betray a trust. But to ignore it is to condemn yourself to a lifetime of darkness."

They're standing so close now that if she turned to face him their proximity would seem inappropriate. Too intimate. But what could be more intimate than the words he just spoke into her ear? When he releases her hand, it feels as if a pressure wave has lifted from her arm. Before she can refuse his gift again, Bastian lifts the candle to his mouth, blows out the flame, and turns his back to her.

"This candle is yours!" he says brightly.

"How will I carry it? I—"

"I'll have someone bring it to your shop before the close of business."

"Mr. Drake, I'm not sure… How much is it? I know what rents are like around here and I don't expect you to—"

Bastian pulls a flattened gift box from a stack behind his desk. "Consider it a gift from one proprietor to another." But he won't look into her eye as he prepares the gift in question.

She'll risk offending him if she puts up any more of a fight, that's for sure.

The skill with which he fashions an elaborate, four-leafed bow out of turquoise and purple ribbon is as disarming as everything else in his shop. But the quickness of his movements suggest he just revealed more about himself than he expected to. Or maybe he thinks the sooner he gets her out of his store, the more likely she is to take the candle.

"The rain seems to have let up. I'd be a gentleman and help you carry those rolls back to your store but unfortunately I am a one-man operation."

"Of course. No. That's fine. Thank you. Mr. Drake, I'm sorry. But I'm just not sure if I should—"

When Bastian Drake finally looks her in the eye, Cassidy's first thought is that a passing car has bounced reflected light off the store's front window and it slid across Bastian's face. But they are facing the inside of a courtyard, not the street. Perhaps a bird flew by outside, or perhaps it's exactly what she doesn't want to believe it was. That some swell of emotion, some insistence within Bastian, caused a bright gold pulse to illuminate both of his eyes so briefly but so completely she's been rendered slack-jawed and frozen.

"Please," Bastian says quietly. "I insist."

Cassidy is surprised she can pick up the rolls of tapestry from where Bastian leaned them against the doorframe. She's surprised she can move her arms, or her legs, or her head. She expected to be hypnotized. She expected time to stand still or jump forward, because in films and T.V. shows that is what happens after someone bears witness to something as inexplicable and impossible as what she just saw. She isn't frightened, just hollowed out.

Is it possible to feel the thing they call suspension of disbelief toward your own life? Because as she hurries from the store, that's exactly what she feels. Between the candle's strange power and the inexplicable illumination within its maker, Cassidy Burke feels suddenly ready to believe anything.

2

"So it's a day for gifts, huh?" Andrew asks.

Cassidy is in the storeroom fashioning small blossoms out of the tissue paper she's just stuffed into a gift bag. Seconds earlier, Clara brought her the store's portable phone and tucked it between her ear and chin so she could continue working with both hands. Now her only employee is back behind the register, making cheerful small talk with their third customer of the day, a doctor from Birmingham who is about to plunk down three hundred dollars for an antique porcelain plate featuring an etching of St. Louis Cathedral.

"A day for gifts?" Cassidy asks. "I don't understand."

"Clara says some guy sent over a candle?"

"Oh. Yeah. That."

"Don't go breakin' my heart with some secret French Quarter love affair, Mrs. Burke," her husband says in a pronounced Georgia drawl.

He knows full well whenever he plays up the accent of his youth, Cassidy's lungs and thighs tend to open at the same time. Most of the Louisiana accents Cassidy grew up with sounded more East Coast than Deep South. Andrew is a native of Atlanta who fell in love with New Orleans, and her, during his undergraduate years at Tulane.

"You're the only man in my life, Andrew Burke. You know that."

She's issued this stock response time and time again over the years. This time it strikes a false note. The only sounds for the next few seconds are the steady rustle of her fingers molding tissue paper. *The only man in my life—except for that guy you made me kiss a few nights ago.*

Remember him? My best friend?

Made her kiss him? That was hardly a fair description. It's not like she put up a fight or asked him to stop.

"So…the flowers?" Andrew asks.

"They're beautiful, as always."

"Yikes. I'm not boring you, am I?"

"No, I'm just busy right now, sweetie."

"I meant the flowers, Cassidy. My gestures of affection? I don't know. You sound less than thrilled."

The steady deliveries of lilies, lavender, and purple tulips have been far more than gestures of affection, she's sure of it. Every day since his Mardi Gras mischief, some new jaw-dropping bouquet has arrived just after lunchtime. And while they certainly make Cassidy's Corner smell better, they're also adding to her dread that the three of them—she, her husband, and Shane—did something dangerous, the consequences of which are somehow irreversible.

Her husband must be feeling a similar anxiety. He has ravished her the minute she's walked through the door every night since she's gone back to work, securing her in his powerful embrace, rattling off a series of politically correct questions ensuring her consent. Then, in the comfort of their bedroom, and their living room, and their front hallway, he's deployed all of her favorite perks: some ice cubes here, a silken wrist tie or two there, and always the intent and studied perfection with which he can devour her sex for what feels like hour after blissful hour. By the time he's done, she's too spent to bring up their little moment of weirdness at The Roquelaure House. (Even after spending most of their lovemaking wondering what it would be like to have Shane's lips and fingers join her husband's dutiful ministrations.)

"So any word from Superboy?" Andrew asks. He gave Shane this nickname when they were still in college, after Shane walked face-first into a sliding glass door at their beach house in Bay St. Louis. "The other night, you said you'd been texting him and he's been…"

"Ignoring me. Yeah. I remember."

She also remembers how quickly Andrew dismissed the topic when she did.

Probably sleeping off his hangover 'cause he spent the rest of Mardi Gras on Bourbon Street. Andrew's brusque response suggested he wasn't ready to talk about what they'd done together. So she dropped it. But she still doubted that's how Shane spent the remainder of the holiday.

Her best friend didn't party like he used to. Not since he'd moved out of that ridiculously overpriced condo in the Warehouse District so he could start investing some of the money his parents had left him. He'd also earned his real estate license and traded in his shiny little Boxster for a sensible Jeep Grand Cherokee more suited to driving clients around the city.

But Andrew's remark wasn't completely off base. For years, Shane was the twist of lemon in their Diet Coke; the guy who brought a bottle of Maker's Mark and some party hats to the hospital room after Andrew's hernia surgery. There had also been a few uncomfortable conversations about which one of Shane's friends was an appropriate guest at their more formal parties. (Gatherings of Andrew's fellow architects were not always the right setting for perpetually stoned tarot card readers who had never met a piercing they didn't like and porn star/dancer/models who had a tendency to go-go dance on any flat surface after consuming two beers.)

But those days were over. Shane Cortland was no longer a portal through which French Quarter eccentricity occasionally made flashy appearances in the midst of their buttoned-down, Uptown lives. These last few months the guy has seemed as career-focused and uptight as she and Andrew have been since graduating college. Cassidy couldn't remember the last time she'd accidentally awakened Shane with a mid-morning phone call on a weekday.

More importantly, Shane was not the one who got all three of them blasted on Kir Royales at a crowded Mardi Gras party at The Roquelaure House. Shane was not the one who steered them to an isolated bench before initiating a make-out session that had rendered her the white-hot center of their dual, drunken passion. That distinction belonged to her husband, Andrew Burke. And if the irony in that fact wasn't enough to make her head spin, Shane, the guy who'd spent most of his twenties seducing as many attractive gay men as he could (and a few straight ones), seemed to be more freaked out about it than either she or her husband.

Or so it seemed, if the smiley-faces, LOL's, and various other emoticons he'd been using to dismiss her text messages could be taken as evidence.

Was Shane, like her, lying awake most nights wondering what would have happened if they hadn't been interrupted by that drunken couple who had come stumbling down the garden path?

Does Shane remember feeling what she saw before it all came to an abrupt end—Andrew stroking the back of Shane's neck while he guided Shane's lips to his wife's mouth? *Her* mouth!

Jealousy should flood her at the memory of this physical intimacy between her husband and another man. Not a delicious heat on both sides of her neck; a heat that flows effortlessly across her cheeks, her lips, even her brow, without a single needle of fear dragging in its wake.

It's here, somewhere. She can't smell it. But she's sure it's to blame. *"Clara!"*

The older woman's face appears around the curtain between the storeroom and the shop. "Yes?" she asks tightly.

"Where's that candle?"

"Up here, under the register. Would you like me to bring it back?"

"No, no. Just leave it up there. And…" Cassidy isn't quite sure what she wants to say next. *Be careful?* With a candle that doesn't weigh more than a pound?

"And what?"

"Nothing. I just wanted to make sure it was here."

"Sure," Clara finally says. "Okay."

"Cassidy…" Her husband's voice trails off. She knows that tone, pregnant with a sense of duty. And he just brought up Shane; she can feel what's coming. Her heart is racing faster than it did when Shane's hand kneaded her breast while Andrew's tongue traveled the nape of her neck.

"We should probably—"

"I need to go, sweetie. There's just a lot going on here right now."

And it's all going on in my head, but I can't talk about it. Because I'm not going to say I didn't want it, and I'm not going to pretend like I don't want more. But I'm terrified it will awaken something in you that I don't understand, something you've never acknowledged. Something I won't be able to control. As for me…?

"Sure, well, when you get home, maybe?" he asks. "You'll be home around six, right?"

"Around then. But wait—" Grateful to be off the hook if only for a few short hours, Cassidy reaches for her iPhone and opens her calendar. "Eight o'clock," she says, when she sees the appointment. "The Preservation Council's letting me set up a table at their luncheon but I have to get in there tonight so I'm not in the caterer's way tomorrow."

"Sounds good. Where are you setting up?"

The Roquelaure House. She bites back a quiet curse. *Well, if that isn't just the most—*

"I'm not sure yet. Clara has the info. Anyway, it should only take an hour or two."

"Sounds good," Andrew says suddenly. "I'll probably swim a few laps or something."

If she's not careful, the thought of her husband's muscular back slicing through their pool, powered by tan, sculpted arms, will have her as dizzy with desire as her visit to Bastian Drake's shop.

"Good. Glad someone's using the pool," she says. *Huh? What is she—his mother?*

"Yeah. Bye, babe. Tonight…"

"Yes. Tonight."

Unsure of what these final words even mean, she hangs up.

The tissue paper blossoms she's been forming with her hands look more like triffids than flowers. She feels like she just lied to her husband in a dozen different ways, none of them individually terrible. But in combination, they are enough to convince her she has to do something. They have to talk about what happened or they have to—

"Clara!"

"Yes."

"Can you bring me that candle?"

A few seconds later, Clara appears, the candle in both hands. She's grimacing. Cassidy has snapped at her twice now for no good reason—both times in front of a customer—and she's preparing to apologize when Clara sets the candle down with a loud *thunk*.

"Smells like pond water," Clara groans, then she picks up the customer's gift bag without being asked.

So it's the smell of the candle she hates.

Cassidy takes a whiff.

It's all here, just as it was that afternoon: vetiver, baking bread, musk—and *men*, there's just no other way to say it. *Her* men. And to Clara this all smells like pond water? One more suggestion that whatever happened inside of Bastian Drake's shop was as fundamentally strange as it felt.

Clara hovers. Cassidy feels the woman's stare as she lifts the label on the side of the glass container.

Light this flame at the scene of your greatest passion and your heart's desire will be yours.

"Remind me to take this with us when we go set up tonight," Cassidy says.

"Suit yourself, boss," Clara says.

Then the older woman is gone in a rustle of tissue paper and Cassidy is alone, staring down into the dark and inviting swirl of the candle's wax.

* * * *

"Are you sure?" Clara asks for the second time.

They're alone inside The Roquelaure House. The tables and chairs for tomorrow's luncheon were set up prior to their arrival. They fill the house's vast double parlor, but they're missing tablecloths and slipcovers, their exposed plastic and wood frames a stark contrast to the sparkling chandeliers and heavy, puddling drapes.

"I'll be fine," Cassidy answers. "You can go, seriously. I just need a few more minutes and then I'll lock up."

The display table for Cassidy's Corner is tucked into one corner of the room, next to a giant étagère filled with the Roquelaure family's pink and white china collection. The tablecloth she and Clara picked matches the china's color pattern almost exactly. She hopes this will make up for how small the table is.

Margot Burnham, the Preservation Council's iron-fisted chairwoman, insisted Cassidy employ the most unobtrusive presentation possible. Hence the small table, the limited collection of sale items, and a tent-sign so tiny and modest it looks like it should be reminding people not to smoke. Should Clara wander from her post tomorrow, it's likely the ladies of the council will stroll right past the spray of silver-plated mirrors, antique picture frames, and candles far smaller and less powerfully scented than the one from Bastian Drake, which is sitting on the floor next to one leg of the table, still inside the gold bag in which it arrived.

Over the years, Cassidy has attended countless fundraisers and parties inside this perfectly restored landmark home. The two-story Greek revival on St. Charles Avenue has also been used by dozens of television shows and movies, most of them stuffed with unbearable clichés about the city; constantly circulating trays of mint juleps, Cajun accents thicker than any you're likely to hear outside of the swamp, contemporary housekeepers dressed in the outfits of plantation slaves.

"Is everything all right, Cassidy?"

"It's fine. I just wish she'd let us bring a bigger table. But I guess it blends into the room in the end. Right? I mean, I can see Margot's point. She doesn't want it to look like we've crammed the entire store into her luncheon."

"Sure. It looks great. I'm just not that crazy about leaving you here by yourself."

"Oh, that's sweet, Clara. But really, I'm fine."

A streetcar passes, its low rumble echoing through the house's large, empty rooms, most of them vast warrens of shadow beyond the halos cast by the chandeliers overhead.

"Listen," Clara begins. "I just need to say there's a reason David and I spend Mardi Gras in Florida now. After a while, it gets so crazy."

"Clara, I'm not sure I understand…"

"I'm sorry, it's none of my business. But you've just been so in your head since we got back. And then all the flowers—I mean, I know you two went to all the parades and a bunch of parties. I thought maybe in all the wildness something might have, you know—*happened*."

"Oh, no! That's sweet of you. But we're fine. I promise."

Wow. Not winning any Oscars for that *performance.*

It's awkward at times, being the boss to a woman twice her age, a woman who worked as a substitute teacher at Cassidy's high school. But never more awkward than it is right now, the two of them staring at each other expectantly, Clara gently chewing her bottom lip and absently rubbing the knuckles on her right hand back and forth across her neck.

"So he's meeting you here?" Clara whispers.

"Andrew's at home."

"No. Not Andrew…"

"Then *who*? Wait—you think I'm meeting *another* man here?"

"Oh, I don't know, Cassidy," she cries. "You've just been so strange!"

"Clara, I'm not cheating on my husband!"

"Well, it's such a beautiful house, Cassidy, and there are so many events here. I would hate for you to associate it with something you'd regret later."

She approaches Clara with her arms out. And in an instant, she's turned her half-hug into a single, steering arm clamped around Clara's upper back. She guides the woman toward the kitchen. "Clara, it is *so* sweet that you're this concerned for me—and for Andrew, and our marriage. But we're fine. Really. Everything's fine. And the event tomorrow will be fine, too, if you just go home and get some rest."

And maybe some wine and half a Xanax too, if it'll help you mind your own business.

"Are you sure?"

No. I'm not sure of anything *right now except I have no plans to cheat on my husband. Unless we're counting, you know,* candles.

"Yes. Of course."

At the back door, Clara gives her one last pleading look. "Text me when you get home. Just so I know you're safe."

"Of course, sweetheart. Of course."

She shuts the door as gently as she can, but it still feels as if she's slammed it hard enough to rattle every window in the house and seal herself inside for eternity.

3

ANDREW

We'll get through this, Andrew Burke thinks.

He soaps his hair frantically. The spray sends punishingly hot water sluicing down the hard ridges of his muscular back.

A little pain is good, he thinks. A little pain will help him forget the frosty phone call with his wife. And it's not like the water's scalding him. It's just hot enough to distract him from the terrifying prospect he might have destroyed his marriage.

If we got through that mess with Joe Lambert's secretary, we can get through this, I'm sure of it.

After all, what could be worse for your marriage than a beautiful woman in your office who won't take no for an answer? A woman who stops you in the parking lot and won't let you get by without forcing her to move—which, oh, by the way, means forcing you to *touch* her; a woman who makes things at work uncomfortable to the point of excruciating, leaving you no choice but to tell your wife about the situation because you don't want her finding out from someone else, and because you're a good husband and a good husband doesn't let a zone of secrecy grow around a beautiful young woman who can't take no for an answer.

All told, it was a six-month ordeal demanding constant uncomfortable conversations with Cassidy, his boss, and even a few lawyers when the woman threatened to make a false accusation against him. But at the end of the day, Andrew got through it without doing anything he might regret someday, all without having some chest-thumping meltdown over the fact that sexual harassment also happens to men and he was one of them.

He also didn't give in to temptation in the first place. It was easy to lose sight of that fact given how long the ordeal dragged on. It was also more than he could say for his old frat brothers, most of whom were in the process of breaking their own marriages.

Andrew, on the other hand, was a good guy. Better yet, he was a good husband. Why should those titles be revoked just because of a few minutes of crazy at some party?

Well, for starters, douchebag, *you actually* did *give in to temptation this time. So what if the temptation* involved *your wife? It was still—*

—still what? He tries to answer himself. *Forbidden? Hot? Inevitable?*

Thirty seconds.

That's how long he planned to spend in the shower. Just a quick rinse to get the product out of his hair, then a nice brisk swim to get the blood pumping. But he's been soaping his head now like a parent trying to delouse their child. Which is stupid because he barely styled his hair at all that morning.

When he'd first started working at Chaisson & Landry, he'd been an every-day-is-casual-Friday guy. Then Cassidy suggested to him that slacks, Oxfords, and a side part would probably earn him a little more respect from his colleagues, most of who are at least five years older than him. But every time she hands him a new tube of her favorite molding paste, she reminds him not to leave the stuff in when he goes to bed. Something about breakouts, she says. Letting the stuff smear across his face during a cross stroke probably isn't the best for his skin either, he figures, so he makes it a habit to wash his hair whenever he's about to hit the pool.

Truth be told, Andrew couldn't care less about his skin, which wasn't prone to acne even when he was a teenager.

No, what matters most to him is that his wife took the time to find the brand that smells the best, that she makes it a point to leave her book club early so she can pick up a replacement for him when he's running low. He doesn't want her to stop doing either of these things because he knows the smallest indicators of love can be the most important, the most lasting, and he figures the way to guarantee this is by following her grooming instructions to a tee so she can see how much her little ritual means to him.

Like now. For fifteen minutes. When she's not even home.

This is nothing, he thinks. *The whole thing. Just a little Mardi Gras...* He's still trying to complete this thought when he catches his own reflection in the steam-splotched mirror beyond the shower door. He's hard as a rock within seconds, a tendril of soapsuds dripping from the bobbing, glistening head of his cock.

Dude! Getting wood over your own reflection? Seriously?

But he stops laughing when he realizes what's really got him boned. Lately, it's become a trend, this *whole not seeing himself when he looks in the mirror* thing. Instead he sees the unconcealed lust that lights up Cassidy's eyes, and then Shane's, when they both catch an unexpected glimpse of his nearly nude body.

His instinct is to flick the suds away with one hand. But he knows if he so much as grazes his dick with his pinky he'll be instantly stroking himself to that hot but haunting memory from their trip to Bay St. Louis over Memorial Day weekend. A memory he's done his best to suppress for a year now, until a few too many Kir Royales at The Roquelaure House brought it bubbling to the surface.

A peaceful day at the Mississippi Coast, with the clapboard house bathed in the deep orange light of late afternoon and his family down at the beach (or so he thought). Just him, a nice long shower, and Ol' Blue Eyes crooning out of the surround speakers in the front room. Andrew was so sure he'd had the run of the place he decided to dance through every room as he toweled himself off, badly singing along with *That's Life*, before he barged in on Cassidy and Shane sipping coffee at the kitchen table while he polished his butt with the towel, his cock and balls swinging in the air in front of him.

The whole thing was a regular crack-up, for sure. They teased him about it for weeks, even nicknamed him *Mississippi Tarzan*, a nod to his terrible, off-key Sinatra impression.

But before the giggling and the friendly name-calling, there'd been a moment he didn't quite have a name for. A moment when his wife and her best friend had looked up from their coffee cups and surveyed his heat-flushed, naked body in the exact same instant. The combination of desire in their stares caused a stirring in his groin so powerful and immediate that by the time he spun from the room, the towel he was holding over himself like an embarrassed little boy hid an erection as throbbing and relentless as the one he was sporting now.

It wasn't the first time they'd done it to him either.

Freshman year at Tulane, the day he'd met them both. *Officially* met them both, after quietly stalking Cassidy for about a week. He just had to know more about the small blonde girl with the big, beautiful eyes, the one who listened quietly during their Intro to Philosophy discussion group before asking a single, precise question that would usually send the T.A. for a sputtering loop. One afternoon, he found Cassidy and some blond guy sitting together on the green, play wrestling and joking around with such casual intimacy he thought they might be boyfriend and girlfriend and he'd just come within inches of making an ass of himself.

But he wasn't sure, so he took a seat a few yards away and pretended to read *Slaughterhouse Five* while he studied them.

After a while, he thought they might be brother and sister. Twins, even, given their tendency to move in synch with one another. Suddenly, the guy sprawled out, hands raised skyward so Cassidy could grab on to them both while she tried to kick her legs up into the air behind her. Their giggling attempt at flight ended when her delicate body thumped down onto his lanky one. Entwined like rag dolls, Cassidy and Shane laughed so hard they briefly drowned out the repetitive strumming of the amateur guitarist a few yards away.

Then, as they righted themselves and brushed the grass off their clothes, Shane flicked both wrists before running his hands slowly through his soft, blond hair with the luxuriant tenderness of a woman showering in a shampoo commercial. *That dude's gay, even if she doesn't know it yet. Even if he doesn't know it,* Andrew thought. *I'm in!*

And then they both looked at him for the first time, the same look that would laser through him years later over Memorial Day weekend.

Their half-smiles fading as desire consumed their amusement, their eyes widening with lust as they examined him shamelessly from head to toe. And in that moment, they radiated a kind of *oneness* that suspended everything he knew to be true about labels or gender.

He had trouble putting a name to it, which was a shame, because he knew if he could name it, he'd be able to dismiss it, and if he could dismiss it, everything would be simpler. But there was no forgetting the way it made him feel; rock hard in his briefs, so hard he wanted to reach down and adjust himself—he couldn't; the back of his neck so hot suddenly he thought he might have moved into direct sunlight without realizing it—he hadn't. And then there was that delicious, anticipatory pressure in his temples, like a head massage from a guardian angel, the same anticipatory pressure he feels whenever Cassidy whispers something naughty in his ear during a stolen moment at dinner with his colleagues.

Sometimes he compares it to that scene in *Ghostbusters* when they all crossed the streams of their ray guns to defeat the evil spirit living atop that old New York apartment building. Only he was no monster, and the raw hunger their combined gaze filled him with was nothing like defeat. It made him feel powerless, for sure, and helpless before a desire he couldn't name. But not defeated.

Defeated is how he feels now, as he drip-dries in the cooling air outside the shower stall, willing his cock to go down.

He's not gay. There's no doubt about that. Sure, there'd been those late nights of sleepover experimentation with Danny Sullivan back in high school. But that was different. They'd been best friends since they were kids. And yes, parts of it had been fun, even hot. Mostly the parts where Danny's racing heart and shivering body made it clear he'd always wanted to explore Andrew's body more than he'd let on. In those moments, making Danny happy had made *him* happy, happy enough to get him hard. And keep him hard. And really, how hard was it to get a man hard anyway?

He'd shared all of this with Cassidy during the full-disclosure period of their engagement. When she wasn't shocked, he was shocked. He was even more shocked when she told him every guy she'd been serious with had eventually admitted to fooling around with another guy at some point in his life. But none of that mattered now. What mattered was that nothing about his late nights with Danny Sullivan had left Andrew with a burning desire for other men. In fact, he couldn't remember a single moment when he'd laid eyes on a strange man and thought, *Damn, I'd hit that.* But just to be sure, he's checked out some gay porn sites, studied a few hardcore photos to see if any of them trigger a part of him that's blossomed over the past few years. Everything he sees there leaves him cold. For starters, there are no women at all, and that's a big problem, and secondly, none of the guys are Shane. None of the rutting, passionless couples he studied have the combined charge of his wife and her best friend.

It's simple, really. Or at least it should be.

Shane is the other half of the woman he loves more than anything in the world. When he was younger, this fact used to make him insanely jealous. Now it fills him with hunger. Because now he's almost as close with Shane as he is with his own wife, except for the part where they…

How could he *not* feel something for the—

Andrew slams both palms down on the side of the counter, hard enough to knock a bottle of contact lens solution onto its side.

Get in the goddamn pool before you rub one out in the bathroom like some horny teenager.

4

CASSIDY

The bench looks the same, perhaps a bit lonelier given there isn't a party in full swing nearby.

Cassidy is surprised her fevered memories didn't exaggerate its slender design or its cast-iron frame. It's in the same spot, beneath the spreading branches of a massive oak, hemmed in by a small perimeter of banana trees sprinkled with uplights. String lights from the party still wrap the oak tree's branches overhead, but they're turned off and probably have been since the event.

The few floors she can see of the condo high-rise next door are dark. A streetcar lumbers by on St. Charles Avenue, its clatter muffled by curtains of foliage. There are scrapes and rustles from the plants nearby, but the loudest sound she hears is the sound of her own breathing as she tugs a matchbook from her pocket.

The candle rests on the flagstones at her feet. She's taken care to stuff the tissue paper back inside the bag and set it aside. She's about to light the match when another thought hits her and suddenly she's pulling her phone from her pocket and setting it on the bench beside her. Now that she's done it, she's not exactly sure why. Maybe she fears the candle will poison her; a few less inches between her and 911 might mean the difference between life and death. It did nothing of the kind while it burned inside Bastian Drake's shop. But this is different. Now she's poised to obey the instructions written on the candle's tiny card; she's going to light the thing at the scene of her greatest desire. Who knows what will follow? The whole thing could be a terrible trick.

Maybe, but how much help could dialing 911 be if it is?

Enough stalling.

The match doesn't light after three strikes.

A little act of self-sabotage, she thinks, bringing a matchbook instead of a cigarette lighter. Then the match lights suddenly. Before she realizes what she's done, she's brought the flame to the candle's wick and shaken the match out with one hand.

She sits back, preparing herself for—she's not sure what exactly. Perhaps a stronger tide of the candle's intoxicating scents?

But what comes next is something else entirely.

At first, she assumes a cloud of delicate, luminescent insects have flown into the halo of the candle's growing flame, circling like lazy moths. But the candle's surface also glitters and glows. The wax looks like a piece of thin mesh stretched over a puddle of hot lava. And the swirl of particles above are fed by little sparkling flecks that drift up into the air, determined embers driven by an impossible, upward wind.

The smell hits her next, far more powerfully than what she experienced in Bastian Drake's shop. She is instantly, fiercely moist. A great wave of pressure has forced her back against the bench. But with this pressure comes pleasure as well, coursing through her with such intensity—it feels as if several sets of hands are caressing her, massaging her body from head to toe. Her nipples are aflame. She can hear herself laughing, the kind of high-pitched, nervous laughter that usually rips from her when Andrew surprises her in the shower with a forceful tongue and a throbbing erection.

As she catches her breath, she sees the golden column above the candle's flame. It towers over her now, at least seven or eight feet tall. Its celestial light bathes the undersides of the thick oak branches above. The glittering particles swirling madly through the body of the column take on distinct shapes.

Bare shoulders, the napes of necks, faces turned away from her— three apparitions appear inside the candle's impossible golden halo, each one worshiping the tiny flame below. As they gain definition, they rise higher toward the branches above, sloughing off more sparkling tendrils.

Their naked backs are turned to her as they spin. Cassidy sees a woman and two men, their heads bowed, their foreheads practically touching, as if they're all staring down at the candle that gave them impossible life. It looks as if they've been placed on a hovering, spinning dais composed of the candle's smoke and light. They rise higher into the air, growing in size beyond any proportion that could be called human.

Then, some threshold is crossed. Suddenly all three figures lift their heads and gaze into each other's eyes. But there is only a deeper shade of gold beneath their eyelids. And while their expressions are serene, the display should be terrifying, this sudden life force that courses through figures that were mere silhouettes just seconds before. But the woman in the trio doesn't look like Cassidy at all, and for some reason Cassidy is too startled by this fact to be afraid. The two men don't look like Andrew and Shane either. She doesn't recognize their faces at all.

Both men peel away from the column before Cassidy can study them further. They lose their human shape, columns of glittering gold, rocketing skyward, the branches slicing through them as they ascend.

Cassidy is alone with the remaining sprit. Almost as tall as the oak branches overhead now, the woman has tuned her placid smile and glittering gold eyes on the bench—and on Cassidy. If it wasn't for that peaceful, welcoming expression, if it wasn't for the warm and welcoming color of her impossible form, Cassidy would be terrified of this…*ghost? Spirit? Angel? What is it?* Who *is it?*

Cassidy has no time to decide. Suddenly, the ghostly woman's face collapses. Her body becomes a single sheet of glittering gold that crashes silently over Cassidy's body like snow in a downdraft. A shuddering orgasm that's been building in her since she first lit the candle explodes inside of Cassidy. She hears her ecstatic cries as if from a distance.

When the darkness returns, it feels as if a blanket has been drawn around her. In contrast to the blinding wash of gold, the garden's ordinary shadows suddenly feel like a jarring supernatural event.

Cassidy shudders and gasps. It feels as if the woman's spirit moved right through Cassidy from her toes to her head, gently dragging her fingertips along every pleasure center in Cassidy's body during the trip.

A stab of guilt tries to pierce the layers of bliss, but fails. An orgasm without her husband? It's not like she was truly alone. Not really. Two other spirits just rocketed skyward, very much like the one that has left her thighs in spasms. But she knows right where they're headed; she's sure. Or *who* they're headed for. The idea that Shane and Andrew may soon share in this intense, ethereal delight fills her with joy. Not just joy, but also a wild and unrestrained hunger for them both.

5

ANDREW

With each stroke, Andrew hopes Cassidy will return home before he exhausts himself. When she does, he'll pull her into the pool by one arm, peel her wet blouse from her breasts with his teeth, grip her hips and squeeze just a little so that her back will arch and her sex will rise up toward him through the bathtub warm water.

In the meantime, he risks temptation swimming in the nude like this. Each time his bare ass breaks the surface, each time water rushes across his cock and balls when he turns off one wall, he's tempted to seize his erection in one iron-fisted grip and finish himself off. But he's saved himself for his wife every night since the incident. It feels like the right thing to do. But it wasn't easy. Especially during long days at the office, when the memory of her gasps as Shane devoured her neck would have him eyeing the only private bathroom at the office to see if he could steal a few minutes of self-release.

Not then, not now. *Save it up, mister. Stroke. Breathe. Stroke. Breathe. Find another word for stroke. Breathe. Find another word for stroke, seriously. Now.*

Their swimming pool is a long, slender rectangle that takes up most of their backyard. To keep the neighbors from getting an eyeful, he left the pool light off. Same story with the row of gas lanterns along the brick wall that hides the neighbor's house.

Hé installed the lanterns himself, which required him to learn more about gas-powered fixtures than he thought it was possible to know. So when the lantern closest to him pops to life like a miniature Olympic torch, the wrongness of the sound halts Andrew in mid-stroke.

They don't come on one at a time. That's not how they work. You hit the switch, and then you wait a few seconds while clicking sounds indicate that gas is being fed down the length of the line. Then all four lanterns flicker to life, gently, sometimes so weakly it looks like they're not going to catch. Never one by one, never with a loud, obtrusive *pop*.

But it happens again. And again. And again, until all four lanterns are lit. An impenetrable radiance fills the glass chambers of each lantern. He can't see the tiny gas flames anymore, just a bright halo of yellow. Fingers of bright gold have emerged from each lantern. They rise snakelike through the night air before converging at the end of the swimming pool, just above the steps to the shallow end. Their movement is steady, determined, unswayed by the humid breezes rippling the pool's surface. Treading water, his rasping breaths the loudest sound in the entire yard, Andrew watches as the glistening, gold tendrils of material he doesn't have a name for form the vague outline of a...*ghost?*

But ghosts are not made of gold.

They're also not real, jackass.

Then the smell hits him and Andrew Burke thinks, *I'm dying. That's it.* And then he thinks, *Dying smells incredible, like every delicious scent I've ever discovered on my wife's body, the floral notes of her perfume mingling with the scent of her juices, a combination of lilac—and candle wax.*

The figure standing at the edge of the swimming pool is not human. Human beings aren't hollow. When they open their eyes, you see pupils and irises, not golden sclera. It's a *he*, for sure, with handsome, defined facial features, but the rest of his identity is a mystery, and wondering about his identity seems insane given that he doesn't have a real body, just a glittering, shifting suggestion of one.

The figure goes down on one knee, lowers one glittering finger toward the surface of the water. But his face is angled upward. Andrew realizes this spirit, this golden ghost, is staring at him expectantly.

"What are you?" Andrew whispers.

He's answered by another burst of intoxicating scents. Only now there's a new smell—it's vaguely sandalwood, earthy. It's Shane. It's both of them, essences of Cassidy and Shane entwined in this impossible bouquet. It washes over him with invisible, overpowering force. The shimmering figure is still down on one knee. One glittering finger, shedding tiny particles of bright gold like delicate embers, still hovers just above the pool's surface.

Waiting, Andrew thinks. *Whoever,* whatever, *he is, he's waiting for my permission.*

"Yes," Andrew whispers.

Instantly, the golden ghost touches one finger to the water. Andrew watches in astonishment as two glittering snakes of light travel under the surface of the pool.

The nearer they come, the more his cock hardens. Then suddenly he feels himself lifted as if a whale is passing directly under him. Pleasure courses through his body from head to toe. The smells of Cassidy and Shane fill his nostrils; they bathe the back of his throat.

Andrew realizes the sparkling gold tide hasn't moved around him and that can only mean one thing.

No, not possible, he thinks. *I'd be in pain, terrible pain. At least, at first. Cassidy's never even put a finger down there.* And it was so fast, and there was no resistance. But the shimmering gold waves are gone now, and there's nothing outside of him that could be sending these waves of radiant pleasure through his limbs. It feels like he's being massaged by several sets of hands. Two sets of hands. But the pressure inside of him is something else altogether; it moves to a different, more powerful rhythm. It was outside of him before, but now it's inside. His balls have drawn up so tightly he knows exactly what's coming next, but he can't believe it. Only one person's ever been able to do this to him with the touch of her hand. Well, two people, if you count *him.* But never, not once, has he ever been able to do what's about to happen without touching—

His seed jets from him. He's so dumbfounded he looks down into the water, tries to watch it happen with his own two eyes. But it's too dark and the orgasm is so powerful it knocks his knees out from under him. When he throws his head back, his scalp touches the water's surface. Will the pleasure literally drown him if he doesn't get control? He flails madly to right himself. But even as he tries to stand firm in waist-deep water, he bellows.

And then, when his breath returns, he gasps the word that was on his lips that night at The Roquelaure House, that word he didn't have the courage to voice then as he watched his wife and her best friend kiss passionately for the first time, a word that filled him with excitement and arousal and satisfaction as he beheld the oneness, the beauty of Cassidy and Shane together at last.

"Mine," Andrew whispers.

6

SHANE

"Are you out of your goddamn mind, Shane Cortland?"

"Easy!" Shane hisses.

"Easy, *nothing*."

Samantha Scott glances around the restaurant to see if her outburst attracted attention from any of the other diners. It did, but she doesn't seem to care. Before Shane can catch his breath, she's back to glaring at him as if he just informed her, a few bites too late, that her shrimp remoulade has magic mushrooms in it.

The wall behind her is covered in antebellum portrait paintings, Civil War muskets, and a succession of gilt-frame mirrors reflecting the crowded dining room. It's certainly an ironic image; the sight of his black transgender friend, decked out in a banded plunge-V Donna Karan dress the color of Merlot, sitting before a collage of artifacts from the slave days. On any other night, Shane would get a kick out of it. But right now, he's so surprised by Samantha's anger he can barely look her in the eye.

Perry's occupies both floors of an old French Quarter carriage house and its expansive courtyard. The most popular tables are outside next to the fountain. But they're sitting inside because he wanted to talk over things with Samantha in peace. He didn't expect the place to be quite so packed. It's a weeknight, after all. He also didn't expect

Samantha to pitch an epic fit when he told her about a wayward moment of sexual fluidity with Cassidy and Andrew.

His veal cutlets swim in some of the finest beurre blanc he's ever tasted. But the slow burn of Samantha's anger incinerates his appetite. She's crossed her hands over her lap like a prim schoolteacher. She's shaking her head and taking deep, dramatic breaths through both nostrils. The only thing she's missing is a Bible and a fan.

"Lord, girl," he mutters. "Calm down."

"She is your *best* friend," Samantha whispers.

"Yeah, well, maybe *you'll* replace her."

"He's her husband."

"Yeah, and *he* started it. Not me. So lighten up already."

"Dark and proud, thank you. It's the one thing God got right the first time."

"Samantha, of all people, I didn't think you would be so judgmental."

"Oh, what? You think 'cause I'm your trans friend that I'm just gonna sit back quietly while you juggle knives? Listen here, Shane. Secrecy is not how the heart operates. Take it from someone who used to wait just a *little* too long to tell a boyfriend my birth certificate said *Stanley* Scott!"

"Wait. What *secrecy*?"

"You telling me you never made a move on Cassidy's husband?"

"*Never.* Oh my God! Andrew? Are you kidding? He's her husband."

"He's also *fine!*"

"Yes, and I love Cassidy and I have a conscience, thank you very much."

"So it just came out of the blue? Andrew has too much to drink and suddenly all three of y'all are making out together at some party?"

"Basically."

"*Basically?*"

How can Shane answer this? *Out of the blue...* They're his best friends, for Christ's sake. He can't think of any two people in the world he's closer to, can't think of anyone who knows more of his secrets than Cassidy *and* Andrew. But there was one secret they didn't know. Samantha didn't know it either. Because no one knew. No one except for the couple he'd shared that furtive afternoon with, on the carpeted floor of the penthouse he'd just sold them. Because they hadn't just been a couple. They'd been his clients, for God's sake. And the three of them had done a helluva lot more than make out for a few minutes on some garden bench.

His cheeks are so hot he contemplates pressing some ice cubes from his water glass to his face. Now he's struggling to sift through a decade's worth of memories looking for signs that this—he still doesn't have a name for it; they're all too scary—was always in the making, the eruption of a long-denied passion that's simmered just below the surface for years.

But Shane is sure of one thing -- Andrew Burke isn't gay.

He's known his fair share of closet cases. Cassidy's husband isn't one of them. No man can fake the adoration and desire Shane sees in Andrew's dark eyes every time he looks at his wife. There's nothing hesitant or forced about the way Andrew grabs Cassidy right in front of him, tickles her on the hips until she collapses in hysterics onto the sofa and smothers her with kisses until she blushes fiercely and asks him to stop because Shane is still in the room.

Did Andrew shoot him a look in those moments Shane didn't read properly? An invitation Shane read as a dismissal?

Hell, maybe that was Andrew's real motive the other night. He wanted Cassidy right then in the middle of the party, and he couldn't be bothered to get rid of Shane first.

But that's absurd! Andrew had been focused on something else entirely during those feverish moments; Cassidy and Shane together, in front of him, under *his* direction. Andrew had wanted those things badly enough to risk the closeness and connection the three of them had built together over the years.

And where had Shane's focus been? On Cassidy, on the feel of her opening, on her racing heart as she offered him the one thing she's never given him, and on Andrew's firm, forbidden grip on the back of his neck.

And maybe that's where he should be looking for signs. Not with Andrew, with Cassidy. Forget Mardi Gras and The Roquelaure House. Try that afternoon last year, when he and Cassidy had been snuggling together on her bed, marathoning reruns of *The Golden Girls*, and suddenly the supple curve of her bare foot had seemed so inviting he dragged one finger across it.

When she squealed and drove her body back against his, something about her vulnerability and frenzied pleasure had started an engine inside of him, an engine that drove him to take her in his arms and flip her onto her back. But once he got her there, once he had her squealing and panting and trying to bat his hands away, a voice in his head had said, *Stop*. The same voice he'd heard that day freshman year of high school, when the sight of Brent Parker running sprints on the football field, his tan skin glistening with sweat, had made Shane feel hungry and tingly and sad all at the same time, a voice that had said, *It's wrong. You don't like any of the names for that feeling. So quit it!*

Years later, he didn't release Cassidy as quickly as he'd looked away from Brent Parker that day. But Shane had been just as startled, just as frightened. It felt like he'd stumbled across a deeper current of desire. But that wasn't right either; it had swept him up without warning. There were unexpected consequences to touching Cassidy in certain ways. How could that be? There was more there, it seemed. And he thought he'd reached a point in his life where if it seemed like there was *more* there with someone, you leaned into it, you didn't pull away. But this was Cassidy. This was different.

"Order a drink," Samantha says and slams her own down onto the table to get his attention back.

"I don't drink during the week."

"Start. It'll clear your head."

"Is this your way of apologizing?"

"For what?"

"For accusing me of trying to break up my best friend's marriage."

Samantha rolls her eyes, lifts a bite of shrimp to her mouth and chews delicately while she considers her response.

Shane's appetite has yet to return.

"You remember Jonathan Claiborne? Used to be a waiter here?"

"Of course I do."

"You hooked up with him, didn't you?"

"I did."

In the past, Shane would have enjoyed remembering his no-strings-attached assignation with one of the hottest guys in New Orleans. Jonathan's smooth, rock-hard body bearing down on his, the man's skillful tongue swirling down the length of Shane's cock, suckling his balls before tickling the edge of his taint while he looked up to gauge the depth of Shane's blissful response with a broad, bright-eyed smile. But now these lustful remembrances do nothing to lighten Shane's current mood.

Or maybe it's something else, he wonders.

When compared to the raw passion he unleashed with Cassidy and Andrew, his hookup with a notorious local hottie seems sort of sweet, but not all that appetizing. Like taking a bite of hard candy and realizing you're chewing more plastic wrap than sugar.

"He's missing," Samantha announces.

"Jonathan?"

"Yep. No one's heard from him for weeks."

"I thought he quit."

"He did and rumor has it he got another job. As a call boy."

"Are you joking?"

"Nope. Quits his job here, starts selling what he's got, suddenly no one knows where he is."

"And you think something bad happened to him?"

"I think he needed to be *special*. I think it wasn't enough for him to just be gorgeous and get up every morning and go to work. He had to wring every last dollar out of what God gave him because being Jonathan Claiborne wasn't enough. He had to go turn himself into the spice in someone's cocktail. And now who knows what happened to him 'cause of it?"

"You're losing me here, Sam."

"Fine. Let me put it this way. I didn't transition so that I could be some magical drag queen people hire for parties. I wanted a foundation of truth under me, Shane. And you deserve the same. What is it those two call you again? The twist of lemon in their Diet Coke?"

Those two, he wants to say. *These are my* best friends *we're talking about.* But instead he says, "Don't be their little experiment. Is that what you're saying?" he asks.

"Exactly. 'Cause when they're done with you, they'll have each other. And you'll have no one."

As usual, Samantha's given eloquent voice to an internal monologue that's tortured him for days. But her logic crashes up against the fevered memories of those few minutes of shocking intimacy like waves hitting a seawall.

Of course everything Samantha has said makes sense.

But for Christ's sake, he's not some random gay dude Cassidy and Andrew met in a bar on vacation and tried fooling around with just to, you know, *see*.

He's their… He is their… Has there ever been a name for what the three of them share?

Third wheel is an insult, and it does nothing to describe their evident love for him. *Friend* is too safe and it barely suggests the amount of time they spend together. And *best friend to a couple* doesn't exactly trip off the tongue.

What's the word for two friends who show up on your doorstep at a moment's notice when the guy you've been dating for a few weeks freaks out on you because he's been sneaking shots of GHB behind your back and you were too dumb to notice? What's the word for the couple who doesn't ask a single question when you call them in a terror, your voice shaking, because you just made the guy leave and on his way out he turned over a lamp, kicked the door frame a few times, and then after you slammed the door behind him, he punched it not once, but twice, and shouted, *I'll be back, you little bitch?*

What do you call the sense of total safety Shane felt as Cassidy sat with him on the sofa, her hand in his, while Andrew checked all the windows and locks in his apartment? How can he describe the feeling in his heart—a lightness, an openness, a kind of lift—when neither one of them rushed out the door that night, when they offered to stay with him until he managed to relax? And when he woke up the next morning entwined in their arms, his nose resting in the nape of Andrew's neck while Cassidy's head rested on his chest, the early morning news playing on a television they'd all fallen asleep watching—what should he have called the combination of hunger and satisfaction the dual press of their bodies awakened in him?

If you're looking for a sign of what was to come, he thinks, *looks like you just found it.*

"Bathroom break," Shane mutters.

"Shane!" Samantha calls after him, regret stitching her features.

He waves at her to indicate he's okay, but just this small gesture makes his head spin.

Shane locks himself in the bathroom, grips both sides of the porcelain sink, and tries to get some breath into his lungs.

He's desperate to blame someone for his current confusion, someone besides Andrew or Cassidy. Or himself. And the only people he can think of are that damned couple, Mike and Sarah Miller.

They hadn't just been clients of his. They'd been his very first clients, and he'd figured their flirtations had just been meant to put him at ease. That's how nervous he'd been during their first day together, apologizing incessantly whenever his cell phone rang, stumbling over his feet in his rush to open every door.

Relax, kid, their lingering smiles and gentle squeezes seemed to say. *Pretend like we're just the cool parents of one of your friends, and not hard-to-please multi-millionaires looking for their perfect New Orleans getaway.*

Besides, they'd both seemed super conservative, hardly the type to initiate what came later. Mike Miller was a high-ranking former military man who'd made a bundle off defense contracts; the guy was a man's man by any generation's definition, gym built, with a high-and-tight haircut and a handshake so firm it could break a wine glass. So what if he liked to give Shane a little wink whenever his wife wasn't looking? Some straight guys have goofy ways of ending a sentence—it was better than a thumbs-up, right?

While her husband charged his way into each room with intense focus, Sarah Miller seemed to float in behind him on a cloud of Chanel. She sported a lustrous mane of golden hair and a perfectly even, store-bought tan. Each time they met, she wore low-cut, sleeveless dresses so shiny and well tailored they probably cost as much as Shane's Jeep. And then there was that husky voice that gave Shane a fluttery feeling in his chest every time she called him *honey.*

Nerves, he'd told himself. *Don't read too much into anything. It's just nerves.*

Besides, maybe clients were always touchy-feely when they wanted you to find them the perfect condo. He tried to get another agent at the firm to buy into this explanation, but the woman laughed in his face instead. "Are you high?" she barked. "Most clients treat you like you're a waiter who screwed up their order five times."

So he shouldn't have been all *that* surprised by what happened when he met the Millers to hand over the keys to their new penthouse.

As soon as the gorgeous couple took a few steps across the threshold, a long silence fell. Shane took that as his cue to leave. But when he opened his mouth, he saw Sarah Miller's gaze roaming the length of his body with undisguised lust.

"What do you say we really close the deal, honey?"

The line sounded lifted from a porn film. And he didn't think women as classy and elegant as Sarah Miller watched porn films. But he wasn't going to say that out loud, not in a million years. Which was a good thing because he couldn't bring himself to say anything at all.

The last time Shane could remember being so aroused he was a teenager and he'd finally worked up the nerve to download a video of two men going at it. Only rarely since then had he felt this same cascade of devastating sensations. The sides of his face felt tingly and numb. A radiant heat spread through his chest. His heart raced so fast he could feel his pulse beating in his ears. And all they were doing was looking at him. Looking at him like they wanted to devour him. Like they wanted to own him—*together.*

"Oh…" It sounded more like a hiccup than an answer, and the couple before him smiled in unison. Then Michael Miller clamped one hand around the back of Shane's neck and pushed him knees-first to the plush carpet. In stunned disbelief, Shane looked up. Mike gave him a warm, half-smile, and freed his thickening cock from his trousers. And then it was filling Shane's mouth and throat. Dizzy from the depravity of it all, he couldn't remember the last time a man had tasted so good, so forbidden.

He had a few gay friends who'd tried threeways with men and women. They'd all told the same story; the minute the woman laid a tender hand on them, bye-bye boner. But that's not what happened when Sarah Miller ran her fingernails up the back of Shane's neck as he suckled her husband's cock. Lightning bolts of pleasure shot up his spine. And after she sank down behind him and carefully unbuttoned his pants, the light scrape of her fingernails as she stroked his shaft felt deliciously exotic.

Then she was on her feet, staring down at him as he slathered her husband's erection with attention. She looked radiant with desire and power. Was it just lustful gratitude he felt? She had, after all, just given him her husband's throbbing, perfectly sculpted cock. When he ran his hands gently up her thighs, pushing the hem of her dress upward in the process, he told himself it was just to thank her. But when he saw her glistening, exposed pussy, saw that she hadn't worn panties in preparation for this very event, his gesture of gratitude turned to unexpected, overpowering hunger.

His first slow, exploratory sweep of his tongue managed to find her clit right at the end. She let out a cry that was as much surprise as bliss—maybe she didn't expect him to go both ways—then she was grasping the back of his head, guiding him back and forth between her husband's cock and her throbbing folds.

Eventually they tumbled to the carpet, breathless, and in the minutes that followed Shane was their ravenous, oral plaything, the taste of Mike Miller's musk blending with the earthy tang of Sarah Miller's flowing arousal on Shane's unstoppable tongue.

In the few moments when Shane didn't leave them gasping for breath, Mike managed to yank his wife's dress down far enough to free her breasts, sucking feverishly at her nipples while Shane deep-throated his cock. By adding Shane to the mix, the married couple had made their bodies taste and feel new to each other again. When Shane added two fingers to the dance of his tongue across Sarah's swollen nub, her orgasm shattered her, leaving her growling and clawing at the carpet on either side of her spread legs. Then Mike was on his feet, pulling Shane's head back as he furiously stroked himself to the edge. Shane fought the desire to open his lips, to take the man's load into his mouth. But the man was a stranger, and some rules still applied.

And then it was over.

No chitchat. No small talk. Just over.

The married couple dressed as if they'd just been woken up from a nap, both of them practically tripping over themselves to avoid Shane's eyes whenever he glanced nervously in their direction.

There weren't a lot of cleanup options; there was no furniture in the place yet, let alone hand towels. But still, the perfunctory manner in which Mike Miller pulled a roll of paper towels from a cabinet and handed it to Shane so he could wipe the man's cum off his face didn't feel deliberately degrading with the intent to arouse. It felt simply dismissive.

You're excused, kid. Sarah and I will now return to normal, heterosexual married programming.

Shane was no stranger to quick, no-strings-attached hookups with other men; he'd fled from all manner of French Quarter apartments at all hours of the night. But to have a kettle of new feelings and desire set to boil by such a sudden, ferocious explosion of lust, and then be cast out immediately afterward—it was more than he could take. And when he finally made it back to his Jeep, after he fastened the seat belt and stuck the keys into the ignition with a trembling hand, he was astonished to find himself blinking back tears. He couldn't remember the last time he'd cried after sex, but that's exactly what he was doing as the few spots of Mike Miller's cum he'd missed started to dry on his face. The Millers had left him as confused and frightened and vulnerable as a deflowered virgin, and here he was, crying alone in his car like some idiot.

But it wasn't just sex he was crying over. It was something more. An awakening he'd never expected, and at the end of the day, it didn't have much to do with Mike or Sarah Miller.

It wouldn't be like that with Cassidy and Andrew. It would be—

But he didn't finish the sentence. *Wouldn't* finish the sentence. *Could never in a million goddamn years finish that sentence.* It was impossible. It was insane. If his head and his heart felt this scrambled after a meaningless threeway with some clients, he didn't want to imagine how crazy he'd be after—

Cassidy pulled her dress back for him, displaying the most secret parts of herself for him, after Andrew took the back of Shane's head in his grip, giving him permission to taste the cock he's been given only brief glimpses of over the years. After he tasted both of them, together. And then after, the two of them holding him, not handing him a roll of paper towels. Holding him in their arms like they did that night he called for their help against that druggie he'd just thrown out of his apartment.

He slammed the sides of both fists against the steering wheel, hard enough to make the horn bleat.

At least he'd stopped crying.

And that's what he does now, weeks later, in the bathroom at Perry's, slams his fists against both sides of the sink. Only there's no car horn he blows by mistake this time. Just the porcelain basin, and it's a lot harder than his Jeep's steering wheel. But a little physical pain is exactly what he needs to stop him from rifling through his entire sexual history looking for more evidence that he hasn't always been the man he thought he was.

Then he looks up and sees a golden ghost staring back at him from the mirror.

8

Shane makes a sound like he's been kicked in the stomach.

When the edge of the toilet slams into the back of his legs, he realizes he jumped backward several feet. Too many things are happening at once for him to make sense of a single one. Threads of gold dust sail out from the four-foot tall mirror as if the glass weren't there at all, as if the gilt frame bordered a window. Before the ghost vanishes entirely, Shane glimpses its vague, shifting features.

Jonathan Claiborne…

A hallucination, for sure. It has to be! Samantha just mentioned the guy so it sort of makes sense. There was something in his food, Shane thinks. Or maybe the stress of the past few days has triggered some kind of psychotic break.

That's all well and good, he thinks, but how does he explain the two long fingers of gold now circling the artichoke-shaped light fixture overhead? Suddenly the fixture comes free, as if a giant hand just tugged it gently from the ceiling.

Shane's hands fly out to catch it before it shatters to the floor. But the intricate glass light fixture doesn't fall. It floats, descending slowly before it lands softly in his outstretched palms. The scents hit him next, so powerful they distract him from the fact that he's rising off the floor. Baking bread, lilac: the combination is familiar. He is engorged within seconds, gasping with as much pleasure as fear.

He spins in place, several feet in the air, the large light fixture balanced in his open palms by the same otherworldly force that pulled it free of the ceiling. It hasn't broken, this precious, intricate piece of glasswork. The prospect of it shattering at his feet was a greater fear than any he'd ever experienced. But it's being supported now—and *he's* being supported, too, by golden fingers of thick and fluid light. And the face of a former trick, apparently.

As Shane continues to spin gently in place, he sees something in the light fixture's glass leaves. It's them, he realizes. They're barely recognizable, and he can't tell if their faces are somehow being projected onto the glass folds or if the images emanate from within. But it's Cassidy and Andrew.

He's holding them in his hands. They haven't fallen. They haven't broken.

If there's a message to this impossible supernatural assault—*assault* seems like too strong a word given how gently he's being handled, but it's the first one that comes to mind—that must be it. He won't drop them. He won't break them. Some force he doesn't have a name for will support them, encircle them, and enfold them. All three of them.

The light fixture rises from his hands, swiftly but smoothly, as if it's being drawn upward by an invisible string.

Shane watches it pop back into place as smoothly as a button being snapped. As soon as his feet hit the floor, a wave of pleasure courses through him, so intense and powerful he has only seconds to pull his cock from his jeans before he empties his load onto the concrete floor.

He chokes back a cry he's sure will bring the entire restaurant outside to a halt if he lets loose. He's never cum like this in his life, jet after jet, never seen anything like it outside of porn films. And as it shoots from him, the vision he just beheld settles into his consciousness with surprising ease. If it was a ghost, was that its intention, to use pleasure to make Shane teachable and open?

You can have them both. Hallucination, spell, or haunting, whatever it was, that's the only meaning he can ascribe to it, to the delicate fixture balanced perfectly in his hands, and the faces of the two people he loves the most reflected in its crystalline folds. *Andrew and Cassidy. You can have them both and nothing will break.*

9

CASSIDY

The house is dark, save for the sparkling footprints dotting the foyer's hardwood floor. Gold flecks swim in each one, waterborne siblings of the luminescent particles that swirled through the candle's halo as soon as she lit the wick. They have to be Andrew's footprints, but she's shouted his name several times and he hasn't answered.

For the second time that day, Cassidy is soaked from head to toe and questioning the nature of reality.

The rain roused her after she lost consciousness. By then, the candle's glass container was completely empty, as if someone had wiped it clean of every last drop of wax while she'd drifted between sleep and waking, utterly drained by the most powerful orgasm she'd ever experienced.

LSD. Acid. Or maybe that Datura stuff Native Americans use for vision quests. Whatever it is, I'm still feeling it.

"Cassidy!"

She cries out. The front door is still open. Shane stands on the porch, soaked from head to toe. When she sees the tiny gold flakes dripping from his earlobes and the tip of his nose, pooling slightly in the hollows of his eyes, her breath leaves her.

Wide-eyed, his jaw tense, he closes the distance between them. He runs an index finger along her forearm and turns up a fingertip glistening with the same gold particles that highlight his face, that swim in the footprints all around them.

"What's going on?" Shane whispers.

"I don't know," she says, the rest of her sentence trailing off. It feels like a lie.

It *is* a lie. She accepted the invitation written on that note; that's what's happening. She lit Bastian Drake's candle at the scene of her greatest desire and now… and now…

Shane's lips are inches from hers. Rain swirls through the open door behind him. Flashes of lightning turn the branches outside into giant claws. But they don't frighten her. They do, however, seem to send a word of warning: *Stay inside. It's not safe to run. The answer, if there is one, is inside this house.*

"Andrew…" she whispers. "We have to find Andrew."

Shane follows her upstairs with bounding strides.

The master bedroom is empty. When she sees the alarm clock's blank screen, she realizes the power's out. She's about to scream her husband's name again when she sees him in the doorway. He is naked and dripping wet. Streaks of gold outline his nipples. They travel the hard ridges of his obliques and fringe the heft of his cock, which jerks from his sudden arousal. The sight of Cassidy and Shane standing together in the shadowed bedroom makes her husband instantly and powerfully hard. While it's too dark to see his face, she can see his muscular chest rising and falling with deep, sustained breaths. He always breathes like that when he's getting ready to pounce. To lick. To taste. To ravish.

"Get on the bed, Cassidy," he says, his voice low and deep.

Yes. Please. Now. If it's a mistake, I'll blame the candle. I'll blame Bastian Drake. But I want it now. Both of them. Here. Now.

In a flash of lightning, she sees Shane's expression. It's a portrait of astonishment and desire as he looks back and forth between the two of them. An expression just like the one he wore when he kissed her for the first time—not fear, but a kind of dazed wonder that life could suddenly deliver something so unexpected and all-consuming.

When Andrew grips the back of Shane's neck, this visual reminder of their moment at The Roquelaure House enflames her desire. Then her husband says, "Take your panties off, Cassidy," and it feels as if her skin has become a thin layer of radiant heat that can no longer contain the desire coursing through her veins.

Hands shaking, Cassidy unbuttons her skirt, kicks her way out of it. It turns into a brief struggle because she can't look away from what's happening in front of her. Bent at the waist, Shane runs his tongue up the side of Andrew's body, following a slender thread of gold all the way up to her husband's pecs. When he reaches Andrew's nipple, Shane sucks it briefly, loud enough to make a pop.

Her husband's low, throaty laugh is gentle. Shane's desire for Andrew is a feeling on Cassidy's skin as she peels off her bra and blouse, a tingly blanket. It feels like invisible hands have just lightly slapped her thighs, squeezed her breasts. As if she is being tweaked and teased and tested by the newness of what they're about to do, by the delicious danger of it. But there are no golden ghosts in the room with them now. It's just the three of them. And while everything about Shane's posture says he wants to suck her husband's tongue from in between his lips, Andrew teases him, gripping the back of his neck, holding their mouths inches apart.

"You're afraid, aren't you?" Andrew asks. "Both of you. You've always been afraid of how much you want each other. Afraid of how it doesn't fit into a neat little box." Their lips inches apart now, the two men she loves the most seem connected by a current of fearless desire, a current fueled by her exposed sex, by her wild passion for them both. "Well, *enough!* Both of you. Enough already. I've had enough of watching the two of you together."

His voice is a low growl and his wording makes her tense. If Andrew is about to punish them, why is he still stroking the back of Shane's neck? Why is he unbuckling Shane's belt with his other hand?

"All that hunger between you two, and it's got nowhere to go. Not anymore. 'Cause I'm gonna give it somewhere to go. I don't care if I have to fuck you both into loving each other the way you've always wanted to, always needed to. I'll do it. I'll do anything for you two, so why not this? Why not, huh? Get on your knees, Shane. It's time for you to taste my wife."

With a light pop, Andrew unbuttons Shane's pants from behind and slides them down his slender hips. All it takes to send Shane knees-first to the carpet is a light shove. Then Andrew sinks down behind him and starts steering him toward the foot of the bed, toward Cassidy's spread legs. He pulls Shane's rain soaked shirt over his head, revealing his lean torso, his perfectly etched abs, that blend of delicateness and hard edges that for years has held Cassidy in a kind of sustained swoon she has channeled into friendship. Her husband's muscular arms are a delicious contrast against Shane's smooth, pale skin. And while she might be the one sprawled on the bed, immobilized by anticipation and lust, they're the ones on their knees. They're the ones poised to worship her.

Her men. Finally. Both of them. *Her* men.

Dazed, Shane grips Cassidy's feet, one in each hand, squeezes them gently, as if he's trying to make sure they're real, that she's real, that *this* is real.

That afternoon she did her best to block out comes rushing back. They were watching television together when Shane suddenly ran one finger across the arch of her bare foot, and then suddenly he was tickling her furiously, and then just as suddenly he stopped, a hungry look in his eyes, as if he'd awakened something unexpected and powerful enough to carry them off in its grip.

I wasn't wrong. It wasn't just me. He could feel it, too. But we were so afraid, both of us. Because with just the two of us, it would never be possible. But it doesn't just have to be the two of us. It will never just be the two of us.

Andrew nuzzles his lips against the nape of Shane's neck, holds Shane in a vice-grip embrace from behind. But his eyes, like Shane's, are focused on her wet heat, even as he reaches down and starts to tug Shane's soaked underwear down over his ass. Shane's hands glide up her legs. His touch is hesitant at first. But then he adds pressure, exploring her. His fingers press down and revisit the places along her inner thighs that make her gasp and moan. Then they graze the edges of her pussy, teasingly. Again and again and again. Slow, matching circles of sweet torture on either side of her mound.

"Have you ever tasted a woman before, Shane?" Andrew asks with a devilish smile only she can see.

Don't, Andrew. Don't remind him he's never done this before just when he's about to finally—

"Yes," Shane answers.

What? When? If Shane's breaths weren't grazing her clit, she would probably bolt upright from shock.

"Superboy," Andrew says, "I thought we don't keep secrets from each other."

"We don't," Shane whispers. "Anymore."

And then, without a word of warning, her best friend's lips encircle her swollen nub. And as the pleasure arcs through her, she has a mad desire to say his name over and over and over again. She's said his name thousands, if not millions, of times before. She's shouted it across crowded restaurants. Barked it while laughing at one of his stupid jokes. But to say his name now, as he probes her with his tongue, would be to change the very nature of it, to change the nature of *him*, to change the nature of the two of them, together. Not just two of them, she realizes when she feels Andrew squeezing her thighs on either side of Shane's head. The three of them.

What starts as a gentle, hesitant nibble turns into a suckling that makes her cry out. Instinctively, she reaches for the back of his head, for that fine blond hair she's run her fingers through time and time again over the years, wondering each time what it would be like if the rules fell away, if labels ceased to exist. If they could have a moment like this. But before Cassidy can grip the back of Shane's head, Andrew grabs her wrist and firmly drives it to the comforter beside her. This is Andrew's lesson to give. For now, Andrew is in control. After all, he's the one who promised to set them free.

"Who was she?" Andrew asks, his voice thick with desire. He pulls Shane's mouth away from Cassidy's pussy. Shane's chin is lathered in her juices.

"No one. A client."

Jealousy, curiosity, and desire move through Cassidy in a swirl that curls her toes. Then her husband begins to lick her juices off of Shane's chin. His tongue finds Shane's. The two men meet in a passionate kiss, sharing the taste of her, and each other, for the first time. Her husband is more than just a director now. He's kissing another man—*with* her. *For* her. As hungry for the feel of Shane's lips as he is for the taste of her very essence.

"Just a client?" Andrew asks.

"And her husband," Shane whispers.

"At the same time?" Andrew asks.

It feels as if Andrew is reading her mind, asking the very questions she would ask if overwhelming desire hadn't rendered her voiceless and boneless.

"Yes," Shane whispers, and then he licks up her folds, finding her clit at the end with a mad flicker.

"And did you like it?"

"While it was happening, yes." Shane gasps. But he's staring down at Cassidy's wet heat, spreading her lips gently with both fingers, taking occasional, exploratory licks along the inside of her folds. Learning her. Memorizing her. Worshiping her. "But when it was over," he says. *Lick. Lick. Breathe. Lick.* "All I wanted was you." With precision and care, he takes her swollen nub in between thumb and forefinger, rolls it gently, then looks up, studying her face, watching the delicious transformation each wave of pleasure sends through her expression. "*Both* of you."

"Shane…" *Don't ever stop. Don't ever leave. Don't ever be afraid again.*

"Both of you," Shane says again. "Always."

As Andrew's tongue travels the nape of Shane's neck, Shane stares into her eyes, hypnotized by the sight of her laid bare to him for the first time. When Andrew's fingers find Shane's hard, pink nipples, Shane shudders and sinks his teeth into his bottom lip. When Andrew gently sucks Shane's earlobe in his mouth, grips it gently between his teeth, Shane gasps. But even then, even as her husband's ministrations threaten to level him, Shane gazes into her eyes, never once breaking their connection.

She knows exactly what he's feeling, knows exactly the cascades of pleasure her husband can release with just his fingers and his tongue. For the first time, she's sharing this experience with the other man she can't live without, and it feels as if their souls have been unzipped from their bodies. As if the three of them are merging in the air above the bed like those golden ghosts that rose from Bastian Drake's candle.

"Cassidy," Andrew says.

"Yes, baby."

"Are you ready? Are you ready to feel Shane inside of you?"

"Yes…"

"Are you ready to watch the expression on his face when he feels how tight and hot you are? When he feels you clutching at him because you want him so badly? Because you've always wanted him?"

"Yes…"

"Are you ready to look into his eyes while you come?"

"Y-y—ye…"

With a devilish laugh, Andrew releases Shane from his embrace. Suddenly there's a loud crack followed by a sharp grunt. Her husband has just slapped Shane on the ass. Hard. Still shuddering from the delicious pain of Andrew's blow, Shane crawls up onto the bed, pressing down on her suddenly. The combination of submission and aggression coursing through his body makes her open for him like a flower.

"Cassidy…" he says, smoothing her hair from her forehead, lips grazing hers. Has her name ever carried so many meanings in a single utterance? She can hear Shane's astonishment that this is happening, his wonder at the feel and taste of her body. She can hear him asking her for permission. Permission to open her, to enter her. And because the answer is yes, she wraps her legs around his waist for the first time, and in response, his body arches against hers. This time, their kiss is pure abandon. The hesitancy is gone. The fear is gone.

Andrew rifles through the nightstand drawer. The sounds should be a distraction, but they're not. Because she knows exactly what he's looking for, the condoms they used for a while when she had to go off the pill because of some routine tests the doctor wanted her to have.

She's in such a rush to have him inside her she hasn't taken Shane's cock in her hand, hasn't explored him the way he's explored her. She grips it. Shane bites his lower lip, looks down, watches her stroke him with joyful disbelief. Each new touch, each new physical connection made for the first time is like another small tremor beneath that will shift the ground under their relationship forever.

"Wow. Not bad there, Superboy," she whispers.

And her teasing tone lights up his face with a broad smile.

"Want to know another secret?" Shane asks.

"*I* do," Andrew answers. Unwrapped condom in hand, he sinks down behind Shane, pulling him upright by one shoulder.

Once Andrew has righted him. The sight of Shane's dick sliding through her husband's powerful, veiny hands thickens the flow of her arousal.

"After I was with that woman," Shane says in between gasps. "You know, my client..."

"Yeah," she answers, but all she wants to do is kiss him, caress his face for the first time.

"I used to watch your face when you were laughing or eating dessert," Shane says. "I used to wonder if I could make you make those faces if I ever..."

"Fucked her?" Andrew asks. He tugs the condom down the last few inches.

"Or made love to her," Shane says softly, with a hint of childlike innocence.

"Yeah, well," Andrew says. He's got one arm wrapped around Shane's waist, but he's gazing down at her. They're both gazing at her. "I'll teach you how to do both."

Andrew leaps off the bed. The next thing she knows, he's sliding under her, hoisting her surrendered body up onto his, keeping her face up. His throbbing cock presses into the small of her back, his mouth finds the seats of pleasure along her neck, his hands knead her breasts, and his fingers find her nipples.

Shane is frozen, his sheathed cock hard and jerking in the air in front of him. When he senses their hesitation, Andrew draws one knee up in between Cassidy's thighs and uses it to open them further. Suddenly Shane's nose is grazing hers. Their lips are inches apart. He presses into her for the first time. Carefully. Gently. Reaching down and aiming with one hand. Never once breaking eye contact.

Once Shane is buried inside of her, Cassidy lets loose a series of wild sounds, unbidden and unrehearsed, only a few of them becoming words.

"Big…" she whispers. "Both of you…such big…boys."

"*Your* big boys," Andrew growls into her ear.

Shane starts to fuck her with long, slow strokes, allowing her to get used to the feel of him. Meanwhile, Andrew's fingers do a dance on her clit he's learned after years of memorizing the rhythms of her pleasure.

Over the course of their marriage, Andrew has taken her every which way from Sunday, but never quite like Shane is doing now; steady, determined, cupping her face in his hands, studying her, their lips grazing, each attempted kiss turning to gasps of pleasure. She has never cheated. For years it has been only Andrew, but now her body is being discovered again and by the man who already knows and loves every other part of her.

They work together. Her husband's hard body rocks up against her in time to Shane's strokes, his cock sliding teasingly in between the cheeks of her ass. For the first time in her life, pleasure feels like comfort, bliss like safety.

There's still a part of her that's convinced Shane might be faking the whole thing. So when he starts to grunt and pull away from her suddenly, she's afraid he might be flipping out. It doesn't even occur to her at first that it could be something else. Something far more obvious. He slides his condom off and unleashes his seed across her heaving stomach, grasping her shoulder for support. His mouth against her ear, Andrew says, "Yeah, yeah, yeah," over and over again. Encouraging, cheerful—the perfect director, the perfect coach.

And that does it. Together, Shane's pained sounding moans mingled with her husband's full-throated grunts of encouragement send the first wave of ecstasy arcing through her.

When she cries out, Shane cups the sides of her face, rests his nose against her nose, as if her orgasm were a shimmering, radiant thing from which he can draw more strength if they're as close as possible.

Andrew's hand slides between their stomachs, and then he slides a finger coated in Shane's cum in between Shane's lips. The debauched sight makes for a shuddering finish. She is wrapped in their heat and in their strength. Shane's body molds into hers. Andrew strokes her hair, then Shane's. Her shoulder, and then Shane's. He's in no rush to add his own orgasm to the mix but his groans are soft and satisfied too, as if he came as well. And for the first time in a long while, Cassidy is rendered silent by something besides fear, by the bliss of a dream realized.

"Belong to you," Shane whispers.

"Both of us, " she whispers back.

"*Always*," Andrew growls.

10

Cassidy awakens to the feel of Shane's breath against her collarbone and the delicious weight of Andrew's arm around her waist. The comforter slid off them during the night, leaving their entwined, naked bodies exposed to the morning sun. Daylight beats through the bedroom window, falling in a precise, accusing rectangle on their discarded clothes. Andrew usually draws the window shade at bedtime. But they slipped into unconsciousness as soon as Shane and Cassidy were leveled by their respective, toe-curling orgasms.

Were they truly exhausted, or was their sudden, deep sleep another result of the spell?

The spell. It's the first time she's used that word to describe Bastian Drake's candle, and it sends a bolt of fear through her.

A spell means it wasn't real. A spell means it was no different from being in a drunken blackout.

Slowly, she rights herself, gently lifting Andrew's arm off her waist. She scoots down the bed in between them. Only when she's free of the sheets does she look back to see if she awakened them by mistake.

Andrew stirs gently and takes Shane into his arms. By the time she's pulled her robe from the closet, her husband and her best friend are spooning. The sight of them together like this would have filled her with confusion and jealousy weeks before. Now it quiets her fears, fills her with a desire she no longer feels a desperate urge to contain or dismiss. The only thing she's wanted more than to be sandwiched between them, as she was last night, is to see them like this, their delicious physical contrasts entwined. It's as if her sun and her moon have met on the same horizon and their combined radiance is neither night nor day, but something almost otherworldly in its ferocity.

Maybe too *otherworldly. But if it were just a spell, wouldn't it have broken by now? Maybe this is*—her mind stutters before it gets to the word *real.* It happened; that's for sure. And it was good—dizzyingly, delightfully good. But if she's going to call it something *real,* that means something will have to come of it, something lasting. And the only way to tell if that's even a possibility is to find out just what the hell Bastian Drake put in that candle.

Halfway down the stairs she can tell the footprints that greeted her the night before are gone. There's not a single trace of gold residue anywhere on the hardwood floor.

How is that possible? Did they evaporate? Or did they disappear? She imagines them wafting up into the air like smoke while she and her two men slept upstairs. This vision sets her heart racing to fear's beat once again. If the spirits that literally moved the three of them to this place abandoned them this quickly, it doesn't exactly bode well for the future of this... What should she even call it? Threeway? Thruple? *Group possession?*

Belong to you...both of us...always. Were those last words the three of them whispered to each other before postcoital sleep the result of black magic? Her gut twists at the prospect.

Someone is coming down the stairs behind her.

For several seconds, she savors the uncertainty of not knowing if it's Andrew or Shane approaching her with quiet confidence, if it's Andrew or Shane sliding his arms around her waist, dipping his fingers under the flaps of her silk robe and caressing the skin underneath. Is it Shane or Andrew kissing her neck lightly, causing her to sway back and forth on her bare feet within the strong confines of his embrace?

"Are we glad or sad?" her husband whispers.

It's an old line that's turned into an old joke. When he was a teenager, Andrew's mother had been a self-help junkie, constantly modifying her parenting techniques in response to whatever faddish book on child rearing she'd read that week. At one point, she became so addicted to what she called "emotional temperature checks," she started greeting her kids every morning with the same question: *Are we glad or sad, dear?*

She turns to face him, and he takes her face in his hands quickly so he knows she's not trying to pull free, that what she really wants is to stare into his eyes, because her one-word answer requires all the bravery she can muster.

"Glad," she whispers.

"Good," he says with a smile. "Me too."

His lips meet hers. Their kiss is long, unhurried, his embrace so tight he's lifting her onto the balls of her feet.

"What'cha doing down here?" he finally asks.

"The footprints last night. You left gold footprints everywhere and I wanted to see if any were left."

"But they're not," he says.

"No. They're not."

"What does that mean?"

"I don't know yet. But someone does."

And it all comes out of her as she guides him to the living room sofa. She describes her visit to Bastian Drake's strange little shop, the candle with the invitation taped to its side. She keeps her voice to a whisper the entire time; the last thing she wants to do is wake Shane. If she's going to make any sense of last night's threeway, she needs to start by having a serious one-on-one with her husband.

"So you think we only did what we did because of this candle?" Andrew asks once she's finished.

"I think it had an effect, for sure."

"So you're afraid it's not real? You're afraid it was just a spell?"

"I don't know what it was. That's why I'm afraid. But what happened to you last night? Before, I mean. I saw the footprints when I got home, but what happened right before then?"

"I thought it was a hallucination, to be honest. It—*something* came out of one of the gas lanterns by the pool while I was swimming. It was a shape. I think it was a person. But if it was anything, it had to be a ghost."

"A ghost. And it came out of the flame, right?"

"Yeah. But, Cassidy, I don't think it was real. I think it was just a—
"

"It's not possible for three people in three different places to have the same hallucination, Andrew."

"Well, we don't know what happened to Shane."

"Whatever it was, it made him come straight here. And his face was covered in the same gold stuff you tracked all over the floor, the same stuff that was all over my arms."

"Yeah. So?"

"*So?* Andrew, I have to find out what I did to you two. There might be long-term effects."

"Come on. It's not radiation, Cassidy."

"We don't know what it was, and we don't know what I did."

Andrew takes both of her hands in his, leans forward. There's a passionate gleam in his eyes, the same fire he gets when he's defending his political beliefs. For the first time since he's come downstairs, she takes in the fact that he's still naked; still beautifully, unabashedly naked. And still there, still *hers*, even after all the rules they broke together the night before.

"What you did, Cassidy," he says, "what *we* did was something we have wanted to do for years. When I fell in love with you, I fell in love with all of you—every part of you. And Shane is part of you. When the two of you are together you make something so beautiful I don't have words for it. And I've always wanted it."

"So you're in love with Shane, too?"

"It's not possible to be in love with you without being in love with Shane."

"Some people would say that's a bad thing."

"Yeah, well, not me. Maybe another man would have run from it. But the moment I first laid eyes on you together—remember? I'd been trying to find you for days after I met you in class, and then I finally tracked you down on the green, and the two of you…the two of you were…you were the most beautiful thing I'd ever seen."

Tell me his tears are real. Tell me he's not crying because of some damn spell.

"But you're not…gay?"

"Honey, you know the answer to that question," Andrew says, and then he slides a hand up her robe and caresses the inside of her thigh. "But I'm always happy to remind you."

"Is it like Danny?" she asks. "The way you feel about Shane?"

Andrew told her years ago about his only sexual experiences with another man, but they've rarely discussed it since then. She's afraid the mention of it now might send him reeling. But no, her husband appears utterly confident, utterly in control.

"Maybe," he says. "A little. My feelings for Danny…they happened over time. He was my best friend. I loved him so I wanted to make him happy. And it became more than that. It became a *desire* to make him happy. And that desire, well, my whole body responded to it. So yeah, maybe it's like what I feel for Shane now."

Or what Shane feels for me, she thinks. But her husband is still speaking so she gives him back her full attention.

"One thing's for sure," Andrew continues. "I've never looked at a man I didn't know and wanted to have sex with him. It's just not how I'm built. So who knows? Maybe I couldn't have done something like this when we all first met. But it's been years since then, Cassidy. Years of watching you two dance together at parties, years of listening to you two singing off-key to the same crappy songs on the radio."

"Why does it always get back to my taste in music?"

"Because you have really, *really* weird taste in music," he says, smiling. "But you know, Spice Girls aside, you're the most important person in my life, and Shane's the most important person in *our* lives. In the life you and I have together. Can't you see? For years we've been building this, and last night the final piece just fell into place. That's all."

When she doesn't respond, he slides across the sofa toward her, slipping behind her and taking her into his arms. It's similar to the reverse embrace he used to spread her open for Shane the night before. This fresh memory causes her head to spin, her breath to quicken. When the relaxing, narcotic effect of her husband's touch starts to wear off, she says, "I have to talk to him."

"Shane? We both do, I think."

"No. Bastian Drake. If that's even his real name."

"Maybe he's not real at all. Besides, it was just a note taped to the side of a candle. So what if you did what it said? How were you supposed to know what was going to happen?"

"His eyes."

"What?"

"His eyes. In the shop. When he was offering me the candle, when I wasn't going to take it, his eyes—they turned gold. Just like what you saw last night, just like what I saw. Pure gold. That's when I knew something… Part of me went into denial. I knew if I lit that candle at The Roquelaure House, something was going to happen. And I only did it because I was too afraid to come back here and talk about what we did during Mardi Gras."

"You were afraid to tell me how much you wanted it to happen again," he says.

It's not a question.

"Pretty much, yeah," she answers. "But still, the candle. I shouldn't have just—"

Andrew rights himself, cups her chin in one hand and draws her face to his. Their lips are inches apart, but his gaze is intent. "This is real, Cassidy," he whispers. "It's real. We're not here having this conversation because our heads were messed with by black magic. We did what we wanted to do. Didn't we? Wasn't it what you wanted?"

"Yes," she whispers. "But now that we've done it, I have got to make sure we're going to be okay." She kisses him quickly and slides off the sofa.

"Now?" Andrew asks. "You're going to talk to him now?"

"Yes."

"All right, well I'm going with you."

"No. You're staying right here."

"Why?" Andrew asks, dropping his voice to a whisper as he follows her up the stairs.

"As soon as he wakes up, Shane's going to freak. I need you to keep him from running. Do whatever it takes to keep him here."

"*Whatever* it takes?"

"Use your imagination if you have to."

Oh my God. Did I really suggest that?

Yes, you sure did. And if you keep thinking about it and don't start moving, you're going to end up in bed with them both again before you manage to track down Mr. Not-Your-Average-Candlemaker.

"How do you know he's going to run?" Andrew asks.

"He went missing for a week after the three of us made out for five minutes. Last night's gonna have him on the first plane to China."

"This was different, Cassidy."

They've reached the closed door to their bedroom.

"Trust me. He'll freak."

"Because he slept with a woman?"

"Because he slept with someone he has feelings for," Cassidy says. "*Two* someones. Look, Shane acts like he's this big player with no feelings. But that's only because he always keeps his feelings out of it. He never plays with anyone he actually cares about."

"And there's no one he cares about more than us."

"Maybe," she whispers, but everything inside of her yearns for this to be true, yearns to believe it with the same conviction Andrew does. She lifts Andrew's hand to her mouth, kisses the tips of his fingers. When she remembers the way he slid one of them in between Shane's lips the night before, her lips get tingly and her thighs flush. "Maybe," she says again, only this time it sounds more like a sigh.

"Cassidy, do you really think Bastian Drake is dangerous?"

"I don't think he's dangerous. I just don't think he's very direct when it comes to his product. And I have to know I didn't do something that's going to end up hurting the men I love."

At the sound of the panic in her voice, Andrew takes her in his arms again, brings his lips to her ear. "Well, I'm not feeling anything right now that feels like pain."

"An hour, maybe two," she says, returning his embrace. "If I'm not back by then, you and Shane can come down to the Quarter with guns blazing. Start on Dumaine Street between Burgundy and Dauphine. That's where his shop is, if it's still there. If I didn't imagine the whole damn thing."

Her husband's compliance is in his silence. But that's not enough. She takes his face in her hands, brings the tips of their noses together. "In the meantime, you do anything it takes to keep Shane from running again. *Anything*. And when I'm back, we'll figure this out."

"Two hours," Andrew says. "Two hours and then I'll call the cavalry."

"I don't think we're going to want to explain any of this to the *cavalry*."

"I don't care who thinks I'm crazy. I just want you back safe."

He kisses her so forcefully her robe slips off her shoulders. She fights the urge to lift her legs off the floor and wrap them around his waist. She almost loses the battle; she's stroking one of his calves with her right heel, and her hands have turned to claws against the hard ridges of his back.

"Two hours," Andrew whispers.

He opens the bedroom door for her like an attentive valet.

Still tangled in the sheets, Shane doesn't wake up as she tiptoes toward her closet.

11

ANDREW

Andrew isn't sure caffeine will be the best thing for Shane's sure-to-be frayed nerves, but puttering around the kitchen beats hovering in the bedroom, waiting for him to wake up. Besides, he could use some coffee, too. It's his reward for managing to get through a quick shower without Shane sneaking out on him. He's only filled the coffee maker halfway when he hears footsteps on the stairs—pounding footsteps that come so fast it sounds like Shane will be out the front door in another few seconds if Andrew doesn't act right away.

In the foyer, he finds Shane struggling into his shirt while he spins in place, surveying the hardwood floor all around him.

"They're gone," Andrew says.

Shane whirls, wide-eyed. Did he think they'd left him?

"You're looking for the footprints, right?" Andrew asks. "She was looking for them too. But obviously they're not here anymore."

Maybe he won't be in such a rush to leave now that he sees Andrew was waiting for him to wake up.

Or maybe not.

When he takes in the sight of Andrew in only loose-fitting pajama bottoms, Shane blushes fiercely and turns his back to him. Then he punches his left arm through a dangling sleeve and starts buttoning up his jeans as he heads for the front door.

Damn. She was right. He's totally freaked.

"Shane…"

"I'm late," Shane says.

"For what?"

"Work!"

"Cassidy'll be back in an hour. Just hang out."

"I need to go. I've got an open house later."

"Open houses are on Sundays."

"I said *later*, didn't I? Sunday's later. Also, I'm going to drop in on my doctor and make sure I don't have a huge brain tumor that's making me see things."

"Quit being ridiculous."

"You're not a doctor."

"Shane, if it's a brain tumor that makes you see giant golden ghosts that give you amazing orgasms, then all three of us have the exact same tumor. And that doesn't seem very likely, does it?"

The part where giant gold ghosts gave them all great orgasms doesn't seem very likely either, but he keeps this to himself. Give Shane an inch of sarcasm and he'll take a mile, a mile that will have him out the door and out of his grasp.

Shane stares at him. He's managed to put himself together now, but it hasn't improved his mood.

"Ghosts?" Shane finally says. "Last night was about…*ghosts*?"

"Somewhat. I think… I mean, yeah. Sort of."

"Well, alrighty then. I guess that explains everything. Anyway, I'm going to work and if I'm not a blithering idiot by the end of the day, I'll talk to you guys later, after I've had about half a bottle of Grey Goose and maybe a Benadryl or two."

"Sit down, Shane."

"I'm not *sitting down*, Andrew," he says, gripping the knob. "Please. I just need to—"

Shane only manages to open the door a few inches before Andrew's on him. He throws his weight against Shane's, forcing him to shut the front door with his chest.

"Let me go," Shane says. But he whispers it the way he might whisper *Don't stop* or *Yeah, right there. That's the spot.* He paws weakly at the doorknob with his right hand, his eyes screwed shut, breathing hard and fast through flaring nostrils. Andrew can feel the gooseflesh his touch sends across Shane's skin.

"Jesus, " Andrew says. "You're really terrified, aren't you? She's right. When was the last time you had sex with someone you actually gave a shit about?"

"I'm not interested in being a prop to spice up someone's marriage."

"*Someone's* marriage? Quit being a dick."

"Quit making promises with yours you can't keep."

"What promises?"

"I can't, Andrew. I just… I can't."

"You can't what?"

"I can't just put on little shows with Cassidy to get you off. This isn't going to be a *thing* with us, okay?"

"I didn't get off, remember?"

"I'm not straight, Andrew. And I can't pretend to be for you or for her. Or for your viewing pleasure, or whatever last night *was*."

"You don't know what you are for Cassidy anymore and it's freaking you the fuck out. That's what last night was."

"Okay. Fine. So I'm a four on the Kinsey scale instead of a five. I admit it. Can I go?"

"I was there, dude. You're a three."

"Only when you're sucking on my neck. And I'd say that rounds me back up again."

This hoarse whisper—the blend of desire and anger in it—makes Andrew's balls tense up. "I promised Cassidy I wouldn't let you leave," he says in a voice that reminds him of his old football coach. "And I've never broken a promise to my wife. Not once."

"Just tell her I didn't feel like hanging out in the kitchen making small talk while we waited for her to come back and say this was all a mistake. A mistake with *ghosts*. So please, for the love of God, just—"

He pins Shane by his shoulder and slams his back against the door hard enough to rattle the frame.

"You little bitch," Andrew hisses.

Shane's blue eyes flare, maybe from pain, or maybe from shock that Andrew's mouth just closed over his. Andrew feels the shuddering effects of the tremulous thoughts ripping through Shane's mind. *Is this cheating? Should I fight? Can I fight?* Kissing Cassidy is like swimming in velvet. Kissing Shane is like rolling the tender sole of his foot gently back and forth over a tennis ball; a delicious, constant tug of war between tension and release.

"What are you doing?" Shane whispers.

"She said I had to do whatever I could to keep you here. So this is me, doing what I have to do," Andrew whispers. He starts to unbutton Shane's shirt before he realizes he doesn't have the patience for every single button. A tug on each flap and the thing pops open, buttons flying. Andrew brings his mouth to Shane's before Shane can look down and count how many buttons he just lost.

Once it feels like he's tongued the fight out of him, Andrew breaks and takes a deep breath.

"You really think I'm that easy?" Shane manages between gasps.

"Sure as hell feels like it," Andrew says.

A single, firm tug on Shane's unbuttoned jeans and Shane's absurdly hard cock bounces up into the air between them. In his rush to leave, Shane forgot to put on his underwear and now he is fully exposed.

With one arm braced across his chest, Andrew explores Shane's smoothness with his other hand, his fingers traveling to places he didn't touch the night before. When he gently traces the underside of Shane's hairless balls, Shane lets out a series of stuttering gasps. To hasten his surrender, Andrew sticks two of his fingers in Shane's lips, then, once they're slick with spit, he circles Shane's hole with them, triggering a wave of pleasure that makes Shane's legs go limp. To keep himself from collapsing, Shane slides an arm around Andrew's shoulders.

The smell of Cassidy's sex still blankets Shane's body, turning into a new and unnamed cologne Andrew can't resist. Andrew sinks to one knee, seizes Shane's cock by the root, runs his tongue down the length of it, tasting Cassidy. Tasting Shane. When he closes his mouth around the head, Shane yelps.

"You can't!"

"I can't *what?*" Andrew asks, standing until their lips are almost touching again. But he maintains his grip on Shane's cock, stroking him slowly and firmly.

Shane gasps, grits his teeth. "If it happens again… It has to be…"

"Has to be what, Superboy?"

"Both of you…always…"

"Interesting proposition," Andrew whispers. He finishes each stroke of Shane's shaft by gently kneading Shane's balls, then sliding his spit-slick fingers leisurely up and down the man's taint. Shane chews gently on his lower lip.

"No…" Shane whispers, but he sounds drunk, on the verge of blacking out from desire.

"No?"

"Won't work…"

"It's working now."

"You won't be able to handle the things I want to do to your body."

"Ha! I know a challenge when I hear one," he says.

Andrew releases Shane, who slides a few inches down the door, gasping, eyes glazed with lust. But there's regret on his face at being suddenly denied Andrew's touch. Andrew saunters into the living room, then, once he's sure he has Shane's undivided attention, he steps out of his pajama pants, one leg after the other, and tosses them aside.

"Prove it," Andrew says.

Shane is free now. Free to disappear for another week, or two, or three. Free to book himself a ticket on the first flight to China. Free to run, to ignore, to deny any of this ever happened. But the sight of Andrew's sculpted naked body, fiercely illuminated by the sunlight pouring through the front window, has Shane stumbling across the threshold to the living room, kicking himself out of his shoes and then his puddling jeans, until both men are standing several feet apart, stark naked, studying each other.

When Shane literally licks his lips, Andrew is surprised by a shiver of pleasure that travels from his balls all the way to his scalp. He's never offered himself to anyone quite like this. Never offered up his body so willingly, so submissively, and his heart races with as much fear as desire.

Not like Danny. This isn't like those times with Danny Sullivan at all. There's so much more here. So much more power. Danny and I were practically boys. But Shane is a—

"The minute you say no," Shane says with a new confidence in his voice. "The minute you resist, I walk out that door."

"All right—but no pain," Andrew says before he can stop himself.

"Some things only hurt for the first few minutes."

"Still, I'm not—"

"Relax. I won't fuck you until your wife asks me to."

Laid low beneath Shane's weight and his thrusts. Cassidy watching, directing. Like last night, only different players in different positions. Husband and wife reversed. Oh Jesus. Oh dear God. Could I? What am I doing?

No man has ever talked to him this way. With Danny, Andrew was always the aggressor, the dominant one. The only thing in play had been their mouths, maybe a finger or two. But the probing, penetrating fingers always belonged to Andrew. Andrew was always the one in control. But now...

Now Andrew is the one blushing, his breaths stunted, and Shane is the one with the wide, cocky grin on his face. Only once in his life has he felt this same blend of fear and arousal, and it was over a silly dream.

When he and Cassidy first started dating, he had a nightmare that he walked in on her with one of his frat brothers, a nightmare so porny and vivid that when he woke from it he was gripping the pillow in jealous anger even as his cock throbbed against the sheets.

"Are you done whining?" Shane asks him.

"Are you done running your mouth?"

"You only get to set one limit today and you just did. Say no, try to stop me from doing anything else, and I'm out the door and you get to explain to Cassidy how you weren't man enough to finish what you started."

"Deal."

Shane points toward the sofa. "Sit," he orders.

But Andrew doesn't sit. Instead, Andrew kneels on the sofa cushions, pitches forward and grips the back of the sofa in both hands, sticking his bare ass out into the air behind him. He gives it a little wiggle for good measure. No way is he giving up all the control. Besides, Shane's probably so hungry for his cock, he won't be able to keep up the dominant routine for long.

"Oh, I see," Shane says, in response to Andrew's small act of defiance.

Now he'll have to flip Andrew over. Now he'll have to show how much he's really hungering for Andrew's dick. And man, he should pull the window shade because if someone comes up the front walk, they're totally going to be able to see us.

"*Shane.*"

It feels like the pleasure sweeping through him suddenly is trapped inside a shell of panic and riding a tide of incredible, unexpected vulnerability. If the shell cracks and the emotions are set free, he'll cross over into some new realm of previously unknown bliss. But part of him can't help but fight it because it feels wrong. Beyond wrong. Beyond forbidden. He didn't know he had so many nerves down there, didn't know they could be used against him this way. Against his ego, his aggression, his masculinity. The gasps and moans coming from him sound genderless and desperate. Andrew reaches behind him, grabbing for Shane's head. But Shane bats his hands away with one swift strike.

"Remember the rules?"

"But wait, stop—you c-can't—"

"Oh, *what?* You thought you could take a little control back? Make me repeat my instructions? Make me beg for your cock? Is that it?"

"Seriously, Shane. You have to sto— You have to…" *Lick. Probe. Lick. Bite. Slap.*

"I tell you to sit and instead you wiggle your hard ass at me like a cock tease, *after* you told me I couldn't fuck it? Well, this is what you get for that, Mr. Burke." Mr. Burke is what Cassidy always calls him when she drags him into the bedroom for some naughty, late-afternoon role-play. Hearing it out of Shane's mouth makes him wonder how many details of their sexual adventures she's shared with Shane, and how many of those details have fueled Shane's appetite for him. The thought of them together, discussing his body, discussing the tender, special spots on his skin, makes him dizzy with desire.

"I can't be—I mean, you have to st-stop or I…"

Shane smacks his lips and draws his mouth from Andrew's ass. "*This* wasn't the limit!"

"Still I…"

Andrew can't speak, because even his mind can't fasten on the words for what Shane is doing. *Shane's mouth, down there. Can't see. Is it just his mouth? Is it his hand? No. His hands are on my cock, on my balls, so it has to be just his— Fuckfuckfuckfuck*fuck… His thoughts spill out into frenzied gasps.

"Fuckfuckfuckfuckfuck—"

"I thought *that* was your limit," Shane growls. Then he goes back to work, his flickering tongue fearlessly traveling the sensitive, unexplored crack of Andrew's ass.

Just like it traveled Cassidy's wet, throbbing cunt. The same tongue, the same flickering motions. The same ravenous hunger.

And the hard shell encasing the pleasure rocketing through him cracks.

Oh, God. Is this what she feels when I taste her, when I lap at her juices? Is this some sense of the bliss she felt as Shane devoured her lips, her folds, her hard little clit?

Miraculously, he's been joined with the waves of pleasure he saw coursing through his wife the night before, all thanks to Shane's skillful, fearless tongue. This realization unleashes something inside of him. His mouth opens against the back of the sofa. The cry that rips from him is as abandon-filled as the one he let loose in the swimming pool the night before. Only now there are no ghosts, no visions, just Shane's unleashed appetite, his ravenous worship of Andrew's body. *Every* part of Andrew's body. Shane's hand strokes Andrew's cock, suckles Andrew's balls, and travels places he's never allowed Cassidy to fully explore.

Two desires fill Andrew—to take Shane into his arms and hold him as tightly as he can, and to fuck him senseless on the living room floor, as hard as Shane fucked Cassidy the night before. While it feels like they should be competing for control—these wild desires—they join with each other instead, forming an overwhelming river of desire that leaves him submissive, gasping and exposed; powerless with hunger under Shane's forbidden, oral assault.

When Shane rolls him over onto his back, Andrew is rag-doll limp, entirely at the mercy of Shane's maneuvering grip on his thighs.

Now he can watch Shane work.

Cassidy knows how to make him feel like a stud, knows the words and phrases that will set him off, knows how to run her hands over his body like he's a statue in a museum come to life and she's the last lustful security guard on duty. But Shane's combination of aggression and worship is a new experience, and it feels as if every cell in Andrew's body is realigning itself to accept Shane's blazing, unexpected gifts.

Dominating Cassidy and Shane together, forcing them to unleash their conflicted desires for one another, has always been his fantasy. But never did Andrew think Shane—his mouth, his ferocity, his beautiful blue eyes and his slender, hard body—could also allow him to experience the same pleasures that ricochet through Cassidy in the bedroom.

Shane sucks him with practiced skill, his tongue flickering across the front of his corona in just the right spot. *He knows just how to do this, how to do me. Because Cassidy told him. Cassidy shared with him every secret of my skin.* He feels bathed in their mutual desire, and this brings him to the edge.

Shane lets out a sharp, satisfied groan at the taste of Andrew's fresh flow of arousal.

"Shane…"

"Give it to me," Shane whispers, unwilling to draw his mouth more than an inch or two off Andrew's cock as he strokes him furiously.

"Shane…"

"All of it, Andrew. Every drop."

It's an order, a command. The feverish spasms of pleasure that await Andrew will lay him open, he's sure of it; Shane must sense this as much as Andrew does. Shane must know Andrew has never come in anyone else's mouth before, anyone besides Cassidy. Not even the women he was with before they met, or Danny Sulliva—

Andrew screams. He'd love to believe it was really a yell or a war-whoop or a bellowing cry. But it wasn't any of those things. It was a scream. His entire body spasms, his legs kicking up on either side of Shane's head, his back rearing up off the sofa cushions, his abs tensing so hard spikes of pain shoot through him, all while his seed gushes into

Shane's mouth. Amidst this wordless pleasure is a fear, a fear that this is the strongest orgasm he's ever had in his life, and it's happening with a man, and does that mean he might be more into guys than he's ever— and then Shane withdraws the finger he deftly slid inside of Andrew's hole, releases the pressure he applied to his prostrate at just the right moment, and Andrew starts to laugh.

Maybe it was the strongest orgasm I've ever had because no one's ever stuck a finger up my ass before.

Slowly, Shane draws his mouth from the root of Andrew's cock, all the way up its length, until the head pops free of his slick, pink lips. He gazes into Andrew's eyes. Andrew can't believe what he's seeing, so he reaches out for Shane's chin, his cheeks, checking to make sure Shane actually swallowed every drop, that none of it is smeared across his face.

After a few minutes of this, Shane reaches up and takes one of Andrew's fingers into his mouth, suckles it gently, as if whatever he tastes on it is quieting his heart, relieving him of the need to come.

"So…" Andrew tries, but his voice is hoarse and he has to clear his throat. "You fucked me without fucking me."

"Yeah," Shane answers, still biting down lightly on Andrew's fingertip.

"So how'd I do? Did I pass my test?"

"It was a good start," Shane whispers.

"Not good enough to make you come."

"I'm saving it for later."

"For Cassidy?"

"For both of you," Shane answers, then he kisses Andrew's fingertip.

Shane goes to stand, and Andrew tugs on his hand. "No," he says.

"I just need to go to the bathroom."

Andrew swings his legs up onto the sofa, pulling Shane down onto the space he's just opened up on the cushions. "You need to stay right here until Cassidy gets back."

"I won't leave," Shane says. "I promise."

"Only one way to be sure," Andrew answers.

Shane plops down on the edge of the sofa, studying Andrew over one shoulder.

Amazing. Just swallowed every last drop of my cum and he's still afraid to snuggle with me.

"Lie down," Andrew says quietly. "I passed my test, now it's time to pass yours."

"I thought last night was my test."

"Nope. There are all kinds of ways to run, Shane. You don't always have to use the front door."

"Ha! So you're a cuddler?" Shane asks. "I had no idea."

"You had *every* idea," Andrew answers. "Admit it. Cassidy's told you everything about me. How else would you know *exactly* how to suck my cock?"

"Experience. Intuition."

"Lie with me, smart mouth," Andrew says.

His breath leaving him in a long, dramatic sigh, Shane sinks down onto the narrow band of cushions in front of Andrew, snuggling into Andrew's chest.

"See. That's not so bad, is it?" He slides an arm over Shane, gradually tightening his grip around his stomach.

"Uh-huh."

"This way, you can't pretend I'm some random guy you picked up in a bar. This way you can accept that this is real. That it's really happening." He kisses Shane's earlobe, then his neck, gently, careful not to arouse too much desire.

In the sudden silence between them, Andrew hears the sudden patter of rain followed by a neighbor's car backing out of a nearby driveway; it reminds him they just conducted a debauched scene in the middle of the living room. On a weekday morning no less!

Shane's breaths are slow and steady. Andrew wonders if the guy's on the verge of passing out again. Then he speaks. "Fine," Shane says. "This is really happening."

"Yep."

"Is it going to happen again?"

"I hope so."

"Me, too. So we're just going to lie here like this until Cassidy comes home?"

"I gave her two hours. She's got one left. But, yeah, that's my plan."

"You have a lot of plans, Andrew."

"I'm an architect."

"You don't think she'll freak out when she sees us like this?"

"Are you kidding? She practically set this whole thing up. Also, have you seen the gay porn on her laptop?"

"Seriously? I *gave* her that porn, Andrew. She said she wasn't a fan. She said the guys were hot, but there wasn't enough of a *story*."

"Guess that's our job then."

"To make her some porn?"

"No. To give her a story."

"I see. You think she'll be okay that you and I…"

"I was okay with you two last night, wasn't I?"

"That was different. You wanted us together."

"If you think she doesn't want us together, then you haven't been paying attention for years now."

In the silence that follows, he expects Shane to dispute this, or at the very least fire up some of his usual snark. "I have been," he says instead. "I have been paying attention. I just didn't think it was possible."

"It is," Andrew answers. "It is possible."

Instead of responding, Shane clasps one of Andrew's hands tightly to his sweaty chest.

"First she's got to figure out what the deal is with that candle, though," Andrew says.

Shane rolls over until their noses are almost touching, looking genuinely confused.

"What *candle*?" he asks.

12

CASSIDY

Closed.

The other stores around the courtyard are open for business, but this small, bluntly worded sign hangs inside the glass front door of *Feu de Coeur*. The shop is so dark there's barely enough light to reflect off the glass containers lining its front window. From a few feet away, it's impossible to tell they hold candles.

Closed? That's all? At the very least, she expected a handwritten sign with calligraphic script saying, *I shall return shortly—Bastian.* Or maybe a miniature clock with plastic arms set to the time the store will open again.

Unsure of her next move, she wanders back out onto Dumaine Street and flips up the hood on the raincoat she found in her trunk.

Lord. Enough already with this damn rai—

—and the rain stops.

She is staring down at the sidewalk in a daze when it happens. The quality of the sunlight changes suddenly. It isn't darker or brighter—it's different. Because the rain didn't just stop, it *froze*. The milky gray light of a cloud-filled sky is now reflected through a thousand suspended crystals of water. The silence is sudden and total. A forest of frozen droplets stretches out on all sides of her.

If it hadn't been for the night before, she would probably be in hysterics right now, curled in a ball on the sidewalk, asking God if she had died. But instead, she reaches into the air in front of her and watches her hand move through the drops as if they weren't even there. And then, through the impossible silence, comes the sound of footsteps.

He's about half a block away, dressed much as he was the day before. A vest of dark brown silk, rather than purple, trousers pressed with a knife's edge, polished brown loafers without a spot of rain on them. The umbrella must be for show, given that he doesn't have a drop of water on him. Indeed, water doesn't seem to touch this man at all; like when he took the wet rolls of tapestry from her arms yesterday without getting a stain anywhere on his clothes. But still, Bastian Drake makes a show of lowering the umbrella to his side, closing it with a soft click, and resting the tip on the sidewalk next to him, Charlie Chaplin style.

"I trust everything went well?" he asks.

"Was it a spell, Mr. Drake?"

"Call me Bastian."

"Is it your real name?"

"It's been my name for eighty-six years, so it might as well be."

"And before that?"

He smiles and studies the street scene around them as if it were just another spring morning.

"Are you a vampire?" she asks him.

"Oh, *vampires*. Please. I can't stand the sight of blood. And besides, they're not *real*."

"But you're real. *This* is real. Can other people...can they *see* this?"

"Only the ones who have enjoyed my gift to its fullest potential."

He's just given her enough information for her mind to grab on to. Her quick calculations tow her from a swamp of confusion.

His name's been Bastian Drake for eighty-six years, but he doesn't look a day over thirty-five. He's a ghost; he has to be. So he must have died at thirty-five, but when he was alive he probably had a different name. Since then he's been frozen in time. And apparently he can freeze time too, which isn't something she's ever associated with ghosts. But it's not like she majored in Ghost Studies in college.

There's a car frozen halfway through the intersection a block away, its windshield wipers arrested in mid-swipe, the driver an indecipherable blur through the crystalline forest. "Is this the same thing you did last night?" she asks.

"Oh, no. Not at all. And I didn't do anything last night, Cassidy."

"Your candle sure did."

"The candle gave you a nudge, that's all."

"Eight-foot-tall ghosts? Spontaneous orgasms? That's quite a nudge."

"It's quite encouraging, isn't it? But still, nothing about it deprived you of your free will."

"So it wasn't forced on us?"

"Did it feel as if it was?"

"I guess not. But what if we'd just freaked? I mean, what if I never went home last night? What if I'd gotten in my car and just kept driving?"

Bastian Drake's smile flickers before it fades altogether. When he speaks again, it's in a more clipped and quiet tone than any he's used with her since they met. "Best not to meditate on the road not taken, Cassidy."

A far cry from what he said to her in his shop the day before. She struggles to remember the words he used. *Take it from a man who passed up far too many gifts in his life. There is no virtue in ignoring your heart's desire. To ignore it is to condemn yourself to a lifetime of darkness.* Even though she's not sure exactly who or what he is, she's willing to bet most of Bastian Drake's existence is spent meditating on the road he didn't take. What else could he have meant by a *lifetime of darkness?*

"That sounds scary," she says.

"All three of you chose to embrace the flame. This is a good thing, Cassidy. When the flame is not embraced, there are consequences for everyone involved."

"I see. So this is what you do with your magic? You help people live out their fantasies?"

"The fantasies that guide them to their hearts, yes."

"I see. And the ghosts we saw last night. Who were they?"

"Well, for starters, they weren't ghosts."

"But you are," she says quickly.

"Clever," he whispers.

"Thank you. So last night?"

"Have you ever heard mention of a place called The Desire Exchange?"

Sure, she wants to say as a chill moves through her. *I've also heard of Bigfoot, alien abduction conspiracies, and all manner of creepy stuff I probably would have laughed off a day ago.* "It's a sex club for rich people out in the swamp somewhere," she replies. "But I don't know anyone who's actually been. It's an urban legend, a myth."

"Ghosts who can stop time are also a myth, Cassidy. But you're speaking to one of them right now."

At least you finally told me what you are.

"Okay. So The Desire Exchange is real. But what does it have to do with the candle you gave me?"

"The Exchange is a place for people to live out their deepest sexual fantasies. Most people visit in the hope of discovering if it's just a fantasy or a calling they've always ignored. A calling that could turn into a new beginning. But many of them learn they need only act it out once and then they're free of it. For these people, it's more of a purge. Either way, the passion and bravery of those who visit The Desire Exchange gives off a kind of energy. I bottle that energy, I blend it, and I place it on a shelf where it waits for someone like you, someone who could use a bit of inspiration."

"Inspiration?"

"A nudge," he says with a bright smile. "Don't worry. This isn't the beginning of a haunting. What you saw last night will never come again. It's up to you to shape your story now. You and Andrew and Shane."

"Just tell me you're not stealing people's souls."

"Oh, for goodness sake! No. What is with this *incessant* belief that the dead want only to hurt the living? It's the great misconception of the plane on which you dwell. The engine of the living world is *love*, Cassidy. Not money. Not pain. Not war. Love. And there are those of us who are senten—there are those of us who are *assigned* to make sure the engine keeps running."

Sentenced. You were going to say sentenced, *not assigned.*

"So last night, those things. If they weren't ghosts, what were they? *Who* were they?"

"*They* are still very much alive, so you needn't worry about them. All you saw was their essence, the life force that sprang from their passion and their desire."

"A woman and two men. Just like me, Andrew, and Shane?"

"Exactly," Bastian answers with a satisfied smile.

"Did it work out? Did the three of them end up together? Or did they just live it out once so they could purge it and move on with their lives?"

"Their story is not mine to tell."

"What about my story?"

"Not just *your* story, Cassidy."

"Sorry. *Our* story. Me and Andrew and Shane."

"Is yours to live," he says.

"But what if—"

"*What*, Cassidy? If you give into fear again? If you refuse to admit that you love them both equally, that you always have, that you've longed for a special sacred place where all three of you could be together, always? Are those the *what ifs* you can't bring yourself to name?"

Belong to you...both of you...always. If she's being haunted by anything right now, it's these words, the words they whispered to each other before they fell asleep in each other's arms. Her heart won't rest until they've spoken these words to each other again, without the sparkling evidence of Bastian Drake's magic threaded across their bodies.

"We can't light one of your candles every time we want to be together," she says. "That's not going to work, is it?"

"You are correct. My gift has done its job. The rest is up to you now."

A gold radiance has returned to Bastian's eyes. This time Cassidy doesn't turn away from the magic in front of her.

She has what she came for, Bastian's assurance that if there are battles lying in wait for her, and for Andrew and for Shane, those battles will pit them against their own hearts, not dangerous spirits. But still, she could stand here all day questioning him. And somewhere along the way, she would probably ruin the whole thing. By the hundredth question, her head would take control of her heart and she would analyze the source of this miracle in such microscopic detail she'd convince herself it was all just a bunch of strange chemicals damaging brain cells, making them misfire.

Also, it seems like Bastian Drake is done with their little chat.

There's a crackling sound all around them, as if the frozen tableau they're standing in the middle of is actually an ice palace that's started melting in the sun. She figures this is Bastian's not-so-subtle warning that he's about to release his hold on the clock of human time. That, combined with the gold radiance that's chased the pupils from the man's eyes, convinces her she doesn't have much time left with him. And maybe he's pulling back for the same reason she believes she should. Maybe he's sensed that the more she discusses his magic, the more she'll wipe its gold dust from her heart. So as the crackling sound around them intensifies, Cassidy says the first words that come into her head.

"Thank you."

Bastian Drake smiles, and then suddenly falling rain wipes him from view.

13

CASSIDY

"Hey," Cassidy says.

"Howdy," Shane answers.

It takes her a few seconds to realize Andrew has handcuffed Shane to the bedframe with a set of fuzzy handcuffs he's only used on her once or twice, maybe because she's a bigger fan of silk wrist ties. The running shower in the master bathroom makes a dull roar.

When she takes a seat on the bed beside Shane, she sees his skin is still rosy from the shower and scented with her husband's favorite peppermint body wash. He's dressed in her husband's clothes too; a pair of his plaid Ralph Lauren boxer shorts and one of the white tank tops he likes to wear to bed.

"How'd you shower in those?" she asks.

"He put them on me after. But he stood guard the whole time so I couldn't get away."

"And did you want to get away?"

"Well, see, he told me this woman I love more than anything went and did something really dangerous all by herself. So I freaked out. I said we had to find her. But he had other ideas. Something about keeping a promise to his wife. That's been the big theme this morning, keeping promises to Cassidy Burke."

"So what was this dangerous thing this woman went and did?"

"She had a meeting with some guy named Bastian Drake."

"Yeah, well, turns out he's not dangerous."

"Okay, fine. But see, this woman, she didn't know that before she went down there, *alone*, did she?"

"Uh-huh. Well, if someone hadn't been ignoring my text messages for a week, I might not have ended up in his shop in the first place."

"*Oh my God. So* not fair, Cass," he says, dropping the sly routine.

"I know. And it might not be all that true, either."

"What do you mean?"

"Apparently his candles find exactly who they need to find. That's how it works. I probably would have smelled it from halfway across the city."

"What did it smell like? The first time?"

"You," she says, staring into his eyes. "You and Andrew, together."

He blushes—god, he's so cute when he blushes. She's always thought so but she's never been able to say so without feeling like a desperate, pathetic, deluded woman hopelessly in love with her gay friend. She expects him to look away from her penetrating stare, but instead he nibbles on his lower lip, meets her stare and asks, "Did I smell good?"

"Very," she answers.

"Have I always smelled good?"

With one bare foot, he drags his toes gently across her bent knee. His cock is starting to rise in the loose folds of her husband's boxer shorts, and she wonders if it's the result of being cuffed, asking her coy questions, the lustful stare she's giving him or all three in combination.

"Yes," she answers.

He slides his foot up onto her leg, and once the bare sole is exposed, she realizes what he's doing, referencing that little moment they shared together, a moment of such unexpected, flowering desire she barely managed to repress her memory of it until they made love the night before. She drags one fingertip along the arch of his foot, and he sucks in a breath through clenched teeth.

"So what did you and my husband get up to while I was gone?"

"Do you want me to tell you?" he asks her. "Or do you want me to show you?"

Her heart races. She grasps Shane's bare foot in one hand. His perfectly manicured, pale foot. Just then, the shower shuts off. A minute later, Andrew appears in the doorway, toweling himself off, trying to appear relaxed and casual even though he's clearly dying for information about her trip to the French Quarter. The sight of them touching brings a smile to Andrew's face.

The smile fades when she starts to recount everything Bastian told her, including a description of the frozen rain that leaves both Andrew and Shane speechless. By the time she's done, Shane is sagging against his handcuffs, and Andrew is wrapping his towel snugly around his waist.

After a few minutes of silence, her husband takes a seat on the foot of the bed, his back to them, as if he needs to stare at the carpet to absorb everything she just described. "Y'all remember my aunt Linda?"

"Of course," Cassidy answers. "She couldn't stand me."

"She called me the *gay one*," Shane says.

"Exactly. You remember how uptight she was, how everything in her house was always perfect. Totally straightlaced, super conservative. Church every Sunday."

"We remember," Cassidy says.

"A few years before she died, she had too much to drink one night. I mean, it was, like, the *only* night I ever saw her have too much to drink. And she told me this story. She was walking her dog out at her husband's fishing camp and this little girl ran across the trail right in front of her, chasing this red plastic ball. There wasn't another house within ten miles, not so much as an access road near the trail. All around was just swamp. Anyway, as soon as Linda tried to run after her, the girl just disappeared. When she got back to camp, she called the cops, described the girl to them, just to, you know, see if there were any missing person reports for a child who matched that description."

"And?" Shane asks.

"There was just one report from the year before. For a girl who eventually turned up dead because her father killed her."

"*Aunt Linda* told you this story?" Cassidy asks.

"That's what I'm saying. She wasn't exactly a tarot card reader. Never read a scary book, never watched scary movies. She wasn't someone who *wanted* to believe in anything except the Lord. But she saw something she couldn't explain and she kept it a secret for most of her life. Ever since the night she told me, well… I told myself a time would come. That something might happen to me too. Something that would change what I believed was possible."

"So you don't think we're hallucinating anymore?" Cassidy asks.

"I didn't think it this morning. I just didn't want you to leave, babe. Anyway, what I'm trying to say is, I think everybody has their Aunt Linda moment eventually. I'm just glad I'm not having mine alone."

"Me, too," Cassidy says.

"Me, three," Shane answers.

"But they weren't ghosts," Cassidy says.

"I hope not," Shane answers. "'Cause I knew one of them."

Andrew turns so quickly at this announcement, the towel slips free of his waist. Cassidy is stunned, waiting for Shane to say he's kidding. But Shane stares back at them intently, nodding.

"I was in the bathroom at Perry's when it happened," he says. "Samantha and I were having dinner. I looked up and there was this golden...*man* staring back at me from the mirror. And it was Jonathan Claiborne."

"The guy you hooked up with?" Cassidy asks. "The waiter?"

"He's not a waiter anymore apparently, but yeah, Samantha and I'd been talking about him before I got up from the table, so I thought it was...you know, I thought I was hallucinating."

"Maybe you were," Andrew says. "I mean maybe the *ghost* was real, but his face was vague and you just filled in the gaps."

"It's possible. I don't know. But you want to know the other thing?"

"Yes," Cassidy says.

"I don't care," Shane whispers. He's looking back and forth between the two of them. When he speaks again, his voice has a catch in it, a catch that brings Cassidy's hand to his knee. "I don't care why we did it. I don't care if it was ghosts or magic or drugs. All I know is that I don't want it to end. I never want it to end. In high school, whenever I looked at a beautiful guy, I would feel this sadness, like this heaviness in my heart. Because I didn't want to be attracted to men. I didn't want to find men beautiful. And then I came out and I was Mister Proud Gay Man and the sadness went away, for a while, at least. But then, a few years ago, it came back. It came back whenever I looked at the two of you together. And that's when I knew I wanted you both, but I thought I could never have you."

Andrew stands up suddenly. What is he doing? Is he about to leave?

"Babe..." Cassidy says.

"I think," Andrew says. "I've made my case to both of you. And quite well, I might add. So at this point, if there's anything standing in the way of this, it's going to be between the two of you. So I'll give you all some time alone."

"Kind of like the time you two had alone this morning," Cassidy says.

"Kinda, yeah," Andrew says with a grin. "Shane here's afraid he's only a four on the Kinsey scale unless I'm chewing on his neck. Given what I saw him do to your body last night, I don't really think that's true. But it doesn't matter what I think. It matters what he thinks. And what you think." Andrew rounds the foot of the bed and gives her a lingering kiss. "So convince him."

His hand reaches for hers. She looks down in time to see him place the key to the handcuffs in her open palm.

It feels like she's about to get away with something. Something her husband just gave her permission to get away with. The door clicks shut behind Andrew, and they're left alone. She's too nervous to look into his eyes. She gets up on her knees and slides the key into the handcuffs.

"Don't." His voice is as tight as a drawstring.

Her heart drops. Is this where it ends? Is the convincing part already over with? Is the prospect of being left alone with her body too terrifying for him to face? When she summons the courage to look down at him, dread swirling in her stomach, she sees Shane's eyes are hooded with desire.

"Don't uncuff me, Cassidy."

The key shakes in her hand.

"Don't let me go," he whispers.

"Shane…"

"Touch me everywhere you've always wanted to," he whispers. "Don't ask for permission. Own me, Cassidy. Own me like you always have."

Her urge is to tear his clothes off, to emulate the way Andrew ravishes her. But that's not the invitation he's extended. Owning him will mean *her* pace, *her* urges and desires. She takes her time pulling the boxers down his smooth thighs, grazing his cock with her fingers. Tickling it. Nibbling the head slightly. No shoving his cock down her throat in some mad rush to deep-throat him to orgasm. Instead, she learns the map of his sensitive spots.

He's told her about some of his special places over the years, but she's unprepared for the cry that rips from him when she pushes his tank top up over his chest, secures one nipple gently between her teeth and flickers her tongue over it, or the near hysterical giggles that rip through him when she teases the edges of his armpits with her fingers.

Every step of the way, she feels a nagging urge to be more aggressive, more masculine. But each time she feels it, she pulls back, reminding herself of his offer.

Own me…

It is her gentle touches and tastes and scratches that push Shane to the brink of ecstasy. Maybe because they're new and unfamiliar, a barrage of delicious shocks to his system. When she drags the fingernails of one hand down the sides of his body, he screams as if he's been penetrated. His throbbing cock jumps against his flat, hairless stomach. She repeats the motions back and forth, just her fingernails, up and down that pale, hairless torso.

"Cassidy!" She ignores the breathless, pleading urgency in his tone, drags her fingernails further down his body, across his hips, down the insides of his thighs. When his hips rise up off the bed, she gives in to temptation, grasps the base of his cock, and slides it down her throat.

His lips part. He's sucking air, trying to make words. "Give me... Let me..." It takes her a moment to realize what he's asking for. Her urge is to let him undress her, but that would mean surrendering her control. Standing over him, she pulls her shirt off, unsnaps her bra. His mouth opens when her breasts are still inches away. As soon as she hits her knees next to the bed, he bucks his head off the pillow, snags her nipple in between his lips, and tongues the sensitive nub. To keep from going over, she grabs the bedframe in one hand, right above the spot where Shane's wrists buck inside the padded handcuffs.

"You like that?" she asks. Her voice sounds like another woman's.

"Give me the other one," he answers with a devilish grin. "Just so we can be sure."

"Bad boy," she whispers.

"Very, very bad boy. Now give me the other one. *Please.*"

"Hey. I thought I'm in charge here."

"Oh, I'm sorry, Mrs. Burke. Is there something you'd like more?"

He swirls his tongue across her nipple, gazing up into her eyes. Those big beautiful blue eyes. For years, she's stared into them for comfort and solace, and now they provide her with something altogether different—pure pleasure.

When she straddles him, he bites the edge of her panties, peels them off her mound just enough that he can begin working his tongue into her folds. The desperate hunger of this frenzied probing has her gripping the bedframe in one hand, peeling the lace to one side with the other hand, giving him full access. Then she rides his mouth, watching his wrists move against the padded handcuffs. She's so lost in the bliss of it, she doesn't hear Andrew approaching, doesn't see her husband until he's slipped the keys to the cuffs inside the lock. The minute he frees Shane's hands they fly to Cassidy's thighs, gripping and pulling so he can angle himself more precisely against her clit. Even with his hands free, he is still her worshipful slave.

Andrew cups her chin in one hand, brings his mouth to hers. She returns his kiss as best she can, even though Shane's hungry ministrations leave her gasping. Andrew is hard as a rock as he turns to dig in the nightstand drawer with one hand.

A defiant, willful part of her mind assesses each swipe of Shane's tongue across her pussy for any sign of resistance, but it doesn't find any. Even if there's some part of Shane that will always be purely, resolutely homosexual, it's being overpowered by a thundering need to give her overwhelming pleasure. These thoughts have her ablaze. Next to her, Andrew tears open a condom wrapper, but the sound seems distant.

By the time she's rolled over onto her back, by the time Shane is on top of her, sliding her soaked, tangled panties down her thighs, his mouth gasping against her neck as he slides into her for the second time in twenty-four hours, she feels separated from the business of her extremities by the delicious, throbbing pleasure in her core.

And then she hears a second condom wrapper being torn open.

A second later, Shane halts in mid-thrust, still buried inside of her as his entire body goes rigid, as his breaths turn into a series of hissing gasps through clenched teeth. Cassidy reaches up to find her husband's chest coming to rest against Shane's upper back. She blinks, sees Andrew's face above her now as well, sees him tenderly kissing the nape of Shane's neck. Her hands travel from Shane's shoulders to her husband's shoulders directly above.

"Oh, fuck," Shane whispers, desperately, pain rippling through his words. "Oh, fuck." But laced through his pain are the sounds of hunger, need, and endurance. Still, Cassidy is afraid, afraid this is too much. She knows he rarely bottoms, has spent most of his adult life wondering if he doesn't have it in him or if he's never met the man powerful enough to flip him.

"Breathe," she whispers, taking his face in her hands. She would call the whole thing off right there if Shane wasn't still rock hard inside of her, motionless and rigid under Andrew's slow but determined invasion, but still hard, still throbbing inside of the condom.

"Breathe, Shane," she whispers. "Just breathe."

Shane winces, tears sprouting from his eyes. She can't tell if they're tears of pain or exertion, but they're *tears*, goddammit, so does it really matter? This was too far, too fast, and she has to end it now before everything flies off the rails.

"Shane, do you want us to stop?"

"No," he growls. "*Never.* Never stop." She feels him drawing back from inside of her, realizes this means he's sliding back onto Andrew's cock. "Belong to you...."

In her head, she finishes for him the words they whispered to each other the night before, when it seemed that shimmering spirits still hovered right outside the bedroom door. *Both of you. Always.* But Shane doesn't finish reciting these vows. His heaving breaths steal the power of speech from his lips, as he slowly, carefully rocks between her clutching heat and Andrew's overpowering penetration. His shuddering body searches out a never-before-felt rhythm, a composition unique to their three bodies, brought together in this way for the first time.

Shane's facial expressions are a wild parade of pain, pleasure, and abandon. But Andrew is pure determination, his arms wrapped around Shane's chest, devouring Shane's neck. She wants desperately to coax Shane past his final wall of resistance. But she knows she doesn't have this power. Not by herself anyway. Together, she and Andrew might be capable of it. But there are no words, no promises they can give Shane that will force him to surrender.

Shane has to choose. Shane has to give himself over to the dual embrace of Cassidy's wet heat and Andrew's unyielding force.

Please, Shane. Please. Give yourself to us. Belong to us.

It's silly to think he's read her mind, but that's exactly what she thinks when she feels the rhythm of Shane's thrusts increase. That's exactly what she thinks when she hears her husband's grunts and realizes Shane's ass now grips Andrew's cock with as much hunger and force as her folds grip Shane.

Cassidy screams with release, her hands clawing Shane's back. And then Shane's cry joins hers as he collapses against her, shuddering with another emotion as she feels him empty into the condom inside of her. Breath returns to her lungs. Andrew lifts himself off of Shane and rolls over onto his side.

Shane continues to sob. When Cassidy opens her mouth to comfort him, Andrew brings one finger gently to her lips, silencing her.

"Give him a minute," Andrew whispers. "Give him a minute to realize he's ours now, then he'll be okay."

She wants to believe him, but she's terrified Shane's tears signal the end of this, that without Bastian Drake's magic, they'll once again be slaves to fear. Shane lifts his head from her chest. Her heart is racing. She's already visualizing him leaping off her and running from the house, from the full, world-changing implications of what they've done together now. Twice.

Andrew reaches up, cups the side of Shane's face in one hand.

Surely, Shane can sense Cassidy's fear, knows full well the look that comes into her eyes when she's gripped by anticipation and dread. Surely, she has the look in her eyes right now.

Shane's eyes meet her own. He brings one of her hands to his mouth, kissing the tips of her fingers gently.

"Belong to you," Shane whispers.

"Both of you," Andrew whispers.

Cassidy's heart slows to a steady beat as Shane settles into her embrace. The words Bastian Drake's candle drew from them have once again rolled off their tongues. But the candle has been out for hours, its spirits and their sparkling residue nowhere in sight. It's just the three of them, their passion, their bravery. And now these words feel like vows.

Not all the words, she realizes. She's yet to add her final line to these, their new vows.

"Always," Cassidy whispers.

Acknowledgments from the Author

I can't thank M.J. Rose and Liz Berry enough for giving me the chance to try my hand at a new genre and for putting together this incredibly exciting new project. I'm also profoundly grateful for Jillian Stein, the amazing social media director for 1,001 DARK NIGHTS. Thanks to these ladies, this is probably the most fun I've ever had outlining, promoting, writing and copyediting a book. Kami Garcia and Delinah Blake Hurwitz gave me some really insightful reads. Thanks also goes to Benjamin Scuglia for additional proofreading and copyediting

I wouldn't be able to work on so many different writing projects while also producing (and co-hosting) a weekly internet radio show without the amazing staff of The Dinner Party Show. A big thank you to my best friend, producing partner and co-host Eric Shaw Quinn as well as our amazing support staff: Brandon Griffith, Brett Churnin, Cathy Dipierro and Benjamin Scuglia (again). If you haven't listened to The Dinner Party Show yet, give us a try. Our goal is to make you laugh until wine comes out of your nose. Even if you're not drinking wine! We're always on at www.TheDinnerPartyShow.com.

Last but not least, one of the highlights of this foray into erotic romance came when Lexi Blake wrote to tell me she was so moved by the first draft of THE FLAME she wanted to include an excerpt from it in her latest novel. This kind of generosity is rare among authors in other genres and I'm still bowled over by it, to be frank. Thanks, Lexi. Thanks for embracing the complexity of Andrew, Shane and Cassidy so warmly and with such acceptance.

About Christopher Rice

By the age of 30, Christopher Rice had published four New York Times bestselling thrillers, received a Lambda Literary Award and been declared one of People Magazine's Sexiest Men Alive. His first work of supernatural suspense, THE HEAVENS RISE, was a finalist for the Bram Stoker Award. His debut, A DENSITY OF SOULS, was published when the author was just 22 years old. A controversial and overnight bestseller, it was greeted with a landslide of media attention, much of it devoted to the fact that Christopher is the son of vampire chronicler, Anne Rice. Bestselling thriller writer (and Jack Reacher creator) Lee Child hailed Christopher's novel LIGHT BEFORE DAY as a "book of the year". Together with his best friend, New York Times bestselling novelist Eric Shaw Quinn, Christopher launched his own Internet radio show. THE DINNER PARTY SHOW WITH CHRISTOPHER RICE & ERIC SHAW QUINN is always playing at TheDinnerPartyShow.com and every episode is available for free download from the site's show archive or on iTunes. 47North, the science fiction, fantasy and horror imprint of Amazon Publishing, recently published his most recent supernatural thriller, THE VINES. And on December 9th, Thomas & Mercer, the crime and thriller imprint of Amazon Publishing, will release new editions of his previous bestsellers A DENSITY OF SOULS, THE SNOW GARDEN and LIGHT BEFORE DAY. He will continue the world of Thee Desire Exchange with a new erotic romance, THE SURRENDER GATE, due out from Evil Eye Concepts in early 2015.

THE SURRENDER GATE
A Desire Exchange Novel
By Christopher Rice

"Arthur has a son who ran away from home years ago, when he was twenty," Emily says. "His name is Ryan. Ryan Benoit. Arthur's written him a letter and he wants me to find him and give it to him."

"As a condition of leaving you his fortune?" Dugas asks.

"It's not a condition. It's a request. And given that he's about to change my life forever, I'd say it's the very least I can do."

There is more bite in her tone than she'd intended, but Dugas seems more aroused by it than offended. "I see. Have you read this letter?" he asks.

"I have not. And I will not."

"Well, that *is* impressive. Certainly more self-control than you exhibited this evening. So you have no idea why Ryan ran away, but you're expected to find him and bring him back?"

"I'm expected to give him the letter. The letter is supposed to bring him back. At least that's what Arthur's hoping for."

"And Arthur has made no attempt to find his son before now?"

"No. I mean, yes. He has, but…"

"But *what?*" Jonathan asks.

"Ryan ran away so long ago that every few years Arthur has an age progression done on computer. Then he hires a private detective to go look for him. A few years ago, one of the detectives turned up what looked like a real lead. But at the time, Arthur didn't want to pursue it. Now that he's dying, he's had a change of heart."

"And the lead was?" Dugas asks.

"The P.I. said a man matching the latest progression was involved with some sort of secret *organization* called The Desire Exchange." Emily watches Jonathan to gauge his reaction to these words. He's nowhere near as startled as she'd hoped he'd be. "I've only heard that name one other time and it was from you. You just sort of mentioned it in passing so I thought—"

"You thought what?" Jonathan asks sharply. "That I was a member of a secret sex cult?"

"I just thought you might know more about it than you were letting on. But you wouldn't tell me unless—"

"—unless you caught me with a client and *embarrassed* it out of me?"

"Children," Dugas says. "Please."

"Emily. *Come on!* Some secret organization that helps millionaires live out their deepest sexual fantasies? It was somebody's idea of a joke. I thought it was funny. That's why I told you. It's not real, for Christ's sake."

"It is not a joke," George Dugas says quietly. His finality silences them both

The man seems incapacitated all of a sudden. By shock? Memories? Emily can't tell. If she hadn't looked to Jonathan so quickly when she'd said those three shiver-inducing words, she might have picked up on the older man's reaction before now.

"And it's *very* real," Dugas whispers.

He rises to his feet, takes his drink in hand, and strolls to the edge of the pool; as if it's wavering blue surface were a window onto the past. "The latest age progression. Describe it to me."

"He was about six feet tall when he ran away, so he should be around that now. Dirty blonde hair."

"Leave out the things he could have easily changed," Dugas says.

"Okay. Bright eyes that have a kind of slant to them that looks almost Eastern European. I guess they'd make him look kind of angry. Or amused, I'm not sure. Anyway, his facial features, they're all proportional, is what I'm trying to say. Especially his nose. He doesn't have one of those big Roman noses that can dominate a guy's face. Everything about him is more classic and all-American."

"Any birthmarks?" Dugas asks.

"Yes. A small strawberry-colored mark above his left collarbone."

This concise description causes Dugas to straighten and suck in a deep breath, as if a wave of pleasure is coursing through his entire body.

"Oh my," Dugas whispers. Then he takes a quick sip of his drink. "Oh, mymy*my*."

Jonathan breaks the silence. "Mr. Dugas, are you a *member* of The Desire Exchange?"

"The Desire Exchange doesn't have members. It's not a club. It's an *experience*."

"An experience you've apparently had," Emily says.

The older man drains the last of his cocktail with several long swallows. The mint sprig catches on the remaining ice cubes as he drinks. Whatever it is, George Dugas has trouble remembering The Desire Exchange without the balm of whiskey and powdered sugar to soothe the hot fires of his lust.

"Have you *seen* Ryan Benoit?" Emily asks.

"How about I give you the chance to see him for yourself?" Dugas says. "For a price, of course. *Several* prices."

When Dugas starts for Emily's chair, Jonathan straightens, watching the man's every move.

"There's the price of admission, of course. That you will pay directly to the Exchange. After I've given you a reference. And make no mistake, you *must* have a reference. The admission…well, I'm sure Arthur Benoit will cover that for you. But he'll also need to give you some sort of fake identity, something that will make you appear to be in line with their usual clientele. Do you think he's up to it?"

Dugas is standing behind her chair now. Jonathan watches the man with the intensity of a cat watching a bird through a window. Emily studies Jonathan's facial expression with the same focus.

"Arthur would do anything to get Ryan that letter," Emily says. "Short of *hurting* people."

"No," Dugas whispers, hands coming to rest on her shoulders. "Of course not. Pain is not on the menu."

"And the price for your reference?" she asks.

Gently, he pulls open the flaps of her robe, exposing her breasts to the humid air. Her eyes flutter shut against her will as she braces for the feel of the man's hands on her flesh. But the feeling doesn't come. He continues to tug on the robe instead until the loose knot in the tie comes undone. Suddenly her thighs are exposed, and then her sex.

Jonathan gazes into her eyes, trying to read her every emotion, ready to spring into action as soon as she gives him the word, she's sure of it. But her head is swimming and there is heat traveling up her sternum. Rather than feeling violated, being gradually exposed this way makes her feel included in a delicious secret.

"The Desire Exchange isn't just about *your* fantasy," Dugas continues. "It's about surrendering to the fantasies of others as well. To do that, you have to let go of labels, of limits. Of fears."

"I'm still waiting to hear your price, Mr. Dugas."

The older man chuckles. "As if you'd ever say no, Miss Blaine. You'd be risking your incredible inheritance if you did."

"I'm risking my incredible inheritance by agreeing to find the only rightful heir. Some of us are motivated by other things than money, *sir*."

"Yes," Dugas says. With one final tug he has separated the flaps of the robe and draws it down over her back, rendering her fully nude and exposed. "Desire."

Jonathan is on the edge of his seat, nostrils flaring, rock-hard pecs rising and falling with his deep breaths. The head of his olive-skinned cock has emerged from the waistband of his briefs, glistening with his arousal. She tells herself it's just Dugas acting the part of the masculine aggressor that has Jonathan engorged. It can't be *her*, for Christ's sake. How many times has he seen her breasts before now? But she's right and she's wrong at the same time. It's not just her. And it's not just George Dugas. It's all of it. All three of them, the setting, the hint of danger, and the act of pure will that brought her here. It's this sudden swirl of desire they've been swept up by, and Emily realizes it's about to render comforting labels irrelevant.

"Nobody does anything for just one reason," Dugas whispers in her ear. "You can pretend you climbed onto my roof because you were after information that will help you find this Ryan Benoit. But you'd be lying. You'd be lying if you didn't also admit you wanted to see the expression on your best friend's face while he was in the throes of passion with a strange man."

Also from Christopher Rice

Thrillers
A DENSITY OF SOULS
THE SNOW GARDEN
LIGHT BEFORE DAY
BLIND FALL
THE MOONLIT EARTH

Supernatural Thrillers
THE HEAVENS RISE
THE VINES

Paranormal Romance
THE SURRENDER GATE: A Desire Exchange Novel

1001 DARK NIGHTS

CARESS OF DARKNESS
A Dark Pleasures Novella

NEW YORK TIMES BESTSELLING AUTHOR

JULIE KENNER

Chapter 1

"Who the fuck are you?"

I jump, startled by the voice—deep and male and undeniably irritated—that echoes across the forest of boxes scattered throughout my father's Upper East Side antique store.

"Who am I?" I repeat as I stand and search the shadows for the intruder. "Who the hell are you?"

There is more bravado in my voice than I feel, especially when I finally see the man who has spoken. He is standing in the shadows near the front door—a door that I am damn sure I locked after putting the *Closed* sign in the window and settling in for a long night of inventory and packing.

He is tall, well over six feet, with a lean, muscular build that is accentuated by the faded jeans that hug his thighs and the simple white T-shirt that reveals muscled arms sleeved with tattoos.

His casual clothes, inked skin, and close-shaved head hint at danger and rebellion, but those traits are contrasted by a commanding, almost elegant, presence that seems to both fill the room and take charge of it. This is a man who would be equally at ease in a tux as a T-shirt. A man who expects the world to bend to his will, and if it doesn't comply, he will go out and bend it himself.

I see that confidence most potently in his face, all sharp lines and angles that blend together into a masterpiece now dusted with the shadow of a late afternoon beard. He has the kind of eyes that miss nothing, and right now they are hard and assessing. They are softened, however, by long, dark lashes that most women would kill for.

His mouth is little more than a hard slash across his features, but I see a hint of softness, and when I find myself wondering how those lips would feel against my skin, I realize that I have been staring and yank myself firmly from my reverie.

"I asked you a question," I snap, more harshly than I intended. "Who are you, and how did you get in here?"

"Raine," he says, striding toward me. "Rainer Engel. And I walked in through the front door."

"I locked it." I wipe my now-sweaty hands on my dusty yoga pants.

"The fact that I'm inside suggests otherwise."

He has crossed the store in long, efficient strides, and now stands in front of me. I catch his scent, all musk and male, sin and sensuality, and feel an unwelcome ache between my thighs.

Not unwelcome because I don't like sex. On the contrary, I'd have to label myself a fan, and an overenthusiastic one at that. Because the truth is that I've spent too many nights in the arms of too many strangers trying to fill some void in myself.

I say "some void" because I don't really know what I'm searching for. A connection, I guess, but at the same time I'm scared of finding one and ending up hurt, which is why I shy from traditional "my friend has a friend" kind of dating, and spend more time than I should in bars and clubs. And that means that while I might be enjoying a series of really good lays, I'm not doing anything more than using sex as a Band-Aid.

At least, that is what my therapist, Kelly, back home in Austin says. And since I'm a lawyer and not a shrink, I'm going to have to take her word on that.

"We're closed," I say firmly. Or, rather, I intend to say firmly. In fact, my voice comes out thin, suggesting a question rather than a command.

Not that my tone matters. The man—*Raine*—seems entirely uninterested in what I have to say.

He cocks his head slightly to one side, as if taking my measure, and if the small curve of that sensual mouth is any indication, he likes what he sees. I prop a hand on my hip and stare back defiantly. I know what I look like—and I know that with a few exceptions, men tend to go stupid when I dial it up.

The ratty law school T-shirt I'm wearing is tight, accenting breasts that I'd cursed in high school, but that had become a boon once I started college and realized that my ample tits, slender waist, and long legs added up to a combination that made guys drool. Add in wavy blonde hair and green eyes and I've got the kind of cheerleader-esque good looks that make so many of the good old boy lawyers in Texas think that I've got cotton candy for brains.

And believe me when I say that I'm not shy about turning their misogynistic stereotype to my advantage, both in the courtroom and out of it.

"You're Callie." His voice conveys absolute certainty, as if his inspection confirmed one of the basic facts of the universe. Which, since I *am* Callie, I guess it did. But how the hell he knows who I am is beyond me.

"Your father talks about you a lot," Raine says, apparently picking up on my confusion. His eyes rake over me as he speaks, and my skin prickles with awareness, as potent as if his fingertip had stroked me. "A lawyer who lives in Texas with the kind of looks that make a father nervous, balanced by sharp, intelligent eyes that reassure him that she's not going to do anything stupid."

"You know my father."

"I know your father," he confirms.

"And he told you that about me?"

"The lawyer part. The rest I figured out all on my own." One corner of his mouth curves up. "I have eyes, after all." Those eyes are currently aimed at my chest, and I say a silent thank you to whoever decided that padded bras were a good thing because otherwise he would certainly see how hard and tight my nipples have become.

"University of Texas School of Law. Good school." He lifts his gaze from my chest to my face, and the heat I see in those ice-blue eyes seems to seep under my skin, melting me a bit from the inside out. "Very good."

I lick my lips, realizing that my mouth has gone uncomfortably dry. I've been working as an assistant district attorney for the last two years. I've gotten used to being the one in charge of a room. And right now, I'm feeling decidedly off-kilter, part of me wanting to pull him close, and the other wanting to run as far and as fast from him as I can.

Since neither option is reasonable at the moment, I simply take a step back, then find myself trapped by the glass jewelry case, now pressing against my ass.

I clear my throat. "Listen, Mr. Engel, if you're looking for my father—"

"I am, and I apologize for snapping at you when I came in, but I was surprised to see that the shop was closed, and when I saw someone other than Oliver moving inside, I got worried."

"I closed early so that I could work without being interrupted."

A hint of a smile plays at his mouth. "In that case, I'll also apologize for interrupting. But Oliver asked me to come by when I got back in town. I'm anxious to discuss the amulet that he's located."

"Oh." I don't know why I'm surprised. He obviously hadn't come into the store looking for me. And yet for some reason the fact that I've suddenly become irrelevant rubs me the wrong way.

Clearly, I need to get a grip, and I paste on my best customer service smile. "I'm really sorry, but my dad's not here."

"No? I told him I'd come straight over." I can hear the irritation in his voice. "He knows how much I want this piece—how much I'm willing to pay. If he's made arrangements to sell it to another—"

"*No.*" The word is fast and firm and entirely unexpected. "It's not like that. My dad doesn't play games with clients."

"That's true. He doesn't." His brow creases as he looks around the shop, taking in the open boxes, half filled with inventory, the colored sticky notes I've been using to informally assign items to numbered boxes, and the general disarray of the space. "Callie, what's happened to your father?"

It is the way he says my name that loosens my tongue. Had he simply asked the question, I probably would have told him that he could come back in the morning and we'd search the computerized inventory for the piece he's looking for. But there is something so intimate about my name on his lips that I can't help but answer honestly.

"My dad had a stroke last week." My voice hitches as I speak, and I look off toward the side of the store, too wrecked to meet his eyes directly.

"Oh, Callie." He steps closer and takes my hand, and I'm surprised to find that I not only don't pull away, but that I actually have to fight the urge to pull our joint hands close to my heart.

"I didn't know," he says. "I'm so sorry. How is he doing?"

"N-not very well." I suck in a breath and try to gather myself, but it's just so damn hard. My mom walked out when I was four, saying that being a mother was too much responsibility, and ever since I've been my dad's entire world. It's always amazed me that he didn't despise me. But he really doesn't. He says that I was a gift, and I know it's true because I have seen and felt it every day of my life.

Whatever the cause of my disconnect with men, it doesn't harken back to my dad, a little fact that I know fascinates my shrink, though she's too much the professional to flat out tell me as much.

"Does he have decent care? Do you need any referrals? Any help financially?" Raine is crouching in front of me, and I realize that I have sunk down, so that my butt is on the cold tile floor and I am hugging my knees.

I shake my head, too dazed to realize this stranger is apparently offering to help pay my dad's medical bills. "We're fine. He's got great care and great insurance. He's just—" I break off as my voice cracks. *"Shit."*

"Hey, it's okay. Breathe now. That's it, just breathe." He presses his hands to my shoulders, and his face is just inches away. His eyes are wide and safe and warm, and I want to slide into them. To just disappear into a place where there are neither worries nor responsibilities. Where someone strong will hold me and take care of me and make everything bad disappear.

But that's impossible, and so I draw another breath in time with his words and try once again to formulate a coherent thought. "He's—he's got good doctors, really. But he's not lucid. And this is my dad. I mean, Oliver Sinclair hasn't gone a day in his life without an opinion or a witticism."

I feel the tears well in my eyes and I swipe them away with a brusque brush of my thumb. "And it kills me because I can look at him and it breaks my heart to know that he must have all this stuff going on inside his head that he just can't say, and— and—"

But I can't get the words out, and I feel the tears snaking down my cheeks, and dammit, dammit, *dammit*, I do not want to lose it in front of this man—this stranger who doesn't feel like a stranger.

His grip on my shoulders tightens and he leans toward me.

And then—oh, dear god—his lips are on mine and they are as warm and soft as I'd imagined and he's kissing me so gently and so sweetly that all my worries are just melting away and I'm limp in his arms.

"Shhh. It's okay." His voice washes over me, as gentle and calming as a summer rain. "Everything's going to be okay."

I breathe deep, soothed by the warm sensuality of this stranger's golden voice. Except he isn't a stranger. I may not have met him before today, but somehow, here in his arms, I *know* him.

And that, more than anything, comforts me.

Calmer, I tilt my head back and meet his eyes. It is a soft moment and a little sweet—but it doesn't stay that way. It changes in the space of a glance. In the instant of a heartbeat. And what started out as gentle comfort transforms into fiery heat.

I don't know which of us moves first. All I know is that I have to claim him and be claimed by him. That I have to taste him—consume him. Because in some essential way that I don't fully understand, I know that only this man can quell the need burning inside me, and I lose myself in the hot intensity of his mouth upon mine. Of his tongue demanding entrance, and his lips, hard and demanding, forcing me to give everything he wants to take.

I am limp against him, felled by the onslaught of erotic sparks that his kisses have scattered through me. I am lost in the sensation of his hands stroking my back. Of his chest pressed against my breasts.

But it isn't until I realize that he has pulled me into his lap and that I can feel the hard demand of his erection against my rear that I force myself to escape this sensual reality and scramble backward out of his embrace.

"I'm sorry," I say, my breath coming too hard.

"Callie—" The need I hear in his voice reflects my own, and I clench my hands into fists as I fight against the instinct to move back into his arms.

"No." I don't understand what's happening—this instant heat, like a match striking gasoline. I've never reacted to a man this way before. My skin feels prickly, as if I've been caught in a lightning storm. His scent is all over me. And the taste of him lingers on my mouth.

And oh, dear god, I'm wet, my body literally aching with need, with a primal desire for him to just rip my clothes off and take me right there on the hard, dusty floor.

He's triggered a wildness in me that I don't understand—and my reaction scares the hell out of me.

"You need to go," I say, and I am astonished that my words are both measured and articulate, as if I'm simply announcing that it is closing time to a customer.

He stays silent, but I shake my head anyway, and hold up a finger as if in emphasis.

"No," I say, in response to nothing. "I don't know anything about this amulet. And now you really need to leave. Please," I add. "Please, Raine. I need you to go."

For a moment he only looks at me. Then he nods, a single tilt of his head in acknowledgment. "All right," he says very softly. "I'll go. But I'm not ever leaving you again."

I stand frozen, as if his inexplicable words have locked me in place. He turns slowly and strides out of the shop without looking back. And when the door clicks into place behind him and I am once more alone, I gulp in air as tears well in my eyes again.

I rub my hands over my face, forgiving myself for this emotional miasma because of all the shit that's happened with my dad. Of course I'm a wreck; what daughter wouldn't be?

Determined to get a grip, I follow his path to the door, then hold onto the knob. I'd come over intending to lock it. But now I want to yank it open and beg him to return.

It's an urge I fight. It's just my grief talking. My fear that I'm about to lose my father, the one person in all the world who is close to me, and so I have clung to a stranger in a desperate effort to hold fast to something.

That, at least, is what my shrink would say. *You're fabricating a connection in order to fill a void. It's what you do, Callie. It's what you've always done when lonely and afraid.*

I nod, telling myself I agree with Kelly's voice in my head.

And I do.

Because I am lonely.

And I am afraid of losing my dad.

But that's not the whole of it. Because there's something else that I'm afraid of, too, though I cannot put my finger on it. A strange sense of something coming. Something dark. Something bad.

And what scares me most is the ridiculous, unreasonable fear that I have just pushed away the one person I need to survive whatever is waiting for me out there in the dark.

Chapter 2

He could still taste the sweetness of her lips, and dear god, he wanted more.

Wanted everything. *Wanted her.*

The irony, of course, was that he hadn't intended to kiss her in the first place, even though from the moment she'd looked at him with those sparkling green eyes it had seemed as if he'd known her forever. But when the tears had welled in her eyes, he knew that he would have done anything to ease her grief.

The kiss had been tender. Almost sweet. But there was nothing sweet about the way he was feeling now. Bottom line?

Raine wanted Callie Sinclair. Craved her. Hungered for her.

Hell, he fucking yearned for her, and that was simply not a feeling he was used to having. Hadn't been for a very, very long time.

Oh, sure, he'd gotten off often enough. Lost himself in a woman. In the feel of her body against his. There was power in the claiming of a willing female, in that hard, rough ride that erased the world, at least for those few singular moments as the sensation built and climax approached.

And when the inevitable explosion came, he'd lose himself in the sharp oblivion that mimicked the death he sought again and again, and yet this death was forged in pleasure and not pain.

But that was all he wanted or needed—just that physical connection to remind him that no matter how dead he might feel on the inside—no matter how hard he chased that escape and no matter how many times he burned—this body still functioned and he still had a job to do.

Because if he could fuck, then he could fucking well survive another day, another year, another century.

Shit.

He ran his fingers over his close-cropped hair and told himself to get a grip. An ironic lecture since he stood like a criminal in the shadows across the street from Sinclair's Antiques, his eyes trained on the now-locked door.

Thank goodness he'd dismissed Dennis, Phoenix Security's driver, telling him to go ahead and simply be on call in case Raine needed him later. He hardly wanted to explain to the eager twenty-three-year-old why the hell he was standing like an idiot, waiting for just another glimpse of this woman who'd gotten so deep under his skin.

Christ, he was pathetic. For millennia he'd not been distracted by a woman. Not since he'd lost Livia, his mate.

Oh, he'd fucked plenty, but that was to escape. Because even after all these centuries, he still craved what he'd lost when she'd been ripped from him.

They'd been bonded, and never once had he believed that he would ever feel that same emotional connection with another female.

And yet this woman—Sinclair's daughter—not only caught his attention, but sparked his awareness.

The intensity of his reaction to Callie had taken him by surprise, and he told himself that he was simply attracted to her beauty. That he just wanted to fuck her—but that wasn't true at all.

He wanted to protect her.

He wanted to have her.

Dammit, he may not have met her before tonight, but he *knew* her. Her heart. Her core.

And that's why he stood there in the dark.

That's why he was watching her door.

And that's why the moment she left the building, he was going to follow her—all the way to wherever the hell that might lead.

* * * *

"Callie, I didn't realize you'd come in. Why on earth are you sitting in the dark?"

I look over at Nurse Bennett and shrug, feeling small and a bit lost. "I just wanted to be here."

"You okay, honey?"

I'm curled up under a thin blanket on the lumpy couch in my father's private hospital room. She sits down beside me and puts her hand on my knee. I expect her to say comforting things. Like how just because the doctors are already talking about transferring him to a nursing home doesn't mean that he might not still pull through.

She doesn't say that, though, and I'm grateful, because I know she doesn't believe it. The truth is, despite what I told Raine, I don't think my dad's going to get better, and I hate myself for that.

"Still nothing today?" I ask, though the question is just for form. Since the stroke, he's spoken only once, and that was to the EMS tech who came after a pedestrian found him sprawled on the street in front of his shop.

"I'm sorry, honey."

"What do you think he was trying to say?" I hate how needy I sound, but I can't help but cling to those last words, as if they were a message for me that, if I only understood, would somehow change everything.

"Don't do that to yourself, Callie. We've talked about this. A stroke is a traumatic event to the brain, and your father didn't just have one stroke but several in quick succession. In that situation, hallucinations are common."

"A pillar of fire with the face of a man? That's common?"

"That's why they call it a hallucination."

"But why that?"

She squeezes my hand. "There's probably no reason at all. You can twist yourself up trying to find meaning where there's none to be found."

I nod because I know she's right. "I'm going to miss you."

"I'm going to miss both of you. Have you decided what you're going to do long term?"

I draw a deep breath. The decision I've made is so permanent, and I hate that I'm making it for my dad, too. But the days keep moving forward, and I have to move with them.

"I talked with a nursing home in Texas. I'm going to stay in New York another week and get his shop closed up and hire an agent to sell the property and talk to Sotheby's about putting some of the more important pieces up for auction. Then I'm going to go home, and I'll arrange for Dad's transport to Dallas as soon as a private room opens up. They don't think it'll take too long."

"Well, like I said, I'll miss you both. But it's good that you're going back to your friends and your work, and that you'll have your dad nearby."

I nod and smile, but the truth is that I'm not sure that anywhere will feel like home anymore. Because right now, all I feel is alone.

Nurse Bennett gives my shoulder a friendly pat as she stands. "I'm going to check his vitals and get out of your hair. Don't stay here tonight, sweetie. You should go home where you can get a good night's sleep."

"I will," I say, though that's probably a lie. More nights than not, I fall asleep on this couch. It's strange, I know, but there's something comforting about the buzz and chirp of the machinery. Even the steady rhythm of the air flowing through the oxygen mask gives me some hope. Because as long as these machines are running, my father is alive. And as long as he's alive, he might return to me.

"I'm trying, sweetheart. You know that I'm trying."

"Daddy?" I search, but I see nothing but the dark.

"I'm right here, baby. But I have to tell you—you have to know."

"Have to know what?"

A low rumbling fills my ears, and I strain to make out words. Nothing is clear, though. Nothing until I hear my father's voice saying, "And you have to be careful."

"I don't understand." There's a frantic edge to my voice. "Daddy, I couldn't hear you. I don't know what you're talking about."

"Look down."

I do, and now I can see my hand in his. He squeezes and fire rises up, flames licking our joined hands.

I yank mine free and leap to my feet.

"Daddy!" The word jerks me from sleep, and I realize that I am on my feet and breathing hard. Even now, I can feel the warmth of the flames and the pressure of my father's hand against my own. But there is nothing there, and my father is all the way across the room, still in the bed and attached to the IVs and machines that beep and hum.

I don't remember falling asleep, but I must have, because clearly I have been dreaming.

I close my eyes and press my fingers to my temples. *A nightmare.* Just a nightmare. Not a message. Not a code. Not a portent.

My father had a stroke, and no matter what I may wish or hope or want to be true, I have to suck it up and deal with that.

I think about what Nurse Bennett said, and I know that she is right. I need to get out of here, at least for a while. Bad sleep and nightmares aren't going to help my dad, they aren't going to help me, and they sure as hell aren't going to heal my grief.

At my dad's bedside, I lean over and kiss his cheek. "You be good, Daddy," I whisper. "I'll see you tomorrow."

I'm doing the right thing—I know that. But once I am outside, the idea of going back to the apartment above my father's store doesn't appeal.

I don't want to be alone, and I consider finding a club. Someplace loud enough that I don't have to talk, and with the kind of heavy bass that pounds through you, almost like sex. A place with no cover for women, and enough good-looking guys to make it worth the bother.

I consider it, but I don't do it. That's not what I crave tonight. I don't want to search for something that I know I'm not going to find. I don't want to pretend that being in the arms of some stranger is going to make a difference.

I don't want fake.

And I have no idea how to find something—or someone—who is real.

So I simply wander, walking from the hospital back toward my dad's store on 59th. I don't have a plan, I don't have a purpose, and it isn't until I turn into a small bar with dark wood and dim lights that I realize I want a drink. Maybe even two.

Hell, maybe I'll have three and ease myself into a dreamless sleep.

It's late on a weeknight, and the place isn't crowded. I take one of the empty stools a few seats down from a couple who are clearly on their first date, then settle in.

"By yourself tonight?" the bartender asks as she puts a dish of spicy nuts and pretzels in front of me.

"Sad but true."

"The hell with that," she says. "Sometimes alone is the best way to be. What can I get for you?"

"Sounds like you've been there, done that," I say after I order a glass of Glenmorangie, neat. I'm leaning forward, my elbows on the bar as she pours, then pushes it in front of me.

"Honey, if you knew my ex, you'd understand that I speak only the truth. Trust me. Ginger knows what Ginger knows, and Ginger knows that alone can be just fine and dandy. Especially if you have a battery operated friend."

I bark out a laugh, almost spitting out my first sip of scotch as I do. "I'll keep that in mind."

I wait until she's walked away to check on other customers before taking another sip. It's excellent, and I lean against the back of the stool and relax, thinking that this is exactly what I need. A good drink. A laid-back atmosphere. And a bartender who reminds me of my paralegal back in Dallas, a wild redhead who's never met a stranger and manages to brighten even the crappiest of days. And when you prosecute homicides and sex offenders, some of those days really can be crappy.

I finish my scotch as I check my phone. My boss has a daughter about my age, and he promised to keep work out of my inbox except in the direst of emergencies. If the state of my e-mail is any indication, the criminal underworld in Texas hasn't completely exploded, for which I'm grateful.

At the same time, I'm feeling a little irrelevant. I can't help my dad and my job is sailing smoothly without me. I couldn't even help Rainer Engel, and now he's probably never going to get his amulet, because I have no idea what it looks like or where it might be. And none of the recent purchase orders and invoices I've reviewed in the store suggest that my father had acquired the thing at all, despite Raine's certainty that Daddy had not only acquired it, but was expecting Raine to come by and get it.

I trace my finger over the rim of my glass as I think about Raine.

You want something real? He's about as real as it gets.

The thought comes unbidden into my mind, and I have a hard time dismissing it, as much as I try.

I don't want to think about Rainer Engel. Not like that. I don't want to remember his mouth on mine. I don't want to think about his hands on my skin. I don't want to remember the way my body fired merely from his proximity or the way his touch had both consumed and overwhelmed me.

He was larger than life, commanding without being overpowering, and his kiss had completely filled my senses, making me feel more alive than I'd felt in a very long time.

I don't want to think of any of that, and yet what choice do I have? Because now that he is in my thoughts, he has possessed me completely, his memory alone as commanding as the man himself, and now I'm feeling antsy and wild and I just want to be home alone in the dark with these wild thoughts and decadent memories.

I toss a twenty onto the bar and stand up. Then I turn—and then I gasp.

Raine.

He's right there, just inches away, and there is a hunger on his face so potent I have to reach for the bar to steady myself.

"With me, angel."

"Excuse me?" My pulse beats in my ear, so loud that it has

drowned out everything except the two of us and the sound of my own breathing.

"You heard me." He moves closer, then reaches for the bar as well. The result is that I'm trapped, with a barstool on one side of me, the bar itself on the other, and Raine in front of me. Between us, the air crackles and pops, alive with the heat we are generating. "You're coming with me."

I open my mouth to protest, but find myself asking, "Where?"

It's a tactical error on my part, and one that isn't lost on the man. His smile flows like liquid sin, and instead of answering, he simply holds out his hand.

"This guy bothering you?" Ginger stands like a pit bull behind the bar, and I can't help but smile at the thought of her going up against the likes of Raine.

Raine's body doesn't shift but I see the storm building in those exceptional blue eyes. "How about it, angel? Am I bothering you?"

I'm bothered, all right. But not in the way Ginger means. Slowly, I shake my head. Even more slowly, I reach for his hand. "It's okay," I say, surprised that there is no hesitation in my voice. "I'm with him."

His fingers twine with mine, and as before, I feel that shock of connection, only this time it seems even more potent, as if this contact is a key, and by merely taking his hand I have opened a door that I may never be able to close.

Chapter 3

Raine held tight to her hand, reveling in the sensation of her skin against his. Of the familiarity of this woman he had only just met—and yet he was becoming increasingly certain that he already knew her deeply. Intimately.

He needed to feel her—to touch her. He needed to bury himself in her and find out if what he believed was true. If Callie Sinclair was truly the miracle he suspected.

Desire and need welled up in him, and he pulled her close, pressing his other hand to the small of her back. He searched her eyes, shining now with emerald fire, and was relieved to see no fear, no hesitation. And yet the worry that he'd seen on her face as she'd left the hospital still lingered, and he was overwhelmed by a wave of fierce protectiveness.

Had he thought he needed her in his bed to satisfy his own craving? He did, yes, but that was no longer his primary desire. On the contrary, he wanted, *needed*, to erase her worry. To ease her. To hold her as she opened up, both wanting him and trusting him.

He needed to build—or rebuild—this connection between them. Because it wasn't just her body he intended to claim, it was the woman—body, mind, soul.

He released her back, surrendering to the urge to brush his fingertips over her cheek. As he did, she closed her eyes, and her soft sigh of pleasure was like ambrosia to him.

"You've had a rough day."

Her eyes fluttered open. "You've been following me." There was no accusation in her voice. She was simply stating a fact.

"Yes."

She tilted her head, as if surprised by his ready admission. "This isn't about the amulet, is it?"

"No, Callie. It's not."

She licked her lips, and he could see the confusion wisp across her features. Confusion, yes. But something more, too. Hope? Recognition?

He shook himself, afraid that all he was seeing on her was the reflection of his own hope and desire.

He smiled to set her at ease. "Is that a problem?"

"No."

The immediacy of her answer bolstered him, and he felt a tightening in his groin. He wanted to hold her close, to feel the press of her body against his and let the thrum of her heartbeat mix with his own.

"It's just—" She gently withdrew her hand from his, and it seemed to him as if she'd ripped the fabric of the world out from under him. "I—I don't usually—"

"What?"

She shook her head as if banishing her thoughts even as a hint of a smile tugged at her lips. "If it's not the amulet, what is it you want from me?"

Christ, what a question. "So many things," he finally said, because that was the best truth that he knew. "Right now, I want to soothe you."

"Oh."

Her voice trembled slightly, and he tightened his fingers into a fist, fighting the urge to touch her. There was a storm building between them, making the air crackle and burn, that spark or connection or whatever it was vibrating in the damp night air. If he reached out—if he let skin touch skin—he knew with unerring certainty that she would come with him, submit to him.

And though he wanted that—dear lord, how he wanted that—he wanted more to have the choice be entirely hers. To come not because she was reacting to the heat, but to him. Not following that thread of connection, but following her heart.

He watched, holding his own breath even as she drew in hers. "What does that mean?" she asked. "When you say you want to soothe me?"

"That depends on you, angel. Do you want me to take you back to your father's house and see you safely tucked away for the night?"

He saw the small frown curve at her mouth and felt a ping of joy that the thought of simply escorting her home did not satisfy her.

"Or do you need something different?"

He could see by the fire in her eyes that she did, and he pressed on, rightly or wrongly using words in the same way that he wanted to use his hands. To caress and tease and pleasure. To bring her close. To make her his.

"Do you need to forget? To get lost in the feel of my hands upon your skin, my mouth on your breast? Do you want to lose yourself in passion, in submission, in pleasure?"

He could see the effect that his words had on her. The flush on her skin. The parting of her lips. The way she moved a hairsbreadth closer to him.

He saw—and he was satisfied.

"I'll give you what you need, angel, I promise you that. But not until you tell me what that is."

"I don't know what I need," she whispered, her head tilted down. "I only know what I want." She lifted her face to his, her eyes burning, and the words she spoke held enough power to bring him to his knees. "Please, Raine. Right now, all I want is you."

* * * *

All I want is you.

The sound of my voice hasn't faded when his hand twines in my hair and his arm goes around my waist.

In one wild, violent motion, he pulls me hard against him. I gasp, both in surprise and pleasure, as my breasts press against his chest. As my hips grind against his.

We are well matched in height, and I can feel the hot demand of his erection against my belly, and when he slants his mouth over mine, I cannot help my moan of pleasure from this sensual assault.

He takes advantage of the sound, using his tongue to tease my mouth open. It takes little effort—I want this, after all. Want his hands, hot and wild upon me. Want his mouth all over me.

And god help me, I want his cock inside me.

The thought shocks me out of myself, and I pull back, breathing hard. "We're on the street."

The grin he flashes is decidedly wicked. "Is that a problem?" There's no denying the tease in his voice, and I don't fight the smile that tugs at my mouth.

"I don't do exhibitionism."

"No?" He looks me up and down so slowly and intimately that it feels as though he is making a liar out of me right there by burning off every stitch of clothes simply with the heat of his gaze. "Then tell me, Callie. What do you do?"

I lick my lips, undone by the sensual images his four little words have conjured in my mind. I have no hope of a comeback. I have completely surrendered. "I—"

But his finger upon my lip silences me. "No. Don't tell me. I'd rather find out myself."

He traces his fingertip gently along my lower lip, leaving my mouth feeling warm and swollen, as if I've been very well kissed.

It is as if he has flipped a switch in me, making me aware of my entire body. From this sensual tingle in my lips, to the tightness in my breasts, to the tiny beads of sweat that have popped up at the nape of my neck. And let's not forget the way my sex clenches in both demand and anticipation of his touch.

In other words, he's made me a wreck, and right then if he repeated his question, I'd have to tell him that I'd do pretty much anything.

We are still on the street right outside the bar, and as my senses return, I notice that we have actually drawn a small audience. Despite what movies might suggest, the kind of wild kisses that mimic fucking are not par for the course on the sidewalks of the Upper East Side. I notice an elderly couple, the man looking at us over the top of his glasses with what looks to me like lecherous interest. I clutch Raine's arm. "If you want this to go anywhere at all, then get me out of here now."

"As you wish," he says, then nods toward the street where a sleek black limo has just pulled up.

I hesitate because it takes a moment for me to register that the limo and Raine are a set.

"You look surprised," Raine says as the driver opens the door for us. I cast a glance between him and the interior. His rough, rebellious looks and sleeves of tats might seem in stark contrast to the pristine leather interior that suggests boardrooms and opera rather than beer and heavy metal. But that isn't what Raine is about, and I already knew that. He has too much control, too much self-possession. A limo suits him just fine.

But I have a feeling he keeps a bike for fun.

"No," I say as I step inside. "I'm really not. I was just thinking that I was relieved you didn't bring your Harley. I'm not in the mood to ride shotgun."

He sits beside me on the leather bench at the back of the limo. There is a bar along the sidewall, and he turns to it, then casually pours a glass of scotch on the rocks. "Actually, it's a Macchia Nera."

I gape at him. "Seriously?"

The fact that I have a clue what he's talking about obviously surprises him. "You've heard of it?"

I take the scotch he hands me, then nod. "My boss is into bikes. That bike is his personal nirvana. He once told me he could either buy the Macchia Nera or a house. When he factored in his wife and kids, he went with the house, but for a while there it was close."

"Fortunately not a dilemma I've faced."

"You'd choose the bike?"

"It would be hard to be homeless. No roof as with a car. But she's a sweet bike. It might just be worth it. Then again," he added, aiming the full force of those brilliant blue eyes my direction, "a man will do most anything to take care of the woman he loves. I imagine that your boss didn't even consider the loss of his bike a sacrifice."

I shift a bit in the seat, then take a sip of the scotch. It's good. Exceptionally good, actually, and I tell him so. "Most men would have offered me wine."

"I'm not most men."

"Yeah. I actually figured that out."

"Clever girl."

I smile at him, enjoying talking to him even more than I like looking at him. But right then, I'm not interested in talking. Or in looking for that matter. All I want to do is feel.

I move to set the scotch aside, but he takes the glass from my hand, then slips his finger into the liquid and slides the digit into his own mouth. My body clenches merely from the sight, and my lips tingle with awareness. "Raine."

He shakes his head, then withdraws his finger and holds it over his lips in a gesture of silence. Then he dips into the scotch again, this time painting my lips with his fingertip.

I almost melt from the contact, and when my lips part on a gentle sigh, he eases his finger into my mouth. I take it greedily, relishing the taste of his skin mingled with the scotch. I draw his finger in, sucking and teasing him with my tongue, and it is easy enough to see the effect that I am having on him reflected on his face.

I meet his eyes, and when I do, the entire world fades away. There is only the two of us, and passion, and need.

I draw him in deeper. I'm greedy now, wanting more. Wanting everything. And so help me, I want to make him come. I want to see this strong, magnificent man lose himself in wild abandon—and I want to know that I was the one who took him there.

Shamelessly, I ease forward, my fingers groping for the fly on his jeans, but he gently shakes his head even as he takes my hand and presses it over the steel-hard length of his erection. "I can't tell you how much I want those lips around my cock," he says as he withdraws his finger. "But not just yet."

I swallow as he takes my hand from him and lifts it to his mouth. He kisses my palm, then repeats the kiss on my other hand. "Sit back," he orders, even as he shifts to face me better. "Eyes closed."

"I want to see you."

"And I want you to feel. Close your eyes, Callie."

There is no room for argument in his voice, and my willingness to comply surprises me, as I do not usually give in so easily to a man's demand.

Raine, however, is no ordinary man, and he is proving that point even now as he sets my entire body on fire merely by the gentle stroke of his finger along my collar. His finger is damp, and I can hear the tingle of ice as he once more dips his finger into the scotch and then uses that digit to paint my flesh. Then I feel his mouth on me, tracing my jawline, trailing down my neck. His lips tease me. His tongue tastes me. And soon enough his fingers descend to the open collar of my shirt.

I'm wearing a blue linen button-down, and as his fingers flick each button open, I know that he is revealing the innocent pale pink bra, though I am feeling very far from innocent at the moment.

He finishes the buttons and spreads the shirt open. I can't help it, and I open my eyes to see that he is gazing upon me as if I am something holy. "You're stunning," he says, and I feel my cheeks heat with the words. "And you broke the rules. Eyes closed, Callie."

I draw in a breath, but comply. Immediately, I feel his fingertip, again wet with scotch, tracing from cleavage to navel. "I think this is my favorite way to enjoy my favorite drink," he says, making me giggle. But my laughter stops when he drips more scotch into my navel, then proceeds to lap it up, his tongue working such magic on me that the muscles in my abdomen quiver with need and I arch my back in a desperate attempt for just a little more contact, a little more connection.

Then his nimble fingers unbutton my jeans and ease down my zipper. I'm wearing thong panties, and he trails his fingertip along my pubic bone, just at the top of the material. Then it is not his fingertip that I feel, but his lips, and my sex clenches with such intense need that I know I am desperately, hopelessly wet.

I want him to take me further, and I bite my lower lip in anticipation of where he will go next. Tongue or finger sliding under the waistband. Easing my jeans down. Teasing my clit with soft kisses. Fucking me hard with his tongue.

My body trembles merely from the anticipation, and there is no denying that he has brought me close, so very close, and I am primed and ready for his next touch.

Except it doesn't come.

In fact, he leaves me entirely.

I open my eyes, confused, to find him no longer sitting beside me, but on the bench seat exactly opposite me. He is sitting up, his legs apart, and there is no mistaking either the bulge of his erection or the heat in his eyes.

"What are you—"

"Take off your clothes."

"What?"

His gaze skims over me, and there is such a feral hunger in his eyes that I swear I almost come right then. "You heard me. I want you naked."

I start to shake my head, but he simply holds up a finger again.

"I want to see you, Callie. I want to see the glow of arousal on your skin. I want to get hard while you touch yourself. I want to bring you to heights of pleasure you haven't even imagined, and I want to hold you while you scream my name and cry out in release."

I am breathing hard, and there is no hiding how fiercely turned on I am.

"You say you aren't into exhibitionism? I'm going to make it my mission to change your mind. So take off your clothes, Callie, or everything stops and I'll drive you home. The choice is yours. But I will tell you that I desperately hope that you do as I say because the night is young, and this is only the beginning."

Chapter 4

Take off your clothes.

His words flow through me, both dangerous and enticing.

Part of me wants to tell him to go to hell, but the bigger part wants to strip bare and get myself off, tormenting him by not allowing him to touch me.

I want to feel this—want to feel wild. Out of control.

I want to take it as far as it can go—but only with Raine.

Across from me, he still sits, silently watching me, his erection so tight I'm surprised he doesn't burst through his jeans.

Slowly, I slip off the shirt, then toss it to the side, leaving me clad in only my bra, jeans, and wedge sandals.

I reach behind me and unfasten my bra, then shimmy it off and drop it on top of my shirt. And then—because I want to run this show at least a little—I cup my own breasts, then pinch my own nipples, gratified at the sound of pleasure he makes. Even more gratified when he puts his hand on his cock and strokes himself through his jeans.

"The rest," he says, and I revel in pure feminine satisfaction when I hear the strain in his voice.

I comply willingly, maybe even too eagerly. I want to be free of my clothes. I want the pleasure of feeling his eyes upon me and knowing that my body excites him.

But I also want this to be a show, a seduction. I have no illusions about who is in charge here, but I do want to keep a tiny bit of the power to tease and entice.

With that in mind, I slide my hand down over my belly to my jeans.

Since he's already very considerately unbuttoned them for me, I only have to lift my hips to shimmy out of them. I do that, moving slowly as I free myself from jeans and shoes.

"You're stunning."

My cheeks warm with pleasure, and I continue this erotic dance, sliding my finger down into my panties and finding my clit, throbbing with a demand for attention.

"Take them off." His voice is clear and authoritative, and just the sound of it—of his command—heightens my arousal. "Then spread your legs and tease yourself."

I do, not the least bit shy. On the contrary, I want this. Everything he has to give and more. And so I do as he says, following his bold words as he tells me to stroke my inner thigh, to tease my clit, to thrust three fingers deep into my cunt.

"Do you like that?" he asks, and I can only moan in assent. "Does it get you off knowing that I'm watching you? That I'm imagining my cock deep inside you? Can you imagine it, Callie? Can you feel me fucking you hard?"

"Yes." It is all I can do to get the word out. I am soaked. My body clenching around my fingers, my clit swollen and demanding. And through all of it, I know that he has his eyes on me. That my show is turning him on, too, and that he is painfully aware of just how much I want him.

"Is it enough?" he asks. "Your hands? Your fingers?"

"No."

"Tell me what you want, angel."

"You. Please. God, Raine. Please."

"Come here."

I practically leap to the other side of the limo even as he rids himself of shoes and jeans and briefs. He still wears that T-shirt, and I remedy that quickly by taking hold of the hem and pulling it over his head to fully reveal his hard, taut body, which is covered in tats. In fact, almost every inch of the man that I can see except his magnificent cock and his face is decorated in wings and talons and the proud faces and beaks of birds that I can only assume are phoenixes, especially with the hint of flames lapping at them.

It's not a look I usually go for, but on Raine it seems to fit. As if it's not decoration, but part of who he is. I don't understand it, and right then, I don't care. I just want to feel him inside me. I want it wild. I want it hot.

Without asking or being told, I climb onto the seat and straddle him.

"That's a girl," he says in approval.

"Condom?" I'm on the pill, but pregnancy's not the only thing a girl has to be careful about.

"I don't have one. But I swear I'm clean. Do you trust me?"

I hesitate, because I have my rules. But so help me, I do trust him. Me, who so rarely trusts any man.

I nod, and I see the fire in his eyes. "Now show me. Show me what it is you want."

I can wait no longer. I lean forward, one hand twining in his hair and holding him steady as I close my mouth over his and capture him in a deep, wet kiss. I slide my other hand down my body, sending an electric shimmer running through me when I graze the pad of my thumb over my clit.

I find his cock, hard and thick and velvety smooth, between our bodies. He's rigid, and I have to rise up on my knees to position him, but when I feel the head of his cock at my core, the sensation is almost enough to make me lose my mind.

I'm desperately wet, and I tease both of us for a bit before lowering myself onto him. But it isn't enough for him, and his hands are at my hips and he's thrusting me down, impaling me hard upon him. I cry out, not from pain, but from the glorious sensation of being completely taken. Utterly fucked.

"Christ, you feel good."

I say nothing. At the moment, I'm really not capable of forming words.

His mouth closes over my breast, and I suck in air sharply at the overwhelming sensation of his mouth sucking hard on my nipple even while he pistons me so wildly. I press my palms to his shoulders, wanting leverage, and bring myself down even harder, faster. I am craving him like a woman starved, and in that moment, I cannot imagine not being connected like this. Not feeling him inside me. Not riding him hard.

"I want to do everything to you." He lifts his head from my breast and tilts up to look at me. His eyes burn like blue flame, and I feel like I could fall inside them. "There is nothing I won't give you. Nowhere I won't take you to give you pleasure."

He kisses me, long and deep, then slides his finger into my mouth. I suck it hard, and with each tug I feel the corresponding pull in my sex and the tightening of my muscles around his cock.

But that is not what he wants, and even as he tongues my mouth, he slides his hand around to tease my ass with his now-damp finger. I cry out in surprise at the intimate contact. I've never gone there—never wanted to with anyone else. And yet I want it with Raine. I want him to fill me completely, and I feel as though there is nothing he can do—no way that he can touch me that I would deny him.

"Touch yourself," he whispers. "Tease your clit. I want to feel the storm building inside you."

That is something else I've never done with other men. Oh, sure, I've gotten myself off after I sent them running, if they failed to take me all the way. But with them watching? That wasn't something I wanted to share.

Now, though, I do not hesitate. As I had done for show earlier, I slide my hand down and finger my clit, using long strokes so that I can not only tease myself, but so that I can feel the slick heat of his cock as he moves in and out of me.

I am lost in a sensual feast. His cock deep inside me. His finger teasing my ass. His mouth on my breast, and my own hand playing with my clit. My legs are wide, and I am riding him hard, and he is thrusting so deep inside me that it feels as though he is completely filling me.

"You're mine." He growls out the words, his mouth capturing mine before releasing it just enough to speak, the words so close that it feels almost as though I'm saying them. "Come with me now," he says, even as he releases into me, his body thrusting violently and heightening my own pleasure.

"Come for me," he growls again. "And come back to me…"

Even as he makes the demand, he thrusts his finger inside me and impales me hard on his cock so that I am utterly and completely filled. And as if I am bound to obey this man, my body soars upward, then shatters into a million pieces that seem to dance and swirl and mesh with Raine, who is spinning up in the heavens with me.

It is wild and wicked and wonderful, and then slowly, so very slowly, I begin to reassemble in his arms.

"Mmm," I murmur, certain I must be the most thoroughly fucked woman on the planet. "*La petite mort.*"

"Why do you say that?"

"That's what the French call an orgasm. The little death. As wonderfully destroyed as I feel right now, I think it's accurate."

He chuckles, then shifts me so that I am more comfortably on his lap. I trace my fingers over his tattoos. "I like them," I say. "They suit you."

"Do they?"

I hear humor in his voice that I don't understand. "What's funny?"

"You're more intuitive than you realize. Those tats are my little deaths."

I frown, completely confused. "What do you mean?"

"It doesn't matter. Right now I don't want to talk. I only want to hold you."

As if in contradiction to his own statement, he presses the button for the intercom. "Dennis," he says. "Take us to Number 36."

He releases the button without receiving a reply, then turns to me. "My home."

I nod, but even as I do, I feel something cold twisting inside me, as if it is determined to push away everything wonderful that I've just felt with this man.

I let him hold me, and in his arms I feel warm and safe. It scares me, in fact, how comfortable I feel with Raine because I have never felt this way before. I'm self-aware enough to know that I sleep with men to fill a hole, but it just seems to get deeper every day. And the truth is, I never walk into sex expecting anything but the physical exhaustion that can take me out of myself.

I certainly never expect a connection. Never expect to fill that hole, even if just a little.

And yet with Raine…

I shift in his arms and sit up.

"Cold?"

"A bit," I lie as I reach for my bra and put it on, then follow with my panties and jeans. He is still naked, as stunningly beautiful as a vengeful god with his marked skin wild against the black backdrop of leather. And even though I am sated, my body responds, even as my mind starts to pull back.

"Is this what you don't usually do? Go home with men you've just met?"

I smirk. "No. I do that more often than I should." My admission surprises me, and I glance at him, but he doesn't seem shocked, just curious.

"Then what did you mean earlier? When you said you don't usually…what?"

I don't usually have expectations other than sex. I don't usually feel anything before being with a man.

I almost tell him that, and I have to cut off my words before I reveal too much of this emotional stew that is filling me.

I tell myself I don't want to go there; I don't want to feel a connection I don't understand.

I am, of course, lying. There's little I want more. Isn't that what I keep telling Kelly? That I feel there's someone out there. Someone who fits me?

And doesn't she keep telling me that I have to open myself up? That burning through men like a book of matches is a bad idea? That I don't have to project my mother's abandonment on every potential relationship.

I know that she is right. I even know what I want.

And yet I also know that the possibility that I may have found it in this man is terrifying.

What if I'm wrong? What if I expose too much of myself? What if I get too close and just get burned?

"Callie? What is it? What did you mean?"

"Just—nothing. I just ramble when I'm nervous."

"Do I make you nervous?"

I pull my still-bare feet up onto the seat and look at him, strong and powerful and entirely in control. "Honestly? Yes."

He reaches for his shirt and shrugs it on, apparently realizing that I've moved into the land of serious conversation. "Why?"

"I—I'm sorry. This is—This is bigger than I expected." I lick my lips, looking with mild panic at the brownstones rising up alongside the limo as it slows to a stop. "It doesn't just scare me. It terrifies me. I'm sorry, but I need to go home."

"Stay." The command in his tone is unmistakable. "I told you, all I want to do is soothe you."

I am tempted. So very tempted. But I shake my head. "This has been amazing. Beyond amazing. But I can't stay with you tonight." I need to get clear so that I can think. Because the one thing I definitely can't do around this man is conjure a cohesive thought.

His hand closes over my wrist, and as I melt just a bit from the contact, I can only wish that his touch didn't have such sensual power over me. "I told you, Callie. I'm never leaving you again."

The words resonate through me, as if touching some deep core, but I force myself to shake my head because I need to run. "I don't know what that means, but it doesn't matter. Because you're not leaving me, Raine." Gently, I pull my arm free. "I'm sorry. But right now, I'm the one leaving you."

Chapter 5

I stand on the street, breathing hard, my thoughts spinning.

My entire adult life I've been looking for something. And for the first time, it feels like maybe I found it.

So what the fuck am I doing running away?

"You crave intimacy, Callie. And yet you run from it." Kelly's words seem to fill my head, and though I try to shut her out, she just keeps on talking. *"Perhaps it stems from the loss of your mother when you were so young, perhaps something else. But until you understand why you're afraid of getting close, you're never going to have a fulfilling relationship. And you are too extraordinary a woman not to open yourself up to love and friendship."*

She's right. I know she's right. And I take a single step back toward the limo. It's still curbside, the door still open. I cannot see through the tinted glass. I have no way of knowing if he is watching me, and yet I am certain that he is. Watching, but not coming after me, and I am grateful for that small mercy because I have to decide this for myself, and I fear that if he steps out of that limo and holds out his hand to me, that I will rush into his arms and let him take me inside Number 36.

I want that—so help me, I want it so badly I can imagine how it feels. The sensation of my feet flying over pavement to meet him. The impact of my body against his as his arms close around me. The hard demand of his mouth against mine.

And yet there's something else, too. *Fear.*

Kelly would tell me to examine that fear and push past it, but as a therapist, that's her job. As an assistant district attorney, I know that isn't always the best thing to do. Sometimes fear is a good thing.

Sometimes fear tells you to run, to save your own life.

Ignore that instinct and you do so at your own peril.

I've seen it time and time again on the faces of too many victims. In the photographs of too many corpses.

I do not believe that Raine would hurt me physically, but I am desperately afraid that the intensity of my desire for him isn't real. That this connection I feel with him is nothing more than an illusion, because how can it be real? How can someone I've known for less than a day have seeped so far under my skin when no one else in my entire life has been able to do that?

The world is already taking my father from me, and I don't think I can stand the pain of being wrong about Raine. Of getting close and losing him, too.

And somehow, I am certain that I *will* lose him. That he will draw me close, and then let me go.

No, that's not entirely true. What I'm certain of is that he already *has* let me go.

I frown because I know the thought makes no sense—I just met the man, and I know damn well he would welcome me into his arms. And yet I cannot shake this certainty. This feeling.

This…memory?

I roll my eyes at the thought. Clearly, the night has rattled me more than I realized. Which is all the more reason to just walk away.

Better to hold tight to the passion and joy I felt in Raine's arms. Better to cherish it like something wild and precious and fragile, and to pull it out for comfort when I feel lost and alone.

Better all that than to open the door to pain and fear and heartbreak.

And so I make the only decision I can.

I turn away from the limo, and I walk away, heading toward Madison, where I can turn and continue toward 59th Street and home.

* * * *

Raine fought back the rising sense of desolation.

She'd left him.

The thought was…well, it was unthinkable. After all this time to have found her again—and, yes, he was certain that he'd found her—only to watch her walk away.

He wanted to run after her, but he quelled the urge. He knew her. He'd recognized her essence the first moment he saw her, and when he had entered her—when she had exploded in passion in his arms—the last of his doubts were swept away. But he understood that the same was not true for Callie.

She had felt a pull, of that much he was certain. But she didn't know the origin of it. And the intensity of the connection scared her.

He may not like that simple fact, but he could understand it. And he could give her time.

She would come back to him—or he would go to her.

Either way, he could be patient.

He'd been alone for three thousand years, thinking her lost to him forever, believing he was condemned to an eternity alone. He could wait a little while longer while he decided what to do.

Not too long, however, as he still had to find the amulet. And to do that, he might have to press Callie before she was ready. Unless, of course, he could find another way.

He considered his options as he looked out the window toward Number 36. The five-story brownstone had been owned by the brotherhood since the late eighteen hundreds, when it had been acquired after the first occupant died in an ill-conceived duel and the property was put on the market to settle his considerable debts.

The first and second floors housed a gentleman's club, Dark Pleasures, which Mal had established in 1895 despite some in the brotherhood's protests. But Mal had been insistent, and one did not cross Mal, especially not after an encounter with Christina, when the rage and regret flowed through him.

And ultimately, all of the brotherhood had to agree that the club served a valuable purpose. There was no denying the usefulness of a central meeting place. A place to talk. To bring potential resources and informants.

And, most important, to be themselves.

Though the club did have mortal members and staff, the brotherhood was selective. And no one but the brotherhood was permitted in the VIP room.

That was where Raine intended to go now. Though part of him wanted nothing more than to retire to his apartment on the top floor of Number 36, he had a duty to discuss the amulet with Liam and Mal, his superiors. And he had the need to discuss Callie with his friends.

* * * *

"Checkmate." Malcolm leaned back in the plush leather armchair, then took a puff from the cigar he held. Across the table from him, Dante frowned as he studied the chessboard. Then he blew out a breath, took a long sip of scotch, and used his thumb and forefinger to topple his king.

"Son-of-a-bitch."

"You should know better than to challenge Mal," Raine said as he approached and took a seat in one of the two empty chairs that surrounded the table on which the chessboard stood.

"What can I say?" Dante replied. "I'm an eternal optimist."

"I think 'fool' is the word you're looking for." Mal's grin was smug and cool, just like the man himself. He calculated everything, never misstepped, and handled the power and responsibility of being one of the brotherhood's two leaders with unerring precision and devotion. Raine loved all of the brotherhood, but it was to Mal he most often turned. And it was Mal who most understood his pain, since he carried the weight of a similar burden.

"And this is all I have to say to you," Dante retorted, displaying his middle finger.

Mal's lips twitched, and Raine sat back in the chair, glad to be back in New York and among friends.

He glanced over as Jessica approached from across the room, then bent down and pressed a kiss to his forehead before handing him a glass. "Macallan. On the rocks. You look like you could use it."

"Thanks," he said, taking a welcome sip as she sat on the arm of his chair and studied his face. He kept his expression bland. Jessica was a healer—and he knew she was searching for injuries—but she had the ability to see so much more than that.

Across the table, Liam settled into the empty chair, his broad shoulders and well-muscled body filling the seat. He was the second leader of the brotherhood, and no one looking at him would doubt that. There was power and control in every one of his movements, and he had only to enter a room to command it.

Now, his eyes flicked from Jessica to Raine. "Just back from the field, and the first thing you do is flirt with my mate?"

"Not the first thing," Raine corrected easily. "And no. I know better than that." He shot Jessica a wicked grin. "She'd beat the crap out of me."

"She damn sure would," Jessica agreed cheerfully, then squeezed his hand before circling the chairs and settling into Liam's lap. He drew her close, then kissed her passionately, and though Raine was used to the way the two of them couldn't keep their hands off each other, tonight it ate at him. As if their affection was eating a hole through his gut that only Callie could fill.

He forced himself to look away and found Mal's eyes bearing down on him, his expression questioning.

Raine met his glance mildly, not yet willing to give anything away.

After a moment, Mal seemed to relax. He leaned forward and stubbed out his cigar, then returned his attention to Raine. "The mission?"

"A success."

"Kirkov is out of the picture?"

"He's dead." Raine pressed his fingertips to his temples. Not simply because he could so vividly remember the Bulgarian serial killer that Phoenix Security had been hired to locate and terminate, but because he knew where this conversation would inevitably lead.

"And the fuerie?" Mal asked, referring to the malevolent energy that it was the brotherhood's sworn duty to hunt. "Was there time for it to transfer?"

Raine tipped his glass back and finished his scotch. "It's over, Mal. I took Kirkov over the Asparuhov Bridge. He was history at impact, and there was no one around the fuerie could enter." He lifted the glass, remembered he'd already finished it, and silently cursed.

"How much of the fuerie's essence was in the man?" Liam asked as Dante passed Raine his glass. Raine took it gratefully and slammed back the last of his friend's drink.

"Minuscule," Raine reported. "Kirkov was fucked up all on his own. Even so, having the fuerie inside him made it that much worse, and now they're both dead. The human monster, and the sliver of the dark within him."

Raine stood. "So that's it. Mission accomplished." He held up Dante's glass. "I'm going to go get us both a refill."

"Wait." Mal spoke softly but firmly, and though Raine wanted to tell his friend to leave him the fuck alone, that wasn't something that he could tell his leader. "Let me see your back."

"Dammit, Mal—"

"Now."

Raine stiffened, taking the time to pull himself together. He knew the rules, and the biggest was that an agent didn't put himself in a position to be killed.

Fuck.

He stood up and lifted his shirt, revealing the newly extended tail feather of the phoenix that marked his back.

"Goddammit, Raine. Didn't I tell you not to take any chances? And you what? Threw yourself over a fucking bridge?"

"I'm still standing, aren't I? I've still got my humanity, don't I?"

He watched as Mal's expression hardened and he pointed at Dante and Jessica, both of whom stood and moved to the far side of the room. After a moment, Liam left as well. Which meant this was going to be an off-the-record conversation and not an official reprimand.

Frankly, Raine wasn't in the mood for either.

"I'm going to crash," he said. "We can do this in the morning."

He started to walk away, but the pain in his friend's voice drew him back.

"Dammit, Raine. I know you want to punish yourself for losing Livia, but it wasn't your fault. You can't keep going into the burn, because one of these days you're not going to come out of it."

"But I will," he said. "That's what we are now, isn't it? We can't die. We can just be reborn in fire." For millennia, he and the brotherhood had been immortal. Blessed—or cursed—with eternal life, death was not the end. Instead, like a phoenix, they were reborn in fire, and with each rebirth, the tattoo that marked them as a member of the brotherhood grew and changed. Raine, unlike his brethren, was almost fully covered with tats.

"That's bullshit," Mal said. "Die enough and you'll be reborn, but you won't be alive. You'll be a living shell. Your humanity burned out. And as many times as you've pushed—as many times as you've burned—you must be getting close to being hollow. To burning out everything human that lives inside you."

Mal spoke the truth. The brotherhood might have defeated death, but there was a price—burn too many times, and a man's humanity could be burned right out of him, too. It was a not a slow process. Not a gradual descent into the void of madness. Instead, it happened suddenly, with little warning.

It had happened two centuries ago to Samson, the most reckless of the brothers, and now he was nothing more than a cold, conscienceless assassin who lived out his days in the brotherhood's German facility, called into service only in the most dire of circumstances.

"Dammit, Raine," Mal continued. "Do you want to end up like Samson? Do you think Livia would want that? Do you think I could stand it? I already lost one friend that way. Would you really have me lose another?"

Raine closed his eyes, drew a breath, then sat back down. "Honestly, Mal, there was a time I wouldn't have cared. When I welcomed each fight, and the more dangerous the better. When I craved a mortal wound. When I longed for death, because I wanted nothing more than to burn the pain out of me. That's what humanity is, isn't it?" He pressed a hand to his heart. "These bodies that are made to suffer. They are the essence of humanity, aren't they? Love. Tenderness. Pain. The wild storm of emotions, and I wanted to simply end it."

"I know," Mal said simply.

"You must understand that." He looked his friend in the eye, knowing all too well that Mal had suffered loss, too. Perhaps even more keenly than he had. Livia at least, was gone in an instant, or so he'd believed until just a few hours ago. But Mal was tormented over and over by the memory of all he'd had with Christina. And everything that he could never have again.

Raine saw the pain play over Mal's face, and he regretted his words. Still, he needed Mal to understand.

Mal, however, was not taking the bait. "Wanted to," Mal repeated carefully. "You said you *wanted* to simply end it. Past tense. Something has changed, Raine. Tell me what."

Raine ran his hand over his close-cropped hair and tried to figure out where to start. "She's not gone. Mal, I swear to you, I've met her. I've held her."

Mal's eyes narrowed. "What the hell are you talking about?"

"Livia. Her essence."

He saw the pain flash across Mal's face. "We lost Livia, Raine. She was thrust into the void. We both saw it."

"We were wrong. Her essence is here, Mal."

"Raine..."

"*No.* Listen to me. This isn't grief or wishful thinking. It's fact. And Livia's essence remains. It's in Sinclair's daughter."

He watched Mal struggle to keep his expression bland. "The antiques dealer?"

"I went by his store after I returned from Bulgaria. Sinclair had a lead on the seventh amulet—no," he added, before Mal could ask about the amulet, "it didn't pan out. But she was there, Mal." He leaned forward, his elbows on his knees. "Callie Sinclair. It's her."

"You can't be certain. Not yet."

"Yes," Raine said, thinking of the way Callie came in his arms. "I am."

Mal leaned back, his expression making it clear that he realized exactly what Raine meant. That he'd already had this woman in his bed. That they'd reached climax together and in that moment when their energies meshed, he had been certain.

"Well," Mal said. "I always knew you moved fast."

"No jokes," Raine said. "Not about this. Not about her."

Mal studied him, then nodded. "And the girl?"

"She feels it too, Mal."

"She knows? She remembers?"

"No." He shook his head, wishing the answer were otherwise. "Not overtly. But she feels the connection."

"Then why isn't she here?"

His friend was too perceptive by half. "She's human. Such intensity so quickly—it scared her."

Mal nodded. "As you say, she's human. If Livia's essence does live within her, it has mingled with the soul of Callie Sinclair. There is no way to untwine it. They are one. And while Livia may have once been your mate, Callie Sinclair was not."

"I was dead until I found this woman, Mal. And now she fills my heart and my head. I may have only just met her, but I know the core of her. She is the woman for me, Mal. And if she doesn't yet realize that, then I will simply have to spend the rest of my very long life convincing her."

Chapter 6

I walk for an hour, even though the store is only a few minutes away, and end up having to double back. It's worth it, though. I needed to clear my head, and when I finally return to the darkened shop and let myself in, I've convinced myself that walking away was the right thing to do.

I have a job in Texas, after all. A good job that's important and that I love. There's something satisfying about being part of a system that makes sure that evil is punished, and each and every time I get a conviction and some lowlife murderer or rapist gets put behind bars, that hole inside me fills a little.

Maybe I don't have a stellar personal life, but I have my work, and it's valuable and important, and it is not going away.

In the end, the only one you can count on is yourself. Haven't I known that since the day my mother walked away? And isn't that lesson being driven home now that my father is dying and there is nothing, absolutely nothing, that I can do to change that?

I can't deny that I felt a profound connection to Raine, but that's part of the problem. Because if it's tearing me up this much to walk away after one day, how much of a wreck will I be when I lose him after a month? A year?

Stop it.

Christ, I'm acting like a skittish colt.

I force myself to push away thoughts of Raine. It's over. Done. I'm going back to Texas just like I told Nurse Bennett. I'm getting my father transferred there. And I'm shutting the door on the New York chapter of my life.

And the sooner I finish inventorying the shop, the better.

It's late, but I'm spurred to action. I consider going upstairs to the apartment above the store and changing back into my yoga pants, but I'm afraid if I do that I'll just get too comfortable and end up camped out on the couch in front of the television with a glass of wine and a book.

So I stay down here, lost in the memories that this shop sparks. I spent my childhood inside this space. My father bought it before I was born, and when my mother left us when I was four, we moved out of the small apartment the three of us had shared and into the cramped little studio above the shop.

I didn't mind how small it was; I wanted to escape the memories of my mother as much as my father did, and having a tiny space seemed to help, as if it kept all my memories and fears boxed in close to me.

I liked it so much, in fact, that my dad made me a playhouse in a faux window seat. He added a hinge to make it open from the front, and I would crawl into the tiny area, just big enough for a little girl to lay on her stomach with a flashlight and books and stuffed animals. I'd even sleep there sometimes, safe in that hidden space.

Though nights were spent in the study and my playhouse, I whiled away my days in the shop, exploring the shelves and listening to my dad's stories. He never considered himself a store owner but a knight. A man on a quest. "There's something bigger than us out there, Callie my love," he'd tell me. And I would sit enraptured—and I would believe him.

He had a deep love of history, mythology, and folklore, and I used to wander the store, certain that I would find fairies living in jeweled pillboxes or angels dancing in the light split by a prism.

I never did, but to this day I still look, and it makes me sad to think that all of this will be going away.

With a sigh, I sit on a velvet-upholstered settee, then immediately realize my mistake. I'm tired, a fact that has become only too apparent now that I have stopped moving. I need to either go upstairs and go to bed or get to work on the inventory, but as I lay my head on the upholstered high back, the only strength I can muster is barely sufficient to keep my eyes open.

Just a quick nap, I think. Five minutes, then a cup of coffee, and then I'll get to work.

Just five minutes. After all, it's not like I'm asking for all the time in the world.

Aren't you?

Though I look around for the source of the voice, I find no one. But the store seems to glow now, and I realize I must have fallen asleep, and the glow is probably coming from the rising sun.

As for the voice, it must have been someone in a dream, though I don't remember dreaming at all.

I start to swing my legs off the settee, but I realize that something is wrong. I'm not in the shop at all. I'm in the middle of a forest, with tall trees and a tangle of underbrush, and everything is on fire.

Frantic, I turn in a circle, looking for a way out. As I do, I see that there are all sorts of paths, and as far as I can tell, each one leads to safety. But I do not make a move for any of them.

I realize that I'm not searching for an exit, but hiding. And waiting, though I am not sure what I am waiting for.

But no one comes, and so I stay hidden in the fire, burning and burning until I am raw and scared and tired and alone and—

Suddenly my ears ring with the clanging of bells, as if I'm surrounded by a ring of old-fashioned fire trucks.

I look out toward the flames, and now I see a face.

Raine.

Relief and joy washes over me. *He came.*

I knew he would come, and he did. How could I have doubted, even for a moment?

And yet when he reaches for me through the flames, I am jolted awake by my phone.

"Find the book."

"Daddy?"

"Find the book, find the path. Look to yourself for the answer, and you will find it hidden in plain sight."

"Daddy? Wait. How are you calling me? What are you—"

I jerk upright and realize that I am holding my hand to my ear. My phone is still on the table in front of me.

I've been dreaming.

With a sigh, I rub my palms over my face. *A dream.*

But even so, I can still remember the joy that filled me when I saw Raine's face. And in that moment I have to forcibly stop myself from running back to Number 36.

Instead, I glance at the many clocks that litter this room. Noon.

So much for my plan to only sleep five minutes. I'd slept through the rest of the night, and half of the day as well. No wonder my head is fuzzy and my dreams strange.

I make myself a cup of coffee, then settle in to work on the inventory. I last about half an hour on that task, but then my mind wanders back to my odd dream.

What the devil did he mean, "Look to yourself?"

I cock my head, suddenly remembering my fifteenth birthday. He'd arranged a full-blown scavenger hunt. Was that what he was doing now?

As soon as the thought enters my head, I cringe. What the hell am I thinking? It was a dream. A stupid dream, not my father actually calling me. Not my dad helping me out.

I should just cash it in and work on the inventory, but now I feel like I'm on a quest, albeit a ridiculous and foolish one.

Look to yourself.

Callie Sinclair.

Could it be that simple?

I head to the bookshelves and look in the C's. Nothing.

I try the S's. Same result.

Apparently, no. It couldn't be that simple.

But then I frown. I've never used my given name; I've always been known by my middle name.

But my first name is Olivia, after my dad.

I go to the O's.

And there, among the tattered covers, is a book with nothing on the spine. Just faded brown leather.

I pull it out, open it.

The first entry is from 2012, and I realize that this is the most current of the series of journals in which my dad wrote his notes about the various pieces he tracked.

The final entry is from last week.

It's curious by its lack of detail, noting only that he had been hired to find a rare amulet. Usually, my father included all known facts about any item he was seeking, including anyone who commissioned the search or who might be an interested buyer.

With this entry, there is nothing other than an additional note scrawled on the bottom like an afterthought:

C—find the rainman. Help him.

With him, what is hidden will be revealed.

I pull the book up to my chest and hug it, and as I do, I realize that I have sunk to the ground. I put the book down beside me and close my eyes.

The rainman.

My father is sending me back to Raine.

And I don't know if I'm relieved or scared.

* * * *

I didn't take a good look at Number 36 last night, and now as I stand in front of it, I take the opportunity to study the red brick building at 36 East 63rd Street. Unlike the wide neighboring buildings with which it shares walls, Number 36 is narrow, with only two windows gracing each of its five stories. The first two floors are convex, as if the building consists of a box sitting atop a cylinder. The brick is a faded red, and the trim around each of the windows is molded plaster, now off-white from so many years of exposure to the elements.

I stand on the street, my hand resting lightly on the iron railing that surrounds the property. Like many brownstones in Manhattan's Upper East Side, the first floor is slightly below street level, and the railing makes a sharp turn and then slopes downward, guiding visitors down five concrete steps to a small courtyard filled with colorful, fragrant blooms.

I have not yet descended those stairs, and yet I have walked past them five times in the last hour, making the trek back and forth between Madison and Park three times, and twice going all the way to Central Park.

Each time I end up back here, as if there is an elastic band around my waist and it is tied fast to this red brick building and the man inside.

Rainer Engel.

It is clear from my father's journal that I need to see him again. And yet, I cannot help the trepidation that grows in me, all the more potent because it is mixed with excitement, anticipation, and most of all, longing.

As much as I have told myself it is best to stay away, to run, I can't escape the simple, basic truth that I want to see him again. I want to touch him and be touched by him.

I don't know what that means, but I do know that I have no more excuses. I can put this off no longer.

Then quit dragging it out. Just go.

I grimace because there is no denying the reasonableness of my own advice. And so I bite the bullet and descend the stairs.

Almost immediately, the din of early afternoon traffic fades and the stale miasma of exhaust and street-side garbage is replaced by the gentle perfume of lavender and jasmine.

It's like entering another world, and I'm honestly not sure if that's good or bad.

The courtyard is lovely, but I barely pay attention to the pots overflowing with flowering vines or the concrete benches set with precision so that there is always at least one seat in the sun and one in the shade. Instead, I move with purpose to the front door. It is solid wood, polished to a shine. A gold knocker in the shape of a bird is mounted at eye level, its trailing tail feathers acting as a handle.

A brass plaque mounted to the brick facade to the right of the door reads:

Dark Pleasures
Est. 1895
Members Only

I don't know what the plaque refers to, but since I do know that Raine lives here, I assume that the residential brownstone was at one time some sort of gentlemen's club, a not uncommon thing back in the nineteenth century, after all.

There is a keypad mounted beneath the plaque, giving the building an anachronistic feel. There doesn't seem to be any sort of bell, however, and so I lift the tail feather and rap sharply on the door.

I hear nothing, but considering how dense the door sounded when I knocked, there could be a brass band playing back there and I wouldn't hear them. A minute passes, then another. I am just raising my hand to knock again when the door opens inward, revealing a white-haired elderly man in black and white livery.

"Madam," he says with a slight bow. "How may I be of service?"

I am not usually the tongue-tied sort, but I'm feeling a bit like I've been tossed backward in time, and it takes a moment for me to thrust myself back into the twenty-first century. I'd assumed this building had been converted to apartments. But considering the limo, now I'm thinking that Raine must own the entire brownstone. "I'm looking for Mr. Engel," I say. "Is he home?"

He studies me for a full minute.

"I didn't realize my question required such thought," I say, then immediately regret it. I'm not generally rude, especially not to staff, but I'm still feeling shaky and this man's odd reaction to a simple question hasn't calmed my nerves.

"May I inquire as to your business?"

I start to snap that it's not *his* business, but manage to bite back my tongue. "I'm Callie Sinclair," I say. "My father is Oliver Sinclair, an antiques dealer. Mr. Engel came to my father's shop yesterday, and I have some information for him regarding a piece he was inquiring about."

"I see. Please, come in." He steps back and holds the door open, allowing me to enter a dark-paneled foyer. The room is shaped like a semicircle, with a set of double-doors facing me from beyond a round marble pedestal. A huge glass bowl sits atop the pedestal, filled with glass pebbles in various shades of red and blue and purple. It's a lovely centerpiece—and provides the only ornamentation in the room—but what makes it truly spectacular is the flame that burns inexplicably inside the bowl, sending tongues of fire licking over the rim, despite the absence of any obvious fuel.

I follow my guide around the pedestal to the doors, and then through them. Immediately, the atmosphere changes. Soft strains of jazz fill the air, along with the muted, almost chocolatey, scent of cigar smoke.

The low buzz of conversation surrounds us, along with the gentle tinkle of ice in crystal. We pass through a lush seating area with low wooden tables surrounded by plump leather chairs. Groups of men and women sit there, sipping drinks and talking earnestly. Many of the men and a few of the women hold the cigars that account for the subtle scent in the air. Considering that the scent is in no way overpowering, I have to assume that there are hidden ventilation systems in the ceiling.

I see a wall of polished wood humidors running perpendicular to a dark mahogany bar behind which is a set of mirrored shelves filled with dozens of bottles of high-end scotch, along with all the standard other distilled liquors as well.

A tall woman in a black sheath dress comes over to greet us. Her gaze skims over me. "Mr. Daley? Is there a problem?"

I realize for the first time how I am dressed. I'd showered before coming here, and now I wear jeans, Converse sneakers, and a T-shirt my father bought me last Christmas that says *Lawyers do it with appeal.*

Bottom line, I really don't fit in.

"I'm sorry," I say. "I didn't realize this was a club or—"

Mr. Daley's sniff cuts me off. "Ms. Sinclair would like to speak to Mr. Engel. Do you know if he is in residence?"

"Callie Sinclair?" she asks, and I nod, a little shocked that this woman I'd assumed to be the club's hostess knows my name. She turns her attention to Mr. Daley. "He's in the VIP room. I'll escort her."

Mr. Daley nods, then leaves.

"I'm Jessica," the woman says, with a bit of a sparkle in her eyes.

"It's very nice to meet you."

"Thanks. I'm feeling a little like I fell down the rabbit hole. I thought Raine lived here. I would have dressed better if—"

"You look fine. Come on."

I follow her through the club, with its dark wood and equally dark leather. A few people frown as I pass, obviously noting how out of place I look. Most, however, pay no attention at all. They are drinking and talking with friends, reading the newspaper, chatting on cell phones.

"What is this place? Dark Pleasures?"

"A very select club," Jessica says. "It provides a sanctuary for those who are granted membership. A respite from the world outside. We have resources for the corporate types who want a working lunch, as well as everything necessary to kick back and just relax for a while. Not to mention an excellent jazz band on Friday nights and the most exceptional Sunday brunch in the city."

"And Raine is a member?"

We have paused in front of a solid oak door marked with a gold placard that announces *VIP access only*. Jessica punches a code into the keypad and I hear the lock release. "Raine? Not exactly. You could say he's more like an owner." She pushes the door open. "Please. After you."

I step inside and am immediately struck by the fact that while the basic decor is the same as the area we just left, the similarities end there. This room includes a number of paintings and antiques that I immediately spot as high-end originals. But despite the money that practically oozes from these walls, the area itself seems more low-key than the main part of the club. There is a vibrancy in this room. A sense of camaraderie. As if I have entered someone's living room and not a public club, even a public club that is select in its membership.

The bar in this room is unmanned, so that anyone can simply make a drink, and it is in that direction that Jessica now heads. "Don't just sit there," she says to the stunningly gorgeous man leaning casually against the bar. "Make Ms. Sinclair a drink. Callie," she says, turning to me, "this is Liam."

From what I can see, Liam is one-hundred percent muscle and about the size of an NFL fullback. He has deep-set eyes and a wide mouth. He's clean-shaven, with raven-black hair that he wears long so that it brushes his collar. He's wearing black slacks and a white button-down and looks as wild and dangerous as a fallen angel.

"What's your poison?" Liam asks.

"Scotch. Thanks."

He grins at Jessica as he pours my drink. "She'll fit right in."

I must look confused because Jessica turns to me. "Scotch and cigars. That's what Dark Pleasures is all about. Though I think you'll learn there's so much more to it than that."

"Oh, no, I just need to deliver a message—"

"I'll go get Raine." Liam passes me my drink, then brushes his hand over Jessica's cheek, and I see both heat and affection pass between them. Something hard and cold settles in my gut. Because I want that, too, and I can't help but fear that I'm going to spend my life making all the wrong choices and never have it.

It suddenly occurs to me that Jessica never told Liam why I was here. "How does he know I'm looking for Raine?"

"It's Liam's job to know everything." She winks. "Makes it damned inconvenient when I'm Christmas shopping." She leads me to two chairs on either side of a small table. "I would introduce you around, but I don't want to scare you off."

"I don't scare easily," I say, though I have to wonder if my words are true. After all, I ran scared from Raine, didn't I?

I turn in the chair to look around. There are four men sitting around a table at the far side of the room. There are papers scattered on the table in front of them, and one—with hair as dark as Liam's, but with a lean, Hollywood bad-boy appearance—is clearly in charge.

"Why so few people?" I ask. "Because it's still too early for the happy hour crowd?"

"The VIP section is extremely exclusive. Consider yourself privileged. We rarely allow guests in at all."

"Oh." I consider that. "And I guess I have a double strike against me since I'm a woman?"

She laughs. "Not in the least. And I'm not the only female VIP member, just the only one who lives permanently on the East Coast. Dagny's in Los Angeles, and Rachel lives in Paris. But on the whole, you're right. A girl gets lonely swimming in a sea of testosterone. Maybe I'll have some company soon."

Her expression is so welcoming and earnest that I can't help but laugh. "You do know I'm just here to talk to Raine about an amulet?"

"And here he is." She nods toward the opposite side of the room from where we entered. I turn in my chair and see that a hinged bookshelf is moving inward to reveal a hidden hallway. And, of course, Raine.

I swallow, suddenly at a loss for words. Yesterday, he'd been dressed casually. Today, I think he could take on corporate America. As he strides toward me in a perfectly tailored suit, he seems to exude the kind of power and confidence that can make things happen with little more than a glance.

"Hello, Callie," he says, but what I hear is "I want you."

I try to reply, but my mouth is too dry. I remember the drink that Liam poured for me, and I take a sip, grateful for both its burn and its wetness. "I—I found something. About the amulet, I mean."

He tilts his head as if debating a thorny question. Then he sits down across from me, making me realize that somewhere along the way, Jessica slipped off. "All right," he says. "Tell me."

"I found a reference to it in my father's journal. Here." I pull the leather bound book out of my purse and pass it to him.

"The rainman," he says. "Me?"

"I assume so. Does the next part make sense to you? 'With him, what is hidden will be revealed'?"

He shakes his head. "No. It doesn't mean a thing."

I frown. "Are you sure?" I'd been so certain that coming here would solve the riddle, and I'm not doing a good job of hiding my disappointment. Then again, neither is he.

I tilt my head as I watch the emotions play across his face. Confusion. Disappointment. Resolve.

"This is more than just a collector's piece to you, isn't it?" I ask.

"Yes," he says, but then he says no more, and we're left with the silence that hangs between us, thick with possibility.

I slip my hands beneath the table and wipe my palms on my jeans.

"Right. Well, I'm sorry it didn't mean anything to you." I push my chair back and stand. "I should go."

He reaches out and takes hold of my wrist.

"Raine, please." I am aware of nothing except his touch. The rest of the world has simply melted away. "Please," I repeat, a little desperate this time. "I need to go."

"No," he says, then stands. He is right next to me, so close that I can feel his heat, raging like a furnace. And dear god, I want to burn. "There's something I need to tell you."

"I—what?"

"I'm going to kiss you, Callie."

I gasp, surprised and, yes, excited by his words.

"I'm going to kiss you, and then I'm going to touch you. I'm going to explore every inch of you, with my hands, with my lips, with my tongue. And then, Callie, I'm going to fuck you."

I suck in a stuttering breath and curse my own reaction that so pointedly reveals my response to his decadent promises.

"I can do that here or I can take you to my apartment. It's entirely up to you."

"And if I walk away?"

"That's up to you, too. I'm sure you've heard of free will. But make your decision soon. Because I don't intend to wait much longer to strip you bare. And Callie, know one other thing as well. I asked you what you wanted yesterday, and you said me. And yet in the end, you ran. Think hard before you answer me now. Because this time if you choose my bed, I won't let you go without a fight."

My heard is pounding, my body covered with a thin sheen of sweat.

Every ounce of reason within me tells me to run. And yet instinct and desire and something I don't understand tell me to stay.

I do.

And I don't even think it was my decision. He may have spoken of free will, but what good is that against the force of nature that is Rainer Engel?

Chapter 7

Raine watched the decision play across her face, desire warring with rationality, prudence, whatever personal albatross she clung to. He wanted to clutch her hand and tell her to simply go with faith. To believe in *them*.

But those were words he could not say. He wanted her in his bed. Wanted her fully and completely. But he would not press her. Once more, the choice would be hers, and he was forced to wait—feeling pretty goddamn impotent when you got right down to it.

He knew she did not overtly remember being Livia. But he also knew that didn't matter. The essence was within her, and so that meant that on some level she did understand. Did know him. Did remember.

But even if she didn't—even if this woman standing before him had not once been his mate—he would still want her. Callie Sinclair amused and challenged him in ways he didn't understand and hadn't expected.

He was a man who had died a hundred deaths and no longer looked into the dark with fear. But at the moment, he was terrified that she would walk out of this club the same way that she had walked away from the limo.

Even as the thought entered his head, she took a step away from him, as if manifesting all his deepest fears.

"Callie." Her name felt ripped from his throat, and he knew that the anguish in it revealed everything. Frankly, he didn't give a fuck.

She hesitated, then held out her hand for him. "Not here." He saw the mischief in her smile. "I'm not into exhibitionism."

The extent of his relief was such that it almost brought him to his knees.

"Where's your apartment, Raine?"

"Come with me."

He knew that the others were watching the exchange from across the club. Knew that Mal especially was looking on, particularly after what Raine had told him about Livia's essence. It didn't matter, and he didn't care. All he needed right now was to get to the elevator. That was his primary objective, and once satisfied, he could move on to the next.

He held her by the elbow, and even that simple touch overwhelmed him. He hit the release for the hidden door, and the bookcase swung open. He led her through, into the simple but tasteful area that at one time was part of a grand ballroom. Now, it served as a reception area for Phoenix Security, which had its own entrance separate from Dark Pleasures at the rear of the building.

That, however, was not where he was going now, and he led her to the small, cage-style elevator, then pushed the button to call it.

"What floor?" she asked.

"Penthouse," he said. "The club takes up one and two. Three is office space. Four is reserved for out of town members. Five is my private apartment."

Unlike his brethren, who had used the money they'd earned and stockpiled over the years to acquire some of the most exceptional pieces of property across the globe, including the two brownstones adjacent to Number 36, Raine had never felt the need. Before Callie, he hadn't felt much of anything. Now, for the first time, he thought about how sterile his apartment was. And how little time he had spent over the last few millennia thinking about making a home. Why bother when all he wanted to do was check out?

Now, he regretted that. He wished that the place reflected him. He wanted her to know him fully and completely, and in every way possible. And the thought that what she would see first was a set of rooms as empty as his heart had once been ate at his gut.

Not that he could do anything about it now, he thought as the elevator finished its slow descent to the first floor and opened in front of them. The only other option was a hotel, but that was where he took other women. It was not where he would take her.

He pulled open the gate and ushered her in. And the moment he'd set the contraption in motion, he pushed her up against the far wall, his mouth on hers and his hand between her legs. "Tell me you're wet."

"I am."

"Tell me you want me."

"I do."

He backed away, breathing hard but satisfied. But in one quick movement, she caught his hand and tugged him toward her, making his cock twitch with excitement at such palpable evidence of her desire.

"Please, Raine. I want what you promised."

"What I promised? To kiss you?" He trailed his fingers softly over her lips, forcing himself to hold back. "Touch you?" He leaned forward so that his lips brushed the soft skin of her ear. Christ, she smelled good. Like vanilla and honey, and he knew she tasted just as delicious. "To fuck you?"

He both saw and felt her tremble, and by god, if he was a lesser man, he would have come right then.

"The elevator's open." His voice was tight, because damn him, he wanted it too, and the elevator was only now approaching the third floor. "Anyone can see."

"I really couldn't give a fuck."

Her words cut through him, making him harder than he could have imagined. And when he closed his mouth over hers, it was like he'd gone to heaven. The kiss was wild, and her responsiveness drove him even wilder. The fact that she so openly wanted him was sexy as hell, and he fully intended to give her everything she desired. To fuck her until she cried for mercy, and then to hold her close and soft until she begged for more.

Right now, this kiss alone was like sex. Their tongues mating, their bodies crushed together. He knew he must be hurting her, pressed tight against the scroll-style bars of the elevator cage, but he couldn't stop, and she sure as hell wasn't complaining.

When the elevator finally opened in front of his door, they were both gasping for breath. He led her inside and just about lost it when she peeled off her shirt right in the middle of his foyer, then dropped it on the polished stone floor. "Touch me," she said as she followed the shirt with her bra. Her voice was breathy, raw. "And then after that—"

"Bedroom." He pointed in the general direction. "On the bed. Arms and legs spread. I want to be able to see how wet you are when I walk in the room." He watched her eyes as he spoke, saw the way they dilated in response to his command, and felt the tug of pleasure in his groin. He could concede power in the bedroom from time to time, but he would not be doing so tonight. Not when Callie was so clearly turned on by submitting to his wishes.

"And Callie—no touching."

He watched her go, and the tenderness that swept over him was at least as powerful as this relentless sexual desire. She was everything. The pinnacle. The source. The goal.

In truth, he had never felt this strongly before, and his only thought was that his earlier, tamer passion with Livia had been the passion of youth. Or that his memory had faded to spare him lingering pain.

It didn't matter. Right now, all that mattered was Callie. Making her happy. Making her satisfied.

And that was a task to which he would turn his full attention—and to which he was willing to devote the rest of his life. Which was a very long time indeed.

* * * *

My first thought is that though the apartment we just walked through is sparse and utilitarian, the bedroom suits him, and I can see bits of the man echoed in the furnishings.

The king-size bed is set against a brick wall, across which is a single wooden shelf filled with books. Above that are several black and white photographs of urban skylines. They are stark and beautiful, just like the room itself.

On the left is a wall of windows covered by vertical blinds. On the right is a wall of mirrors, though I can see that Raine's closet is behind the sliding sections.

The floor is a rich, dark wood that is polished to a sheen, and a plush white rug fills the space at the foot of the bed, topped by a bench upholstered in black leather.

With one exception, the room seems perfectly put together, so precise that it could be a hotel or a showroom. But the bed is unmade, and there is something incredibly intimate about the rumpled sheets and tossed back comforter.

I leave the rest of my clothes on the bench, then climb onto the bed, my body trembling with anticipation as I position myself as he directed.

The truth is, I've been trembling since the first moment I met him, mostly from desire, but also a bit from fear.

Right now, there is no fear. There is only the sweet anticipation of knowing that he is coming and that he intends to take the time to very thoroughly fulfill his promise to me—kiss me, touch me, fuck me.

Oh, god.

My thighs are slick with the evidence of my arousal, and though I want to touch myself, I obey his orders and do not.

That restraint only turns me on more, just as his command did. There is no denying the fact that Rainer Engel is a man who likes to be in control; I saw that the moment he walked into my father's shop.

But what I didn't know then is how much I wanted him to turn that trait to me—and how much I would respond when he did so. How willing I am to surrender to him and let him take me where he wants me to go, trusting that it will be farther than I have ever gone before.

For a woman who usually keeps as tight a control on her sexual encounters as she does her caseload, this is strange territory. But then again, whatever is happening between Raine and me is strange as well. Strange and exciting and wonderful. And dammit, right then, all I want is more.

All I want is Raine.

I start to call out to him, but I manage to hold my tongue. I know damn well why he is taking his time. More than that, it's working. I'm so aroused it's painful, every cell in my body primed.

I am living, breathing anticipation, and I fear that if Raine doesn't walk in here soon, I'll explode simply from wanting him.

"Now that is a pretty picture."

I lift my head to see him leaning negligently against the doorframe, still in that insanely sexy suit.

"Raine."

"I like my name on your lips. I like it better like this, when it's not just a name but a plea. Tell me, Callie, what are you pleading for?"

"You know. It's your promise."

"Remind me."

"Touch me," I say, because he wants me to beg. "Please, please, touch me."

"With pleasure." He moves slowly to the bed, as if we have all the time in the world, but all that does is make me whimper and squirm. "I like you this way. Wanting me. Waiting for me. Wide open for my pleasure and your own. Tell me, Callie. Do you like it, too?"

"Yes." My word is breathy and so soft it seems to float away on the gentle breeze from a slowly turning ceiling fan.

"Why?"

"I—" I pause to think about it, but he shakes his head.

"No. No analysis. No outline. Just tell me."

"Because I never surrender. Because this is safe. Because you want me to, and—"

"Yes?"

"And because it turns me on to please you."

His sensual mouth curves up into an easy smile. "Does it? In that case we have a lot in common. Because it turns me on to please you. To touch you," he adds, "just as I promised. Close your eyes, Callie. Close your eyes and feel."

I do, feeling first the way the bed sags as he gets on beside me. Then I shiver at the first contact of skin against skin as he draws a single fingertip from the base of my throat all the way down, down, down to my sex. He teases me, lightly stroking my clit, then easing his finger deep inside me as my muscles contract violently, wanting even more than he is yet giving me.

My arms are stretched to the side, and I know better than to move them. But I have to fist my hands in the bedclothes in order to stay in place, and as Raine teases and torments me with one simple finger, I dig my heels in, clutch the bedspread, and arch up, seeking both satisfaction and relief, trying to make the sensation of his hand upon me bolder and brighter, and also trying to escape this intense, slow-building torment that is almost like pain in its persistence.

When he withdraws his finger, I sag onto the bed, already exhausted and more turned on than I can ever remember being simply from this sensual touch…and the anticipation of so much more to come.

"I'm going to touch you everywhere, angel. I want your body as aroused as your cunt. So vibrantly aware that I could brush your shoulder and make you come. I want to watch your skin prickle from my touch, your nipples tighten. I want to see the way your belly constricts as you try to hold in pleasure. I'm greedy, angel, and from you I want everything."

As he speaks, he has moved, and now I feel the bed shift again. This time, I hear him set something on the bedside table, and moments later, I feel his palms upon my ribcage. They are oily, and as he moves them over me, stroking and massaging, I lose myself in the pleasure of being tended by this man. A pleasure that only increases when the oil heats from the friction of his hands.

The sensation of the heat and the scent of the oil's spice is somehow both soothing and arousing—but when he teases my nipples, there is nothing soothing at all. Instead, I want to beg him to close his mouth over my breast. To suck my nipples that are now so potently in need of attention. Again, I bite back the urge, and I allow myself to get lost in the near-pain of this pleasure.

I don't know what is in the oil, some type of mint if the scent says anything. But I do know the effect it has on my tender flesh, and as his hands ease up my calf, my thigh, and toward my sex, I can only bite my lip in anticipation, and then cry out his name when he palms my cunt, making my sex heat and tingle, even more needy than before.

But it is when he strokes circles on my clit, making it throb with unfulfilled need, that he almost drives me over the edge. And I whimper as I feel the coming release, but know also that Raine's expert touch will not allow the explosion until he brings it on.

"So slick. So sweet." I hear the struggle for control in his voice and take some satisfaction from that. He may be the one in charge, but I have a hold on him, too. "Christ, angel, I want to drive my cock into you."

"Yes," I whisper. "Please yes."

"I want to possess you," he continues, as if I haven't spoken. "Hard and fast and furious, until there is no question that you are mine. But not yet. Not just yet."

My moan of protest dies in my throat when I feel the brush of his beard stubble against my inner thigh, and then the stroke of his tongue on my sex. He plays with me, his tongue dancing circles over my clit. But then his mouth closes over my sex in a full-on kiss, and his tongue thrusts inside of me. I cry out, surprised by this sensual assault that has only made me more wild, more desperate.

Though my hips buck, he doesn't yield. Just holds me in place, forcing me to accept the sweet torment that he is rendering with his mouth. But as the pleasure grows—as I start to shatter—he pulls back, and I do not have to open my eyes to know that he is grinning wickedly when he says, "Not just yet, angel."

He flips me over, then treats me to another sensual massage, though this time he focuses mostly on my shoulders and back. Eventually he moves to my thighs, but there are no more small caresses that come close to my sex. No touch that is going to send me over the edge.

And somehow, because I am waiting for it, the absence of such erotic caresses arouses me even more.

"On your knees, angel," he says, and I scramble up, eager for whatever he has in mind next. My mind is awhirl, my body at his disposal. And when he eases me down to the foot of the bed and pulls me toward him so that my rear brushes his slacks, I realize what he intends, and my sex clenches with greed.

I hear the distinct metallic sound of his zipper, then feel the pressure of one hand upon my rear as his other teases my sex.

He starts slowly, opening me. Entering me. He keeps his hands on my waist so that he can control the way I move. But the pleasure is too much for both of us, and his tempo increases with the heightening pleasure.

He bends over me, so that I feel him inside me and on my back. Now he has one hand on my breast and the other teasing my clit as he thrusts hard and deep, and I rock backward to meet him, wanting him to go deeper, wanting him to fill me up completely.

He is fully clothed, and there is something so decadent about me being naked and him being dressed that it adds to my arousal. "You're mine," he says as I fly. "Mine," he repeats as I go spinning off. And when he finally explodes inside me, he takes me with him, and it is as if he has catapulted the two of us to the stars.

And then, when he pulls out and lays beside me, drawing me in to curl against him, I say the one thing that I know he wants to hear: "Yours."

Chapter 8

He leads me into the shower, then cleans me up, washing my hair and tending to me so that I feel wonderfully cherished. Afterwards, he dries me off with a fluffy towel then wraps me in a robe that smells like him. I breathe deep, relishing the scent of it. We end up on the couch, wrapped up lazily in each other's arms as we flip through the television channels in a ritual that I would consider uncomfortably domestic with any other man, but with Raine feels just right.

He stops on a football game, and I have to laugh. "Seriously?"

He lifts his brows in mock offense. "You'd prefer what?"

"We passed at least a dozen great movies. *Singin' in the Rain*? How can you resist Donald O'Connor?"

"Actually, I never could. The man's as charming in person as he is on screen."

I cock my head, amused. "Is he?"

For a moment, he looks surprised, then his expression clears and he brushes his finger teasingly down my nose. "I read a lot of biographies. O'Connor's one of my favorite stars." As if to prove the point, we back up to the movie, and he holds me close, then kisses me softly when the movie ends with the billboard of Gene Kelly and Debbie Reynolds.

I sigh. "A shame the world doesn't break out in song like that." I see him watching me and narrow my eyes. "What?"

"I adore the way you think. And I also promise that you don't want me breaking into song. I would scare small animals."

I laugh, but I also can't help the little tingle of pleasure at the compliment.

He clicks off the television then stands, holding out his hand for me.

"Are we dancing?"

He pulls me into his arms and dips me. "That wasn't my original plan, but I can certainly see it as a possibility." He starts to hum, then spins me before moving me artfully around the room. Considering I can't dance to save my life, I'm impressed by his ability to lead, and by the time he dips me again by the bedroom door and then draws me back up for a kiss, I'm laughing and clinging to him, feeling happier and freer than I have since I came home to New York after my dad's stroke.

"Thanks," I say.

"For what?"

I want to say for making this about more than sex, but that seems both odd and presumptuous. "For making life a movie musical, even if just for a few minutes."

He studies my face, and in that moment I am certain that he knows what I had originally intended to say. But all he does is brush a kiss over my lips. "Get dressed," he says. "And let me get you some food."

I half-expect that he's going to cook, but he laughs off that prospect, assuring me that cooking is not in his repertoire. As it's not in mine either—and since the mention of food has reminded me that I am starving—I defer to his suggestion that we go back to the club.

"It's not formal, but jeans and T-shirts aren't allowed. Not even in the VIP area. We decided a long time ago that we needed to keep a certain feel within the place."

"Sadly, I didn't pack a bag."

"You're about Jessica's size," he says, heading out of the bedroom and down the hall to a guest suite. "She won't mind if you borrow something."

I hesitate, not wanting to seem possessive of him so soon, but feeling entirely possessive anyway. And wildly jealous. I *liked* Jessica, after all. And what the hell was she doing leaving her clothes all over Raine's apartment, especially when she was so obviously attached to Liam? And why—

"You're thinking so loudly I can hear every word."

I scowl up at him, still determined not to say a word because it would make me seem petty and jealous. Even though it is obvious that he is reading my face just fine, and I already seem petty and jealous.

"She and Liam moved to a loft in the Village two years ago. They thought it would be an adventure. But when I'm out of town, they sometimes stay here. It seemed easier for them both to just leave some things in the guest room."

"Oh." I clear my throat, feeling foolish. "That makes sense."

A grin dances on his lips.

"What?"

"I like it that you're jealous." His voice is low, with enough heat that it is clear he likes it very much.

"Oh," I say again, but this time it's not foolishness I'm feeling, but something much more provocative. I rise up on my toes and kiss him. "You can fuck me again," I say boldly. "But first you have to feed me."

He laughs. "Then get dressed and let's get some food."

I pick out a knee-length blue dress with a full skirt and matching blue flats. I'm still uncomfortable about borrowing Jessica's clothes, but Raine must have given her a heads-up because the first thing she does when I walk in is make me do a circle, and then sigh.

"Well, damn. I think you look better in it than I do."

Since Jessica is one of the most beautiful women I've ever seen, I doubt that. But I'm no slouch either, and I'm willing to concede that I look hot.

There's a phone by the bar that calls the kitchen, and Raine orders us both burgers and fries, and I have to smile at the dichotomy between the atmosphere and the food. But I like it. It makes the club comfortable rather than stuffy, and it bolsters my initial impression that this is the place where friends gather.

As I sit in one of the plush leather armchairs and look around, I have to say that I think that is true. As far as I can tell, the men are all close, and Jessica moves seamlessly among them. Friends with each. And much more than friends with Liam. There's only one, in fact, who shoots both Raine and me a flat look before leaving the room not long after we enter.

"Who was that?" I ask when Jessica comes over. "I got the impression he and Raine aren't going to be doing the guy bonding thing anytime soon."

"Trace. And you're right."

"What happened?"

Jessica waves the question away. "Ancient history, so don't worry about it. And Trace is only in New York a few more days. He divides his time between here, Los Angeles, and Paris."

"Nice."

"He doesn't like feeling tied down. At any rate, I'm being paged." She waves to Liam, who is tapping his wristwatch. "And Raine is coming back with your burgers." Her smile is just a little bit wicked. "Have fun, you two."

The burgers are as delicious as burgers in an exclusive, centuries-old club should be, and the company is just as awesome. Mal and Dante join us, and we talk about everything from old movies to architecture and even a few quick references to the company they all work for, Phoenix Security, though the comments are vague enough that I have no sense of what the company actually does.

As we talk, Mal and Raine play a game of chess, and though I keep my expression neutral, I'm secretly thrilled when Raine wins.

"Anyone for another drink?" Dante asks as he rises.

"No thanks," I say, then notice the time on the ornate clock on the far wall. "Actually, I should go. I want to see my dad tonight. And I should probably work on the inventory a bit, too."

"All right," Raine says.

"All right?"

"I'll come with you. Hospital. Inventory. I can't think of a better way to spend an evening."

"Broadway comes to mind," I tease. "But I'm glad you're such an easy date."

"So long as I'm with you, you'll find I'm very easy."

I see Mal and Dante exchange looks and have to laugh. "Your friends are going to think I have you wrapped around my little finger."

"That's okay," Raine says, standing and offering me a hand. "You do."

The hospital is a short walk from Number 36, but Dad is sleeping when we get there.

"When he's awake, I read to him or just talk," I tell Raine. "But I don't want to wake him."

"We'll come back tomorrow."

I glance at him, grateful this is an outing he's willing to repeat. "Thanks. I'd like that."

Once we're back on the sidewalk, I glance sideways at him. "So you're home during the afternoon and tomorrow you have time to go with me to the hospital. You drive around in a limo and live in the penthouse apartment of one of the nicest brownstones I have had the pleasure of visiting. Forgive me, Mr. Engel, but what kind of a company is Phoenix Security? Or are you simply one of the glorious elite who lives off piles of money gathered by the family over the last gazillion centuries?"

"As a matter of fact, I do have those piles of money gathered over centuries. They provide a nice cushion and allow me to buy roses from street vendors without breaking my budget." He stops at a street vendor and does exactly that.

"Thank you, kind sir," I say, taking the rose he hands me.

"But Phoenix also provides a nice income."

"So what does the company do? By security, you don't mean stocks and bonds, right? You're talking about stuff like wiring people's houses? Motion detectors and video surveillance?"

He looks amused. "Not stocks, correct. But as for the other, I'd say that we're more...specialized. The company's been around a very long time. We provide exclusive services on an international scale."

"Sounds exotic."

"It can be."

"Dangerous?"

"That too."

"Well, what do you know?"

His brow furrows. "What?"

"Turns out I'm falling for James Bond."

"Is that right?" He's laced his voice with a British accent and I laugh, delighted.

"Do you mean *is that right* that you're really like James Bond?" I ask. "I couldn't say. You haven't given me enough details of your missions."

He lifts our twined hands to his lips and kisses my fingers. "I mean, is it right that you're falling for me."

"Oh." I bite my lower lip, then tilt my head up to smile at him. "Yeah. That's right."

"That's very interesting information."

"I'm very glad you think so." I can't seem to banish the grin that is determined to spread across my face.

"I think it's fair to say the feeling is mutual."

I ease up next to him as he hooks his arm around my shoulders. "I like this," I say. "It's been ages since I've just walked around the city, and even when I was living here, I never seemed to come to the park enough."

"Nor do I."

"I have a radical idea," I say. "Let's blow off inventory and just continue what we're doing."

"I love your radical idea."

"I'm glad. I forget how nice it is to just look around sometimes."

He nods. "Funny that I have all the time in the world and yet I never seem to find the time to enjoy it."

His words hit me like a sting, and I tug him to a stop. "What do you mean, all the time in the world?" I know he can't be speaking literally. And yet for some reason I don't understand, his words have shaken me.

His brow furrows, and I think that he must be as confused by my reaction as I am. "I just mean that I've filled my days with work when I should be filling them with this. The park. A stroll. A beautiful woman by my side."

He presses a kiss to my temple and I squeeze his hand in response, feeling just a little bit foolish about the direction my thoughts were going.

"And you? Do young, brilliant assistant district attorneys manage to fit love and leisure into their lives?"

"Very little leisure, even less love." I tilt my head so that I am looking at him, knowing that my next words are probably inexcusably bold. "Before now, love was never on my radar."

His smile is slow and easy and full of both heat and understanding. "Is that so?"

"It is." And because now I'm starting to feel a little too exposed, I take his hand and urge him further into the park, aiming us along the trails toward Central Park South.

"Thanks again for coming with me to see my dad." It's my best effort to change the subject. "What about your parents? Where do they live?"

"They're gone." I hear the loss clearly in his voice. "It's been a very long time."

"I'm so sorry." We have arrived at the end of the park, and now we step out onto the sidewalk. I glance around, then smile. "Your parents, my dad. I think we could both use some cheering up. Come on."

I lead him to Fifth Avenue and FAO Schwarz, then wave my finger in an *ah-ah* gesture when he starts to protest. "Haven't you seen *Big*? The big piano is an instant mood enhancer."

"Better than sex?" he deadpans.

"No, but we can do it in public without getting arrested." I tug his hand. "Come on."

As it turns out, we have to wait in line for ten minutes behind a gaggle of seven- and eight-year-olds. We are, by about two decades, the oldest people in line.

Frankly, I don't care. And after I start out doing a truly crappy job of playing *Mary Had a Little Lamb* by hopping from one note to the next, Raine joins me and, as expected, completely shows me up by playing the opening riff of *The Entertainer*. And getting a standing ovation from everyone in the store.

Honestly, it's pretty cool.

And as we step back outside and start up Fifth Avenue toward 63rd Street and Number 36, I can't help but think that this is the most fun I've ever had with a man. For that matter, it's the most fun I've had with anyone in a very, very long time, and I'm quite sure that my grin makes that very, very clear.

"Home?" Raine asks, and I nod automatically.

It's only when we have reached Number 36 and are back in the penthouse that I realize that this is where I expected we were going. And yet this isn't home. Not for me.

But still...

"What is it?" Raine asks, seeing me pause by the window.

"Nothing," I say. "It's just—you came here, and that felt right to me. And I—"

"You feel it, too." He moves closer to me, and that heat that always seems to be bubbling beneath the surface with us seems to crackle and pop. "That tug. That connection."

I nod slowly. I know exactly what he means. "It should scare me. But it doesn't."

"Maybe it would with someone else. Maybe it doesn't scare you because it's right with me."

"I think it is," I say. "Right, I mean." I press my hand to the glass. "This is moving so fast, Raine, but it doesn't feel strange. It feels as though I've known you forever. As if—I don't know. As if we're picking up where we left off somehow."

He is staring at me, his expression managing to be both earnest and astounded.

I shake my head and hold up my hand. "I'm sorry. That was way too much. I shouldn't have said anything. I don't want you to feel weird or think that I'm moving too fast." I'm rambling, but I don't care. "I just wanted to tell you that, and now I'm thinking that maybe I should have just stayed quiet, because I really don't know where that came from."

"Livia," he says.

"What?" I have no idea what that means.

"Where it came from. It came from Livia."

I lick my lips, an odd sensation twisting inside me, almost like fear. As if I do understand—but I just don't want to.

"What are you talking about?"

He shakes his head. "No, I'm sorry. I shouldn't have said anything."

"Why not? If you understand what's happening between us, why we're moving so fast, why it feels so right, then please tell me. I want to know."

I can see the debate play out on his face, but I don't understand it. Or, at least, I don't understand it until he finally speaks.

"She was my mate," he says, and I stand completely frozen. "My wife. Many years ago. She died, Callie. But part of her lives inside you."

I force myself to breathe in and out. Is this a joke? Because I pushed him to tell me something before he was ready?

"You're saying your dead wife was what? Reincarnated inside me? That the reason you're attracted to me is because I'm walking around with your dead wife hitching a ride?"

"Reach inside, Callie." His voice doesn't waver in the least, and I realize that this isn't a joke. He believes this bullshit. And I'm not sure if I should sit down and cry or run away in terror. "Search for the core of our connection, and you'll know I'm telling you the truth. It's why this feels so right."

I shake my head, not quite sure I can manage words right now.

"Please," he presses. "Don't you see? It explains why it feels to you as if we're picking up where we left off."

"No." The word is ripped out of me. "All this explains is why I was so scared of finding a man I connected with in the first place. Because all that does is open me up to nut jobs. *Fuck.*" I slam my palm against the window so hard I'm surprised the glass doesn't break.

"*Shit.*" He runs his fingers over his scalp. "Dammit, Callie, I'm sorry. I shouldn't have said anything yet. But I thought...I know you feel it as profoundly as I do. I thought you would understand it, too. And it's so damn easy to talk to you that I forget that your perspective is so much different than mine."

"Perspective?" I repeat. "You mean the view from sanity?" I am blinking madly, trying to hold back tears. I'm destroyed. That's the bottom line. Everything I wanted. Everything I let myself believe, and it's all gone in one puff. Like pulling back the wizard's curtain to reveal the truth.

I force myself to draw a deep breath and keep my voice from shaking. "I'm sorry, Raine. Whatever you feel, it isn't real, and I'm not going to ride along just to be part of your game. Because I can tell you right now, there's no way that I can win."

Chapter 9

My head is swimming as I stumble out of the service entrance off of Raine's kitchen. I find myself in a whitewashed corridor, and I turn frantically, looking for an elevator. It is at the end of the hall on my left, and I race that direction, then jab the button. I press my forehead to the wall next to the elevator and will myself not to cry. And I pray that Raine doesn't come after me, because right now, I don't know what I would do.

His mate? He'd thought he'd lost me? Her? I carry her essence inside me?

It was insane.

In a rush, I remember my fear that first night in the limo. That my desire for him was only an illusion.

It turns out that wasn't what I should have feared—*my* desire is real.

It is Raine's desire for me that is an illusion.

And this is all some sort of horrible psychological mind-fuck wherein he thinks I'm his dead wife or something.

It breaks my heart. And, yeah, it scares me, too. Because I'd thought what he felt was real.

And because he so obviously believes that what he said is true.

Oh god, oh god, oh god, how could I have been so stupid? How could I have let myself get so close because now it feels like he's taken a knife and sliced me in two?

The elevator doors open and I hurry inside, then jab the button to make the doors close.

But it is not even the knowledge that I allowed this to happen that eats at me the most. That I broke my own rules and allowed myself to get burned.

No, the worst is something I can barely admit, even to myself. And that is the tiny, buried, lingering feeling that he's telling the truth. That he believes it not because he went over the deep end in grief, but because it is true.

Damn me, he's gotten so under my skin—he's managed to twist me up so completely and thoroughly—that I am actually tempted to buy into his psychosis. I can almost even convince myself that I feel it, too, some deep primal connection that extends back to even before he walked into my father's shop.

But that's absurd. And despite my childhood searches for fairies and angels, I know better than to think that such things truly happen.

Don't I?

I'm still lost in my confused and swirling thoughts when I hit the street. It's dark, but not terribly late. Still, the street seems strangely empty, as if everything has shifted and I'm now living in some sort of netherworld that traps people whose dreams have died.

I don't like it, and all I want is to get to the shop, go upstairs, and sleep for a year.

I hurry that way, intent on my goal.

So intent, in fact, that I let my guard down. Which is why I have only myself to blame when the burly man in a windbreaker jumps out from the small passage between the shop and the next building.

I barely have time to make a sound before he has a hand over my mouth and has yanked me into the shadow-filled corridor. A cold sweat breaks out over my skin and my heart is pounding so hard I can hear nothing other than my own blood thrumming through my veins. In fact, I only realize that he is talking to me when he shakes me and I see his mouth moving.

"The amulet, bitch. Where the fuck is the amulet?"

"I—I have no idea." I have always had the illusion that I would be strong in a fight. But I'm not strong now. I'm terrified and it is all that I can do to focus and breathe so that the world doesn't turn to gray and I pass out right now.

I pray that someone passing by will see or hear us. The passage is filled with trash bins, and because of that, we are only a few feet off the lit sidewalk. But the night is quiet, and as far as I know, we are all alone.

"You don't know? You don't *know*? Well, maybe this will remind you." He pulls a knife from his pocket and thrusts the blade toward me. But he doesn't even make it an inch before something that looks like a thin strip of flat red light lashes out in front of me, slicing not only through his chest, but right through the metal blade as well.

The scream that I'd been holding in erupts, and I whip around to find Raine holding something that would be a sword if the blade didn't appear to be made out of...what? Light? Flame? Heat?

I don't know. Frankly, I don't care. I'm just grateful that he's there, and I take an unsteady step toward him. As I do, I hear the sharp report of a gunshot, then see the shock on Raine's gorgeous face.

He steps forward as if drunk, then turns. As he does, I see a second man, standing less than a foot away.

"Stay...the fuck away...from her." Raine's words sound like they are being forced out through water, and I run toward him even as he manages a burst of strength and spins, thrusting that strange sword right into the gunman's heart before yanking the blade free and collapsing onto the ground, blood gushing out of the bullet wound that has opened his back.

The gunman falls, too, but I am not concerned about him. I only care about Raine.

But though I try to get to him, it is as if I have hit a wall of air, and I can't move forward. *Shock*, I think. *I'm in shock.*

And then, when his body begins to rise and spin and burn, I am certain that it is shock and that I am hallucinating.

And the last thing I remember before the world goes gray is Raine's body, black and charred as it writhes in dancing tongues of fire.

* * * *

"So you just told her?" It's Mal's voice, but it seems as if it's floating in a cloud above me. "What? You had her in bed and that was your idea of pillow talk? You tell her she's got the essence of your dead mate inside her? No wonder she bolted."

"Boys..." Jessica's voice now, stern yet hushed.

"An error in judgment, I admit," Raine says, his voice soft. *He's alive. Dear god, he's alive.* "She said she felt the connection, that it seemed to her as if we were picking up where we left off. And I just couldn't—"

"What?" Liam asks. "Couldn't wait to terrify the girl?"

I try to open my eyes, to see Raine. To touch him. To tell them all that I'm in here, but I can't seem to get any part of me to function properly. I'm trapped inside myself, and I want so desperately to come back.

"Stop it, you two. When was the last time you saw Raine so happy?

And she's the reason for it. Of course he wants her to understand. And you," she continues. "Do you love me?"

"You know I do," Liam says.

"So you'll share your crazy-shit beliefs and ideas with me and expect me not to bolt, right?"

Liam says nothing.

"That's what I thought. Of course you will. So cut him some slack. Both of you. The man's in love, and love makes men fools. And as for you," Jessica continues, and from her softening tone, I am sure she has turned her attention back to Raine. "She may have felt it, but she doesn't really get it. You, Rainer Engel, have been alive for thousands of years, but you've forgotten how to be subtle. So go easy on her, okay? And just keep reminding yourself that she doesn't understand any of this yet."

She's right, I think. I don't understand. But I want to. Because unless everyone at Number 36 is as crazy as I thought Raine was, then it's me who is missing the bigger pictures, and not them.

I saw Raine burn and yet he is alive. And now Jessica is saying he's been alive for thousands of years.

So yeah, it's fair to say I don't get it. But I very much want to.

"Thanks, Jessica," Raine says.

"You're welcome. And now, gentlemen, I think we should leave."

"It's okay. You don't have to."

"Yes," she says. "We do. Look." Her voice softens and I feel a gentle pressure as she takes my hand and squeezes my fingers. "Welcome back, Callie. You're going to be just fine."

"Callie?" Raine's voice is urgent, and it is his hand I feel next. Strong and warm and safe. Despite everything—or maybe because of everything—I am certain that he will keep me safe.

"Come on, angel. Open your eyes. I'm fine, and you're fine, and I need you to open your eyes. Everything else can wait, but I need to see you. I need to know that you're okay."

I hear the urgency in his voice, the fear and the pain, and it twists at my heart. And somehow I manage to claw my way up through the fog.

My eyes flutter open, and the first thing I see is Raine's gorgeous face. The tight line of his mouth matching the worry in his eyes. And then it fades, and those beautiful blue irises shine even as his mouth curves into a smile of pure relief.

"Thank god," he says, then lifts my hand to his mouth and gently kisses my palm.

"You came after me."

"I did. I almost didn't. I've told myself so many times that no matter how much I want and need you, that I can't force your hand. And yet I couldn't simply stay back. Not with you running from me in fear. I had to at least make sure you were okay."

"I wasn't. Those men." I shudder. "Thank you."

"It was my pleasure. Except of course for the dying part. That is never much fun."

"That really happened?" My voice is coarse, my throat raw. "I didn't hallucinate? You really burned?"

"I really burned."

I frown, trying to wrap my mind around that, then take a sip from the glass of water he holds for me. As he bends close, I see the wing of a bird peeking out from his collar to rise up his neck. "That's new," I say, reaching out to stroke it.

"It is. *La petite mort*, as you said. With each death, I get a new mark."

I shake my head. "I feel like this should be making sense, but it's not. The only thing I'm sure of is that you were telling me the truth—although I still don't entirely understand what that truth is. And I didn't believe you. I'm sorry."

"You have no reason to be," he says as I scoot up on the bed, moving back to make room for him beside me. I take the opportunity to look around and don't recognize the room.

"The guest quarters. I wasn't sure you'd want to go back to my room."

I can't help but smile. Even with the horrible things I said to him, he is still taking care of me.

I draw a breath. "So back up. You die. And when you do you burn? And when you burn you get a tattoo?"

"A nice summary, though it leaves out some of the finer points." He traces up and down my fingers, and though I don't pull my hand away, the contact is both intimate and distracting. "What do you know of alternative dimensions?"

"About as much as you know about Tom Hanks' movies."

I'm grateful for the smile that flickers on his lips. "Then I'll give you the concise version. There are other dimensions that exist parallel to ours, and with the right technology, they can be traveled. In my world, a very long time ago, I was part of an elite team sent to recover a malevolent energy that had become uncontained."

"A bad guy."

"Very much."

"In our dimension, energy is sentient." He frowns, obviously trying to figure out how to make that more clear. "You don't need a body. You just need what in your world might be called a soul."

"No body? No physical love."

"Not as you understand it. No skin on skin, body against body. But that didn't mean we couldn't feel passion, connection, sensuality. Even climax. It just means that there is no point of reference that can help me explain what it is like to make love in my dimension."

"I feel like I should understand," I admit. "Like I almost do, even. As if I'm reaching for something in a dream."

"Livia," he says, and I nod. Because like it or not, I now believe that is true, though I am no closer to fully understanding it.

"So you didn't have a body?"

"Again, it's difficult to explain. Yes, and no. We had form inside the consciousness. Like an avatar. Or a dream. It wasn't until we arrived here in this dimension and on this planet that we acquired this human form." He grins. "And while I will not say that one is better than the other, I will say that the pleasure that can be had with a body of flesh and blood rises to a level that I never imagined in my youth."

I smirk. "You must have liked it. From my perspective, I'm willing to bet you had a lot of practice."

He smiles in response, and I know that I'd said the right thing, lightening the moment just a bit. Because this is heavy stuff we are talking about, and though I know I won't understand all of it, I am trying. Both to understand, and to believe.

"So you became human after you chased the energy—"

"We call it the fuerie."

I nod. "Okay. So you chased it to this dimension?" I'm proud of myself for keeping that much straight, and I say a silent thank you to reruns of *Star Trek* and my love of science fiction movies.

"Exactly. You don't need to know all the details, and to be honest, I don't want to relive them. Suffice it to say that there was an accident. We crashed here, on earth, and so did the fuerie. We melded with a party of traveling warriors and wise men and women sent by an Egyptian prince to follow a comet they had seen racing across the sky."

"You."

"Us," he affirms. "I'm human now, albeit immortal."

I nod, figuring that I could get more details on all of that later. "And the bad guy?"

"It crashed nearby and forced itself—or bits of itself— into unwilling human shells before riding to our location to attack." He drew in a breath. "The battle was hard-fought and many of the humans who had traveled with the warriors' party were killed, and many of the fuerie escaped. And until we can reopen the void and send it back, it is our duty to track down the fuerie and destroy it, in whatever form or forms it has taken."

"You can send it back?"

"The amulet your father was searching for is the last of seven pieces that can reopen the void and direct the fuerie back to our dimension."

"So that's why you wanted it."

"That," he says. "And so that I could go back."

"Go back?" Something cold, like dread, washes over me. "You're going away?"

"No." The word is harsh and firm and I am instantly relieved. "Not anymore. But I won't lie to you. I've been lost. Reckless. I wanted to get back because I thought Livia was lost during the battle. The fuerie created a rift, and I thought that she'd been thrust into it. I thought she was gone. Neither in this dimension nor any other." He meets my eyes. "For creatures made of pure energy, that is the essence of death."

I nod. "So you were grieving."

"I was, yes. But it was more than that." He runs a hand over his head. "In our world, when two beings mate, it is a permanent melding that even death doesn't shatter. How could it when, for beings of pure energy, death does not exist?"

I frown, not sure I'm following.

"Don't you see? I was grieving for Livia, true. But I was also grieving for myself, and my knowledge that I would spend eternity alone."

I suck in a breath as understanding washes over me. "That's heartbreaking."

"It's part of who we are. Or who we were. Those of us in the brotherhood aren't truly one or the other anymore." An ironic smile tugs at his mouth. "It's a brave new world."

Since I don't know what else to do, I squeeze his hand, and am gratified when he squeezes back.

"And in all this time, you never once felt her presence?"

"Not once. But keep in mind that the world is a very big place. And three thousand years passes in the blink of an eye to a creature made purely of energy. Even to those of us in the brotherhood, time moves at a different pace than for pure humans."

"I think my head is spinning. I want to understand it all, but I have so many questions and all the answers are coming at me at once."

"I know. Suffice it to say that for a very long time, I was lost. I was reckless. When I lost hope that we would ever find the final amulet, I chased death. I took unnecessary risks."

"But you're just reborn," I point out. "Not fun, maybe. But why is it a risk?"

"I wanted the pain," he says, his voice so low I can barely hear it. "And eventually, I wanted to just be hollow."

I shake my head. "I don't understand."

"A body can only take so many deaths. Then something switches, usually with no warning. I had a warning tonight. I am running out of free passes. Too many more burns and I will be hollow, my humanity lost."

I swallow as cold fingers of fear grab me. "You risked that for me?"

"I would risk more than that for you."

"Because of Livia," I say flatly.

"Some part of her essence is inside you, yes. We call it transference."

"And that's different than you? The way you—what did you call it?—melded with the wise men?"

"The prince was a man who had visions, and he had sent his wise men prepared and with a mission. We merged with them at a genetic, bodily level, and with their consent. But transference remains a process of energy. Like you think of a soul. Or what you might call reincarnation."

The thought makes me shiver. "So she's just there? Inside me?"

"Yes and no." He frowns. "These things aren't easy to understand or explain. She is there, yes, because energy can neither be created nor destroyed."

"Einstein."

"He got that right, yes. But it can be changed. And at least some of Livia—of her essence—is part of you. Inseparable now. And dormant, though that is the wrong word, as it suggests she is only sleeping and could wake and take over. She can't. She is you and you are her."

I hug myself, feeling overwhelmed. What I'm not, however, is freaked out.

I'm not entirely sure if that's a good sign or a bad.

"You thought she was gone." I pause because I'm trying to organize my thoughts. "But she didn't know you believed that. She thought you left her."

"I suppose."

"No," I say with certainty. "She did." I meet his eyes. "I think that fundamental belief is an ingrained part of me. Not just because my mother left me, but because that fear of being loved and then pushed away is deep inside me."

"Oh, god, Callie." The pain is clear in his voice.

"It's not your fault," I say. "It was a mistake. And honestly, I'm glad to understand."

Raine, however, looks unconvinced, and very guilty.

Since that wasn't my intent, I cast about for another question. "The men who attacked me—why were they looking for the amulet?"

"The fuerie was inside them. They want to open the void as well. If they have all the pieces of the amulet, they can escape this world and run wild across all dimensions. If we have all the pieces, we can send them back through to a containment center. Or we could open a rift and thrust them into the netherworld between dimensions, essentially destroying them."

I nod, thinking that over. "Okay. But how do you know for sure the fuerie was in them? Maybe it was just an old-fashioned mugging."

"I could see it in them."

That surprises me. "Really? So does that mean you can see Livia, too?"

"No. As I said, you and she are one, though I can feel her essence in the core of you. In order to survive, Livia made a choice all those years ago. The fabric of your dimension doesn't allow us to remain unbound as energy for long. So Livia had to either allow her energy to merge with a human's, or fill the human and remain separate. But that is violent and disrespectful, and is not our way. It is what the fuerie did."

"Possession," I say. "When you hear a story about demonic possession, it is the fuerie?"

"More often than not," he affirms. "As much as I've told you, I'm still only scratching the surface."

I nod because I've already figured that out. How could he possibly explain in just one conversation everything there is to know about how beings of pure energy interact with our world?

I cast about for a less complicated question. "So when you see the fuerie, what does it look like?"

"Flame. Heat. Energy. It's the foundation of our world. You could have seen it too, if you were properly trained. I'm surprised you didn't, actually, since you were scared. Often adrenaline triggers the reflex."

I frown because something about that sounds familiar. I can't imagine why, though, and I temporarily push the thought away. Right now, I'm about to go into information overload. Still, I can't stop asking questions. "You killed them? With that weird blade?"

"A fire sword. It's a weapon of the Phoenix Brotherhood. I go nowhere without it."

"You don't really have a security company."

Now his grin turns boyish. "Absolutely we do. And we have one hell of an elite clientele. It's a useful cover for our search for the fuerie. And many of our cases are entirely legit and unconnected to our original mission."

"So can I see it? The fire sword."

He laughed. "It burned in the fire. Usually I manage to toss it clear before collapsing, but not this time. I'll have to forge a new one. But I promise to let you watch."

We share a smile, and I feel something between us click back into place. I like it. And something in that gentle moment triggers the thought I'd been searching for earlier.

"Dad told the paramedic he saw a face in flames."

I can tell I've hit on something interesting by the expression on Raine's face. "Did he?"

"Why could he see them if you have to have some of your world's energy inside you?"

"Because of you."

"Me?"

"Livia."

"Oh." Automatically, I hug myself, then tug the blanket up higher on my legs.

"I think she must be attached to your family."

I nod because things are starting to make sense. "So when Daddy came to me in a dream, it was real?"

"It was real," Raine says. "And you can speak to him as well." He squeezes my hand. "It will be dreamlike at first, but with time you can communicate as easily as talking."

It takes me a second to process what he's saying. "So even if Daddy doesn't wake up—"

"So long as he's in there, he can get out."

I close my eyes, and warm tears spill down my cheeks. "He knows that, I think." I sniff and wipe the tears, then manage a watery smile. "He gave me a clue about where to find the journal. It was filed under my name. Not C, but O." I meet Raine's eyes, then hesitate, not sure I want to tell him the rest.

His brow creases with a frown. "What?"

I take a breath and tell him. "My given name is Olivia."

For a moment, he just looks at me. "And your father is Oliver." He nods as a slow smile spreads across his face. "Another piece of the puzzle slips into place."

He shakes his head as if in amazement. "Dear god, I have loved you for an eternity, and I will never lose you again."

He pulls me close and holds me tight, but despite the fire that I now know burns in this man, I still feel cold, and the shiver that runs through me is one of apprehension and fear. And, I think, of loneliness.

Chapter 10

An hour later, I'm curled up in one of the plush leather recliners in the VIP room at Dark Pleasures. Beside me, Jessica is telling me about the last mission she went on with Liam.

"To Prague, which was an absolute treat as we stayed a week even after the job was done. We'd lived there once, but that was well before indoor plumbing, and this was a big improvement."

I like the stories, and I definitely like Jessica, but I feel as though she thinks she knows me, but of course she doesn't. Livia, perhaps. But I am not her. And I can't help but fear that all of the brethren, Jessica included, have forgotten that very basic fact.

Across the room, Liam and Dante are bent over the chessboard while Raine and Mal are deep in conversation at a small table tucked into a corner.

After a few moments, Raine comes over, and I hold out my hand. He bends to kiss me in greeting, the gesture warm and comfortable and familiar.

"They all think they know me." The words are out before I have time to think about them, and I realize that this has been bothering me more than I have let myself realize.

"You're mine. Of course they want to know you."

"They think they already do."

He nods slowly. "But that's true. At the core of it, at least." He bends to kiss me, and I curl my arms around his neck, wanting something more from him, though I'm not sure what.

"I love you," he whispers, voicing the words for the very first time.

But instead of filling me, the words seem to hang heavy inside me.

"I love you, too," I say, then brush a kiss over his lips to camouflage my confusion and strange, dark thoughts. I shift in my chair, then lever myself up, feeling suddenly antsy. I smile, as if there is nothing in the world on my mind, and ask him if he wants a drink. Then while he takes the chair, I go to the bar and pour myself a shot. I toss it back, and as I do, I see my reflection in the mirror behind the bar.

Me.

Callie Sinclair.

So why do they all see Livia?

I look harder, and I cannot deny that I can find her inside me. The truth is there—Livia is part of me. Her core. Her essence. Her soul. Whatever you want to call it, it has become a part of me. And perhaps that piece of her is part of the reason that I fell in love so quickly and completely. But that does not make me her.

She is not who I am. The girl in the mirror is not Livia.

I close my eyes because although Raine might understand that with his head, until his heart understands, I can't make this work.

"Hey." His hands press against my shoulders and I look into the mirror to see him behind me, his lips brushing my hair. "You're crying."

It's only when he says the words that I realize they are true.

"I'm sorry." I draw a breath and turn to face him because this isn't something I can say to his reflection. "I love you, Raine. Maybe it's been fast, or maybe it's been growing over centuries. I don't know and I don't care, because I am certain of how I feel."

I watch the smile bloom on his face, only to die with my next words.

"But you're not in love with me. You're in love with a memory, Raine."

He shakes his head. "No."

I take his hand and hold it tight. "I can't do this. I'm not Livia. Maybe a part of me was, but that was a long time ago, and I have no memory of it. Not really. Do I feel a connection to you? Do I love you? Desperately. Passionately. But I'm not going to reduce the truth of that feeling by saying it originates from another woman's past. It doesn't Raine. It's me. All me."

He watches me intently, but says nothing, and I press on, because I have to get this out.

"Maybe there is some of her in me, but it's no more than the atoms of dinosaurs. You talked about energy, and I understand that. Everything is connected, sure. Energy can be neither created nor destroyed. I get all of that, and it's part of why I believe that what you've told me is true. But I can't be some other person simply because that's who you lost so long ago and who you want me to be."

"That's not what I want." He is speaking carefully, as if a wrong step will send me away.

But he doesn't realize that I'm already gone. What matters now is whether he can get me back.

I take his hand. "Isn't it? The woman you loved is dead, Raine. I'm Callie, and I do love you. God, I love you so much it terrifies me. But that isn't enough to keep me here."

"What are you saying?"

"I'm saying I can't stay here. Because I can't be somebody else, Raine. Not even for love." I brush away a tear and draw a stuttering breath. "Not even for you."

****

Raine couldn't sleep. He'd paced his apartment all night after Callie left, finally giving up even as the dark surrendered to the light.

He'd come down into the club an hour ago and decided that seven in the morning was a damn fine time for a drink.

Now he filled his glass yet again, then tossed back the contents, relishing the burn as the liquid flowed down his throat. He couldn't get drunk—a side effect of his particular brand of immortality—but he could damn sure try. And maybe if he tried hard enough he could turn the buzz into an alcohol-induced haze.

And maybe if he managed that, he could forget.

Except, of course, he didn't want to forget. On the contrary, he wanted to hold her close to his heart. Hold them. Both of the women he loved. His Livia. His Callie.

How the hell had he lost them both?

"Careful." Mal stepped up to the bar, then leaned against it, the casualness of his stance belying the concern on his face. "Finish off the Glenfarclas and Trace will have your head. He was friends with John Grant, you know, and was there when it was distilled. Not to mention that bottle cost a fucking fortune."

Raine managed a small smile. "Trace has wanted my head for centuries. About time I gave him an excuse."

"Don't do him any favors." Mal reached over the bar and grabbed a glass of his own, then held it out. "And don't drink alone."

Raine lifted the bottle and poured a shot into Mal's glass.

"She thinks that I'm in love with a memory."

Mal took a long, slow sip. "Are you?"

Raine's eyes shot to his friend, and his words came out cold and harsh. "Hell no. Christ, Mal, I loved Livia—I did. I do. And whatever part of her is still within Callie, I love as well. But that isn't why I love her. God, she's in here." He slammed his hand against his chest. "In my heart, under my skin. There was a spark the moment I saw her, and when we made love the first time, I knew without a doubt that I've known her forever—and maybe I do have Livia to thank for that—but it's not what's in our past that grabbed my heart."

His friend said nothing as Raine poured another shot, then finished it off. "Livia was my mate, and I loved her beyond all reason." He had, too. But they had been mated before they crossed the void, and that relationship had a different feel, a different cadence. They'd been bound, their energies meshed. And he had been sworn to protect her, while she was sworn to serve him.

The relationship was symbiotic, and yet sterile in so many ways. And perhaps they would have grown past that in their years on earth, bound in human flesh for so long that he'd all but forgotten how it used to be. But he'd lost her the day of their arrival, and so he would never know.

With Callie, he understood what it meant to not only love, but to be in love. To feel not only passion, but playfulness.

He had loved, Livia. But with Callie it was so much more. With Callie, *he* was so much more.

"I loved her," Raine repeated. "But Callie is a partner, too. A friend. Perhaps there was no room for that so many years ago, when our mission was so closely bound to every moment of our lives. But I found laughter in Callie. And life, as well. And if I have any regrets, it is my recklessness over these past years."

He rubbed a hand over his tattooed arm, remembering each and every death that they marked. "Because now I fear that if I go into battle and fail, I may lose myself. And in losing myself, I will lose her as well."

Still, his friend said nothing.

"Dammit, Mal, say something."

Mal reached over and clenched his shoulder, his gray eyes sharp. "It's not me you need to be talking to, Raine. And you damn well know it."

* * * *

It's nine in the morning and I'm on my fifth cup of coffee. I didn't sleep last night, though I'd curled up on the couch in my father's hospital room and hoped that the beeps and chirps of the machinery would sing me to sleep. I'd wanted to find my father in dreams, but it hadn't happened, and now I feel bereft, as if I'd lost both my father and the man I loved.

I'd left with the sun, walking back to the store as the city awoke, and as soon as the clock struck nine, I'd called my office in Texas.

Now I'm on hold because I'd foolishly forgotten about the time change, and the receptionist told me to wait while she calls down to the gym to see if my boss is there, going through his usual early-morning workout.

I'd considered simply calling back later, but I want to do this now. I want to let him know that I'll be back to work bright and early Monday morning, and I want him to officially put me back on the docket as soon as possible.

I force myself not to think about the reason. About why it even matters to me. Because I do not want to even entertain the possibility of staying in New York. How can I when everything about this city reminds me of Raine?

And all I do is remind him of Livia.

Frustrated, I wipe away a tear that has escaped my cheek.

He didn't stop me.

I told him what I needed to hear, and he said nothing. He let me walk out and keep on walking. And now it's the next day and he hasn't come, and dammit I can't help the stupid tears because my heart is broken. And I'm cursing my own stupidity for falling in love in the first place, and I'm wishing there is a way that I can just get him out of my head, because whenever I think about him—

Fuck.

"Dammit, Claire, get back to the phone." I tap my foot, then start pacing. I've reached the end of the store when two things happen. The front door opens and Raine steps in, and Claire comes back on the line.

"Just another minute," she says. "He's on his way up."

"Thanks. I can wait." I look up at Raine as the hold music begins again. I clutch my fingers tighter around my phone, as if that alone can give me the strength not to run to him. "My boss. I need to take this."

"Later. We need to talk."

I shake my head. "We don't."

"Yes." He moves closer, then takes the phone from my hand and disconnects the call. "We do. Because I love you. *You*. Callie Sinclair. Not a memory. A woman."

"It's been hours," I say because, yes, I am hurting. "You let me leave. You let me just walk away."

"I needed to get my head around how much I feel for you. Because it's so much more than I've ever felt before. For Livia. For anyone."

I look at him, wary, because I want so much to believe, but I don't know if I should.

On the desk, my phone starts to ring. I know it's Claire, wondering what the hell happened.

"No," he says. "Give me this chance to tell you that I love Callie Sinclair. That I want nothing more than to touch her. To make memories with her. I want to laugh with her and I want to watch her cry out in passion. I love you, Callie. Your humor, your heart. Everything that makes up the woman standing in front of me."

He pauses only long enough to draw a breath.

"Is Livia's essence within you? Of course. Did I love her? I did. But that was a long time ago, and now her essence is only the string that drew me to you. Strings can be cut. But you could sever that string and I would never leave you. *Never*," he adds fiercely. "You are everything to me, angel. Don't you see? For centuries, I've craved death. Sought it out. Wanted to find that goddamn amulet so that I could go back home, even though that world no longer is mine. I don't want that anymore."

He takes my hands. "I want to stay. I want you."

I swallow and blink, trying to hold back tears because his words have filled me to overflowing.

"I love you, Callie. And I'm sorry if I'm saying it wrong, but I need you to believe me. Because you hold the power to destroy me. Please, angel." His voice is gentle. Pleading. "I need you."

"I believe you," I say, and I don't think I've ever spoken truer words. "And I love you, too."

Chapter 11

"I love you," I say again, because it is real and huge and I want to say it as many times as he wants to hear it.

He pulls me close and kisses me hard. "I was so afraid I'd lost you forever, and—"

I close my mouth over his again, silencing him. I don't want to hear about being apart now that we are together. That, to me, is the wrong kind of fantasy.

"Make love to me." I'm breathing hard, my heart pounding. His is too, and as he pulls me close I can feel it pound through me as if our two hearts are united as one. As if we are blurring the line between where I end and he begins.

His hands go to my shirt even as mine attack his jeans. "The windows," I gasp, though right then I truly don't care. He can slam me up against the glass and fuck me blind if he wants. I just want to feel him against me.

In one motion, he scoops me up. "Where?"

"The studio. Upstairs." I nod to the back of the store and the simple door that leads the way to the living quarters. He goes, carrying me easily, and I cling tight, reveling in the feel of his body pressed against mine. Of being carried. Tended to. It feels right, this moment.

It feels like coming home.

I tense, realizing something.

"Callie?"

I make a frantic motion with my hand. "Wait. Wait. Let me think."

He continues up the stairs, his expression wary, but I say nothing.

There's something important, and though it's flitting around in my mind, I can't quite grasp it no matter how much I—

And then I remember.

"My playhouse," I say, twisting my hand into his shirt collar as if that will make him understand what I'm talking about. "I think Daddy hid the amulet in my playhouse."

His brow creases. "What does that have to do with me? The journal said, *With him, what is hidden will be revealed.* I don't even know what your playhouse is."

"But you're with me, aren't you?"

He cocks his head. "And you think your dad knew that we would be together?"

"If Livia is in him, too, then yes. I think maybe he knew—maybe *she* knew—that in the end, we would make this work."

We've reached the landing at the top of the stairs and he pauses outside the door to the studio, then puts me down.

"What?" I ask because he is looking at me with such intensity.

"I just love you." His voice is gentle but firm, as if he has just stated some immutable law of the universe. And when he kisses me, threads of fire spread through me, filling and warming me, making me feel safe. And, yes, loved.

I have no idea what I said to prompt this, but I do know that I like it.

"So if it's in the playhouse, where is the playhouse?"

I reach for the door to the studio and open it. It's a typical loft apartment with no isolated rooms. My father put up a bookshelf to separate my area from his when I got older, but before that it was just open.

The back wall is made up of windows in front of a wooden bench. It's not a window seat, and that had disappointed me as a child. Until my dad decided to take pity on me.

I signal for Raine to come over, and he does. Then I kneel in front of the bench. I run my finger along the bottom until I find the hidden latch. I flip it, then lift the wooden panel. It rises on the hinges hidden just under the top to reveal a cavity just barely big enough for a little girl to use as a playhouse. Inside, I find my stuffed animals, a blanket, three flashlights, a pillow, a copy of *Alice in Wonderland*. And a cardboard box that I do not recognize.

I tug it out, then glance at Raine, who nods.

I pull off the lid, then suck in a breath, awed by the magnificent fire of the opal that makes up the center of the amulet. "It's stunning," I say. "Hang on. Let me get my dad's jeweler's loupe. The fire in this stone is incredible."

I clutch the box in my hand, intending to just run down the stairs and get my dad's loupe out of his desk, but I don't get that far.

The moment I step outside the door, I hear a sharp *crack*. For a moment, I just stand there, confused. Then I hear Raine scream my name. I try to turn, but I seem glued to the spot. And, strangely, when I look down I see blood on my shirt.

My blood.

I fall backward, realizing as I do that someone has leapt from the stairs to the landing. He's grabbed the box, and he's racing away.

I try to focus on why that matters, but everything just seems so fuzzy. Even Raine, who is at my side now, his hand tight around mine.

"Hang on!" he cries. "Dammit, Callie, you hang on."

But I'm not sure how he expects me to do that, because everything is so slippery, and I'm sliding away faster and faster.

"Don't you dare. Don't you dare leave me."

I focus on his words. On their meaning. And as I do, I realize what's happening.

Dying.

"Raine? I think I've been shot. I think I'm dying."

I see the tears flood his eyes and the way his jaw clenches with determination, and I know that I am right.

I try to shake my head, but I'm not sure I'm managing it. But when I shift sideways, I can scoot just a little bit closer to him. I can't stand to be away from him. I can't stand to lose him now that I've just found him.

"Raine?" My voice is so thin I can barely hear it. "I don't think I can hold on. I love you."

I think I am hallucinating now because I see a wild flash of colors. Then I realize it's not a hallucination. It's the blade of a fire sword.

"You said I could watch you forge it."

"This is Mal's. I also said I never go out without one. Listen to me. *Listen to me.*"

I force myself to focus. To not let the gray take me.

"They have...the amulet," I say.

"Right now, I don't give a damn about anything but you. I need you to move. I won't be able to do it for you once I slice my throat, and the fire will throw me across the room if I die too close to you. It won't risk accidentally taking a mortal. One foot, Callie. Can you crawl one foot into the flames?"

His words are coming at me fast, and I can barely process them. But I have heard enough, and it is the surge of adrenaline that gives me more strength because I have to make him stop. "Die? The flame? What are you talking about?"

"Come into the flame with me. If my mate enters, she will become immortal, too. Come into the flame, Callie, and live with me forever."

"No. Raine, *no*. You said you didn't have many burns left. This could destroy you."

The words, ripped from me in fear, have exhausted me, and I let my head fall back as I gasp, trying to draw in air.

"I can't bear to lose you," he says. "And if the price of your life is my sanity, then I will pay it to know that you are safe and whole."

I open my mouth to protest once more, but it is too late. He holds the base of the fire sword and with one flick of his wrist, the blade extends, slicing across his throat and spilling his blood.

I hear a scream and realize that it is my own.

He falls to the floor, and for a moment nothing happens.

"Raine... Raine..." I try to scream his name, but I do not have the strength.

He is facing me, and I see the light dimming in his eyes. And then his lips move. Just one word.

Now.

The word still hangs in the air as the flames start to rise around him. And I know that I must go now. The flame will not last forever, only until he is reborn.

I either try or I die.

And I cannot bear the thought of losing him. And so I struggle toward him, using all my strength. Pushing with my feet. Pulling with my arms. Until I am so close I can feel the fire cooking my skin, and I do not know how I can do this. How I can go into the flame and suffer that pain?

Except I know that I can endure it because Raine has, time and again. And twice now for me.

I can survive it for him.

I count to three, then force my body to roll, screaming in pain as I do from both the pressure on the wound and the fire that has now sparked my clothes. But that is good, I think, because I need the flame. I need to burn. I need...

I need...

And then there is just black. Black and pain.

Then something soothing. And a light. Blue and yellow and a deep, blood red.

Shining. Healing. And rising into the sky on jeweled wings.

Illusion? Or reality? Or is there even a difference?

I do not know. I don't even know if I am alive or dead.

All I know is that the pain has stopped but the black has come. So deep and thick that I know that Raine was wrong. This is the end.

This is death.

And death is cold and black.

* * * *

"Time to wake up, sweetheart."

"Daddy?"

I'm surrounded by black, the floor beneath me cold and hard.

"You did good. You found the amulet."

I search for him, but there is only his voice and the black.

"We lost it."

"You survived. You're alive. And you're with Raine."

"I love him, Daddy."

"I know. And I love you."

"I miss you."

"I'm here. But right now, Callie, you need to leave this place. Follow the path, Callie," he says, his voice fading as a faint, golden path seems to shine on the floor.

"Daddy?"

I reach for him, but he's gone, his voice drifting away down the path. I crawl that direction, and as I do, the blackness turns to gray, and then the gray turns to light.

And I open my eyes.

I'm on the floor of the studio, gasping and naked in Raine's arms.

I look down at my chest, right were the bullet got me, so close to my heart. The skin is completely unmarred.

Beside me, Raine stirs, blue eyes overflowing with relief. And with love.

"We're really safe?" I ask. "We're really alive? Are you okay?" And not just alive, but immortal. The thought is still too big for my head, though I am certain that if I am going to tackle immortality, I want to do it with Raine beside me.

"I am. We are." He brushes his hand over my hair, his eyes still focused on my face as if he can't believe I am here.

I understand completely. "Make love to me," I beg. "Please, Raine. Please prove to me that I'm really alive."

"Oh, angel, you're alive. More alive than you've ever been." He brushes his hand over the curve of my shoulder, his expression filled with awe.

I look too, and when I see the vibrant, colorful phoenix tattoo my breath hitches and I feel something that I would call joy, except that the feeling is too big to fit into such a small word. "It's true? I'm really immortal?"

"It's true," he says, but I do not really need his answer. I can feel it. This new energy swirling inside me. The connection that I have sought for so long. And the full feeling inside me that has completely conquered that horrible sense of emptiness.

Raine.

He is my mate, my love, my life.

And I will never be alone.

"You're smiling," he says.

"I have reason to." I shift on the ground so that I am straddling him. The floor is hard, but I don't care. I'm desperate for him, overwhelmed with the need for our bodies to prove what my heart already knows. That this is real. That this is forever. And that this man is a part of me.

I move my hips in a slow motion. "Let me give you a reason to smile too," I say huskily.

I see passion light those ice-blue eyes. "Angel, I'm already smiling."

He pulls me close and closes his mouth over mine. The kiss is wild and deep and bruising. I don't care. I want the bruises. I've already got the tattoo, now I want to be marked by Raine as well. Marked by him. Filled by him. Taken by him.

I feel wild—hell, I feel alive—and I break the kiss and then sit up, stroking his hard, thick cock even as I rise up on my knees and position his head at my slit, and then lower myself slowly, so painfully slowly, so that I am teasing us both.

"You're killing me, angel," he says, and then takes hold of my back with one hand and my rear with the other, and in a surprisingly fluid movement, flips us.

Now I'm on my back and he is on his knees. And I'm gasping with pleasure as he holds my hips and pistons into me, hard and fast and deep.

He is taking me higher and higher, and we are joined now, body and soul. And when I explode in a thousand pieces, he is right there, too, merging with me, dancing with me, filling me completely.

When we both finally come back to earth, I snuggle close, my head on his chest. He reaches into the playhouse for the blanket and pulls it over us.

I frown, remembering what else was in that playhouse. "I'm sorry about the amulet."

"We'll get it back. It's as useless to them as it is to us without all seven pieces."

"Thank goodness."

I sigh and press closer to him, then trail my finger over the tats that mark his chest. "So am I different now? After the fire, I mean?"

"You're immortal, like me. Other than that, you are still you."

I smile again, both amazed and content that I will never leave this man. But something in his words makes me wonder. "Does that mean you're more than immortal? Do you have powers or something?" I feel a little silly asking, as if I'm trying to turn him into a comic book hero. I expect him to laugh off the question, so his answer startles me.

"You might say that."

I sit up. "Really? More than your power to make me feel very, very good?"

He laughs. "Energy. Within certain limitations, we can manipulate it."

I frown, trying to understand. And then I remember. "That first day. I *did* lock the door."

"It's an electronic keypad lock. I simply told it to open."

"That is pretty damn cool."

"What can I say? I'm a very cool guy."

I roll over and kiss him again. "You're a hell of a lot more than that," I say. "You're *my* cool guy."

"I am," he says. "Forever."

He strokes my hair and looks into my eyes, and the tenderness in his gaze makes me melt all over again.

"I love you," I whisper.

"And I love you."

"Make love to me, Raine. Slow and long. I want to feel you inside me. I never want to stop feeling you."

"Anything you want, angel." He brushes my lips with a tender kiss. "We have all the time in the world."

Epilogue

Mal continued to study the chessboard as Liam dropped into the seat across the table from him, then put his phone down.

"Just heard from Raine. Callie's now a New York County Assistant District Attorney."

"That's excellent," Mal said as he considered the position of the rook in relation to the bishop. "It can only help Phoenix Security to have someone in the DA's office."

"Agreed," Liam said, and then said nothing else.

Mal closed his eyes, silently cursing, then looked up. "Something else?"

"I don't know. Is there?"

Mal said nothing, just waited.

"Dammit, Mal, you need to talk to me. You've been brooding for two days, sitting over this damn chessboard, half the time without an opponent."

"There's always an opponent," Mal said.

"Jessica's worried."

At that, Mal bit back a smile. "Jessica?"

"Fine. I'm worried, too. Tell me I don't have reason to be."

Mal sighed, then combed his fingers through his hair. "I've been thinking about games. About strategies."

"Mal. Don't do this to yourself."

"To myself?" A sudden fury burst through him, and he lashed out, sending chess pieces flying. "Do you think I want this pain? Dammit, Liam, not a day goes by that I don't think of her. That I don't crave the moment when I will see her again...even as I dread it."

Liam drew in a breath. "I wish I didn't have to tell you this. But she's back. She's in New York. "

Mal's body turned to ice. "Are you sure?"

"Dante saw her. She was at least a block away, so he could be wrong, but—"

"He's not," Mal said flatly as the cold settled into his bones. He turned his attention to the now empty chessboard.

"Do you think it doesn't destroy me, too? She was your mate, but she was my friend, my crew. But there's no other way," Liam said, accurately following Mal's thoughts. "There is no other strategy, no trick we haven't thought of. There is only one way."

He stood, and Mal could see the pain on his friend's face, as potent as his own. "You have to kill her again, Mal. Because if you don't, she'll end up destroying us all."

Acknowledgments from the Author

For Liz and Kim … who jumped through hoops and bent over backwards and saved my sanity in the process!

About Julie Kenner

J. Kenner (aka Julie Kenner) is the *New York Times*, *USA Today*, *Publishers Weekly*, *Wall Street Journal* and International bestselling author of over seventy novels, novellas and short stories in a variety of genres.

Though known primarily for her award-winning and international bestselling erotic romances (including the Stark and Most Wanted series) that have reached as high as #2 on the *New York Times* bestseller list, JK has been writing full time for over a decade in a variety of genres including paranormal and contemporary romance, "chicklit" suspense, urban fantasy, Victorian-era thrillers (coming soon), and paranormal mommy lit.

Her foray into the latter, *Carpe Demon: Adventures of a Demon-Hunting Soccer Mom* by Julie Kenner, has been consistently in development in Hollywood since prior to publication. Most recently, it has been optioned by Warner Brothers Television for development as series on the CW Network with Alloy Entertainment producing.

JK has been praised by *Publishers Weekly* as an author with a "flair for dialogue and eccentric characterizations" and by *RT Bookclub* for having "cornered the market on sinfully attractive, dominant antiheroes and the women who swoon for them." A three time finalist for Romance Writers of America's prestigious RITA award, JK took home the first RITA trophy awarded in the category of erotic romance in 2014 for her novel, *Claim Me* (book 2 of her Stark Trilogy).

Her books have sold well over a million copies and are published in over over twenty countries.

In her previous career as an attorney, JK worked as a clerk on the Fifth Circuit Court of Appeals, and practiced primarily civil, entertainment and First Amendment litigation in Los Angeles and Irvine, California, as well as in Austin, Texas. She currently lives in Central Texas, with her husband, two daughters, and two rather spastic cats.

Caress of Pleasure
A Dark Pleasures Novella
By Julie Kenner

I'd thought that he was mine, the dark, arresting man who commanded not only my body but my heart. Dante had swept into my life, and I'd succumbed to the burn of passion in his arms.

I'd believed we had a love that would last forever, but he'd shattered my dreams and broken me into pieces when he'd walked away, taking a piece of my soul with him.

Now he has come back seeking my help, and though I try to keep my distance and protect my heart, I cannot deny that the fire between us burns hotter than ever. And I cannot help but fear that this time our passion will reduce us both to ashes.

Also from Julie Kenner

Erotic romance

<u>As Julie Kenner</u>

Caress of Darkness
Find Me in Darkness
Find Me in Pleasure
Find Me in Passion
Caress of Pleasure

<u>As J. Kenner</u>

Stark Series novels
Release Me (a *New York Times* and *USA Today* bestseller)
Claim Me (a #2 *New York Times* bestseller!)
Complete Me (a #2 *New York Times* bestseller!)

Stark Ever After novellas
Take Me
Have Me
Play My Game

Stark International novels
Say My Name
On My Knees
Under My Skin

Stark International novellas
Tame Me

The Most Wanted series
Wanted
Heated
Ignited

Other Genres

Kate Connor Demon-Hunting Soccer Mom Series (suburban fantasy/paranormal)

Carpe Demon
California Demon
Demons Are Forever
The Demon You Know (short story)
Deja Demon
Demon Ex Machina
Pax Demonica

The Protector (Superhero) Series **(paranormal romance)**
The Cat's Fancy (prequel)
Aphrodite's Kiss
Aphrodite's Passion
Aphrodite's Secret
Aphrodite's Flame
Aphrodite's Embrace
Aphrodite's Delight
Aphrodite's Charms (boxed set)

Blood Lily Chronicles **(urban fantasy romance)**
Tainted
Torn
Turned
The Blood Lily Chronicles (boxed set)

Devil May Care Series (paranormal romance)
Raising Hell
Sure As Hell

Shadow Keepers Series (J. Kenner writing as J.K. Beck)
When Blood Calls
When Pleasure Rules
When Wicked Craves
Shadow Keepers: Midnight (e-novella)
When Passion Lies
When Darkness Hungers
When Temptation Burns

Sign up for the 1001 Dark Nights Newsletter
and be entered to win a Tiffany Key necklace.

There's a contest every month!

Go to www.1001DarkNights.com to subscribe.

As a bonus, all subscribers will receive a free
1001 Dark Nights story
The First Night
by Lexi Blake & M.J. Rose

Turn the page for a full list of the
1001 Dark Nights fabulous novellas...

1001 Dark Nights

WICKED WOLF by Carrie Ann Ryan
A Redwood Pack Novella

WHEN IRISH EYES ARE HAUNTING by Heather Graham
A Krewe of Hunters Novella

EASY WITH YOU by Kristen Proby
A With Me In Seattle Novella

MASTER OF FREEDOM by Cherise Sinclair
A Mountain Masters Novella

CARESS OF PLEASURE by Julie Kenner
A Dark Pleasures Novella

ADORED by Lexi Blake
A Masters and Mercenaries Novella

HADES by Larissa Ione
A Demonica Novella

RAVAGED by Elisabeth Naughton
An Eternal Guardians Novella

DREAM OF YOU by Jennifer L. Armentrout
A Wait For You Novella

STRIPPED DOWN by Lorelei James
A Blacktop Cowboys ® Novella

RAGE/KILLIAN by Alexandra Ivy/Laura Wright
Bayou Heat Novellas

DRAGON KING by Donna Grant
A Dark Kings Novella

PURE WICKED by Shayla Black
A Wicked Lovers Novella

HARD AS STEEL by Laura Kaye
A Hard Ink/Raven Riders Crossover

STROKE OF MIDNIGHT by Lara Adrian
A Midnight Breed Novella

ALL HALLOWS EVE by Heather Graham
A Krewe of Hunters Novella

KISS THE FLAME by Christopher Rice
A Desire Exchange Novella

DARING HER LOVE by Melissa Foster
A Bradens Novella

TEASED by Rebecca Zanetti
A Dark Protectors Novella

THE PROMISE OF SURRENDER by Liliana Hart
A MacKenzie Family Novella

FOREVER WICKED by Shayla Black
A Wicked Lovers Novella

CRIMSON TWILIGHT by Heather Graham
A Krewe of Hunters Novella

CAPTURED IN SURRENDER by Liliana Hart
A MacKenzie Family Novella

SILENT BITE: A SCANGUARDS WEDDING by Tina Folsom
A Scanguards Vampire Novella

DUNGEON GAMES by Lexi Blake
A Masters and Mercenaries Novella

AZAGOTH by Larissa Ione
A Demonica Novella

NEED YOU NOW by Lisa Renee Jones
A Shattered Promises Series Prelude

SHOW ME, BABY by Cherise Sinclair
A Masters of the Shadowlands Novella

ROPED IN by Lorelei James
A Blacktop Cowboys ® Novella

TEMPTED BY MIDNIGHT by Lara Adrian
A Midnight Breed Novella

THE FLAME by Christopher Rice
A Desire Exchange Novella

CARESS OF DARKNESS by Julie Kenner
A Dark Pleasures Novella

Also from Evil Eye Concepts:

TAME ME by J. Kenner
A Stark International Novella

THE SURRENDER GATE By Christopher Rice
A Desire Exchange Novel

SERVICING THE TARGET By Cherise Sinclair
A Masters of the Shadowlands Novel

On behalf of 1001 Dark Nights,

Liz Berry and M.J. Rose would like to thank ~

Steve Berry
Doug Scofield
Kim Guidroz
Jillian Stein
InkSlinger PR
Dan Slater
Asha Hossain
Chris Graham
Pamela Jamison
Jessica Johns
Dylan Stockton
Richard Blake
BookTrib After Dark
and Simon Lipskar

9 781682 305720